I Think of You

A Pride and Prejudice Variation

María Elena Fuentes-Montero

I Think of You

To contact the author, please use the following address:
mariaelena.fuentesmontero@gmail.com

ISBN:1477601589
ISBN-13:9781477601587

To Mexico

"You have ruined everything. All is lost if he finds out!"

"He will not. They all participated. They will not dare."

"Yes! I have betrayed too hard to allow it!"

The sound of broken bones and an excruciating scream culminate the unsettling scene that comes to my mind every time I hear talk about Derbyshire. Yet, accustomed to doing what it is expected and push aside any reminiscence of the past, I assume the role of the second Miss Bennet.

What else can someone in my position do, except pretend? What better disguise than an indifferent one?

María Elena Fuentes-Montero

Chapter 1

Hunsford, 10 April 1812

Oh God, I need to write this down. I am lost without my diary, my books, my Jane. I should not have come to Kent! It has been four months, and the nightmares are more intense, my sense of reality thinner. I feel it again, that I do not belong anywhere. I thought that Charlotte's presence would reestablish my peace of mind, but there is little to expect if I am incapable of rational thought.

I have been taking long walks in Rosings Park, in the hope of distracting my mind from all that I want to forget or resign myself to. It is for naught. As much as I have put miles between Meryton and myself, I cannot run away from this. Everything reminds me of my mistakes, all that I care to do is prohibited, all my accomplishments are unladylike, and my hopes — my hopes are pathetic.

Of course, I have rebuked Lady Catherine's insults and I have behaved, in the best of my ability, as a gentlewoman should. And I have flirted with him, I cannot deny it.

I know I should have not. Nevertheless, it felt nice to be admired by such a man. It was gratifying to be in the presence of an educated person that had no reason to scorn me. I did it regardless of the consequences. I thought it was harmless, because I am 'not handsome enough'. But it seems I was wrong: today Mr. Darcy proposed, and I rejected him, as I knew I should.

It hurt.

My arguments were convincing, oh yes, very rational. However, my words were hard and filled with all the resentment I was capable of. The resentment against myself — all directed at him, as if he was the one responsible for my impossibility of being able to marry anyone.

His wounded expression, reflecting the injustice of my opinion of him, I cannot forget — an opinion so far from the one I actually feel.

STOP THERE, ELIZABETH! His proposal was insulting: to speak of Mother and Father as if he knew anything about them! About all they had been through! No, it was well done. And if he knew the real me, he should be disgusted. I did him a service. He will put this behind soon.

And finally, I have written my troubles in a concise way. I should be capable of some sleep.

****

This is the first page of the diary I started so many months ago, before Mr. Darcy's unsuccessful letter and my escape. I was in an awful mood, convinced of my unworthiness and of his ungentlemanly behavior toward Jane. I read it now, and cannot stop my feelings of regret. If I were the keen studier of character I had let people believe I am, I would not have misjudged him so grossly, and so many tears could have been spared.

However, I had been haunted by those dreams, and all I could see was the face of the people who knew about it and hear their reproaches: *"Only an orphan behaves like this. She is a shame to her family. Who knows who her father was."*

Perhaps I should start at the beginning. My first memories are from the time I was about five or six years old. Mother and I lived in a town named Bakewell, in Derbyshire. Mama was the nurse of the apothecary of the village. We were alone at that time, just the two of us in a small cottage, and her brother Edward Gardiner joined us from time to time. I do not remember my father, a soldier called Willoughby, because he left us almost immediately after my birth. Mama says that I was a lovely baby, but I guess he could not stand the screaming and crying in the nights.

For many years, I remained locked inside the house (while Mama was working), although, sometimes I managed to escape to the streets and played a little with the children that I could befriend. I *so* enjoyed those precious hours of freedom and always returned home with scratches in my arms, my dress in a mess of dirt and mud.

When Mama found me like this, she scolded me gently. She understood that I was bored at home, having no one to speak with.

The best times were when Uncle Edward brought with him Cousin Jack

Sthieve, a boy three years older than me. His father (my mother's brother-in-law from Scotland) wanted him to learn the profession of a merchant, so he traveled with our uncle almost everywhere. For me, he was like a dream, with his stories about the world and knowledge of foreign languages. We played pirates, climbed trees, even practiced some fighting with our fists.

When I was seven years old, mother and I went to my uncle's wedding in the village of Lambton. He was marrying Madeline White, the daughter of the local parson. I was so excited about assisting, about meeting the bride, about my new dress, about traveling! I looked forward to the date from four months prior, and Mama was almost hysterical with my ramblings about the upcoming event.

When we arrived at the Lambton Inn, I met Aunt Philips and their three sons. They were all older than me, and the only company I was comfortable with was Jack. Thus, I unsuccessfully tried to follow him everywhere. In the week previous to the wedding, the adults spent most of the time with the preparations. The bride and the arrangements of the church seemed like coming from a fairy tale. All the cousins escaped to the woods and rambled from side to side of the country with the local boys. I was excluded from their games and adventures.

This festive occasion was also when we met Mr. Thomas Bennet, the best man in the world. I cannot stop smiling at the memory of Mama flirting with him and their occasional escapades from public eyes. She explained that he was a widower, and had four daughters and an estate named Longbourn, located in a faraway place.

The day of the ceremony was warm, and it appeared to me the whole town was in the church when the Gardiners said their vows. I remember the expensive dresses and hats of some ladies, the beautiful carriages and the flowers everywhere. I also felt the prettiest girl ever with my dress with feathers and my beautiful curls with new ribbons. The wedding breakfast was held in the open space near the parsons' house, and all the children could play and run through the land. I tried to follow Jack as always, but the boys were too fast and strong for me to catch them.

This is the part where I have the most inconvenient blackout.

I only recall the aftermath — Mama crying with me on her lap, women whispering under their fans, and our urgent removal from the celebrations. Mr. Bennet took us to our home in Bakewell, and after a few weeks, we were taken away to the town of Meryton with my Aunt and Uncle Philips.

The happy coincidence is that the village of Meryton in Hertfordshire was a few miles from the estate of Longbourn. It is easy to follow that Mama and Mr. Bennet found that most convenient for their romantic interludes. After not many months, they were happily married, and I was welcomed into a family where finding playmates was never an issue again.

Mama took the responsibility of being the mother of five girls with her characteristic enthusiasm, and Mr. Bennet easily earned the title of "Papa" from me, with his tales and book room full of adventures. My childhood became remarkably different with the steady presence of my sister Jane and the liberal instruction of my new father. I learned the basics of math quickly, and in a few years, was helping with small estate matters. Mama took the role of being the Mistress of Longbourn with eagerness, although she was a little troubled about her impossibility of getting with child.

At the age of eleven, I was so fascinated by algebra exercises and natural science books that I started to dream about numbers in my sleep. This was all right, until Mama heard me one night, and decided it could lead to the worst impression in a future husband. She started to dedicate more time to my instruction in more feminine pursuits, and long speeches about proper behavior (with belated comments about that fateful day when I was scorned by everyone).

Papa, on the other hand, instructed me in the fine art of laughing at human follies.

****

The day after Mr. Darcy's proposal, he approached from nowhere during my walk, a letter in his hand and a disheveled attire. It was so unexpected, I turned around and started running like mad through the forest to the parsonage. I never looked back. If he went after me, I did not realize, or if he just stared at my retreating figure, I cannot tell.

After some minutes catching my breath, I went to see Charlotte and implored her not to ask me to go to Rosings Manor or to any other place until my uncle sent for me.

The only entry in my diary those days is the following.

Hunsford, 15 April 1812

Mr. Darcy and Mr. Wickham are from Derbyshire. They could know about what happened in Lambton woods. How am I to consider befriending either of them?

No. No. NO! You must keep pretending!

Elizabeth, take into account that being a recluse has its advantages: you do not have to live up to anyone else's expectations.

****

Life at Longbourn was very much the same when Jane and I arrived. I kept my promise to Mama of not doing anything unladylike, at least during the day: just my walks and practicing the pianoforte. But in the nights, I escaped to my father's library and tried to understand the fascinating books of natural philosophy that were almost entirely covered by dust.

Some of them were intended for engineers. I could see that the principal scope was about teaching math and physics in a convenient way that could be employed to build war machines. At first I was scandalized that they should use Archimedes's, Galileo's and Newton's discoveries to do something so evil. Then, I reminded myself that *that* was the occupation of the first one, the second one was almost burned by the inquisition for his arguments against the church, and the third one was a tyrant.

Maybe my mother is right, and I should not like this.

Except, it was the only way to avoid the nightmares and memories that would intrude. Exhausting myself kept the dreams at bay, and doing calculus operations distracted my mind from remembering the scenes that I so regretted.

Two weeks after my return from Kent, the most unexpected visit happened. Mr. Bingley appeared in the neighborhood. Jane was shy, and his call did not last long, but the days that followed led to the irrevocable change in her demeanor, as said gentleman came each of them. At the end of the month, they were courting openly, we were calling each other by our given names, and my father gave his consent in a short interview where they established the wedding date for three months hence.

My sister was shining with beauty and more talkative than ever, and I wondered if this unexpected return of Mr. Bingley, and the absence of the superior sisters, had anything to do with a certain gentleman that haunted my every night.

With the hope of seeing him again, I eagerly anticipated the visits to Netherfield. Of course, after each, I scolded myself for this foolish infatuation and his obvious reluctance to return to the place that should represent such unhappy results. I reminded myself of his celebrated pride and the fact that his good opinion, once lost, was lost forever. Although, I could not help straining my ears when Charles spoke about him or anything related.

This way, the weeks passed in the blink of an eye, with mother's wails about the shortness of time and preparations for the wedding trip. Jane and I were planning for her role as Mistress of Netherfield and conspiring to avoid Mama. She promised to take me to her home when returned, for who would teach their children to climb trees and write very ill? I told her perhaps Charles would not like the intrusion, but surely when I was the most anticipated old maid, could join them joyfully.

What I did not reveal was that I dreaded the time when I should see the wedding of Mr. Darcy to some pretty, accomplished lady from the *ton* which, due to the connection with Charles, was an unavoidable scene.

The entry that I have in my diary is about Lydia:

Longbourn, 16 June

My little sister was invited to accompany Mrs. Forster to Brighton with the militia. Amid the preparations and upcoming events, Father's permission was denied; not without a lot of histrionics and wailing from her though.

The departure of the regiment left a yellow scar on the field where they had encamped, merchants with empty pockets, and several broken hearts. I could not but rejoice, because the presence of a charismatic and popular Lieutenant caused only apprehension in me.

****

The week before the wedding, Mr. Darcy was expected to stay with Charles. He was going to stand by him at the altar, and he was going to bring his sister too. Thus, I made the vow to avoid Netherfield at all costs. I could always use the excuse that his sisters, Louisa and Caroline, were arriving any time from now, and it was a widely spread wisdom that they did not like me.

Chapter 2

The first day that announced the arrival of the Darcy siblings to Hertfordshire, I decided to employ my time in the gardens, which were blooming beautifully at this time of the year. I had just lost my scissors under some spiny bushes when I heard a carriage approaching. Hurrying to sit on my knees I tried to reach through the branches. Soon I found myself with no escape, with my hair and sleeves entangled in the sharp herbage.

Oh, God. Why was I so clumsy!?

In vain I tried to liberate myself from the claws that were holding me. In a few seconds, my position was so awkward that I started to panic, forgot about everything and cried for help with all my might. Thinking that things could not get worse, I was emphatically contradicted.

"Miss Bennet, are you well?" There was a hint of sarcasm in Mr. Darcy's inquiry.

Please Earth, swallow me!

"Brother! Do not be unkind! Do you not see that she needs assistance?" came a very welcome response from a feminine voice behind me.

"Yes, of course, of course. Give me a second, Miss Bennet," said he. "I always bring a penknife with me."

Immediately, I felt warm fingers in the small of my back trying to unhook my dress. I heard some fabric catch and a low curse. When I started to feel him carefully working on my neck, shoulders and upper arms, I could not hear anything but my heart galloping.

After what seemed an eternity, when my sleeves were almost free, I was sweating so much, I can declare that if it rained, my body could not have gotten any damper. Thanks to the Almighty, at some point, only my hair remained tangled, and four hands worked diligently with my curls.

When they were finished, I dropped myself unceremoniously to the ground and covered my face. The siblings seated themselves beside me, breathing hard. Mr. Darcy hid something dark in his pocket, and they shared unintelligible words at my back.

After a moment, realizing the folly of my attitude, I reasoned this was the best way to meet him after so many months. Because, how awkward it would have been to meet at the altar during Jane's wedding for the first time since Kent!?

Thus, I started to shake with chuckles. A small hand grabbed my elbow, and when I uncovered my face, they were looking at me with an earnest expression that was soon substituted by mirth. We started to laugh almost at the same time, so loud that it became contagious. When Jane approached, even she could not stop her giggles.

"Brother, please, could you introduce me? For I do not think this was a proper introduction," the girl beside me stated with a grin.

"Oh yes. May I present my sister, Miss Georgiana Darcy," he said with a flourish. "This is Miss Jane Bennet, and her younger sister, Miss Elizabeth Bennet, my dear."

Jane and I curtsied and replied simultaneously, "It is very nice to meet you!" and a new wave of chuckles started.

After some minutes of silly banter, we went to the house. Once inside my room, the dress had to be discarded due to several revealing cuts. I hurried to put on a new one.

He has come! He has come!

In front of the looking glass, I found there were some tiny scrapes on my neck. One thick braid had been cut by a half — nothing that could not be fixed rearranging the tresses.

Coming back to the parlor, my sisters were there, and Mama was asking about Miss Bingley and Mrs. Hurst.

"They are already in Netherfield," was the timid response of Miss Darcy.

So, that was why they were taking refuge here.

Mr. Darcy turned around from his customary place in front of the window. "I know you are busy with the many preparations, but I feel that my sister has spent too much time indoors during her stay in London. Could any of you show her the village and the countryside during our stay?"

"Of course, Mr. Darcy, all except Jane can do that tomorrow if you would like!" was my mother's eager response.

My sisters answered enthusiastically as well, and it was arranged that we would all stop by Netherfield about nine in the morning.

Poor Mama, she was trying to behave like a grand dame in front of Miss Darcy. She could not see that walking three miles to Netherfield was far from what was considered proper in Mr. Darcy's eyes. It did not matter to me; it could not be worse than what had happened before!

After some unsuccessful starts, I managed to find a topic of conversation that interested the girl at my right. It was music. I discovered she could play not only the pianoforte, but the violin as well — a fact that surprised me, as some people considered this particular instrument inappropriate for women — and that her brother was proficient in drawing portraits from memory. This particular theme did not last long though, because Mr. Darcy was uncomfortable with being the subject of our tête-à-tête.

****

That night, I went to bed with the feeling that not all was lost, that maybe someday I could tell Mr. Darcy the truth about my parentage. If he still wanted his sister to befriend me, it could mean that he was not so frightfully angry at me.

And I committed the mistake of going to bed early.

Longbourn, 26 July

I decided I should put in black and white the dreams that are so insistent in intruding in my head. Maybe this way I can solve the puzzle of what happened. In all of them, I could see that I caught Jack after some chasing, and that someone else was with him — another lad.

This boy reminds me of somebody that I have met recently. Yes, I have seen this face. Or a parent? There is a strange look about him. Strange eyes.

****

Natural Philosophy is about finding patterns in nature. A law or an equation is a way to put the world in a simple language. When you find a pattern, you say that you understand a certain class of phenomena. That was my aim: to rationalize my sentiments and find the truth about my past, to make a simple model. Can that be accomplished with human feelings?

****

The next day, I was up about six o'clock, so, when the time to visit Miss Darcy came, I was quite impatient. My sisters were not yet awake, and I decided to go by myself. We could pass by later, if my new friend was interested.

When I arrived at Netherfield Park, Mr. and Miss Darcy were already seated on a bench outside the manor. I had an odd feeling of satisfaction seeing them there. Maybe they were impatient for my arrival, and it was a sound decision to leave my family at home.

"Good morning, Miss Bennet." Mr. Darcy stood and helped his sister up.

"Good morning. What would you like to do today?"

"It is dry, and not extremely hot. I suggest you take my sister to Oakham Mount, if you are not particularly tired, of course."

"Very good. We can arrange some other day to spend with my sisters in Meryton, for I am poor company when shopping, and they are poor company when they have to walk a long distance."

"Is that why they are not with you?" asked the girl, and I could sense that she thought they did not like her company enough.

"Well, they are also late because they cannot be ready this early! You see, only we, accomplished ladies, can be up with the Sun. Did you put on your hundred mile walking boots?"

"Oh yes, look," said she, slightly lifting her skirt.

"Then you are ready," proclaimed Mr. Darcy with a wave of his hand. "Off you go!"

Miss Darcy gave him a quick kiss, and we departed like two young girls looking for adventure.

The walk served to get to know Ana better (the pet name she preferred), and Mr. Darcy by inference. I discovered her to be a clever girl, with a warm way of looking innocent under a dry wit. We were not so different: we were both looking for acceptance and craving someone with whom to share confidences, without the consequences of a relation with family. We could be comforting strangers.

After reaching Oakham Mount, I decided to tell her a little secret.

"Do you see that land at the east?"

"Yes, what about it?"

"That is the first place I spotted your brother, a few months ago." As my disclosure could be misconstrued, I rushed to add, "and Mr. Bingley, of course."

"My brother told me, you met at an Assembly."

"Yes, because I was doing some sort of experiment on that tree and did not want to be found out." I signaled a short leafy elm that served well for determining Earth's gravity*. "They would not have seen me, even if they were a few steps from me."

"Would you care to climb it now?" said she, with an eager expression.

"Oh, no! We cannot. What would your brother think? He will not let you come with me again!"

"But he taught me himself. And it is a small one. He does not have to know."

Oh dear, what have I done? "What if tomorrow we visit a secret place? A place that no one has seen and have a picnic there? This way we do not conceal anything from him, and will manage to keep another dress wholesome."

"Yes," she whispered with her head downcast.

"What if we go to Longbourn to see if my younger sisters are up now? It is the same distance as to Netherfield, and we may ask for the carriage to take you back home."

"Can we send a note to my brother in that case?"

I took the hand of the little manipulator. "We will do that as soon as we arrive."

Once at home, we joined Mary in the music room. She was practicing some new songs, and the aid of Miss Darcy was most helpful. After some time of listening to her performance, we realized how diligent she must be in her studies to be this proficient. My other sisters soon joined, and happy music banter started. Ana played some duets with Mary, others with me. We all sang. Our chorus was out of tune and Lydia changed the lyrics now and then, but it was great fun.

Mama invited Miss Darcy for lunch, and when Mr. Darcy came to pick up his sister, we were all sleepy, chatting about shopping on the morrow.

"Brother, so soon?" Ana suppressed a yawn.

"Soon?! You have been here all day. And I can see that you are tired."

"Yes, but we were very busy discussing important matters of feminine pursuits and lace."

"And pray, enlighten me, what is so important about lace?"

"Oh, this is a serious matter," I said, doing my best imitation of Miss Bingley. "We need to determine how much fabric is necessary for a turban. Would you care to share with us your point of view? What is your preferred color?"

"My preferred color? It is …" he paused, looking me in the eyes, and then turned his face to his shoes. "No, I am sure I do not have a preferred color."

Oh, Elizabeth, you should bite your tongue, it is mean to mock his friend's sister.

"Well, we can finish that conversation tomorrow," interjected Jane.

"Yes, what is the plan?" asked Lydia.

It was agreed to go to the haberdashers and milliners on the next day. Mr. Darcy offered his carriage for the venture, and they parted to Netherfield right away.

Well, he had no problem with his sister befriending me, but he certainly did not want to be in my company!

****

The trip to Meryton was exceedingly noisy — just how it should have been in a carriage full with six young women. My younger sisters ran to the shops just after being handed out, and Jane, Ana and I walked behind them. After some time going from one shop to another, I excused myself a moment to go to another shop. They were all entertained with a new set of fabrics celebrated as the latest fashion, and they surely would not notice my absence. Thus, I surreptitiously escaped to the post office.

The motive for my secrecy: I was expecting a package whose content I did not want Mama to discover.

I rushed across the street and entered the place, breathing heavily. Running directly into the owner, I asked about my parcel. He handed it to me, explaining it had just arrived and he had planned to deliver it during the day. I was in the process of thanking him, "No, I will take it home myself. Let me see if it is what I am expecting," unwrapping the envelope, when the door opened and a shrill voice startled me.

---

*The gravity constant g is a one of the most popular physical properties known all around the World. It is easily measured using a simple pendulum. The rigorous name of this magnitude is "acceleration of gravity" and its value on the surface of the Earth (around $9.8 m/s^2$) differs from one place to another. The experiment Lizzy is referring to was designed by Galileo in 1602.

Chapter 3

"Miss Eliza, what a surprise!"

Turning, I covered the package with some haste, as Miss Bingley and Mr. Darcy appeared at the door. My heart contracted as I observed that she was firmly attached to him — a familiar expression of ownership on her face.

"Good morning, Miss Bennet," said Mr. Darcy.

"Good morning, Mr. Darcy, Miss Bingley."

"What a coincidence, Eliza, to run into you in this place! Were not you *supposed* to be taking care of Miss Darcy? Why are you not at your home with her?"

"Excuse me?" Why was she interested about my whereabouts? She had the best prize at her side.

Mr. Darcy disentangled from her. "Miss Bennet, I can see your package is from Longman and Co.; I am expecting a delivery from them as well. Is it a book? Can I see it?"

I handed it to him reluctantly.

Miss Bingley looked over his shoulder trying to catch the title. "*Dear* Eliza, are you taking the job of the delivery boy? What are you doing with a book in a foreign language? Look at that inscription. It is not Italian, not French. What idiom is this?"

"It is Russian."

"Is it? Let me see it." She took the book from Mr. Darcy's hands. "It is truly a strange book; look at these tables and diagrams. I hope you do not burn your brain with that."

"It is for my father. You can consult him, if it is of your interest what he reads."

"Let me ask for my correspondence. I would like to inform Georgiana that it is already here." He passed the book back to me.

Outside of the post office, Mr. Bingley's carriage was a few yards away, and said gentleman was coming out from the modiste's shop with Jane — all my sisters following them in a cloud of giggles and batting fans. They came across the street while Mr. Darcy and his companion were walking out with the mail in hand.

"Lizzy, there you are! You were with us one minute, and the next you disappeared." Jane grabbed my hand, exultant as she always is when with her betrothed. "I see you finally have the book you have been looking for."

So much for being discreet about my book.

"Dear Georgiana, finally I can catch up with you! I thought we would never see each other today!" Miss Bingley walked briskly to the girl that flinched at the unrequited familiarity.

"Miss Bennet," saluted Mr. Darcy from my back.

"Darcy, you were lucky with your assignment," responded my future brother.

"Good Morning, Mr. Darcy," curtsied Jane. "You are here also! What a happy coincidence; and Miss Bingley as well."

"Yes." *Why is he so laconic now?*

"Excuse me, I should say hello to my future sister." Jane drew her fiancé where the rest of the girls were chatting amiably.

"Miss Elizabeth," called Mr. Darcy, "I must apologize for what happened. I was trying to distract Miss Bingley from the subject of Georgiana, and ended up focusing her attention on something that is a personal matter for you. It was most ungentlemanlike, I am sorry."

Oh, do not remind me of that. Those words were undeserved and cruel. I could not think of them without abhorrence — lost in my own web of lies. "You do not need to. As you can see, everything is well. This coincidence is all my sister needed for this to become another perfect day."

"Yes. I am glad Bingley's plan worked rather fast."

"Fitzwilliam!" Georgiana approached. *Thank God.* "We have had so much fun. I bought several trinkets and ordered a new bonnet. It is going to be the same blue shade as my new pelisse. You will like it."

Mr. Darcy recovered from our conversation immediately, hiding his package behind his back. "When are you going to show them to me? I have something for you, as well."

"Hmm, do not try to trick me, brother. There is no way you are taking me home so soon. I am having the best of times." Ana dragged us to the rest of the group, where Miss Bingley was doing her best to keep that 'certain something' in her air.

"Charles, if you are going with them to Longbourn, I am going back home with Mr. Darcy. I have much to do, and Louisa is awaiting me. We have a wedding ahead of us. There is no time for these girlish amusements."

Mr. Darcy became rigid, and Georgiana took him aside once more.

"Come, Caroline," Jane encouraged. "We will send for Mrs. Hurts too."

"I certainly shall not. Unless I am particularly acquainted with the company, I detest paying calls. I shall go straight home to do what is planned." She directed herself to where Mr. Darcy and Georgiana were standing.

"Thank you, thank you! You are the best brother ever." Ana was jumping and hanging into his neck. "Thank you for coming with us."

"Where?" All the colors disappeared from Caroline's face.

"With the Bennet sisters, of course."

Miss Bingley took three deep respirations and grumped a goodbye.

After following her angry movements, we regrouped to decide how to go back home with only one carriage. The solution was straightforward: Jane and Charles wanted to be alone, and a crowed carriage was not to their liking. Mr. Darcy and I would act chaperones; the younger girls did not want to break up their merry party, nor walk either. Ana was visibly happy with the sheets of music that had come in the new package, and was planning with Mary to practice as soon as they reached Longbourn.

****

We strolled by the lane in silence for some time, giving the love birds enough space. Sporadically, Mr. Darcy would remark about the good time they were having in Hertfordshire. I could not find any subject safe enough, until he ventured, "Miss Elizabeth, I believe we should have some conversation. It would look odd to be entirely silent for half an hour together."

His present mood was still an enigma to me, and I followed the game. "What think you of books, Mr. Darcy?"

"Books — oh! No. I am sure we never read the same, or not with the same feelings." He handed his parcel. *Must he remember everything!?*

I looked up at him and then at the title. "It is about philosophy! — What a strange subject nowadays, when all I hear gentlemen speak of is the war on the Continent!"

"Why? I do not see any problem in learning any field, from history to alchemy. You do not need to invest anything but your time and intellect. I am sure you would find it immensely interesting."

"Are you complimenting me, Mr. Darcy?" *Bite your tongue; bite your tongue — do not play with fire!*

"Do you want to be complimented, Miss Elizabeth?"

"It depends." *Oh dear.* "Only if it is deserved."

"So, let us put you to the test." He straightened in a pose that reminded of Michelangelo's David before battle. "Do you think we must believe in what we can measure, or in what we intuit?"

"In what we can measure, yes. Definitely, I believe in what we can measure or observe somehow."

"You do not believe in that which you have not seen, then? How do you

20

account for the existence of God, or how can you be sure of what you see, if there are different points of view inherent to whom the observer is?"

"Well, it certainly depends on the subject at study. The existence of God is an act of faith — there is no rationality involved in this." I paused in order to organize the ideas. "My rational mind is put at rest when I talk with God. On the contrary, the problem of the observer's point of view is easily overcome using adequate instruments. If we can prove something — really prove following the laws of nature — then, I think it true."

"So, you think everything has to be proven to believe in it?"

Such a statement had many ramifications. I took the coward's way out. "Well, Mr. Darcy, at this very moment, I only believe that we have arrived and that I shall have to earn my compliment at some other time."

"I look forward to it."

Entering the house, I excused myself for a couple of minutes to hide the book in my room. Soon afterwards, the betrothed couple was already in the parlor, chatting with Kitty and Mama. Lydia, Mary and Ana were not in sight. In view of Mr. Darcy's bored expression and hearing some scattered notes, I guided him to the music room.

We encountered the girls with the sheets in their hands. Mary was studying one of them intently, and trying some chords on the pianoforte. The other two were planning something for the next days. My younger sibling was a little put out about the impossibility of having Georgiana all for herself.

"Lydia, I have plans for tomorrow morning. Please understand."

"Sister, she will be available by the time you awaken in the morning. We are not going far," I came to Ana's rescue.

"Where are you supposed to go tomorrow morning, Poppet? I have not been informed of this," said Mr. Darcy.

"Oh, Fitzwilliam, Lizzy has promised to take me to a special place."

"And what about me? I have not seen you in ages. Are you planning to abandon me all the time in Hertfordshire? You agreed to go riding with me one of these days."

"Lizzy, do you think my brother could come tomorrow?" Ana rushed to ask.

"My sister never rides. She has such a fear of horses, that she always rounds the carriage by the rear," Lydia mocked. "I do not think you can convince her to agree to your plan."

"Then, I am sure my brother can enjoy an early walk as well. Pleeease."

This girl was a skilled negotiator. I should learn from her! Was she trying to push me toward her sibling?

"All right." I directed to Lydia. "And, it would do you good to walk now and then. Do not you want to go with us?"

"La! It is a waste of time." She turned on her heels and went out.

"Child, I think that we are imposing on Miss Elizabeth," intervened Mr. Darcy.

"No, no," I said a little too eagerly. "We need someone to carry the picnic basket."

"So, I am the pack animal instead! I am wounded." Mr. Darcy pressed a hand over his heart.

"Oh, brother!" Ana slapped his arm lightly.

"I should invite Mary. Excuse me a minute."

I retreated to the pianoforte as Mr. Darcy whispered to Georgiana, "'Lizzy', eh?"

****

Longbourn, 28 July

Something turned on a trigger in my mind today. I remembered a part of the dialogue. I still cannot identify the other boy.

"This is a boy's game, only for the big and brave," said Jack dismissively.

"I am brave, very brave!" I cried.
"Brave, eh?" He smiled a little sarcastically.
"Yes, I can do anything."
"Anything?" asked the other boy.
"Yes!"
"I do not think so," Jack intervened more seriously.
"I can, I can. Try me!"
"No, Lizzy, no."
"Why not?" I insisted.
"Yes, why not? Let us put her to the test."

Here I rouse with heavy perspiration. I do not know what to think anymore.

****

The unknown lad could not be him!

On the verge of screaming, I compared the voices in my head. "So, let us put you to the test," and, "Let us put her to the test." No, no, no!

He was not like that. No more thinking! *Shut your mind. Stop!* I ran downstairs to the music room.

Relax or you will wake up everyone.

One of Ana's new music sheets fitted my purpose well: Ludwig van Beethoven's "Sonata Pathétique."** Yes, that word coincided with my behavior. What was I thinking while flirting with him again yesterday!? Today I would restrain myself. I had to!

****

I practiced and practiced, putting all my heart into the performance: the tune was melancholic, and it suited my spirit. It was exactly what was needed for me to understand the center of my problem: regrets. I would regret all my life not making the next step.

Thus, after I do not know how many hours, dawn came. I was going to climb the stairs to put on my morning gown, when Mary came already changed. It was too early for her to be up, but understanding came to me when she took the papers possessively.

She turned to the pianoforte and started to practice the same melody without a word toward me. Too tired to give consequence to this strange conduct, I left. They were used to my early play. She could not be angry for waking her up.

Once back in the music room, my sister was visibly frustrated with her performance. To encourage her, I sat in the bench. First, I just told her to be patient, that it was a difficult piece. She looked at me and shook her head. Poor child, so demanding of herself.

She stumbled through the notes, hitting the keys with too much force. I decided to explain the technique. My fingers played the first movement, until I gathered that it did not have the desired effect on my companion.

"It is easy for you. You are left handed!"

"Mary, take it easy!" I took her arm, trying to stop her from leaving.

"No!" She elbowed, throwing the papers to the floor as she rose. "Do you know how it is said in Latin, Lizzy? — It is 'sinister'. That is what you are!"***

We heard a gasp from behind us and turned to see Mr. Darcy and Georgiana at the door; which provoked Mary to run out of the room, barely avoiding colliding with the siblings.

"Good morning," he said, as I collected the music sheets.

"I am sorry, Ana. I am sorry," I told the girl that was somewhat perplexed.

Mr. Darcy bent down to assist, as he scrutinized me. "Nothing happened, Miss Elizabeth. It is all right. We also fight all the time."

"Yes, you are right. Let us forget about it." I laid the papers on a side table. "Are you ready?"

Mr. Darcy helped me up. The excursion started.

****

"Do you approve?" I asked, when the building came into view.

It was an old church, resembling a cottage from Snow White's tale, covered in creeper to the roof. It was taller than it was wide, and some ruins reminded it had not survived some fire that happened many years ago.

Georgiana covered her mouth, amazed, and Mr. Darcy studied the remains.

I ran slowly down the gradual slope before them. When I reached the entrance, I looked back. They were smiling broadly. *Good choice, Lizzy.*

It was humid and cold inside — so welcome after the long walk. I closed my eyes to breathe the peaceful atmosphere of this favorite place. I could almost feel the tiny dust particles suspended in the air, and, when I opened them, I corroborated the image with scattered light rays that intruded in this sanctuary, dancing in my hair.

Shifting, I saw Georgiana touring the perimeter, touching the walls, studying the blurry paintings, measuring the tower height. She finally came to stand closer to me and said, "I see why it is a secret you guard so well — it is magic," she turned to point at her brother, who was still in the entrance, staring in our direction. "Look, he is spellbound."

"I am happy you like it. So, where would you like to take the picnic?"

Mr. Darcy awoke from his reverie. "Oh! I think I left the basket in your home, Miss Elizabeth."

Ana and I dismissed the apology, "We left very hurriedly. It is not your fault. We all forgot until now."

"Well, I saw a plum tree in the vicinity, what about that kind of refreshment?" said he, walking out again.

Georgina followed him, and I used this time to ponder all that was in my mind. I knelt in front of the altar and prayed for courage. I would never be easy with him until I explained the truth about my parentage.

After managing to push down the knot in my esophagus, I headed outside. They were not far. Ana was catching the plums that were dropped from above. His coat was laid on the grass. I neared the tree to see him skillfully climbing and plucking the fruit. If he were less handsome, it would make things so much easier!

In no time, we were back, sitting around the plums. Moment of truth. *Keep your courage, Elizabeth!*

"I must tell you something. An issue is weighing on my conscience which cannot be delayed any more."

"Good God! What is the matter?" cried he, with more feeling than politeness. "You look pale."

I raised my palm, asking him to wait, then let go, "I am not my father's child, I am the daughter of a soldier. I am not born from Longbourn. Mr. Bennet is my stepfather, the Bennets are my stepsisters, and from my real parents, I only know Mama. She was Mrs. Willoughby before becoming Mrs. Bennet. My real father abandoned us when I was a newborn. We have never had other news from him, I ...I..." the contraction in my throat did not allow me to continue. I covered my face.

I felt Mr. Darcy rise and go to a faraway corner, and Georgiana enveloped me in her arms. And I cried, oh God, I cried with all the resentment accumulated from so many years masquerading myself as another. I cried for the child that was rejected by her real father. I cried for the scorn I received as Elizabeth Willoughby, and for all the lonely hours I spent locked in a cottage.

Georgiana soothed me with sweet words for a long while, whereas Mr. Darcy stood apart. He seemed scarcely to hear us, and started walking up and down in earnest meditation, his brow contracted, his air gloomy. I observed, and instantly understood it. His opinion of me was sinking; everything *must* sink under such a proof of family weakness, such an assurance of the deepest disgrace. I could neither wonder nor condemn, but the belief of his self-conquest brought nothing consolatory to my bosom, afforded no palliation of my distress. It was, on the contrary, exactly calculated to make me understand my own wishes; and never had I so honestly felt that I could have loved him, as now, when all love must be vain.

"I am afraid you have been long desiring my absence," he said and strode out of the church.

A while afterwards, Georgiana and I were walking companionably silent back home, whilst Mr. Darcy followed alone. I did not dare to look back at him. Not once. *He must hate me now.*

---

*Sonata Pathétique or Piano Sonata No. 8 in C minor, Op. 13 was written in 1798 when the composer was 27 years old.

**The etymology of Sinister is as follows: early 15c., "prompted by malice or ill-will," from *sinistre* "contrary, unfavorable, to the left," from Latin *sinister* "left, on the left side" (opposite of *dexter*), perhaps from root **sen-* and meaning properly "the slower or weaker hand". The Latin word was used in augury in the sense of "unlucky, unfavorable" (omens, especially bird flights, seen on the left hand were regarded as portending misfortune), and thus *sinister* acquired a sense of "harmful, unfavorable, adverse". *Bend* (not *"bar"*) *sinister* in heraldry indicates illegitimacy and preserves the sense of "on the left side." (from: http://www.etymonline.com).

Chapter 4

Arriving home, Jane took care of our guests. She sent me upstairs. Physically and emotionally tired, I fell asleep quickly. Thankfully, I did not have any dreams.

Once awake, I observed that the Darcys must have left.

The new book would serve to silence my memories. I took it from under the pillow and scanned the title. I could not understand a single word: "Рассужденіе о твердости и жидкости тѣль," author: "Михаиломъ Ломоносовымъ."* I opened the book and understood one thing: 1760 — The publication year. I should be able to figure out all the symbols and graphs.

The language of science is mathematics — it is a universal idiom that does not depend on the country you live in. Any person that understands it should be capable of communicating his ideas with other people just using numbers, equations and graphs. Or so I thought at that time. Consequently, I was tremendously vexed when realized, after scanning the highly anticipated book over several hours, that it was almost impossible to discern its content. Caroline was right, I would burn my brain with this — headstrong, headstrong Lizzy!

I annotated in my diary:

Longbourn, 28 July, afternoon.

Today I started to peruse the book that I received yesterday after five months of expectation. I know the actual name in English from the previous reference; it is "Reflection on the solidity and fluidity of bodies." So I infer that:
Рассуждение = Reflection;
о = on;
твердости = solidity;
и = and;
жидкости = fluidity;
тѣль = bodies.

But it could be all wrong. I know Papa has a book about the Russian Empire in the library; tomorrow I am going to look up at the alphabet to learn more.

****

When it was almost time for supper, my dear Uncle and Aunt Gardiner arrived with all their children. When I heard the commotion, I rushed down to welcome them. The two girls of six (Amy) and eight (Rose) years old, and the two younger boys (Michael and David), ran to me, crashed and hung around my neck so hard that I was pulled to the ground. Laughing and hugging, we tickled each other; I finished up all disheveled, my mood restored in no time.

The family reunion was a happy one, father and uncle dueled with jokes, and a joyful spirit surrounded us as if it were Christmas time. I ended up sleeping with the two girls curled around me in my bed. It felt so good!

****

The next day, I spent almost all the time playing with the four young soldiers under the orders of Admiral Lord Nelson — Kitty — that were visiting directly from Cape Trafalgar. A tent was constructed in the gardens with the help of Georgiana, the tallest of us, using a large piece of fabric attached to some bushes. We simulated every scenario, real and fantastic: the surround of enemy ships, the assault to 'La Armada Invencible', Nelson's death, the flight of the Spanish cowards and the conversion from marine to evil pirates of the loyal and fearless British Royal Navy. Mary and Lydia were the perfect damsels in distress; whereas Lydia preferred the Army men, Mary fell in love with the pirates.

At the end of the day, when everyone else was resting a little, and Ana was preparing to leave, I accompanied her to the carriage.

"Lizzy, what you did yesterday showed a lot of courage. I am impressed and honored that you told us. I would like some day to have the strength to tell you something that happened to me not long ago." She took my hands in hers. "You are the only person that could understand why I did it."

"I am willing to listen, but I think you should consult with your brother. He does not agree with you about me being brave at all. He certainly must think I am an inappropriate friend and counselor for you." I shrugged my shoulders at the questions in her eyes. "Please just ask him first; I do not want to intrude in your life."

"See you to-morrow then."

****

The next day I woke up in the most unconcerned and happy manner ever: my smallest boy cousin was riding on my stomach as if I were one of Napoleon's horses! He screamed, jumped and played with such energy that the bed hit the wall as in an earthquake.

I took his tiny hands in mine. "What is…?" Oh Dear, it was late, "Where are your sisters?" He jumped harder. "David, little storm… Oh, OUCH!"

"Attack the French! Hey!" He hit my sides with his feet. "Hey, there is a fort ahead! Hey!"

His joyful mood was so contagious I could not but comply, and we started to move up and down in coordination until my belly ached.

"Well, little one, I think the rest of the troops are waiting for us to have breakfast," I said while handing him to a maid in the hallway.

I changed to a simple morning dress and went after the boy. "Come with me."

Once we were downstairs, I realized I had really overslept. It was because all this playing had tired me — good remedy! "Let us see where your siblings are." After finding Aunt Madeline, mother and Jane inspecting the wedding dress in my sister's chamber, we continued on to the other rooms. Uncle and Papa were in the library, Mary playing the pianoforte. "It seems they are all with Kitty and Lydia."

"There you are, Lizzy!" was the eager greeting. "Thank God! We need you."

"Whatever for?" They seemed a merry party with the girls arranging Lydia's hair in a mess of lace and braiding, while the other boy read in Kitty's lap.

"Come, come Lizzy," Amy grabbed my hand and directed where my sister was, "we will make you look like a princess."

"Yes, Lizzy, my head hurts. I cannot take it anymore!" Lydia stood up from the vanity and sat me there instead. "They will make you the prettiest ever. Kitty and I are going to the gardens with the boys."

At the broad smiles of the children, I obliged happily.

Imagine the funny picture afterwards, when my aunt came into the girls' room and encountered half of my hair on the face, and the rest arranged in twenty tresses with ribbons and colored clasps.

"You never looked more charming."

"Do you think so, Mama?" one girl asked, and the other suggested, "Let us go downstairs Lizzy, so everyone can see how beautiful your hairstyle is!"

Agreeing, I volunteered to fetch the boys from the gardens. It was surely going to rain in a short while.

My sisters and cousins were finishing a high structure of wooden blocks under the tent.

"Dear ones, your Mama is calling for you. Go inside." I waved them off, staying to pick up the toys.

The blocks were ordinate cubes, but on the floor, I found a wooden puzzle that intrigued me exceedingly. I remembered seeing it before in the form of a star, but now it was disarrayed, and I was curious about how to put back the smaller pieces into the previous configuration. I tried and tried, again and again, many shapes for naught. Geometry was not my thing.

"Good morning, Miss Elizabeth. Let me help you." Mr. Darcy stepped into the tent and knelt in front of me.

I handed the pieces to him. "Good morning."

"I see why you are lingering here. These toys were my favorite when I was a lad. My father told me, they were Chinese art crafts." The precise movements of his long fingers were captivating. "I came with my sister and Bingley. He cannot stay away a single day."

31

And you, why did you come? I did not dare to ask.

He finished and handed the toy. I laid it on the basket and started to put the other blocks in.

"Miss Elizabeth, I am not good at this…That is, I want to apologize for my abominable speech at Hunsford. I could not have been more wrong, your relatives merit my utmost respect. You belong to a family where everyone is loved and treated as equal. I cannot even imagine how difficult it must have been to raise you all, against the misconceptions about adopting, about orphans…"

I tried to interrupt his apology, disbelieving my ears, but he stopped me.

"No, no, please, let me finish. I understand now why you have been avoiding me. It is wholly deserved, I was disrespectful, and your words: your conceit, and your selfish disdain of the feelings of others," he cited, "they could not be more justified."

"Please, please, Mr. Darcy, I am not avoiding you."

"You are not avoiding me? You do not have to spare my feelings, Miss Elizabeth. I would rather know the truth than be in the wrong forever."

"You are not angry at me?"

"Why would I be angry?"

Because I treated you disrespectfully, because I befriended your sister. I — someone so far below you…

He seemed to guess my thoughts, and said exactly what I needed to hear, "I have been a selfish being all my life, in practice, though not in principle. As a child, I was taught what was right, but I was not taught to correct my temper. I was given good principles, but left to follow them in pride and conceit. Unfortunately, an only son (for many years an only child), I was spoilt by my parents, who, though good themselves (my father, particularly, all that was benevolent and amiable), allowed, encouraged, almost *taught* me to be selfish and overbearing; to care for none beyond my own family circle; to think meanly of all the rest of the world; to wish at least to think meanly of their sense and worth compared with my own. Such I was, from eight to eight and twenty; and such I might still have been but for you, dearest, loveliest Elizabeth! What do I not owe you! You taught me a lesson, hard indeed at first, but most advantageous. By you, I was properly humbled. I came to you without a doubt of my reception. You showed me how insufficient were all my pretensions to please a woman worthy of being pleased."

He had such a yearning look, I had to explain, "I never meant to deceive you, but my spirits might often lead me wrong. How you must have hated me after *that* evening?"

"Hate you! I was angry perhaps at first, but my anger soon began to take a proper direction."

"And now, after the disclosure of my family connections?"

"Now?" He looked up at my hair. "I think you are the most fashionable lady in the neighborhood."

I touched it and remembered my appearance. "Oh," a giggle escaped my lips as some rain drops were heard, "I am told this is the latest style for Royalty."

****

When what seemed a light rain, developed into a biblical storm, all the guests were invited for luncheon. We were gathered in the dining room, the Gardiners, the Darcys, Charles and my family when Mama's complaints began.

"Oh Jane, this cannot be. Your wedding dress will be ruined! What are we going to do now? The carriage may even stick in the muddy roads, and we will have to go walking, and your dress, oh God, your lovely dress..."

"Something like that will surely scare the groom away," replied Papa dryly.

Charles was momentarily startled, but recovered soon. "I think in the event of such circumstances, I would carry her!"

"All the way back home or to the church?" Uncle hid his smile under a napkin.

My aunt tapped him under the table, and Jane changed color. Poor sister, she was always too serious.

"I am sure the bride will look so beautiful in her wedding dress that, in case he abandons her, there will be countless candidates to take Charles's place," came the clever response from Georgiana, while Mr. Darcy looked at her (apparently amazed by his sister's ease).

"And what if it is still raining by tomorrow morning?" Mama waved her handkerchief dramatically. "No one will attend. We will be alone in church, with all the flower arrangements and breakfast for thirty families."

"In that case, you may raise the opportunity to marry one of your other daughters to the vicar, or any other unfortunate soul that passes by," counterattacked Papa.

"Oh, Mr. Bennet, you delight in vexing me!"

This way we expended a couple of hours at the table, while I tried not to look in Mr. Darcy's direction. My sisters talked about their elegant clothes for the morrow, my uncle and father made sport of us, and the object of my observation smiled to himself now and then.

Could he be starting to like my family?

****

The rain did not relent soon. Mary and Aunt Madeline decided to distract Mama upstairs, while Papa and Uncle Gardiner went to the library. The rest of us were confined to the parlor, trying to entertain the children. After some time, we managed a semblance of peace when they agreed to listen to the book of "Gulliver's Travels: A Voyage to Lilliput and Blefuscu."

Michael, the smaller one, fell asleep in my lap while Kitty was reading. The rest were quiet for some time, until they found that it would be much more fun to enact the story. The part of the habitants of Lilliput fell on the two girls and the boy, and it was little David's idea that Mr. Darcy should be an excellent actor for Gulliver. Lydia and Kitty agreed cheerfully, followed by Jane and Charles (Lilliput's queen and king).

The main role would have been vacant if Ana had not insisted that such character was tailored for his brother, for he had the right stature and commanding voice necessary to terrorize the enemy fleet — this was how the always proper Mr. Darcy found himself laid on the floor, with three children pulling his hair in all directions.

To everyone's consensus, the best part was when Gulliver pulled the enemy ships, screaming a terrible AAGGRR while standing up with the three Blefuscudians and swinging them around.

The performance attracted the attention of the rest of the household; it finished with the actors bowing proudly to a loud ovation.

Who was I kidding? I was enchanted by this man.

****

When the Netherfield party had decided it was time to depart, for a wedding was on the morrow and it would not do to have the bride and groom with dark circles under their eyes, I followed Jane toward the foyer.

The Darcys pulled me aside to give privacy to the couple.

"Oh, Lizzy, it has been a wonderful day. I have not had so much fun in ages!"

"Yes, Ana, it has been great indeed, thank you for coming."

"It is a pity that tomorrow we have to leave," she gazed at his brother, asking a silent question.

"We cannot stay here if the Bingleys are not at home, Poppet."

She breathed out and Mr. Darcy rolled his eyes, "May we write to you? I mean, may Georgiana write to you, when we go back to London?"

"Yes. We are becoming the best of friends."

****

Longbourn, 30 July, midnight.

Today Mr. Darcy called me "dearest, loveliest Elizabeth." I know it is improper, and I should have cautioned him, but he said my name with such gentleness that I could not.
"Dearest, loveliest Elizabeth." Nobody has ever called me that.
Can he, in spite of everything, be interested in me? What am I going to do if he is?

Mama is still talking to Jane in her bedchamber. I suppose they are speaking about the marriage bed. What takes them so long, I do not understand. If the instructions are: "You have to be brave and it will be finished soon," how it is that they have been speaking for hours?
I pray Charles will be gentle with Jane, and it will not hurt so much.

****

Mama walked out of my sister's room, and I surreptitiously entered to find her already in bed.

"Jane, are you awake?"

"Yes, come." She moved to leave enough space for me to lie besides her.

"Are you well? What delayed Mama so much? Is she still worried about the rain?"

"No, Lizzy. I think she has all but forgotten about that."

"Mmm," climbing under the covers, I attempted to reassure her, "Do not be scared about tomorrow. Charles loves you — he will be understanding."

"Oh, I know that. As a matter of fact, I anticipate our wedding night with eagerness."

Then, it was not about 'that' that they had talked about. "I am happy for you then. Where are you going for your wedding trip?"

"I do not know! Charles wants it to be a surprise. He only told it is on the continent, and that I need a lot of clothes, because it is going to last at least three months. I am so excited about it! 'Tis too much! By far too much. I do not deserve it. Oh! Why is not everybody as happy?"

I embraced her lightly, still worried about the intimate parts of the voyage, and hoping that she would stay content nevertheless.

My sister turned to face me with a broad smile. "And you, Lizzy? What about you and Mr. Darcy?"

I was startled by the question and feigned surprise.

"Do not look at me like that; you know what I am talking about. He stares at you all the time!" *Oh dear, what am I going to do!?*

It seemed Jane had sensed my panic, since she held me closer. "All will be well, Lizzy. All will be well."

---

*Why is Lizzy studying this difficult subject? — England is in the middle of Industrial Revolution, which is based on machine tools. For example, in 1812, the first gas lighting utilities were established in London.

The book she is studying here was written in the Old Russian language. The Russian alphabet changed in the early years of the twentieth century.

Chapter 5

Next morning, the uproar for the wedding made Longbourn seem as if we were being invaded by aliens. Mama was pacing up and down the house, "supervising" all of us, fussing around Jane and frantically giving orders to all the servants. Poor Mrs. Hill was after her, trying to put forth some semblance of equanimity and carrying all the clothes Mama discarded. I dressed up in my new pearly gown as fast as I could, but she was not pleased and made me arrange my hair several times. All in all, I must say she was right, the final touches to my style gave me a different appearance: I looked pretty.

After preparing the children, we were almost ready. The Gardiners boarded their coach; Mary, Kitty, Lydia and I climbed into Mr. Bingley's carriage.

Mother, father and Jane were going to linger a little to give the pretense of being fashionably late to the bride.

When we arrived, Mr. Bingley and Mr. Darcy were already near the altar. The picture they made was a handsome one: the bridegroom was in a light green waist coat along with dark green tails, and his companion was a vision to behold with his black and white attire. My sisters went to the family pew with my aunt and uncle, who were explaining to the children the importance of behaving properly during the ceremony.

The Minister, Mr. Parker, neared the gentlemen at the same time as I. "Miss Elizabeth." He bowed. "Messieurs, come please, I need to speak with you in the sacristy."

Charles looked nervously in my direction, and Mr. Darcy and I interchanged greeting smiles.

"You too, Lizzy, you too," commanded the vicar, showing the way.

After crossing the hallway, we arrived at a small room, and he positioned himself behind an enormous table.

"This is a serious matter I should have addressed before, but as you know already, I have not been in good health lately, so better now than never." He gazed at the groom that was sweating profusely. "Lizzy, you first. What can you tell me about Mr. Bingley?"

"About Mr. Bingley?"

"Yes. I understand that you met last autumn and spent a few days together at Netherfield. Am I right?"

I nodded.

"Then I suppose you know him a little. By the way, why were you staying there?"

"My sister Jane got sick after riding over for a dining invitation with Miss Bingley. I had to attend her," I remembered with mirth.

"Were not Mr. Bingley's sisters capable hostesses?" Oh Dear, he had spies everywhere.

Mr. Darcy saved me from replying with an eager proclamation, "She is an affectionate sister, Mr. Parker."

More confident now, I gathered my nerve to inquire, "May I ask to what these questions tend?"

"Merely to the illustration of Mr. Bingley's character. I am trying to make it out. He is carrying away the brightest jewel of the country."

Recalling a similar conversation a year ago, I could not help answering, "He is a sensible and amiable friend, but I could wish, Mr. Parker, that you were not to sketch his character at the present moment, as there is reason to fear that his performance would reflect no credit on him."

"If I do not take his likeness now, I may never have another opportunity." *You, Old Gossip! You are having your amusement at the expense of my future brother!*

"I can answer your enquiries more precisely, Reverend, as I am his friend of long duration." Mr. Darcy said with a conspiratorial glance at me.

Mr. Parker seemed intimidated by the accusatory tone used by the latter. "In that case, I prefer to speak to the groom. If you could please wait for him in the main chamber?"

With no other solution at hand, we complied. Poor Mr. Bingley. He would be asked every detail, from if he pulled his sisters' ribbons to if he bathed weekly.

Once in the small corridor, I chuckled quietly. "Did you see Charles's face?"

Mr. Darcy looked in the direction of the door. "Please, Miss Elizabeth, a minute? We may not have another prospect to be alone before my departure."

This likelihood stopped my strides, as he offered a little book from inside a pocket of his coat. "I just want to give you this. I know how much you enjoy reading foreign tongues."

Intrigued by this characterization, I saw it was a compilation of poems. I could not figure out the language, though.

"It is in Spanish, I hope you like it."

"Thank you, it is harmless, not like the other one I have in my room." I put it inside my reticule. To which, he beamed radiantly while we walked out. *You should smile more often, love.*

****

By the time Charles joined us at the altar, the church was full of people, and it was difficult to discern who was where. I had eyes only for Mr. Darcy, and almost missed the moment Jane walked through the aisle on the arm of my father. I stood by her proudly during the service, entranced by the words of commitment that were exchanged. I also permitted myself to dream that this moment could be for me as well, reciting the vows silently while stealing glances in the direction of the man in my thoughts. Our gazes met several times, and I was sure this was one of the happiest moments of my life.

The ceremony ended in a blink, and the new married couple was soon directing their steps to the many well-wishers standing by the corridor. I felt his tall figure at my side instantly, and his fingers taking mine in the crook of his arm. I looked up, knowing already that he had a gesture of satisfaction in his visage, while he patted my hand with familiarity.

It was in this perfect instant that I had a quick look forward to the crowd and saw *him*.

****

The day of Jane's wedding turned out to be the worst of my days ever. When realization dawned on me, I could not handle the reality. An excruciating pain of needles crossing my throat and belly doubled me in half, and I had to loosen Mr. Darcy's arm in order to run to the adjacent room and seclude myself in it.

The incredible spasms were surely going to make me vomit at any moment. I heard him ask through the closed door what was happening, but I could only mutter that I wished not to go back.

I closed my eyes tightly, until someone unlocked the entrance and steps rushed inside.

"Lizzy, what is it? Does anything hurt?" Mama came with the rest of my family. "Girls, move, give her some air. Mr. Bennet, open the window."

"I will get the apothecary." It was dear Mary, so solicitous.

The door screeched again, some voices were arguing outside.

"I should fetch my doctor! " — This was Mr. Darcy in the corridor.

"No. Wait until we know more. Her family is with her," Charles was with him.

"Calm down bro…" Georgiana started. The door was slammed back.

Recovering when the pain finally subsided, I realized I was sitting on a small sofa in the vestry.

"Darcy called us," Papa said with worry. "What happened?"

Oh God, I turned my face to avoid their scrutiny. *I cannot tell!*

Interchanging glances with him, Mama said, "Girls, you should go outside, and to the wedding breakfast with Mr. Bingley. We have already made enough of a spectacle. Your father and I will stay here until the apothecary comes."

Jane looked at her, astonished. "But…"

"No buts, you must go. Lizzy will be well."

I extended my arm to squeeze my sister's. "Jane, today is your wedding. Enjoy yourself. This is nothing. This is because the children have sapped all my energy."

"Come when you feel you are ready. Do not over task your body."

"Go, girls, go. Everyone must be outside wondering what has become of us."

My younger sisters kissed my forehead. "We will see you there," said one. "Rest all you need," said the other.

They walked out while Mary came in with the doctor.

"What happened, little pirate? What trouble did you get yourself into this time?" Mr. Thomas was smirking at me with the same jovial tone he had used when I was an infant.

"Her stomach aches." Mama became her usual self. "My Lizzy is not prone to being weak. I do not understand."

The doctor approached and laid me down, in order to check my abdomen through the fabric of my dress. Not finding anything unusual, he opened one of my eyes, then the other. "Have you been sleeping properly?"

"More or less, Sir."

"And eating?"

"Oh, I have noticed lately that she leaves half the plate full," she fluttered.

"That is not the Lizzy I know. What is the matter?"

Like a child being called to the carpet, I cast my eyes down. "I do not know. I have not noticed."

He inspected my nails, then my eyes again, and concluded, "This young lady is anemic. The only thing she needs is to eat properly and rest more; nothing that a caring family cannot accomplish."

Papa glanced at me. "Well, that is easy, Elizabeth. Do you think you can abide by the directions?"

"Yes, Mr. Thomas. Thank you."

"Then everything is in order. We must return to the wedding party." The men agreed to see each other outside.

Mama inhaled deeply, "Lizzy, it seems everything is all right. We should go now with Jane."

No, no! My mind cried as I shook my head.

"Why do you look so panicked, Elizabeth?" Mary questioned.

I was silent for a second, figuring out an excuse. "I do not feel like going. I... I am a little dizzy. I would like to go home."

"But we have to go to the wedding breakfast! It is mandatory for me to be there. No, no, Lizzy, this cannot be. We have to go now and pretend nothing happened. It will not do to fuel the gossip that must be already spreading all around!"

"If Lizzy faints, it will help nobody," my sibling interjected wisely. "I can go with her, and if she feels better, we can come back later to the celebration."

"A-h, n-o, a-h..." my mother stammered.

Mary gave me a supportive glance and continued explaining, "Mama, listen, you can go to Netherfield with Papa now in the carriage. Lizzy and I will wait here. If she is recovered by the time the carriage comes back, we will join you. If she is not, then I will accompany her home. Hill will take good care of her for sure."

"But you do not feel that bad, do you, Lizzy? You will come soon." Poor Mama, between her duty to me and her dreams about marrying us all.

"I promise to go when I feel better. Do not worry about me. It is just a passing thing. It is nothing." I put forth my best mask of contentment.

"Well, then wait here until someone fetches you."

Mary and I waved her goodbye and sat side by side quietly.

After a short while, Mrs. Hill appeared at the door. "Miss Lizzy, here you are! What happened to you?"

"Hill? What are you doing here?"

"I was summoned by Mr. Darcy's servants. I came in his carriage to take you to Longbourn. They said you were ill. Are you strong enough to walk to the road?"

"Yes, I think, so." I stood up, grabbing my reticule.

They helped me out, and then we were handed in. Observing the interior, I could not help the quiet longing. This was his. He sat here and slept on these cushions on long journeys. My fingers touched the beautiful leather. How would it feel to be in this close space with him? How would it be to share stories and argue about philosophy for a few hours of travel? I strived to memorize the last scent I would be allowed from him. *You will never know, Lizzy.*

When we arrived home, Mrs. Hill and Mary almost carried me upstairs. Changing to a nightdress, they took down my hair from its elaborate styling. The necessity of staying home overwhelmed my mind and I exaggerated my dizziness quite a bit.

"Lizzy, I see that you must stay in bed for the day." My sister covered me with a sheet.

"Yes, Mary, all will be fine. You can go and let Hill take care of everything. You know she will spoil me the whole time." *Please.*

"Then I should let you be. I am going to tell Mama that you are fatigued, but will soon recover. Good bye."

She hurried to the hall, and the sound of the carriage driving off was heard.

"Well, Miss Lizzy, what is it that you are trying to do with yourself?" Mrs. Hill startled me.

"Excuse me?"

"Oh, yes, I know you are up to something. I do not know what it is, but what is ailing you is not something from your body." She took my face in her hands. "What is bothering this pretty head of yours?"

"Nothing. I do not know what you are talking about."

"If there is anything I know about you, it is that you would not miss this day with Miss Jane. Something decidedly strange is happening, and you are taking it upon yourself not to share it with anyone. I will leave you alone, but do not pretend to me that all is well."

****

Longbourn, 31 July

God, please help me! This cannot be! This cannot be true!
I should not have awakened today. This day should not have happened.
What a shame, what a shame!
He is here. Jack is here.
Why, why? Why did I do that?
I want to erase this day and that day from my mind.
Please God, help me!

I was seven years old, Jack was about ten:
"Let us put her to the test."
"Try me: I can lift heavy things, I can run, I can climb."
"And what about nasty stuff, like eating mud? Or swimming in a dirty pond?" Jack knew I would hate spoiling my new dress.
"Yes, look!" I swallowed a handful of mud.
"And fighting?" the nasty one said.
I hit him in the stomach with all my force.
"Wou, WOU!" He withdrew. "I see. Well, one last test. Are you old enough? Can you bear pain as a woman does?"
"Yes!"

****

The idea that something terrible happened that day would not fade away. Why were people whispering? Why did Mama cry so much? What did I do? What did I allow them to do?

What is Jack doing here in Hertfordshire?

And Mr. Darcy? What does he think of me now? He seemed scared when talking with Charles.

The book. He gave me a book.

I extracted it from my reticule. "Poetas Hispanos" — the title of a miniature volume, with a leather cover. I examined the first pages. It was a collection from several authors. There were three words in a polished handwriting in the first page: *"Elizabeth, July, 1812."* A sob flew from my chest.

****

After some hours of coming in and out from sleep, I heard a carriage arriving. Dearest Jane, she had come to say goodbye.

I dried my cheeks quickly and dressed in my most concealing dressing gown while hearing my sister climbing the stairs.

"Lizzy, how are you feeling?"

"I am well. It is nothing."

"Mama said you had *anemia*, but she does not know what that is."

"Mmm, does it mean she is making up some dreadful consequences and wailing about my death already?" She nodded timidly, and I took her hand. "Do not worry, sister. I am only sleepy."

"And why did it happened? I did not hear that anyone was infected... I..."

"No, no Jane, it is nothing like that. It is something related to the color of the mucous, or so I understood. It is cured by eating — nothing else!"

"Well, that will not be a problem for you."

"Yes, yes. Now, what are you doing here and not with your husband on a beautiful ship to the Continent!" I led her down to the first floor. "And where is my brother that I might give him some advice?"

"Some advice?"

"Yes. Little things, like your cold feet, and that he should throw those horrible wool socks you knitted overboard."

"Oh, Lizzy!"

"Brother!" I hurried to say something in Charles' ear, "Did you take smelling salts with you?"

"What? Whatever for?"

"Do not you know?"

He looked at my sister for help, but she just cocked her head.

"Jane, have not you told him? — Mama is going with you. She says she has never been abroad and sea air will improve her health."

He looked dumbfounded and sniggered when he realized it was a bad joke.

"Lizzy, you are incorrigible!" Jane admonished, "Come, give me a hug."

Mr. Bingley genuinely seemed besotted with her, and we parted affectionately. *It is what she wanted, Lizzy. It is her dream.*

Determined it was time to shake off my sadness — because the others would arrive soon, and I did not want to answer any questions — I climbed the stairs.

After a while, loud exclamations of my family's arrival were heard. I could discern that the Gardiners were preparing for their long trip to London, and my sisters were gossiping about the people they had seen at the wedding breakfast. Something about it being the success of the *ton* and meeting elegant ladies and handsome men — the usual talk. Nothing outward happened because of me.

Then, I heard my mother's steps approaching. "So, girl, what was this business of you in the church?"

"What are you talking about? I did not do anything on purpose!"

"No, no, child. That is not what I meant. I mean, one minute you were happy, and the next you were absent with Mr. Darcy calling for help. I have to declare, it was quite the scene."

I covered my face, imagining the fright I gave him, while she kept rambling. "We were all around Jane and Mr. Bingley, and then, I see this huge man pleading…"

"I will tell you, Mama. Stop, I will tell you. I saw Jack in the crowd. I fled when I saw *him*."

"Jack?"

"Yes, Mama, Jack Sthieve."

After some internal deliberation, she seemed to realize my predicament. "Lizzy, he is part of the family. You will see him often these days. He has some dealings with your uncle Philips, and he is not going to hide for your sake alone. Get used to the idea."

"Mama, Mama," I took her hands imploringly, "tell me what happened that day, please!"

She detached and turned her back, concealing her tears. "No, Lizzy, I cannot."

Chapter 6

That night I was scared of writing down what was bothering me, but it had always helped to clarify my thoughts. After many hours trying to relate the incomprehensible flashes of Jack shaking his head and the other boy doing a strange gesture with his tongue, turning sleepless in my bed, I decided to do it.

Longbourn, 1st August

There must have been something I did that was shameful. My mind can no longer deny it. But what? And more importantly, how can be assured that no one will ever know?

We could be so disgraced by this.

Maybe it would be better if I just stay at home and sever all my interactions with the outside world.

Yes. It is mandatory to avoid people seeing me, especially Jack, who is the only witness of that moment. I hope, I beg you Dear God, to spare my family this humiliation.

The next day I awoke with a huge headache, attributed it to the sporadic sleep I had had over the last several days. I asked my family to let me be alone until it diminished, and was irrevocably turned to the sad musings of the previous night.

Without the help of music or something else to occupy my wits, I decided to turn to the book that seemed more welcoming. I pulled it from under my pillow, and started to peruse it again. The first pages seemed easier than the one in Russian. Many Spanish words had a similar root. The subject of many poems could be discerned; they were on the splendor of nature, praising God, and reaching the second half, I found several were about love. This was the part that gave me both a pleasant and sad surprise: there, in a carefully folded paper, was a translation in the hand of the man that was foremost in my dreams.

I think of you.

I think of you, you live in my mind
single, stable, relentlessly, at all times,
though an indifferent face
does not reflect on my forehead
the flame that silently consumes me.
And stiff in my murky fantasy
Shines your image peaceful and pure,
like the beam of light that the sun sends
through a gloomy vault
of the broken marble of a tomb.
Silent, motionless, in deep stupor,
it sizes and commands my heart.
And there, in the center vibrates dying
when, between the vain noise of the world,
the melody of your name sounds.
With no struggle, no desire and no regret,
without shaking in blind frenzy,
without uttering a single, a slight accent,
the long hours of the night I dream
and think of you!

José Batres Montúfar*

The tenderness of his declaration, the coincidence in the turn of our minds, the similarities of our thoughts and the impossibility of expressing them, battled with my resolution to forget him. Despite my despicable words at Hunsford and my low connections, he loved me.

But he does not know, and I hope he never will.

****

That week passed more or less without incident, just nursing my sentiments of guilt and hoping that a solution would eventually come around. I posed like the well-behaved lady my mother always wanted, because, "God help us if any eligible bachelor sees that you are a bluestocking," and studied the Russian book during the nights. A strange fatigue was taking command over my daily actions. At that time, I did not make the connection with the anemia symptoms, but the doctor explained the relationship to me later.

****

Once, my father asked me to come to his library. I expected it to be for one of his talks of the absurdities that he collects, but it turned out to be something almost out of character.

"Lizzy, why are you indulging your mother in everything? Are you trying to distract her from something? Does it have to do with your problems sleeping or eating?"

Papa had noticed; I should be more careful. "No, I am not up to anything. I am well."

He stood up and came to sit in the chair next to mine. "Then, should I assume that you are finally bending and looking for a husband as your mother dreams?"

Ridiculous. Nothing could be further from the truth. "No. Why do you say that?"

"You are always in the parlor, no ramblings through the country, no hiding from your sisters. You spend time doing needlework. The only thing that you enjoy is playing the pianoforte, and even in that, you are not indulging yourself enough. Where is my wild Lizzy?"

"There is nothing the matter, I just miss Jane."

"That might be true, but if you do not spend your time doing what you like, it will only make you sadder. One cannot be happy if half of the day is used pleasing others."

"It is not that."

"There is something else, is there not, my girl? Does it have to do with a certain gentleman visiting the neighborhood? Or with another one that just left?"

"Oh, Papa! You are making fun of me!"

"No. I talked with your mother, and she explained you were apprehensive about Jack being here. She told me, you were inquiring about the day of the Gardiners' wedding, and that you were troubled by it."

I had to look down, all the shame of my actions washing over me. To speak with Papa about this. How humiliating! NO, I could not!

"Child, come here." He made me stand up to sit on his lap, reclining on his chest, "Why cannot you leave that behind?"

"What if I see Jack?"

"I do not think that is so very terrible. You have to keep on as you always have, smile and say something witty. You have always been courageous and smart. I am sure you can deal with him."

Not now, Papa. Not now, that I knew what my self-confidence led me do.

"Lizzy, listen. He is not a bad man, and I am sure he was not a bad boy either; people do strange things under certain circumstances, but they go on, they overcome their mistakes. I am sure he has almost forgotten that day… as you should."

I was trying hard not to cry. I just concentrated on his reassuring words and on not remembering. "Have you ever tried to not think about something? To erase your memory or turn your mind in another direction?"

"Oh yes! What do you think books are for?"

"So, is that your recommendation? — to hide myself with a book in your library? Are you willing to share?"

"Well, young lady, I am willing to lend you all the books I have. There is no problem with you running away with them. Just do not invade me here, because then, it will not be hiding."

"What about Mama?" I tried to negotiate something else, like every spoilt child.

"I will talk with her. Take all the dictionaries from this room and go!"

****

Two weeks after Jane's departure, a package came for me in the morning. I was happy to see it was a letter from Ana and some music scores. I laid those papers aside, expecting to find a balm in the words of my friend:

Pemberley, 7th August

Dear Lizzy,

We have finally arrived home, and I am anxious to know about you. Please, please Lizzy, tell us what happened to you in the church and how you feel now. I do not understand the explanation we heard from your mother.

My brother has also been acting strange. He was anxious when you felt unwell and, since the wedding breakfast, his attitude has changed from concern to irritability and anger. Why should he be so angry for a whole week? I do not know. I hope he gets back to his old self soon.

He is calling for me to join him right now. I will stop this letter and resume it later. Do not think he is rude with me or anything like that; I just do not want to give him another motive to be irritated.

Pemberley, 8th August

I could not finish this missive yesterday, but it was worth listening to my brother's improvement in spirit. Apparently he has come to make peace with whatever bothered him. He explained I should do the same, and start by sharing what weighs on my mind with someone that is worth my trust.

Thus, I have gathered my courage up to write to you. It is easier this way; I do not want to see your shocked expression when you hear it all.

This is something that happened to me with a man you know already — George Wickham, my father's godson.

Last summer I went with my former companion, Mrs. Younge to Ramsgate; and thither also went Mr. Wickham. At that time, I retained a strong impression of his kindness as a child. I believed in his declarations of love, and I let him persuade me to a shameful thing: an elopement. My brother providentially joined us a day before and stopped it.

You may imagine how Fitzwilliam reacted. Regard for my credit and feelings prevented any public exposure. He wrote to Mr. Wickham, who left the place immediately, and Mrs. Younge was removed from charge.

According to him, with the elopement, Mr. Wickham's chief object was my fortune, which is thirty thousand pounds.

These are the facts that I wanted to convey to you. Nevertheless, what bothers me the most is the contradiction between his manner of addressing me during our courtship and his subsequent attitude. He was so very tender, so full of kind and caring words, so full of love. I remember him holding me, whispering sweet nothings, making up stories of the felicity we should find when married. And when he called me "Georgie," it was with such a tone of adoration — almost reverential.

Why, WHY did he leave me without a word? Is it possible that he felt nothing, absolutely nothing for me? I admit he can be mercenary; but how can a man lie like that? How can he pretend attraction and passion? How can he live with the memories of our moments together and go on so easily? As if nothing had happened!

I just cannot understand. Can you help me with these feelings of betrayal? Can you help me find a rational explanation? Am I so easy to deceive, to manipulate? Am I so undeserving of being loved?

Now, I think I have made a mess of this letter; I am so confused! I do not know if I am misusing you or taking advantage of your generous heart. However, this is the account of the events and feelings I wanted to share with you. I sincerely hope you will not judge me too harshly, although I know I deserve it, and be kind enough to send a reply. I wait anxiously for any word; I have run out of friends since I left my former school.

Yours, etc.,

Georgiana Darcy

P.S. There is enclosed a little present. My brother says you will enjoy that particular piece.

****

Georgiana had been courageous in writing to me and confronting her mistakes. She was ill used and exposed to the vile machinations of a man ten years her senior and, I realized now, a consummate profligate. Although, what weighed the most on my conscience, was the knowledge of my ill judgment and harsh words toward Mr. Darcy the day of his declaration. To be compared to such a rake and be rejected with appalling and mistaken arguments!

My attention was suddenly drawn to the window by the sound of an arriving carriage. It was too early in the morning when the visitors invaded.

"Where is that girl? Where is Elizabeth?" Lady Lucas cried.

Her husband hushed her and apologized to my mother, but to no avail. The next diatribe was expressed with vehemence, and the sure purpose of being noticed by all the inhabitants of the house.

"That bastard has brought the worst disgrace to my family! She, YOU ALL, have shown my Maria the wrong way with your brazen attitude. I knew it; I knew it from the beginning! Nothing good could come from admitting into a respectable family a child whose father is unknown. Accepting and raising as a gentleman's daughter the offspring of a nobody could only bring disgrace to this village, and my poor girl is paying with undeserved consequences."

What was she talking about?! Her verbal abuse sprang to dress speedily. *Please, God, do not let this be related to Jack!*

"My poor child, my poor dear Maria had nobody to take care of her. Why did they ever let her go out of sight? I am sure there was some great neglect, for she is not the kind of girl to do such a thing, if she had been well looked after. I always thought they were unfit to have the charge of her. I am sure my Charlotte has nothing to do with it, because she must be working in the management of the house and parish all day. It is all the influence of the unfit example given by this family. I will make sure the Collins's will turn you out before long. When Mr. Bennet dies, before he is cold in his grave, they will come to Longbourn, and Elizabeth will pay for her disregard…"

She could not insult my family like this! While she trailed off, I reached the parlor with my chin high. I saw her seated next to Sir William Lucas, her visage was full of wrath.

My sisters were consoling mother, who was thrown on the couch lamenting about the destructive speech.

"There you are, ungrateful spawn!" Mrs. Lucas stood up, pointing at me. "You are to blame for my family dishonor and my girl's desolate future. You are the one responsible for it all!" She walked toward me. "You will pay for this!" she slapped me hard in the face.

Momentarily taken aback by this display of disproportionate violence, I stood petrified while Lady Lucas (frightened and in shock by her own behavior) retreated.

After some silent seconds, the gathered group divided in two bands: the Lucases in a corner, the Bennet's around me. Mother was out of her senses with concern. Mary, Kitty and Lydia were angrily stating they had no right to behave like this. I could hear them, but I was not listening, until I saw Mama separate from us and go menacingly in the direction of the couple.

In that precise second, my father's commanding voice stilled the room: "Stop where you are, Mrs. Bennet! I want an explanation of what is going on in this house right now!"

Almost immediately, my sisters and Mama surrounded him, groaning at the same time.

"Wait, wait, one at a time."

"This, THIS SHREW dared to slap MY Lizzy in the face!" mother accused loudly.

"Slow down. I do not understand a word you are saying. Lucas, what is this visit about? What were those defamations I heard your wife scream at my daughter?"

The always good humored Sir William Lucas was at the moment another man. He guided his wife to the sofa nearby and stood looking at father and me with an expression that made him look ten years older. "My daughter Maria is with child," he said — shoulders down with resignation. "We do not know who the father is, or when it was conceived." A collective gasp and low murmur spread in the room while he sat holding his crying wife. "We… we are desperate, looking for the bastard that did this to our girl. She does not say a word; she will not even say where it happened. Nothing. We think she was seduced in Kent, because we never let her alone here. That is why we came to your house; we need to find the man and make him marry her at once. She has all the nausea and signs of an early pregnancy, she... There is no doubt," his voice was inaudible by now, and Lady Lucas' lamentations about her teenager and the scandal that could befall them were the only words we heard.

My father paced the room twice and then directed, "Girls, go with your mother to her room. You, Lizzy, sit here with me." He guided me to a nearby chair.

I did not want to be seated. I wanted to give her a piece of my mind!

"Papa, we want to know what happened to Maria. She is our friend, too," complained Kitty.

He shook his head guiding them out. "Now, Lizzy, I know you are as surprised as all of us in this house, but we need you to relate *everything* that happened in Kent, and the people you met there."

What? Was he not going to defend me, to make this woman apologize for what she said, what she did? I looked up at him, and saw his face of, "Trust me on this."

AGRRRR.

All right Papa, you win. I was utterly disheartened by the defamations and the pain in my cheek. On the other hand, what was happening to Maria was something really dreadful.

After recollecting my thoughts, I started the tale which I suppose, was similar to the one Maria Lucas related when coming from London last spring.

At the end, the four of us were silent for several minutes. Sir William was the first to speak, "So, apart from Mr. Collins, the only men that you saw were Mr. Darcy and Colonel Fitzwilliam?"

"And the servants, of course."

"Oh, no, no. My child would not involve herself with that class," Lady Lucas' brows wrinkled offended.

My father rolled his eyes, and Sir Lucas pressed his wife's hand. "We need to evaluate all the possibilities, dear."

"My poor, poor child. No, no, I am sure it must have been Mr. Darcy. He does not deceive me with his airs of superiority. He must marry her. Make them marry at once, Lucas!"

---

*José Batres Montúfar (1809-1844) was a Guatemalan writer, politician and military figure. (The writer is taking the liberty to cite some Hispanic poets that weren't even born in 1812.)

** According to the etymology dictionary "anemia" is a word coined around 1800 — 10; comes from Neo-Latin or Greek *anaimía* — want of blood.

Symptoms found in case of Anemia caused by vitamin B-12 deficiency, which were not known in Regency times, are:

- A tingling, "pins and needles" sensation in the hands or feet.
- Lost sense of touch.
- A wobbly gait and difficulty walking.
- Clumsiness and stiffness of the arms and legs.
- Dementia
- **Hallucinations, paranoia, and schizophrenia.**

Chapter 7

This could not be! "YOU mercenary witch!" I stood up, hovering menacingly over Lady Lucas.

"ELIZABETH!" my father pulled me back to the seat.

"No, Papa, no. I will not stay peacefully, hearing her insults any more. She has no proof, no indication, not a single reason to suspect that Mr. Darcy is capable of such sordid conduct. He is a loyal friend, the best of brothers, an admirable man. His only fault is being aloof and shy, if it can be considered a failing; and of course, he has ten thousand a year. How convenient it is to find him guilty! Why they do not consider Colonel Fitzwilliam as a suitable suspect, or any of the other thousand men that live in Kent? Why him? Why not one of the soldiers that were encamped here for several months? It could be anyone!" Having uncorked all the accumulated fury that resided in me, I did not relent. "Ah, but Mr. Darcy is certainly a good scapegoat! He would not ridicule or expose them in public, and is generally disliked. Is he not, Lady Lucas? And let us not forget how rich and how great your daughter will be! What pin-money, what jewels, what carriages she will have!"

Papa stood between Lady Lucas and me. Grabbing my shoulders, he walked me out of the parlor and into his library.

"ELIZABETH, you will not talk like this to them! You have no idea what that family is going through. You do not own all the truth! Stay here, and we will have a long conversation when I finish. Think about what you have done. You, young lady, should be ashamed of this behavior!" The door cursed behind him.

"Fine! Go with them! I do not need anyone!" *They are just after his money. It is not him. Not him! He would not touch that girl with a feather. He has a sister of her age, for God's sake! He is not a rake. He loves* me*!*

Me!

They have no proof. They have no proof... I repeated these words in my mind again and again.

Yes, that was what I had to find. My own evidence. I would refute their accusations. On a white sheet from Papa's desk, I started to write my statements:

Proofs:
He could have anyone he wants.
He is a moral man.
He has had countless women who have fawned over him.
He was not in Maria's presence alone, not once.
Maria was always in Charlotte's presence.
He is a good brother.
He is a good friend.
He accepted my refusal without resentment.
Colonel Fitzwilliam defends him.
He loves me!

Good Lord! Nothing of this was an evidence of his innocence. I knew it was all true, but I had to verify all of this.

I read the first sentence: "He could have anyone he wants." — This was the easiest one; he could buy half of England.

Second: "He is a moral man." Several comments from Netherfield came to mind, until I remembered the one that spoke the most of his character: "Disguise of every sort is my abhorrence." Then, another statement from Colonel Fitzwilliam tarnished it, "He likes to have his own way very well, but so we all do. It is only that he has better means of having it."

The next one: "He has had countless women who have fawned over him." There have been Caroline, Anne de Bourgh,… Could Maria Lucas be after him as well? I laid my head on my hands. I had to admit that possibility. He was handsome and educated. He could have impressed her with his station — It could be, but they never spoke a word at Rosings. He did not show her any affection. An image of him standing behind the girl, whispering in her ear, came to my mind. It could not be! No, no, NO!

Returning to concentrating on my list, I fanned the burning air. "He was not in Maria's presence alone, not once." No one could affirm this. We met alone in the park several times, and nobody knew about that. Oh my God!

"Maria was always in Charlotte's presence." Only her sister could state this, not I.

"He is a good brother." Ana looked up to him as a father, but then, this had nothing to do with the kind of man he was with other women. I had nothing!

I started to walk around the room. Next, "He is a good friend." Of this, there was plenty of proof, except the fact that he often made decisions on their behalf. He was almost altruistic. "Towards him, I have been kinder than towards myself," I remembered the hurtful words tattooed in my memory. I wondered if he told Charles to come back after Jane. I should have asked! *AHHH!*

"He accepted my refusal without resentment." What did I know about this? "And this is all the reply which I am to have the honor of expecting! I might, perhaps, wish to be informed why, with so little endeavor at civility, I am thus rejected." Oh yes, he was irate at me when I refused him. Except that he was not resentful; on the contrary, he promoted the friendship between his sister and our family. Which turned my mind to Ana's letter. *Why would he be irritable and angry for a whole week?*

"Colonel Fitzwilliam defends him." Colonel Fitzwilliam — the other suspect.

Wait, what was I talking about? There was nothing here. I was speculating without a single clue! The Colonel was as a good candidate as any.

"He loves me."

At least he said so, "How ardently I admire and love you," and his poem, "I think of you, you live in my mind, single, stable, relentlessly, at all times." But those were just words! — like the ones George Wickham told Georgiana.

I still had nothing! Frustrated, I crossed out the word. ~~Proofs.~~

These were my littered thoughts when Papa finally came into the room. "Now, Elizabeth, sit down and explain to me this aggressive behavior!" he went behind his desk. His visage was severe, his eyes piercing me.

Seeing no other option, I sat on the edge of the seat. Well, I had no proof, but neither did they.

"Papa, I think I am blameless. Lady Lucas entered this house insulting our whole family, saying the most hurtful things, and slapped me in the face. You cannot suppose me to behave as a harmless damsel when I face such violence, both physical and verbal. They deserved every word I said. I am not ashamed of the feelings I related. They were natural and just. Do you expect me to accept her threat to leave us in the streets after you die? To stay calm when our moral standards are questioned? To be called a bastard, a brazen woman, and subject to who knows how many other monumental lies, without defending myself?"

My father frowned in a way that means 'Do not take me for a fool'. "I would have expected that kind of response immediately when you were slapped. Not after you calmly related for several minutes the events at Kent. No, when you started your tale, you were well on the way to forgiving the offenses laid at our door. You know well that Lady Lucas expressed the misguided sentiments of many people in this village. You know they are in the wrong, and it has been a long time since you have disregarded them all. No, what triggered your temper was the charges to Mr. Darcy and I want to know why."

WHAT?! "What exactly are you accusing me of?"

"Of defending a man wholly unconnected to you, a man you barely know, with innermost vehemence and disregard for other people's feelings."

He had me trapped. I had never been more at a loss to make my feelings appear what they were not. It was necessary to laugh, when I would rather have cried. And I had no energy for this pretense anymore.

"So, I hit a mark, did I not, Elizabeth? I see you have taken a fancy to this man. Let me advise you to think better of it. I know your disposition. I know how exceptional, how different you are. Your are smarter than anyone I know, and yet, very inexperienced. You have a propensity to misunderstand social situations. I know you could be neither happy nor respectable with him. Your talents would place you in the greatest danger in an unequal or irregular relationship. You could scarcely escape discredit and misery. You know not what you are about."

An irregular relationship? What could Papa mean by that? I wanted to argue, but he approached to bend down in front of me, changing his tone from scolding to a loving one. "Do not let his verbal skill deceive you, or be dazzled by consequence and station. Guard your heart, my child. Guard your heart. Talk to me. This shell in which you have secluded yourself in is not going to do you any good. It only creates distrust between us."

His earnest expression disarmed my equanimity, and I started to shed some tears. "You are right. It was wrong of me to express myself as I did. The Lucases are in a dire situation now, and I only poured more salt in their wounds. I was wrong. I am sorry."

"You know you are worth a lot, my girl, do you not? I want you to remember we parents want to see our children always protected from the outside world. If it depended on us, we would have you in a fantasy place surrounded by toys and candies. Unfortunately, children have to grow up, and we have to prepare you for real life. I hope you will not be too harsh with the Lucases the next time, and that you will remember that with the severity that you judge — you will be judged afterwards. You do not know what is ahead in your own life; better be careful and take care to keep a clear head."

I closed my eyes and let his words sink into my thoughts. *I will be faithful to you, Papa.*

****

While holding Georgiana's music scores, I could not help feeling we had something in common. We have both made mistakes with dangerous consequences. Jack was possibly a righteous man; he had earned his bread since he was a lad. Mr. Wickham was mercenary, dissolute, good for nothing. I did not remember him doing anything except gossiping, playing cards, and flirting with everyone that wore a skirt. No, Ana was not to blame for what had happened to her. Her fault was not the same as mine.

"Apassionata*
"Ludwig van Beethoven's Piano Sonata No. 23 in F minor, Op. 57"

It seemed a cheerful piece and so very difficult, with those ups and downs. I searched if Mary was nearby. She was in the kitchen with the rest of the women of the house. Luckily, they were all focused in the plans for the visit to the Philips's on the morrow, and only the one I intended to speak with raised her eyes to look in the direction of the door. I signaled her to join me, and she immediately agreed. Dear sister, she was in so much need of someone noticing her.

"Are you coming with us to the card party?" asked she with joyful anticipation. I shook my head 'no' while we entered the music room. "How are you feeling, Lizzy? Papa said you had a headache, that we should not disturb you."

"Do not worry about that."

She took the papers from my hands. Directing her steps to the pianoforte, she asked while sitting on the bench, "I guess it is from Georgiana; there is a letter for the four of us. Mama has it."

Mmm, Ana thought about everything. "Thank you, I will read it later. Let us see what this piece is about first."

It was really, really complex. The chords varied in scales rapidly and unexpectedly, with a lot of emphasis in the use of both hands. The first movement made recurrent use of the deep, dark tone of the lowest F on the piano. I spent almost all the afternoon practicing this part of the sonata, realizing that it was composed in a state of the deepest turmoil. It was as delightful as it was happy. It was as passionate as it was desperate. It truly was an exquisite piece of music.

****

IT IS HIM. OH, GOD. IT IS HIM.

DO NOT. DO NOT. DO NOT. DO NOT DO IT!

I woke up desperate after *the* realization. I ran down the stairs and rushed out into the night. And I ran. Ran. Ran through the forest until my lungs were out of air and my legs did not respond.

"Can you bear pain as a woman does?" I collapsed to the moist ground on all fours, breathing hard. I wanted to die. I WANTED TO DIE. It was George Wickham. The boy at the wedding was George Wickham! The boy that…

Oh God. Oh No.

Along with the understanding that I was losing all my hopes and dreams with this recognition, the acutest pain settled in my chest. Lord, please do not let him remember. Do not let Wickham remember!

How many hours did I cry? I do not know. I just recall the sting and despair provoked by this new knowledge. "Everything is lost," I repeated once and again. I could not write to Georgiana. I had to cut all ties with them, with him. Everything was lost.

****

I wandered in circles until, at dawn, realized it was time to go back home. Fortuitously, I was not as far as I thought, and the walk was only awkward because of the state of my clothes. I entered tiptoeing, although Hill saw me. The rest of the house was still asleep. I bathed and changed with her help without being noticed by anyone else.

Striving to think about something until breakfast time (anything to keep my memories at bay), I tried the Russian book, Ana's letter, my diary. There was no solace even in the poem in Mr. Darcy's hand. Nothing could take away the recollections of Wickham; the image of his cynical, self-assured, roguish side smile, "Anything?" How disgusting!

Translating others from Spanish — that should work. I reached for the dictionary and perused the poems for a short one. Title: "Versos sencillos. José Martí**." I looked up the meaning: "Simple verses" — Nice.

I wish to leave this world
By its natural door;
In a tomb of green leaves,
I would be carried to die.
Do not put me in the dark
To die like a vile traitor;
I am good, and like a good man
I will die facing the Sun.

"Lizzy," I was startled by Jane's call, "Liiizzyyyy?"

Jumping from bed, I turned to look at the door. I saw the tail of a dress and went after it. In the hallway, I heard it again, "Lizzy come, I made a dress for your doll." The sound came from her room, so I followed there. Opening the door, I saw nothing. "Here, Lizzy, here. Look how beautiful she looks now."

"Jane, where are you? Why can I not see you?" Perceiving a shadow behind the bed, I approached the other side of the room. She was cross-legged in the floor, with her beautiful hair down and dressed in her night robes, handing me with a proud smile my favorite toy, "Does she not look like a princess now?"

"Yes. She looks beautiful. She resembles you on Sunday." On Sunday? I closed my eyes, comparing the image of the girl in front of me and the last memory of Jane. "Why are you here?" I asked, eyes still shut. "Where is Charles?"

Silence.

Jane was not here. I was unaccompanied in this room.

---

*Ludwig van Beethoven's Piano Sonata No. 23 in F minor, Op. 57, colloquially known as the *Appassionata*, is considered one of the three grand piano sonatas of his middle period. It was composed after Beethoven came to realize the irreversibility of his progressive deafness. There is some controversy about if it was named *Appassionata* before or after the author death.

**José Martí is the National Hero of Cuba. He is famous for his literary works.

Chapter 8

Longbourn, 23 August

Thank God, today after breakfast I could extract a small confession from Mama. She was not in the mood for much talk, but she told me some vital information; although I did something dreadful the day of the Gardiners wedding, as my dress was a mess of dirt and mud, there was no blood.

She also came with a piece of advice that I rejected at first, and now have to think over: to go away from Hertfordshire for a couple of months. "Maybe to your cousins in Scotland — the Sthieves? I know my sister and my brother-in-law will be happy to receive you," she tried to cheer me up. "I am sure there are plenty of handsome soldiers to catch your fancy there. You even could find a husband and forget all about this wretched business."

Dear Mama, to think about soldiers at this time! It certainly is her Achilles' heel.

Exasperated, I thanked her for being thoughtful. The idea of going with those cousins is out of the question. How can she expect me to go with Jack's parents? — I do not understand; yet, leaving Longbourn is something I must consider now.

Although it causes me an enormous amount of pain, my rational mind says this is the solution to my present troubles: to go away. Alone.

Alone — this is the hardest word.

****

The next day, I had a hard time getting up from bed; to confront the day and the world. I got up lazily, one leg at a time. *Come on, come on, and put on a happy face. As Jane says, "If you try enough, showing a cheerful spirit, you will end up getting one!"*

With those ideals, I managed to go through the morning, learning the second part of the Beethoven sonata and listening to an excited Mary. My dear sister was looking forward to the evening with uncharacteristic enthusiasm. I wondered why.

She said that since Jane had left I had been a recluse. "You are the one blind to all that is going around, and the one who sees everything through a dark veil. The more you read, the lonelier you become, and the less you understand people. You should come with us. We are all going, and surely everybody will be suspicious that you, once again, are not."

Later, after lunch, I went upstairs with the intention of working a little more on the book by Lomonosov. I managed to extract the meaning of a paragraph I believe is a cornerstone of the dissertation:

*"All changes in nature are such that inasmuch is taken from one object insomuch is added to another. So, if the amount of matter decreases in one place, it increases elsewhere. This universal law of nature embraces laws of motion as well, for an object moving others by its own force in fact imparts to another object the force it loses."**

The first two sentences were clear to me. If something is not where you left it, it necessarily has to be in some other place. The second seemed an incomprehensible puzzle of words. What does the author means by "own force," or by "imparting to another object the force it loses while moving others?" Does it mean that, when the Earth attracts another object, it loses its 'force'? It could not be — if it were true, everything around us should be floating in space. Because by now, the planet must have loosened all its force! *It is wrong, it is wrong!* I crumpled the paper. So many hours spent translating — for NOTHING!

Hence, the subject that had seemed so attractive when the package arrived was losing its charm day by day. I tried some Calculus — it did not work either. My mind would not relent. Time after time, the images of Wickham replayed in my mind.

Seeing nothing could catch my concentration, I gave up cheating myself, and took the book that did catch my interest. Avoiding the previous author, I found there were several verses written by a nun, Sor Juana Inés de la Cruz**.

While finishing, I heard my sisters downstairs, arriving from the village, and discerned that there was news about Maria Lucas, "How romantic! Can you imagine receiving secret letters?" Kitty was saying.

"I do not think so! Poor Maria, she does not know if her lover is going to come back. What is the point of receiving them, if she is the one taking up all the blame and discomfort? Everyone in Meryton is gossiping behind the Lucases' backs, and they are not being invited to social activities anymore. I do not see where Christian charity has gone," responded Mary, as I was reaching the first floor.

"La! He writes that he is coming soon and is going to take her to the Derbyshire Peaks and show her his home and…"

I started climbing the stairs back. Maria's seducer was Mr. Darcy! No, it could not be. *Yes he is. Did you believe he was serious about marrying you!? Right! You, Elizabeth Willoughby!* But he was honorable; he was not like that. Why not? Look at Georgiana, she was pretty sure herself, at least enough to elope. He never showed any partiality toward Maria! Could he have written the same poem to her?

My head was spinning. I grabbed the railing to keep from falling. *You are nothing to him. You are nothing.*

****

After two or three days mulling over my doubts, Papa received another call. It was Jack Sthieve.

Their interview seemed interminable. Why was he here? Why?!

At last it was finished, and father called us all to the parlor for an announcement, "Jack has come to request the hand of our Mary. Congratulations child! I have consented to it."

What?! This could not be! This was one of father's jokes.

I waited for it to be contradicted, explained. To no avail. In a couple of minutes, Mama was already planning the wedding, Mary and my sisters were talking about the many travels she had ahead, and Papa was sharing his bottle of port with Jack. I covered my ears. Papa was serious. When did this happen? How?

Then it dawned on me: Jane married almost a month ago, they had been courting all this time I spent isolated here. This is what Mary was referring to when she said I was blind. This is why she was so happy the other day.

But she does not know him! No. No. What was I going to do? I could not see him every day until the wedding. Oh, Papa, why did you consent to this?

"I am not feeling well," I rushed up the stairs.

Reaching my bedchamber, I started to beat the mattress fiercely. *It simply cannot be!* Why did you have to come to Meryton, Jack? Why did you come? Everything was right; everything was going on smoothly, until you came! I had to do something. This could not be.

I was going to expose this. Yes! I was going downstairs now, and I was going to ask him what WE did! What I agreed to do! It did not matter if my sisters knew about this! I was not going to hide anymore! I was going to tell Mary. I directed my steps decidedly in the direction of the door, until I hit the tall figure of my father.

"What are you doing? What is the meaning of this attitude? Why did you leave us in the parlor so uncivilly?"

"You! You! You consented for them to marry! How could you do this to me? How? How! You are condemning me to spend my life away from my family, from everything that I love. I will no longer see Mary and will avoid all family gatherings. Why?"

"What are you talking about? This is madness! What does any of these have to do with you?"

"This has everything to do with me! Everything! Ah, but I am not going to wait idly anymore. No. I am going to ask him the truth, and, when Mary knows it, he is going back to wherever he came from. I am going to have my family back. He is not taking this from me, too. I am not letting him do that."

"Elizabeth, be careful. You are accusing him of taking something from you?" Papa was worried now. "When, did it happen if you never leave this house? You are not making any sense."

"In Derbyshire, of course! Thirteen years ago, when you met Mama. Ah, but I suppose you were too busy. That is why you do not remember he was there, that Wi…"

"You do not know what you are talking about," he looked to the window. He was hiding some thought. "You are making assumptions without support, and you have no indication of his character after so many years."

"What if he does something awful to Mary? What if he wants to do something immoral to her? You know she is always attentive to these matters. She will not like being exposed to a man."

He inclined his head with his 'be patient with this child' face. "I do not know where you get those ideas from. You are intruding in their intimate life, and it is not your place. You are not qualified to understand married couples," he concluded, retreating.

I ran to his side, "But Papa, Papa, what if he is depraved? What do you know about him, about his habits? Why do you trust him?"

"I see you are having one of those impulses of thinking meanly about everyone. I do not know where this comes from, but you ought not to see everyman as a rogue; and YOU should trust MY judgment!" His words were final and abrupt and, as he closed the door, I knew that I had become even more of a recluse than ever.

This is wrong. He does not understand! AHH! I reached for the Russian book, and started to tear the pages fiercely. This was all wrong.

****

Despite how busy she was, a couple of weeks before the "happy event," Mama found time to sit at my side in the bed and share some of the gossip in Meryton. "Oh, Lizzy, the most unexpected rumor is being circulated. It is said that Maria's lover is none other than George Wickham. Can you believe it? That charming man is being secured by the Lucases? How can this be? Are they to take all the good prospects from us; first Mr. Collins, now Mr. Wickham!"

Relief. Overpowering relief. It was all I could feel. Mr. Darcy was not the one that seduced Maria.

"Ah, but we caught Charles and Jack. Are not they more handsome and rich?" Mama was rambling again.

I closed my eyes to shut her down. It was not him. He was not a liar. He was not a rascal. He was blameless.

"Lizzy, are you listening to me? What is happening to you, child? Are you dizzy again," she said while forcing my eyes to open with her fingers.

"Why would you think I am dizzy? No, Mama, do not touch me," I removed her hands from me. "I am well."

"Sorry I am a little scared by your illness. You are pale and have lost a lot of weight. I think getting out of this house will do you a lot of good. You are not the kind of girl to stay indoors so much of the time — that is what is killing you."

Yes, <u>that</u> and not knowing, and indecision, and thinking too much! "You are right, Mama, I will resume my activities soon."

She left, and I replayed the conversation with Mama in my mind's eye: He did not lie to me. He was not Maria's lover. It was Mr. Wickham. Do not laugh, Lizzy, do not laugh. Poor girl. Still, nothing could refrain from this feeling of recovery, and I did it. I reclined on the headboard and laughed freely, like a child.

****

Longbourn, 14 September

Today something happened that I have missed a great deal. I took a nap after lunch. I do not know what made me fall asleep, but I thank God for this precious present.

Also, while dreaming, I had an unusual remembrance. I was little, maybe less than six, playing with some of the boys of my age in Bakewell. We were in a spacious yard near the church, and I am 'It' in 'Blind man's bluff' — I am enjoying myself a lot. Several of my playmates are around me, pulling and pushing, making a lot of noise to catch my attention. I am a bit disoriented, but it is part of the game.

Suddenly I hear hooves very close, and immediately afterwards, I am knocked down by someone heavy. I remove my blind cloth, and I see Jack is recumbent over me on the ground, yelling insults at the retreating figure of a horseman.

The other children are regrouping around us, praising my cousin for his bravery while he helps me up. "Lizzy, are you well?" I nod silently, and seeing I actually am, he resumes his complaints while angrily brushing the dirt from his pants. "That man almost killed you. The devils take him! Blast!"

I see now that Jack saved me that day, and I wonder; did he risk his life to do that? Did someone try to kill me?

Later, with the news about Maria Lucas, I felt compelled to reread Mr. Darcy's poem and Georgiana's letter. It has been a month since I received the last; Ana must have been terribly disappointed without a response. Poor dear betrayed twice: by Wickham and me. And what is Mr. Darcy thinking? He ought to be regretting the advice he gave her. I did not stand up to the challenge of being his sister's friend. She needed someone to trust, someone who could be sympathetic with her loss. I failed her — I failed him. He must feel it like a betrayal too.

What if I just write her a small note? Something about being honored by her trust, but I cannot write anymore. I could say I cannot explain my reasons and still make her feel how much I appreciate her. She is a sweet girl. She needs a friend. She needs someone to tell her that she is guiltless, that what happened to her is not her fault.

I am tempted by this idea, however, this kind of letter could trigger a different effect.

No. No. Do not back up on this Elizabeth! DO NOT! What if she shares the letter with Mr. Darcy? He might imagine your health has worsened. What if he comes here to see if anything is the matter with you? You will only make things more difficult. How will you explain them in person?

You cannot!

You have to find another way to help Ana.

You have to do this for him. You need to wound him this much for him to forget you. Do this for him, Elizabeth. He deserves someone better than you. He deserves to be happy. Push him away!

I remember his wounded expression the day I rejected him. He is so handsome; even when he is angry he is handsome. And when he smiles — when he smiles it is like if I could see the boy that is still there, in his tender heart.

We were so happy the last afternoon they visited here at home! I replay the scenes of those days and feel accepted; more — appreciated, admired, and loved. And the next day it was all lost.

When I remembered the scene at the wedding, at first, I was inclined to blame Jack. I realize now that my wrath should be directed at Wickham. The rascal! What he has done to Georgiana, and to Maria is despicable. Not only a scoundrel good for nothing, but a degenerate! Coward! Snake! With his snake tongue and snakelike slim body taking advantage of innocent women.

Where can he be now?

---

*Lizzy doesn't know that what she is reading is a historical document: it is the first time two laws of nature are stated as independent principles. The first two sentences are the law of conservation of mass and the last one is the law of conservation of energy. See more about this subject in the appendix of this book.

** Some sonnets of the Mexican extraordinary woman that was known as Sister Juana Inés de la Cruz, are translated to English here:
http://monasticmatrix.usc.edu/cartularium/article.php?textId=2317

Chapter 9

Replaying my memories, I see now the sadness that invaded me before the extraordinary measures I took that day was not solely the result of an illness that drained all the energy from me, but mostly the consequence of believing that happiness resides in knowing what is coming ahead.

While listening to Mary's performance, I heard voices from the foyer and refocused on the excited words of my younger sisters arriving from Meryton:

"I say he must come tomorrow or the day afterwards, as the banns are already published." Lydia was coming into the room, followed by Kitty.

"It is a pity that he must be coming alone. I would so much like meeting Captain Carter again!"

"La, Captain Carter? What is he compared to Mr. Wickham? He is not nearly as handsome, not as congenial."

"And what is that to you, if you are not the one marrying him?" Kitty seemed annoyed, when comprehension dawned on me: *Wickham is coming.* The Lucases must have found him, and must have demanded that they marry at once! How I did not see this before? *He must be traveling from Brighton at this moment!*

Oh God! I sprang from the couch deciding to take action this time. Tomorrow was Sunday. He might see Jack in church and remember everything. *I must do something right away! Think Elizabeth, THINK!*

I looked around and observed my sisters. Mary was well; she would be married and away from the rascal in no time. There was no risk in that quarter. But these two — I observed the teenagers arguing — what was I going to do with them? They were staying in Longbourn. Lydia was eager to meet him. She was ignorant of the danger she was in. She was even planning how to flirt with the... with the... with the snake, the vulture, the... I fidgeted restlessly with the fabric of my gown. *Focus, Elizabeth, focus!*

Let us start again. What was I going to do? Tell Papa? Tell Mama? What? What to tell them!?

AGGRRR, this noise was going to drive me to Bedlam!

After leaving the music room, I sat at my desk and opened the diary.

Hazards:

He can remember.
He can spread the story.
He can blackmail my family.
He can take advantage of Lydia or Kitty.

Realizing the jeopardy my family was in, I started to think of solutions. What could trigger his memory? How could I avoid that from happening?

What was what started to trigger mine? I did some math. The dreams started about a year ago. No, no, a little later… a little later — when the regiment came. Then, it would be easy for him to remember if he saw Jack or… or if he saw me. I balanced the probabilities of both events: If he were here tomorrow, it was not likely that he would go directly to the church.

That led to two basic questions.

> *How am I to avoid seeing him?*
> *How am I to prevent Lydia and Kitty from falling in one of his traps?*

The solution for the first one was to stay at home — I would do it all my life if it was what it took to avoid him.

Wait, how do you know he has not remembered already? My lungs could barely retain the shallow breath.

No, no, calm down, Elizabeth. Calm down. If he knew, he would have asked for money a long time ago. He had no memory of that day. Not yet.

The argument between my sisters downstairs could still be heard, so I focused on the second question. "How do I to prevent Lydia and Kitty from falling into his trap?" HOW? I tapped the table hurriedly with my fingertips. I could relate to them the little I remembered about that day. No, no, no; that was too humiliating. *NO!*

I focused on the facts. What did I know about him?

Facts:

1. *He was the instigator of the ordeal in Derbyshire.*
2. *He seduced Georgiana.*
3. *He seduced Maria.*
4. *He tried to marry Mary King after she inherited her fortune.*

The first one I knew for sure, but that was exactly what I did not want anyone to know. *You do not know what that test was about, for God's sake Elizabeth!*

I read the second one. No, NO. I could not trade my reputation with Georgiana's. I crossed out this sentence several times until it was illegible. *You are walking in circles, Elizabeth. Break it. Go on.*

Then, there is number three and four. There was plenty of proof of that. But Lydia knew this already, and she did not realize the danger anyway! I started to tear the page from my notebook. *This is not working.* I yearned for a solution to materialize in my vision, when my thoughts of the twenty third of August appeared behind today's page.

The advice from Mama, it was written, *"To go away from Hertfordshire."* To go away. To go away.

I repositioned today's page where it belonged and perused the previous ones. I found the notes of Jane's wedding day and started to alternate between the dates. Thirty first of July and twenty third of August: the tale of what showed up so far in my dreams and the counsel from Mama. Could I advise Papa instead? Could he prevent Lydia and Kitty from running into Wickham? I disentangled the tight plait I had arranged a couple of hours ago. *I cannot tell Papa.* An image of his look of disgust materialized in my vision. I would rather die than go through that indignity!

"To die" — I wrote that down too. How easy it would be to climb the bell tower in my cherished church and jump. I visualized the fall; the effortless way to end it all. Just die… Just peace.

"Peace"

I might design it in a way that Meryton neighbors would believe it was an accident. If I were to die, I could write Papa and explain the few things I remembered from that day. Leave the letter in his desk tomorrow morning during the mass — no shame to confront. Arriving at home from church, he would find it in his book room... *NO, no, no. Elizabeth, what is the matter with you?! Are you out of your senses?* "'Tis insane!" I cried aloud. *You would make them more miserable than what you are trying to protect them from!* I stood from the chair and reached the window. *Just go away!*

I grabbed the frame tightly. If I were going to go away, I ought to plan it to look like I had been kidnapped, or stolen by the gypsies. I racked my brain for a good explanation to prevent a scandal as a result of my escape. *Yes, that might work, I heard there is an encampment right now just outside of town.*

****

Standing, sitting and passing in my room alternately, I gave some thought to traveling to London, to live with my uncle. It would prevent the scandal. However, I disregarded this after realizing they would ask for an explanation themselves.

Perhaps to the north? To Scotland? To the Continent? I wanted to look at a map in the library, to ascertain which places abroad were not at war, but dreaded anything that could make them suspicious. *Just take the post that travels northwards. Take all the money you have saved and see what happens next.* I regretted making such momentous decisions in a hurry!

The time when all my family was at mass was the perfect time to board the coach. It passed by the road that was about two miles to the east around twelve o'clock. Tomorrow was not a busy day. It would probably be almost empty. Then, another question assaulted me. How was I to travel safely?

I looked around for a disguise. The simplest option was to dress like a servant girl. Not knowing what had happened to me so long ago, I continued to fear of being further harmed at the hands of men. *No, it must be something different.*

Several options were contemplated until the one that appeared least dangerous prevailed. I could travel like a young man of my station. Maybe I could pass as a fifteen-year-old boy. I took into account my high, hoarse, childish voice and my lack of womanly assets. Even Lady Catherine, with all her wisdom, believed me younger than I was.

I should have dedicated more time to planning for a safe trip. The truth is my thoughts were wandering in circles. How should I convey to my parents the facts about Wickham?

Deciding what to take with me, I perused my clothes (choosing only one summer dress) and my old diaries. The first one had few legible entries from Bakewell; the last one brought many memories, most of them happy. They were about playing with Jane, the conversations with Charlotte and reading with Papa. Only the passages about Mrs. Parker, the reverend's wife, and her Sunday School class were painful. *Not now Elizabeth, not now. Leave those recollections for another day.*

****

Late that afternoon Mama came to my room. She seemed tired from her job of arranging issues related to Mary's wedding.

"Lizzy, have you eaten today?" She threw herself on the bed. "Hill says she has not seen you. What have you been doing?"

"Nothing, Mama, I have been here all the time." She could not possibly know my plans.

"Why do I have the feeling you are hiding something from me?" *What?* "No. I will feed you myself." She stood up and cried through the hall. "Hiiill, BRING ME A PLATE FOR LIZZY."

Take it easy, Elizabeth. Distract her. Better ask her about Mary. "Are not you afraid of my sister marrying Jack?"

"Jack? Why would I be afraid of Jack? Are you digging in your memories of the day of my brother's wedding again?!"

"Yes. He was there. Was he not?"

"Yes, he was. He was in the wedding, but he had nothing to do with anything!" She wiped her brow, signaling that I was draining her patience.

"How many times have I told you to drop this subject? How many times, Elizabeth?"

"But I want to know!"

"Yes, you want to know. You want to know everything, as always. Like when you were eleven, and you were hidden in your father's library." *What is she talking about? What does that have to do with this?* She stood up and walked to get my plate from Hill, asking to bring some water as well.

She came back, denying handing the full dish to me. "No, miss, I know you are not a baby anymore, but I do not trust you. Now, open your mouth."

She was fussing unnecessarily over my health. She would end with a speech of how she had to take care of everything, and nobody helped her.

"Now, resuming the subject of Mary marrying Jack; I truly think you are forgetting the many times you played together, while he took care of you in Bakewell. Do you not remember that?" She gave me another bite so that I could not answer her. "No, I would trust him with your life. As a matter of fact, what happened in Lambton would not have happened if you had stayed with him." *What? How can that be?*

"Are you sure Jack was not there?"

"Yes, of course. <u>He</u> told me so."

"Jack told you that he was not there!?" Did he abandon me with Wickham in the woods?

"No, not Jack," Mama responded distractedly, whilst reaching for the glass Hill just brought.

"You do not make any sense. Who is 'he'?"

She opened her eyes in irritation. "Take this bite and do not ask me about this anymore! As a matter of fact, I do not want to hear about it ever, EVER again!"

Spoon after spoon, the benefit of chewing and swallowing was not offered. "There, now, go to sleep while I take care of what is left to do in this house. You know that, if I do not take problems into my own hands, they are not done right."

If Jack was not there when Mama saw me, why did I have this conviction that he betrayed me?

****

Finally, practicality overtook me at night, and I started to pull together what would be needed for tomorrow. I went to the place where some of my father's old clothes could be found, and collected what appeared a costume from his youth. It was a larger size than what I could wear, but unable to find anything better, I took to the task of sewing it and arranging it to my form.

One key problem of the disguise was that I should travel like a man, and be able to go back to my feminine appearance once in the place where I should establish my living. Wherever it was.

I would cut my hair to an intermediate length, and keep Papa's trousers long enough to cover my boots. *How are you going to make a living, Elizabeth?*

Later, think about that later, one step at a time.

Trying not to dwell on the risks that were to follow, I felt asleep doing what became my favorite pastime: translating poems.

****

Saying goodbye to my family was as painful as if an elephant foot stepped on my thorax. Undecided between savoring those precious last moments and the risk of being discovered, at the end, I waved my hand to the retreating carriage.

Another difficult decision was what to take: my diaries or the poems? — the poems. It would fit between my breasts. I would change in the church and hide the notebooks there. Without much further thought, I cut my hair, wrapped my bosom tight, dressed in father's pants and a summer gown over it.

I wrapped the other men's clothes in a small parcel, while figuring out what to put in the letter to my parents. I imagined Mama's shock when she discovered I was no longer there. Poor dear, she had wanted me to marry Mr. Collins because she was sure it was the best someone like me could aspire to; and now, I was leaving her without anything. Not a slight thing to congratulate herself for.

Stop, Elizabeth! She would understand: it was the same <u>she</u> did that day. We ran away from Lambton after the incident. I was not going back on this! I was not going to immerse in self-pity, not going to spend a tear over this. *Go and get done with that letter right now!*

At least a small amount of scandal was unavoidable. To minimize it, I suggested three choices: they could spread the rumor that I went visiting with some relatives or that the doctor recommended traveling to the sea, or that a kidnapping could be considered as well.

I tried to convey I was traveling safely, and would write as soon as I found a place to live. I also mentioned I had enough money to get to Scotland. I scribbled my apologies for the hurt I was causing and warned about Mr. Wickham, citing his treatment of Maria Lucas solely. I reasoned for the hundredth time I had no conclusive arguments about his mistreatment in Derbyshire.

So far I only had flashes that indicated I allowed Wickham to put me to a test, and that I was frightened; that being Wickham and seeing I was almost desperate to play, I must have agreed to something dreadful.

No, Papa would dismiss anything I had against him, like in Jack's case.

Once finished with this task, I went back to my room. Grabbing my few things, I took one last glance at what I was leaving behind. I would never find another home like this.

You are doing this for them. Hurry up.

All the servants were busy when I left the house. Without being noticed, I managed to get out of sight quickly. Nevertheless, on the way to my favorite hiding place I had to stop a lot to catch my breath — the consequence of spending so much time indoors. I arrived barely in time to do all I needed to accomplish. Angry at the fact I could not walk as rapidly as I wanted, I weighed the idea of burning the diaries, but decided against it for two main reasons: there was not a minute to spare, and I was not ready to kill my past that way. *I might be nobody again, an orphan, like before; but like before, I am going to find my way!*

The best place was the bell tower. Where there was a small wall collapse — no one should hazard going to that place. Taking into account it was a risky ascent, I climbed it carefully. I took off my dress, and packed it in the place of the male clothes in which I dressed. I found a brick to put my diaries under, in front of the window. *It would be so easy to jump now.*

Stop it! STOP IT!

I did my best to check my appearance. Then, holding the cross I carry around my neck, I murmured a small prayer. Feeling the treasured book close to my skin, I ran in the direction of the road.

I reached it with time enough to see the mail coach approaching from the distance. *Please, please, I know this is not a scheduled stop*, I begged internally, signaling the driver to stop, and in my best imitation of a manly attitude, asked for the final destination. He looked at me from the bottom up with a frown and answered shortly, "Newmarket." A little bit to the east, but northwards, nevertheless.

Once inside, I found enough space between one of the windows and an old couple. Two man servants were snoring in front of us. As this was the best method to avoid conversation, I covered my face with Papa's old hat and pretended to sleep. We arrived at Newmarket past midnight.

Too late for another trip, I looked for the nearest inn. It was not elegant, and, realizing it was almost empty, I asked to be given the farthest room. I paid for it beforehand, with the innkeeper's scrutinizing gaze, not leaving any doubt as to the direction of his thoughts, 'What is a lad of this age doing here alone?'

Once in my chamber, I closed the door and placed a chair under the knob, securing it. It did not feel much safer, excluding it should make some noise if anyone intended to intrude. Climbing into bed, I decided against undressing. The walls had many inscriptions of the travelers that had visited before. Some were just names, but some were unkind, to say the least. What kind of inn was this?

During the night, I heard someone hitting the adjacent wall rhythmically — the reason I could not sleep well, and was up early in the morning. Little

David had provoked the same noise when he jumped on my belly. Who could be playing with a child at this hour?

Leaving that place was a priority. I looked immediately for the next post. There was one scheduled for Scarborough in two hours. It was a trip of about three days, and taking into account the nights at the inns, seemed expensive as well. Yet, it was the best seaport if I was to travel to the Continent. My current money was not enough to journey safely. I racked my brain for a solution, and the only one I could find was selling my cross. *I will have nothing from my family if I do it.* I sighed, *and I will have a broken family if I do not.*

In the empty streets of this town, I had some difficulty finding someone to ask about the location of the pawn broker the inn's owner previously recommended; as soon as informed, I went directly. It was situated in a faraway part, almost in the woods. The proprietor greeted me. He was solicitous about my whereabouts and bought my cross necklace for the price of the gold. I packed the payment, and made plans to board the coach right away.

Looking for directions back to the inn, I was startled by the appearance of about five lads of my height in dirty clothes, walking in a straight line my way. I did not have time to get suspicious. One of them pushed me to the ground, and, whilst I tried to put my hands in front of me to soften the fall, the other four took my reticule and the rest of my belongings, disappearing a second afterwards.

Sitting on the pavement of the deserted street, all I could do was curse my stupidity for being such easy prey. *What were you thinking, Elizabeth, keeping the money in only one place?*

The single thing I was left was the book in my chest.

****

After some hours of swearing and hitting the facade behind me, it was necessary to eat something — which was a difficult task taking into account I had not a single penny. I went to the woods nearby and found some apples. They tasted exquisite, delicious, like the forbidden fruit in paradise.

Once my belly was half full, I started to weigh my alternatives. There were not many, and only two seemed viable: to ask for a job in the office for the hiring of servants, or to go to the church and ask for help. I hated both, but decided that the first was the less degradation.

I went almost crawling to said establishment the following week. I was always received with scrutinizing stares and impolite answers. The other servants looked at me as if I was an other-worldly bug, and the employers did not even notice my existence. I slept in the woods and ate what could be found there.

My stomach ached horribly, and I got light headed frequently. The sleeping hours were the worst, with the cold and the interminable nightmares and hallucinations. I do not want to relate them; there is no point in that. And it would be exceedingly difficult in any case, because I did not have my diary to register those days. Suffice it to say, it was a confusion of circumstances where I felt trapped between branches (immobilizing me to the ground), or lost in an infinite land (an empty field without colors or trees). I dreamed about God and the Virgin Mary, about my dear family, and about Mr. Darcy.

Finally, on Sunday, my mind gave way to panic. I was scared of the hunger and dirt I was living in, fearing getting pneumonia.

The worst of it all was the increasing sensation of losing the sensitivity in my arms and legs, followed by the soiled feeling from not bathing in almost a week. This was what pushed me towards my next step.

I went to the local church with the chief purpose of stealing all the hosts in the altar. I waited for the service to conclude, and the parishioners to retire. After what seemed a prudential time, I entered the building, and not seeing the vicar or any other person around, I approached my goal. There, in a shiny gold cup, was the personification of temptation. White, round, soft.

They melted like honey. To the first followed another, and another, and another, and so on; all of them cloying with its taste.

Until, doubled over in cramps, my stomach gave in and I started to vomit in the worst place ever.

The sound must have been what called the attention of the clerk and his wife, who appeared in front of me, astonished at the horrible spectacle I presented. With the certainty that I was going to past out, I heard them say something unintelligible; and through blurred vision, realized I was being carefully carried to a near room.

Chapter 10

Once in the new chamber, I was sustained by my shoulders by the reverend, while the lady rushed to find something in another room. "Here it is." I heard her come back, my eyes still closed, unsuccessfully trying to regain my balance. "Lay her on this cloth." She helped to put me down slowly over some fabric on the floor.

"But Beth, we should not let a vagabond in here!"

"What vagabond?" She removed my hat. "It is a girl. Look." *AAHH! How easily she found out!*

"It does not matter. She is dirty, and she could rob us."

"Nonsense." The woman gently brushed the hair away from my face. "She was just hungry. Besides, if she wanted to thieve something, there is plenty of gold on the altar."

I listened to his low complaints while she was trying to remove some of the mud from my clothes. Feeling like eavesdropping, I could not shake the dizziness.

"What could have happened to her to be in this state?" Her hands moved my head from one side to the other. "Thank God, she does not seem injured."

"I had better look for someone to clean up all the mess she made out there… and bring some water."

"Thank you, it is very thoughtful of you. Her throat must be hurting. And bring a wet towel!" she called to the retreating steps of her husband.

By this time, my embarrassment was more than my lightheadedness, and I ventured to open my eyes. When doing it, I saw a tall, beautiful woman of dark hair of my mother's age, reaching for a cushion from the armchair nearby. She approached again and positioned my head carefully over the soft piece. "There you are. How are you feeling?"

"Better. Thank you, madam."

"You are welcome. What is your name, child?"

"I am…" *You did not even think of a man's name while making up this disguise!* "Elizabeth. How did you figure out I am not a boy?"

"Easily. You are too beautiful to be a boy." *Me?* Was she mocking me? "Now, where is your family? Where are you from?"

I did not want to lie to her; thus, I just kept silent.

"I see. Well, I am Beth Cochran, the vicar's wife." She directed to the door. "Speaking of which, where is that man?"

She left, and I raised myself a little to observe my surroundings. It seemed like a classroom, or a place for small meetings, with chairs of different styles and some pamphlets scattered over them. Should I run from there? Would they treat me like a robber? I tried to stand up slowly, and realizing it was hopeless to think about walking (much less running), sat again. If there was any punishment, it was well deserved! What was I thinking, stealing from the house of God?! Better pray they did not take it to heart.

I decided to wait, to be patient for a change. This place was much more comfortable than any other I had visited the previous days. These generous people surely would give me some food and directions for a way out. The woman seemed a grown up Charlotte. Smart and practical.

I reached the nearest chair for one book and saw the cover. It read: "Essay on the Slavery and Commerce of Human Species by Thomas Clarkson*." Strange subject.

Just before perusing the content, several people's steps in the hall startled me. Until seeing Mrs. Cochran's grinning face peering in the door and asking two of the gentlemen to help me stand up, I was a little bit afraid.

They took me to a nearby chamber, which was arranged in a homelike fashion. I was laid on a big settee, and she took the chair of an old desk in front of me, when the men left.

"I suppose you ran away from home, and do not have a place to live." She handled me a glass of water.

I nodded, while drinking the welcome liquid.

"Well, you will bathe first, and then I will bring you some food."

"Are not you going to surrender me to the authorities?"

"To the authorities? That crook, who is in cahoots with the criminals in this town? No. Not if I want one less thief on the streets." She stood up and was walking out. "Remember to eat slowly. I will send you broth and a little plain bread, but you cannot binge; otherwise you will vomit again."

A while later, I was helped and instructed by a servant, who apparently had very few words to spare — just her name, Helen — how and where to take my bath. She handed me a simple and clean dress, and I had one of the happiest hours.

This fine lady was a cherub sent to help me and the cold water was a paradisiacal waterfall. I begged God for this luxury every day.

Leaning on the wall, I walked back to the room that was assigned before. I decided to lie down again, just to save some energy, when I heard loud voices in the next room, which apparently was the one I had visited before. Scattered parts of several heated speeches could be discerned, like: "It is mandatory to take action — to buy weapons!"; "Why invest our time in this venture? It is a Quaker idea!"; "Clarkson was nearly killed by a gang of sailors paid to assassinate him by the slave trade!"; "What are those negroes to us?"

I would like to say I did not strain my ears to know what they were talking about, except that it is not true. The oratory of these men was so intelligent, the arguments on both sides so well established. I could not but admire the way they put their hearts in each declaration.

In the end, I was much interested in educating myself on the subject.

****

The same girl-servant brought the food. I ate it slowly, savoring every bite. When I had almost finished it, said Mrs. Cochran entered the room and asked if I enjoyed my meal. We spoke about trivial things for a couple of minutes, until she got to the central point of her wonders: "Am I going to get into trouble for letting you stay here?"

"No. I promise to not take anything else. I... I am sorry for the trouble I caused before... I..." How was I to apologize for something so scandalous?

"Shhh, shhh. You do not need to explain. It is easy to see you have been starving for a while. I am grateful to the Almighty that He brought you here. You can stay as long as you want, or at least until you recover some of your health. I cannot allow you to stay idle once you are ready to work, or whatever you were planning to do before coming here. However, if you stay away from the altar, and you do not bring any other person with you, I can keep my husband occupied in more urgent things than caring for who sleeps in one of these empty rooms. Now, one last thing, what should I do if anyone from your family comes asking for you?"

My chest contracted at this thought. Papa and Mama were surely sick with concern. I had promised to write shortly, and I had not done so yet. And the gossip? Were they dealing with any scandal? *I must find a way to send a letter without giving the address. I...* Mrs. Cochran lifted my chin, refocusing my attention on her question. "Do not worry about that, madam; my family does not know where I am. They live far away."

"And, are you of age, young lady?"

"Yes, I am. That I am. I have just turned one and twenty. And I do not think my parents have resources to find me, anyway." Papa would only look for me in London, and not for more than a week or two.

"Well, then, it is settled. Sleep now, and let me know if you need anything else."

I caught her hand hurriedly. "Thank you, Mrs. Cochran. I will not be a burden for long, I promise."

"Nonsense. You do not know how much I enjoy disagreeing with that man."

****

I spent a couple of days very bored, recuperating my health on that enormous couch. From time to time, I wandered between the small room assigned to me and the altar chamber. I discovered all there was to know about the chapel and encountered the reverend on infrequent occasions. Was he avoiding me?

Most of the time, I was thinking how to let my family know I was well, without giving up my whereabouts. I could not find any solution.

I also chastised myself for leaving my home without a plan. *What were you thinking! You are not a child anymore, to escape running, like when you got in trouble with the boys in Bakewell!* The memory of a bunch of lads breaking a window or stealing bread from the baker intruded.

I could not do that now, nor adopt a stray dog to combat the boredom like when we lived in the cottage. I remembered the many hours spent alone when Mama was working. No, I could not build a tent here to pretend I was a gypsy either.

I also had the bliss on occasions to help the servant girl, taking care of her six-month-old baby. Michael was a wonderful boy with blond curls on the top of his head, and the rest bald. Although I did not have to employ all my babysitting skills (which are many) for that task, because this child was not as active as my cousins.

One of those nights, I read a pamphlet about abolition. In it, Mr. Clarkson considered the question of the slave trade in the British Empire. He described meeting and interviewing those who had personal experience of the slave trade and slavery; the way Africans were taken from their homes, betrayed by compatriots that served to guide the white hunters, or sold by other tribes. I also read how it was cheaper to let them die and buy a new one, than to cure them; and about the many humiliations they suffered when working. However, the image that impacted me the most was the one about the ship where the slaves were transported. They were packed in berths, lived for months inside crowded rooms within totally unsanitary conditions, and drowned when their keepers considered it necessary for one reason or another.

I hate the humiliation! I hate it! I hate it!

On the other hand, thinking about ships also led to happy thoughts, picturing Jane on her wedding trip. What would she think of my absence when she found out? Where on the Continent had Charles taken her?

****

By Thursday, I was almost recovered, eating freely without nasty repercussions and being able to do normal daily activities. I could even take the baby boy for a small stroll in the gardens, and helped in organizing and fixing the clothes destined for charity works.

"Mrs. Cochran, I think I must resume my journey shortly. I want to ask you for advice of how to do it more safely than the last time. Please, could you help me find a better disguise?"

She looked at me for a couple of moments and sat down in the nearest chair, with her hands on her knees in a gesture of tiredness. "You know you are not well yet. What is wrong with staying here until you get better? You have water, you have food, you have clothes, a bed and shelter. Why do you need to go?"

"Mrs. Cochran, I am so indebted to you for all you have done for me. Those things you have enumerated are precious, and I do not want to give them up. Still, I cannot live here forever; I have to earn my living."

"In that case, I could help you find an appropriate job — something that does not require much force. Maybe you could start as a teacher here in Sunday School. I have noticed you are good with children, and a scholar. Although this is a job you would do for free, your gentle accomplishments could be useful if a nice family notices you, and wants to take you for their employment. And lessons are a duty I am tired of, anyway."

I shook my head shyly, not wanting to appear ungrateful (I hated Sunday School). "I hope to make more money than is paid to teachers or governesses. I believe I could find a job that is more lucrative in the north."

"Who has told you that women get better money in the North than here?"

"Maybe an employment as a housekeeper can be found. Or better yet, in a library; in one of the rich, extensive properties that are there." *There must be other landowners like Mr. Darcy.*

"Dear, you are truly naïve if you think you can just knock on the front door of those big palaces, and ask for the best position. They do not know you, and if they had one of those positions vacant…" she extended her hand for me to approach. "If they had one of those positions vacant, they also have a long waiting list of trained servants to do those jobs."

She was right. *Who do you think you are, Elizabeth?*

"Why do you need a disguise for travelling, in any case?"

"It is just an old story — an old memory from my childhood. Nothing really."

"If it is nothing, why do you take so much trouble in looking like a man?" Mrs. Cochran seemed rather exasperated.

"It is an experience that was hard for my mother," I lied. "An event that marked our lives forever. It is her secret, though."

Resigned, she knelt in front of the pile of clothes we were working before. "You are right about being dangerous for a gentlewoman to travel alone. We can find something adequate for you here. Help me find a coat with big shoulder pads, and a hat that would cover your head better. I do not know where we are going to find boots of your size yet, but it will come out somehow."

After a short while, we had almost the best attire that could conceal my womanly features (not that there were many left after losing so much weight), and my companion was in better spirits as well.

"This should serve for you to achieve two things at a time: to conceal you are a girl and to look wealthier than a simple servant. Because we do not want people to treat you like a runaway lad, or like a person without resources to pay for your transportation."

Three complete changes of clothes and two coats appeared more than perfect to me. "Thank you so much, Mrs. Cochran. I do not know how to pay you back for your kindness, but I will. I…"

"You should start by calling me 'Beth'. Mrs. Cochran is my mother-in-law, and although I respect her, I do not like to think that I am old as she," she said while striving to arrange my hair in a small bow. "I do not know how are you going to fix this either. You had better think of how to make your face less feminine. Think about drawing a scar or the shade of a mustache."

"I will do it." I hung the clothes on my shoulders, showing more bravado than what I felt, while she neared the door. "Mrs. Beth?"

"I have to go now."

I approached and kissed her cheek. "You are my new angel."

****

In the afternoon, I met some of the gentlemen that gathered in the adjacent room. I understood they had a kind of fight, and it had ended up with a division in two smaller groups. The men led by Mr. Cochran were definitely against the slave trade, and planned to take action with the already strong national movement. The others were not willing to risk that venture, and were going to withdraw from these unions.

I did not have to strain my ears much. Actually, it was necessary to cover them. Very impolite and hard words were said behind closed doors.

Resolved to achieve better results this time, in the night, I started to work enthusiastically on my new disguise. The part of arranging the clothes to my size was not difficult, but the part of changing my face was. How was it that I had gotten into this trouble, if I was not considered a beauty? The flat cap would successfully cover a significant part of my head. Of course, under the hypothesis that I had a lesser amount of hair.

A window glass served as a mirror, and I tried all the possibilities that came to my mind; some of them crazier than others — all unsuccessful. Drawing on my face seemed out of question: what if it rained, or what if I could not make exactly the same line every day? The worry of being found out was deeper now than in my previous attempt. And I did not want to starve again. Anything but that.

****

The next day, when I was taking care of little Michael, Mrs. Cochran came with the craziest idea ever.

"If you do not want to draw your face, there is always the solution that should make you look absolutely ugly. Will you dare to shave your head — to be bald?"

Incredulous, I followed the line of her vision. She was observing the baby in my arms. "You must be joking! It only looks beautiful in a child of his age. No, no, no. This is all I have left!"

"All you have left? Left from what? Is it not your intent to look like a man? To not look beautiful?"

"Yes. But I want to be able to go back to my previous appearance once I am finished travelling."

"What if I can find you a job here — a job that only men can do?" She claimed in full Charlotte-style. "If your disguise truly works, you could make better money than any woman."

"What kind of job can be enough to buy..." She could not be serious. No, no. To give up who I was forever? To dress like a man every day? To resign being a lady!?

"I could convince Mr. Cochran to ask his friends from Cambridge to see if there is anything for you. Would you not like to work there? To work in one of the universities or private institutions? Maybe in one of the libraries?"

"In Cambridge?"

"You know, it is not so far from here, and I could help you in case you needed anything. You could come every weekend and see Michael and me."

"But, why do I have to be bald? BALD!" I almost cried. "Is there no other way? Are there not any other women in Cambridge?"

"Oh yes, there are. Except, if you want a lucrative job, you will need to draw attention to your assets."

I was slow to understand her meaning, and when I did, I suppose all my disgust showed in my face, because Mrs. Beth's mocking grin was quite self-assured. "You see, it is better to be a man."

****

After a while pondering Beth's ideas — What a clever woman! How did she figure out just the place I would LOVE to be able to work? The place where so many scientific discoveries were achieved? — And, gaining anything from my thoughts, I decided some fresh air was in order. I positioned Michael on my hip and went for a stroll in the gardens. I could not go far due to yet suffering from weakness when straining a little; hence, we sat comfortably on a bench to play some silly games with our fingers. *If I were to stay here, I would...*

My ramblings were cut by the sound of rapidly approaching hooves. A messenger got off the horse and stapled an ad, from the many he had wrapped in a side bag, to the giant oak next to the church entrance.

Called by curiosity, I waited for him to leave and approached the tree. There in elaborated black letters was promised a reward for any information regarding the woman in the charcoal portrait: me.

---

*Thomas Clarkson was an prominent abolitionist, you can read about him here: http://en.wikipedia.org/wiki/Thomas_Clarkson

**There was a famous female writer that lived in this period, Amantine Lucile Aurore Dupin, who dressed like a man regularly. She is better known as George Sands. Sands was a remarkable feminist and also played a vital role in Chopin's life.

Chapter 11

When I saw the picture, my natural impulse was to run. However, with the baby in my arms, it was impossible. I only made it to the front of the church. Then, realizing that avoiding people was of the essence, I went back and snatched the poster.

I looked at it more attentively now, my mind jumping between contradictory feelings. He was looking for me. He found out I left my home. The boy in my arms mirrored my sad smile. *How did he find out?* Michael frowned a little. *Oh, my! Wickham remembered!* I panicked. The baby started to pout. I hugged him to my chest. "Shhh. Shhh. This is nothing, sweetheart. This is nothing." *Oh, God. Not that. It must be something else. Maybe. Maybe someone contacted him. Maybe he was in London if Papa searched there.* Only Charles knew where he lived. How could father contact him? I gazed at the beautiful drawing on the paper I was clenching together with the child. He did not even like Mr. Darcy!

Dear Lord, he must be thinking the worst of me!

****

Leaving Newmarket was a priority. Yes, even if I did not have any money and was not yet healthy. Frustration from the fact I could not make it far with this illness dampened all my plans. *You should not do it like the previous attempt, Elizabeth! Take your time.*

I tried to relax a little bit, reading the poems, comfortably laid in the big couch; except that it was almost impossible with the insufficient light. If I could at least write to my family and Georgiana without giving up the current address.

Maybe once in Cambridge, I would be able to send letters, somehow.

Cambridge — what a tempting idea! I would see the place where William Oughtred made the slide rule. Learn about the scientific method established by Francis Bacon. Read Isaac Newton's original works about the laws of motion. Understand how Henry Cavendish measured the density of the Earth and of inflammable air. So much knowledge was prohibited for women and at an arm's length for men.

Nothing came without a cost. I knew that very well, since the previous transformation from Elizabeth Willoughby to Elizabeth Bennet. Yes, it was difficult, but it was worth the effort — one thousand times! I would not trade the years in Longbourn for a lifetime of adventure in Bakewell.

Being bald was not such a high price to pay. An image of the picture I presented to Mr. Darcy the afternoon we arranged the toys in the garden came to my mind. Yes, he liked my hair; but I was not going to see him again. What would I need it for?

The couch became a little more uncomfortable than before. To stay in England, which was the best solution (taking into account I would speak my mother tongue), I needed a reliable disguise.

The ad of the reward helped to build my resolution. Not a soul would recognize me without the hair.

This was a new life. It was compulsory to get rid of all my previous belongings to start anew. This was the right decision.

And, I had Beth. Walking from one town to another was not an impossible task. Otherwise, I would be a lot more alone. *Do you think you will find another person like her easily, Elizabeth? Surely not.*

****

I struggled with those thoughts almost all weekend, being distracted only by the eloquent speech of the reverend on Sunday:

"The word 'man' defines all rights. Everything that divides men, everything that specifies, separates or pens them, is a sin against humanity.*"

After the mass, I was surprised to see the vicar approach. "My wife told me, you were looking for employment in Cambridge. Is that correct?" I nodded, attentive to his next words. "I think I have the right position for you." *This was fast.* "There is a convenient service you could perform in the library of King's College."

"A service?" Incredulity and expectation were filling my wits.

"Yes. An employment that comes with a shelter and a comfortable salary for a young man eager to work." *What arts and allurements did this woman use to convince the reticent Mr. Cochran into helping me?* He pointed for us to sit down in a pew, implying he was going to describe the characteristics of this deal.

He carefully explained that I should not mention his meddling in this affair. He was not used to presenting women like men. He was trying to help the current *Pro Cura Bibliothec*, who was an old friend of his, in finishing the cataloguing of a newly arrived collection. This was a temporary job, and if I did it with diligence, surely some other occupation could be found later.

"I only have one condition. You must start right away. Go tomorrow, first thing in the morning."

Mmm, this was what stimulated this speedy solution. He was still afraid of housing a thief in his parish. "Of course, sir. I am immensely grateful for this opportunity. I will not let it flee from my hands." Feigning my most soldierlike attitude, I was fighting the urge to scream 'thank you, thank you, thank you' and jump from the satisfaction working in such a library provoked in me.

"You should appreciate it is a unique one. This is not an employment requiring straining yourself physically, and you will be under the protection of the Church."

****

Mrs. Cochran, immediately after I was finished dressing in the masculine robes, came magically to my room with the right pair of boots in hand. It had to be the vicar's doing as well.

"It is good you are trying them now. I know the provost in that school, and he is a respectable fellow. And Mr. Falcon, the librarian you are going to help, is such an amiable man. He is slowly losing his eyesight — that is why a young person like you is needed — but apart from that, he is capable and patient. I am sure you will learn quickly how to do the work, and will find time to read and study all you want. You will be well."

I listened, imagining the place she was describing, when an essential question came to my mind. "Mrs. Cochran, I am afraid we have not considered a problem that is paramount in this scheme. I am very grateful for all you are doing for me; still, there is another favor I must ask you."

She gestured to stop wandering in circles and say what I had in my mind.

"I am not sure how I am going to handle my courses." I looked at the fabrics in my hands, trying to convey the difficult task that would be to clean and dry the pads in a place where a man was supposed to live.

"This is nothing. Helen will arrange to have a fresh set for you each month. It will give you a reason to visit. Come, come. Let us get done with the issue of your hair."

I am not sure if that is needed, Mrs. Beth. Would you remind me why? — I wanted to protest, but did not dare.

"I have been pondering a new idea. What about trying first an extremely short cut? Yes, I can try making it one fourth inch, or even shorter. And, if it is not to our liking, we have the last resource of shaving. What do you say to that?"

Was she trying to convince me, or herself? This did not leave room for doubt: no woman in her right mind would do something like this. "Can you do that? Anything is better than shaving."

****

Once finished the troublesome task, she turned me to look at myself in the window glass. "You see? The only thing you must work on now is mimicking the students."

Good God, I look like Mr. Collins! I saw the less than attractive shape of the boy in the reflection. There would be no problem convincing the people around me. I put on the hat to see if it could cover my head. It did.

"You are remarkably convincing. This is a handsome attire that will serve you not only to keep you warm," she turned up the lapels, "but to cover your face in case you want to be unnoticed."

"'Unnoticed' is exactly what I am looking for," I assured her. "Mrs. Beth, I promise I will pay you back soon. I will save every penny to do it. You will not regret helping me."

"Who ever told you that you have to pay anything back? When are you going to learn to receive God's gifts without questioning if you deserve them?"

I was momentarily surprised by her scolding.

"Oh yes. Do you think I have not noticed how you carry the guilt of the entire humanity on your back? That is a trait close to conceit. Be careful. It will not do you any good."

Not understanding the relationship between those two statements, I changed the subject asking how many miles it was to Cambridge.

"You are not walking there, Elizabeth. You are not that healthy yet. I am accompanying you tomorrow."

"But. But…"

"No buts."

****

The next day, true to her word, Mrs. Beth came (in a rented coach) to take me to the town of bridges over the River Cam. She carried a bulky basket.

"These are just some snacks. Sadly, they will not last long. It should help you survive until your first pay," she said at the end of the voyage.

I looked inside and found some bread and cheese. "These are my favorite. You are amazing! Thank you."

"This is nothing. Take care, and do not get into trouble!"

"Yes," I responded, seeing that she was trying to hide some emotion while turning to the carriage. "I will."

"I will pray for you." She climbed and absconded behind the curtains, signaling to drive away.

Making sure my hat was in place — *this is it* — I turned around to observe the imposing church façade with superior gothic style. Worthy of a King indeed.

I walked the few steps to the wooden door and entered a little awkwardly (due to the two packages I was carrying) into the enormous main chamber. The cold of the interior caressing my arms, I looked up to the high ceiling and the beautifully decorated windows with medieval stained glass. My five senses awakened with the peaceful atmosphere. Why was it that when a place is silent, one can see, smell, feel, hear and even taste every small detail? Amazed by the magnificence and directed by the familiar aroma of old books, I found one of the side chapels of the Great Chapel.

Mrs. Cochran said this was the place where I should find Mr. Falcon. It was almost without students. Maybe because it was still too early Monday morning.

Moving toward a counter, I asked a curate who was diligently arranging some papers, "Can you tell me where I can find the Pro Cura Bibliothec?" I asked with my best imitation of a secure voice.

The middle aged man peered at me from head to toe over his spectacles. "Who is asking?"

"Michael Ellis, the new Second-class Assistant. He is expecting me."

With what seemed a masculine version of Lady Catherine, he indicated, "Mr. Falcon is in the next room, doing *your* duties. I expect you to do them neatly and diligently for now on." He positioned the papers on the desk and stood up, leaning on his knuckles, to hover over me. "And not to prod around the Fellows of the College."

I nodded while heading to the place he had indicated. This was not the right moment to be impertinent, Lizzy. I pictured how Papa would mock this priest, giggling. There would be plenty of time to comment with Beth about that ridiculous wig!

Once in the entrance of the forth side room, I found a clerk with remarkably white hair arguing with what I presumed was the cleaning lady.

"Mrs. Smith, come here, please," he indicated with his cane at the chains on the floor. "They are in the middle of the aisle — they are in the way." I followed the offending object until I understood the origin of this problem: the books were chained to the bookcases. What kind of archaic library was this?

"This is the best I can do with those. They are too long and heavy to fit over the books," the lady answered in a tone of voice that showed she was far from intimidated. "You should make them shorter or get rid of them."

"Get rid of them?" the man frowned, like if she was speaking Chinese. "And risk losing the books when one of those so-called gentlemen deems it necessary to take them home? Nonsense. Do as I say and do not argue in front of the students," he signaled with his eyes for the woman to look in my direction.

He walked past her, and from her low complaint, I understood this argument was an everyday occurrence.

"What can I do for you?"

"I am Michael Ellis, sir. I am here..." How to avoid mentioning Mr. Cochran now? "To help you with the cataloguing of the books that just arrived."

"Oh, well, that is excellent news. I am Frederick Falcon." He approached and threw a confident arm over my shoulder. *Do not freak out, Elizabeth, you are a boy now.* "How is that grumpy old man, Cochran, ah?" I looked up at his mischievous smile, and realized they were probably close friends. *Well, I did not disobey the vicar; his colleague is the one that mentioned him.*

****

Mr. Falcon directed me to a side exit of the chapel and indicated to wait for him outside. While trying to look comfortable with the weight that was causing cramps in my arms, I saw him explain to the other clerk that he was taking me to my accommodations in the Gibbs' building.

Once he joined me on the sidewalk, I realized said building was but a few yards away. He guided me to the stairs, neighboring the corner.

I must say I was a little bit afraid, while slowly climbing after the old man, until the chamber that would be all for myself came into sight. This place looked like the quarters of Merlin the wizard!

The so called 'attic' was actually a store of all that is old and extraordinary. I was not sure if everything here even had a name. I tried to discern books from portraits, portraits from fabrics, fabrics from furniture, furniture from instruments, instruments from casseroles, casseroles from… a telescope? I approached said object, touching it lightly. "Does it work?"

The curate shrugged and indicated he remembered one of the lenses was broken."I think it is not something irreparable." Walking to the wall where a window allowed lots of light, he signaled to a large iron structure, "That should be your bed. It is a solid piece, almost unmanageable to move, but useful nonetheless."

Said object was impossible to reach at the moment, I arranged my things over a desk that seemed in acceptable conditions. "Are there any cleaning tools?"

The man nodded, signaling for me to accompany him to the door. "Yes, Mrs. Smith can help you with that. Though, it must be later. After we pretend your efforts are urgently needed in the library."

Once again in the big church, I saw the clerk I supposed was the principal in the library.

"It was about time," growled he, without a scrape to his airs of superiority. "Here are Mr. Bryant's books." He indicated a stack of large boxes. "Remember to catalogue in different records the ones that pertain to Natural History."

Deciding *that* was enough instruction, he glanced around like someone that does not want to touch anything, and went out pompously — like a peacock (unaware he looked more like a duck).

Mr. Falcon and I interchanged conspiratorial glances and neared the mountain of work. "Well, as you have heard, we need to catalogue and arrange this library in the old bookcases. Then, you should take one of the big notebooks over there," he signaled to a worn desktop and chair, "and write down by subject: title, author, publisher and publication year of every book. Right?"

I nodded and asked for the pen and ink.

He opened the drawer, showing an overflowing stack. "Now, do not worry about Wightwick." He signaled up with the eyes to the top of his head for me to recognize who he was referring to.

It was almost "Wig-wig." What an appropriate surname!

"He is harmless. He is just the provost's secretary. And he leaves at two o'clock every day."

****

Starting to work immediately, I planned ahead as much as I could. Opening some packages and advancing in the idea of how to arrange the books better. I was diligent in trying to classify all the subjects correctly and divide the shelves accordingly. However, at two o'clock, like a synchronized army, five employees took their belongings and walked through the back door.

Mrs. Smith handed me the mop and broom as if she were delivering a polecat. "There you are boy," she said, wiping her hands on her apron and arranging her cap. "Keep it all you want. If you manage, in the meantime, to lose them — all the better."

I looked at her questioningly until I realized what she meant.

Well, this was not bad. The routine in this place was comfortable. I would wake up with the Sun every day, work until early in the afternoon, and the rest of the time was all for myself. I approached the staircase leading to my 'apartments,' and looked once more to the beautiful yard behind me. Yes, I could very well get used to living surrounded by palaces. Well done, Mr. Ellis!

****

Once at the top of the stairs, I stepped in and observed my surroundings. This place certainly needed a lot of work. Today I would focus on the principal things, like having a bed, arranging my belongings in the massive wardrobe, and cleaning.

It would be fun.

And so I did. The bed was immovable; cleaning the adjacent area was the only option. Some of the old fabrics I saw before were well packed and played the role of bed linens. I considered hiding my book of poems in the writing table I previously used, but reasoned the wardrobe had a key and should be safer. Then, I moved said desk close to the window.

When exhausted by the hard work, it was quite late. *Get the water before darkness settled down. Hurry up. You cannot linger like this.*

I found a bucket between the things that were still messy, and went downstairs following the direction signaled by Mrs. Smith. Once in the pit**, a servant from one of the schools nearby helped to get the water. Thus, I was on my way back sooner than what I had previously calculated.

****

This thing is heavy! I was bringing the full bucket down the lane. When I turned the corner near my staircase, I glanced to the street that led to the front door and perceived an elegant carriage. I placed the bin on the floor so that I could breathe; supported on one arm, I looked again to the street.

Oh my, HE was here! I edgily reacted, seeing the shape of the man I could make out in a crowd. Hide, hide! I sprinted, trying to reach the stairs fast. I tripped over the bucket and hurried on. I reached the stairs. Was I out of sight? I tried to catch my breath, clutching the rail. Straining my ears, I heard heavy footfalls outside. Up! Up! Climb to the attic! Two at a time. To no avail — in less than a blink, his fast steps echoed in the narrow walls. I tumbled again and leaned on one knee and a hand. He caught my ankle. No way out. I turned around, sitting, and tried to shake his grip. I began throwing kicks. He took my legs with both hands. I threw a rain of punches. He arranged his legs in either sides of my feet and grabbed my fits too. In a flash, I was immobilized from head to toes with his head on my belly. *Oh, God.*

---

* This is a phrase from a speech of José Martí.

**According to The Regency Encyclopedia, "Many people still brought their water in jugs from a nearby public pump, a practice which in time of cholera, ensured that the whole neighborhood was soon infected."

The information about Cambridge was kindly provided by Anna Cook, Senior Library Assistant, King's College Library:

-According to John Saltmarsh, in his "King's College: a short history" Cambridge, 1958, in 1744, the library occupied the fourth, fifth, sixth, seventh and eighth side chapels on the south side of the chapel. Until 1777, all books were chained.

The archivist, Patricia McGuire, has provided with the following information about the library staff from college records:

-The 1812 accounts say Mr. Vince was paid (5 shillings per term) 'pro supervis bibliothec', and Mr. Saunders was paid a pound per term 'pro cura bibliothec'. Samuel Berney Vince (1802-27) was a Fellow (he was Vice-Provost 1819-26, Tutor 1816-26, Minister of St Edward's Church across the street in 1813-16 and died in 1845.) Saunders would have been an administrative clerk. Probably he was the chapel clerk, because he was also in receipt of chapel expenses for washing surplices, polishing plate etc. In 1805, Bryant's library was arranged by Messrs. Barrow and Briggs, who were voted in Congregation to get 20 guineas each for their trouble, and 5 guineas to Briggs for a catalogue. Saunders later got 10 guineas for unpacking and arranging Bryant's library.

-The following collection has been recently completed:

First and early editions of Jane Austen.

Chapter 12

How could I get out of this situation? I rested my head on the step behind me. He had me. I looked down and saw his dark curls. His body was clutching mine; one arm around my thighs, the other effectively securing my two hands over my chest. His weight was preventing me from catching much needed air. Rest a little, Elizabeth.

I tried to inhale once more. He was heavy — so heavy. I bent my neck to notice him tilt his head and shut his eyes. I looked to the constricted space. We had to move from here. Someone could see us!

"Mr. Darcy, please, let me free."

He squeezed his eyes tighter, and his grip became more intense. I rested my head on the step again. This was not working.

"Mr. Darcy, Mr. Darcy, please. I promise not to run any further."

He shook his head against my belly, without retreating an inch in his arrangement over me. *Oh My!*

"Please, Mr. Darcy, look at me." He turned, supporting his chin on my navel. His orbs bore such intensity. "There is nowhere I can go from here except the attic."

"Can we go there? To the attic?"

"Yes, we can."

He stood up, while offering his help for me to rise. Dear Lord, he was frightened of my appearance.

I checked if my hat was still on. Fortunately it was. I arranged it better to cover my ears, "Follow me please."

Once in the last floor, after opening the door, I walked to face the window. How did he find me? Why was he here? I DID NOT WANT HIM TO SEE ME! Not like this!

Keep your courage, Elizabeth. Face him!

I turned to find his gaze alternating between the strange objects in the immediate area and me. I studied him in much the same way as he was studying me. He looked thin. What had happened to you Fitzwilliam? Why do you have those dark circles under your eyes?

He stepped into the room, not leaving the vicinity of the door yet. His lips in a thin line, his hands clenched, not a sound coming from him.

So, it was my duty to start this conversation. "Mr. Darcy, what are you doing here?"

"I am here on behalf of your family. They are desperately looking for you. You must come with me."

On behalf of my family? This made no sense knowing my father's reservations about him. "I cannot do that, sir. I will not!"

His features went from contradiction to powerlessness to incomprehension. "You cannot be serious. You are not the kind of person to disregard the wishes of your family. You must know they need to find you. You must go home."

"No, sir, you do not understand. I cannot go home. I cannot!"

He approached in two long strides, only the small couch standing between us, "Miss Elizabeth, do you know what your family is going through? I think you underestimate their suffering. Your mother is out of her wits trying to find you. She even traveled to Bakewell!"

Poor Mama! She had always been afraid of returning there. I covered my mouth. Wait, Bakewell? "How do you know about that place?"

"Do not look at me like that. I could not help finding out about your family's past. I arrived the day you disappeared. They were all in a state of shock — arguing and crying. They came home from mass to find you gone! GONE!"

He was in Longbourn the day of my escape?! Why?

"After your father read the farewell letter, I cannot..." He strove to keep his composure. "I do not know how to describe the fear, the desperation, the utter turmoil your letter provoked."

My dear Mama must have been frantic. Why did he have to witness this? I wanted to hide, but he continued, "They know you are ill. They know you are traveling alone. And they do not have a clue of where you are. They do not even know if you are alive!"

"But… but… what does any of this have to do with you? Why were you in Hertfordshire that day?"

"You could not expect me to leave them in that dire situation. I helped them the best I could," he declared, his palms up, emphasizing that he thought this was what was expected from him.

"Yes, I saw what I presume was a portrait made by you. Nonetheless, Mr. Darcy, you should not be here. It is a family issue." You should have given up when I did not reply to Georgiana.

"On the contrary, Bingley is not there to do this job. I <u>had</u> to step in. They needed someone young who could make the search. I would have done it for any of you. For any of your sisters. Your letter was heartbreaking. They do not understand. Your father went to all the places he knows. He looked for you restlessly in London. Your family from Scotland has been contacted. They have asked about you in all the villages around Meryton — the places you have been all your life." He started to pace the room agitatedly, like mimicking the search. I could see that he was desperate, his thoughts battling a war. "And your health, what about that? You almost fainted in my arms in your sister's wedding, for God's sake. You are ill! No. You must come. This search must over. It has been insane looking for you all over Hertfordshire and London. I know what you have been through. Everything you are running from has a solution. I know why you are here as I have found your diar…"

"Mr. Darcy, you take too much upon yourself," I halted his tormented speech. "You can give up the quest now. You see I am well. Nothing is the matter with me. I will live in a comfortable place. I am surrounded by books and educated people. I will be happy here."

"Happy here! You are not even a shadow of what you were. You look like a teen lad. You are thinner than when I saw you last. And this place! You call this cold place 'comfortable'?! An attic! No servants, no fireplace, and surrounded by men! No, this is no place for a lady." He stepped closer and held me gently but firmly by my elbows. "You must come. YOU WILL COME!"

There was a strange feeling of ferocity in his eyes. I was not giving up so easily! NO! "Would you force me, Mr. Darcy? Is that the way you are going to behave toward me now?"

A flash of anger and regret crossed his face, and he let down his hands. "No, never." He claimed and turned around, his shoulders moving slightly up and down with every intake of air.

Poor dear, he had not realized yet the finality of my resolution. He did not perceive I cut my hair so very short that I could not be presented into polite society. I stroked my head still covered by the concealing cap. Must I do this? Must I wound him thus?

Yes. I walked to stand before him. "I think you do not understand. I cannot go back." I took my hat off and looked down, not wanting to see his face of rejection. Please God, give me strength.

He dropped onto the couch, heaved a sigh and clutched his head with both hands. I leaned on the wall to observe a new wave of wrath, but only could see how this new knowledge was hurting him. The pain — physical pain — emanating from every feature of his body. *I am sorry, love.* There was nothing left for me to do. He must go now.

Apparently, he read my thoughts. After a minute or two, he stood up and walked out of the room.

I had effectively pushed him now. There was no way back. He would not want to see me again. Ever. Not after this. Not after seeing me like this. How it hurt! I had tried to accomplish this so many times. Except that seeing it, seeing the transformation, seeing him go from caring to pain, and finally to feel sorry for me, was more cruel than what I pictured it would be.

Although I promised to myself at Longbourn not to cry over this resolution, I must admit this was one of those times I could not control my feelings. Between tears and moans, I made myself review the questions that were permanently placed in my mind for many days. Was there another way to avoid Wickham? Would anyone tell me what happened so I could act accordingly? Could I have confided in Mama that Wickham was in Derbyshire the day of my uncle's wedding? Why was it that she did not know he was there, that Wickham was there? Why did she not recognize him when the Militia was in Meryton?

And what was I going to do now? Now that Mr. Darcy knew?

I needed to light a candle first. I managed to dry my eyes while looking for a tinderbox. That was a considerable accomplishment, because it was a small object in this huge place, and I had to find it in. In the meantime, I found the candles and went to retrieve the bucket. It was probably empty, and I would not be able to get the water this late, but at least I would have it.

Maybe it was not a smart idea to sleep in a place where Mr. Darcy could inform my family I was in attendance. Should I wait until tomorrow? Should I find some other place to sleep today, and ask Beth for help later? Maybe I should go abroad somehow?

To my surprise, in the street, what I found was the bucket upside down, and Mr. Darcy seated on it with his back to me. This answered my questions. *Go back and start packing, Elizabeth.* I retreated as silently as I could.

I was going to be so happy in this place! I hurriedly took the robes I had previously arranged in the closet. Why had he found me?! This was the perfect place for me. I hid the book of poems inside the coat pocket. And how am I going to get out of here without being noticed?

When taking some of the food that Beth had prepared, I felt a warm hand stopping my frenetic movements. *There is no way out.*

He guided me to sit on the bed, keeping that strangely sad visage around him. "I have a deal for you. You will not run away from here, and in exchange, I am not going to tell your parents where you are."

I looked down, trying to think clearly. He was here again. What were my alternatives? My only gateway was walking over the roof with the hope of finding another attic and escaping downstairs. And then what? Where would you be going from there, Elizabeth? "Would you keep my secret for a couple of days while I reflect about it?"

"Will you promise not to run away in the course of this temporary agreement?"

"Yes."

He nodded in agreement. The cold emptiness of the absence of his touch, when he removed his hand, was hard to bear. I heard him approach the door at my back. "A servant is going to get the water now and bring you some food. Sleep well, Miss Elizabeth. Also, please, do not hesitate to ask anything from him. He knows where I am staying, and will always be nearby."

I wanted to tell him that it was not necessary. Be that as it may, when I turned to look at the stairs, he was already gone.

****

Sleeping was a hopeless task. I resumed organizing the place. Step by step, I was able to make something more or less cozy of my sanctuary. Amongst the many unrecognizable objects stored there, I found a strange piece of furniture that could only be compared to a cradle and a chair together: it had in the bottom the semicircular part of wood that is used to swing babies to sleep, but it was a chair nonetheless. A rocking chair — I liked it. I also found a notebook to start a new diary, and many, many other things.

Writing letters was mandatory. Thus, I started my compositions to Longbourn and Georgiana, not knowing yet if I would have Mr. Darcy's help to post them. Both were difficult in different ways. To my family, I tried to reassure them about my safety and good health. Please stop looking for me. I asked about the way they decided to convey my absence, and if they knew anything about Jane.

Writing to Ana — I do not know how to describe how complex that was. She was the victim of a man without scruples. In the end, she had done the right thing — she had talked to her brother. It was difficult not to think that things could be dealt with differently, and not to feel guilty about one's decisions. Then, I thought about the hurt it must have caused to Mr. Darcy the knowledge of her failure. *Poor girl, striving to be worthy of such a brother — a man without fault indeed.* At the end, I narrated the past weeks' events. Asking for her discretion and apologizing for the long time it took for me to write back.

It was not necessary to convey my motives for running away from home; it would only hurt her more to know that Wickham was back in Hertfordshire, and probably married to Maria Lucas. Furthermore, I would not risk Mr. Darcy knowing of those motives.

****

The next day started with a welcoming sun shining through the window of the cold attic. Finding a new bucket with water next to a carefully wrapped sweet bread (my favorite breakfast) Mr. Darcy's servant left at my door, I had only to do my toilet in what appeared to be a seldom visited part of the Gibbs' building.

I started early on my mission of cataloguing the books — such a spellbinding occupation, I could do it my entire life.

When Mr. Falcon arrived, I could see he was not feeling well. His pale skin, his distorted movements and shaking hands, a sad indication of his deteriorating health. Instead of continuing with my previous assignment, he asked me to help him with another task: taking care of the room filled with students while he went to the relieve himself. I had to get used to this familiarity between men.

In the other side chamber, the most common arrangements of the students was in small groups. Why did they not study separately? It was easier to read alone. However, the strangest thing was their vocabulary, with a great deal of "blasts," "damns" and other unkind words I will not put down in writing.

For example, the chair Mr. Falcon gave me to rest upon was near to a table where four young men sat. I could not help learning their surnames: Lennon, McCartney, Harrison and Starkey*. I also heard a lot of complains about how much homework their tutor gave them the previous day.

Later on, statements difficult to understand were said, like, "the woman screamed as a horse" by Mr. Lennon (which was apparently funny for the rest of the quartet). Mr. Harrison alleged, "my father would not allow me" in response to an odd proposition, as well.

They talked about playing a joke on some newcomers. Something about carrying them far from the village and dropping them there, to find their way back by themselves. As long as they did not do it in winter, it was almost harmless fun. I shut my eyes and pictured the younger boys they were talking about asking directions.

To my surprise, closing my eyes came with a revelation of a different kind. This was what I heard in my dreams: a murmur of a few male voices. This was the sound I could not connect to any image. Yes, there were boys' whispers after Wickham's proposition!

The first impression of this thought was extremely unsettling. Why was it that I could only <u>hear</u> those voices, and not see their owners? The walls nearby seemed heavier. I walked outside the building. *Do not worry, Ellis. That is in the past. You are a man now.*

Then, I saw the same servant that had brought the bucket with water. Mr. Darcy was not giving up; he thought I would still escape. He was even more stubborn than me.

****

Cambridge, Tuesday, 29 September, afternoon

I find this town fascinating. I would so much like to walk all the streets! I will do it as soon as the weather is warm enough.

In the meantime, several books can fill my hours. I have found in particular, one that seems to be about the composition of air. It is in German, by Alexander von Humboldt.

I will also use a scientific method to discern about what is slowly appearing in my dreams; it is easier now that it cannot affect my family and my life. Let us start:

Place: Lambton woods, near the Church, Derbyshire

Time: Around Easter, 1798, Uncle Gardiner's wedding.

Events:

1. I run after Jack and Wickham until I reach them in a part of the woods that has an average slope.

2. I agree to some bargain with the latter.

3. I feel fear meeting the terms, but I feel safer because Jack is nearby.

4. I hear some other boys and a low murmur. There is always a recurrent pain in my throat and belly every time I remember this.

5. Much later, my mother is crying with me curled in her lap. My dress is a mess of mud. There is no blood on it, although I am sure there were some scratches in my skin.

6. Mama asks Papa to help, although they are not yet engaged.

7. We ran from Lambton right away.

This list should hopefully grow with time.

The bread and cheese Beth gave me and the vast amount of food from Mr. Darcy was a godsend, although I would like to find some fruit. I think I saw apple trees in the road from Newmarket.

Still, I need my poems.

Challenge, by Julio Flórez

If because at your feet I drop,
defeated like a servant,
and timidly, nearly fearful
I beg a gaze from you;
if because in your presence,
I become ecstatic with emotion,
you believe my heart
is breaking in my chest,
and I will eternally be
of my passion a slave;
You are wrong! You are wrong,
fresh and fragrant rosebud,
I will break your pride
the way miners break the rock.

If to fight you provoke me,
I am ready for war.

If you are foam, I am sea
that trusts in its frenzy.
You make me cry, but one day
I will make you cry too.
And then, when surrendered
you offer your entire life
asking mercy at my feet.
Because my anger is
colossal in its excesses,
do you know what I will do
in those moments of resentment?
I will tear out your heart
and smother it with kisses!

I must admit, being in a place where I do not know any familiar face had made me miss Mr. Darcy. Although, how could I expect him to want to see me after yesterday's discovery?

I have the consolation that nobody can take away the memories of us (not even him).

There is also one last thought that has been in my mind all day and deserves to be in these pages. I should participate in the antislavery movement. Yes, I will find the way to be useful to those brave men.

****

Next day, Mr. Falcon invited me to a drink to celebrate Michaelmas. I had to comply; otherwise he would think I am not a man.

That morning, I had the chance to help those boys that I observed on Monday. Mr. Harrison asked for some aid finding calculus books. They were looking for some of Mr. Bernoulli's or Mr. Euler's works, however, I recommended Mrs. Agnesi** instead. They were naturally impressed by the knowledge that *her* books are much more easy to understand than the classics.

It felt good to show them a woman can be a brilliant mathematician too.

Once back in the attic, I was longing for two things: fruits and a bathtub. The second was the most difficult to accomplish. My only hope: that the piece left abandoned in the farthest corner could be repaired easily. So the first took precedence.

I walked out of the building, heading to cross the river through some of the bridges at the west. Looking back, I waved my hand in salutation to the servant that had to follow me everywhere and started walking in said direction. Mr. Darcy had given him an uncomfortable task.

It wasn't too far, but once I choose the direction of my walk, the chap gave up. I knew he was not *that* interested in following his patron's orders. He was surely tired of this useless occupation.

I followed a little-used path for around half an hour, until I reached the place that seemed most solitary, and also more likely to have some apples or pears.

This fruit orchard reminded of Longbourn. I climbed a tree. Father was right in calling me a monkey; I comfortably installed myself on one of the branches and reached for my first apple. *Mmm, remember to not gorge.* I took a tasty bite. *At least not too much.*

When I was having my second fruit, my hands a little sticky with the juice, a bee appeared in the tree. She fluttered and fluttered around me. *Stay calm Elizabeth. Do not move a hair.* Until she decided to land in my apple! *Do not be scared, she will move on quickly.* Then she jumped to my wrist. My God! She jumped again to the apple. She liked sugar. That was why she came after me. I looked at my hands. I ate with both …and my face. Her random flight proved she had not decided where to settle. She could bite my face! She was going to land on my face! I dropped the apple and started to move my hands hysterically around my head. I was going to fall. Oh, no. I managed to attach one leg in a near branch. I lost balance.

I ended up side down in an instant, with only a hooked boot preventing from hitting my head on the ground. What could I do to disentangle myself now?

Think Elizabeth. I tried to bend upward. AGRRR. I was not strong enough yet! I tried to reach the ground with my hand. It was too far. I looked around and nothing seemed to help. I knew: I would undo my cravat and reach a solution with it. I could not help being mad for finding myself hanged on one leg because of a bee!

I was fighting with the tie when a loud laugh was heard behind my back. Oh, dear! This was not true. I turned a tad to look at him. He was a few steps away, walking toward me, showing such a satisfactory mocking grin I could not help being angry. He thought this was funny! Finding me at my worst had become his favorite pastime! I finished with the knot and threw the fabric to the nearest branch. I would show him not to laugh at me!

"Do not worry. I am always ready to help you out of your gardening problems." He swiftly grabbed me by my back and unhooked the shoe with the other hand. *Look how easily he can lift me!*

I ended up being held in his arms. I looked into his warm eyes, and for just a moment…Well, I did like being here. I…No, no. *Elizabeth, you must be angry at him.* "Mr. Darcy," I looked up at his silly teasing smile again, "Thank you. I think you can let me back to the ground now."

"Whatever for?"

"Because I need to go back before dusk!"

"We can do that together." He started to walk in the direction of the buildings.

"You have to free me, Sir. This is a public place."

"I do not see anyone around. We are far from the river."

I tried to free by myself unsuccessfully.

"There is no way I am going to let you do that. There is no point in letting you go." *What? This man is crazy.* "Oh, yes. You see, if I let you free you will run away in the very minute you touch the ground. Then, I will have to catch you, and we will end up in this same position. I would rather skip a step."

"Really? And when are you going to let me free then?" He had to realize this was an intimate position nonetheless.

He looked at me and appeared to be considering a witty reply, "When you tell me how you got that job?"

---

* Mr. Ringo Star's real surname was Starkey.

**Euler transformed the differential and integral calculus in a formal theory of functions where no longer was needed the support of geometry. The Bernoulli family has a wide spectrum of discoveries: from hydrodynamics, to mathematical physics in general. I am referring here only to Johann Bernoulli, who in 1696 posed the so called "The brachistochrone problem" (the problem of finding the curve on which a particle takes the shortest time to descend under its own weight without friction. This curve is called the brachistochrone). Maria Gaetana Agnesi (1718 — 1799) was an Italian linguist, mathematician, and philosopher who is credited with writing the first book discussing both differential and integral calculus.

Chapter 13

"How did I get my job? That is an easy tale." *Well, better do not rely on that.* He would drop me the exact moment he knew I attempted to rob a church. "But, you will acquaint me with how you found me in return." I challenged him. "Do we have a deal?"

"That is a good deal, except that you will stay this way until I finish."

"I imagine you will not think the same when I do," I warned him.

His playful visage changed immediately to a frightened one, as he tightened his grip.

I prolonged the story as much as I could, unsure, while he walked in the direction of the river. "Now prepare yourself for something very dreadful," I got to the final part. "I stole the hosts in a nearby church due to my hunger, and was shamefully found by the vicar and his wife, vomiting at the altar. They were the ones that assisted me in obtaining this job." I clung to his lapels, to prevent hitting my head.

The fall did not happen.

Contrary to my expectations, he lightened up. His chest started to shake slightly, and when I looked up at him, he was laughing again, with a liberating quiver I never thought could come from the scowl he wore before. Who could understand this man? I just said I had behaved like a thief, and he found *that* a good reason to relax.

"Mr. Darcy, are you all right?" I saw him take the route to the farthest bridge. Now, who said women were the ones difficult to make out?

"Better than ever." He slowed his chortle. He had to be imagining the ridiculous scene of throwing up on the altar.

"Well, now it is your turn, sir." Oh, yes. We all had our moments to be ashamed. There had to be something grave about his tale too; otherwise he would not have asked to stay in this position until he finished his tale.

"The day you disappeared, we only had time to search for you discreetly around Meryton. Subsequently, your family began in the places they thought you hide in the country, and I did so in London. Some of the places in the worst neighborhoods. After many unsuccessful enquiries, I realized you had put your heart into not being found. And that you are too smart to do anything that can be guessed easily." *He found me easily enough.* Poor dear, he was not able to speak about this coherently. "After racking my brain, thinking about the most unlikely places, I tried journeying with the same means you had at your disposal that day. This is why I looked for the itinerary of all the post coaches that traveled near Longbourn the day of your escape. I studied them and decided the one heading north was the one you must have taken — there is not much land to the South. When I reached Newmarket, I guessed you probably spent the first night in some of the inns of that town. So, I looked in all of them with no success. Nobody recognized your portrait, although I was sure you arrived too late to be able to keep traveling the same night. Thus, I went to other kind of establishments. I looked in the places where you might have bought food, and in the places you might have purchased new robes. It was useless again.

"Just before giving up searching in Newmarket, I tried the pawn broker. You might have had some difficulty with your finances." He nodded at me to ascertain it was a logical thought. "The owner of one of those places recognized the picture and showed me your garnet cross."

"That was a fine gentleman. He paid well for it."

"A fine gentleman?" he shouted incredulously. "That man robbed you of all your belongings, Elizabeth!"

"What?" I could not believe it. That man had my most precious token, and he wanted even more from me!?

"Yes. He tried the same trick with me after I bought it. When I left that shop, I was attacked by the same boys as you."

"Oh no, they robbed you too!"

"They could not take anything from me. Do not be scared." He inspected our surroundings and ascertained there was not a soul between the many trees. "Anyway, I managed to catch one of the rascals and extract from him the truth about who was their leader." His countenance transformed from concern to full repugnance. "When I found out what that man did to you.

When he confessed he took advantage of your innocent ways. And finally, when he told me the other place you visited that day. His words, 'she probably went to sell her charms again' brought me to the brink of killing him."

"The man said I sold my charms? Where did he get that crazy idea from?" This was not true. I was not dressed provocatively.

"The man disclosed where you spent your first night."

"Yes. It was the nearest inn to the post station," I hinted he should have searched there first.

"The nearest inn? It was a house of ill repute, a place where men go to meet women with the exact purpose of having an affair!" *Dear God. Only courtesans go to that kind of place.* "When I went there, the owner spoke about you in the rudest ways. He said you were wearing man's clothes. That he was sure it was part of your routine during the act of..."

I could not hear anymore, "You thought me a...?" No. This could not be. "You thought I spent the night in that place doing...?" I started to shift and hit him with my elbow with all my force, "LET ME FREE!"

When he dropped me, I ran through the solitary slope wildly. He dared to hold me all of this way, since he thought I was an easy woman! I felt Mr. Darcy grabbing my hand and turning me around to face him. *There is no way you are going to stop me this time!* I threw both, a kick to his genitals and a punch into his face with all the force of my left hand.

The leg failed to reach that high, but the blow did not. In a heartbeat, I was crying from the sting his iron chin brought.

I shifted to hide the tears. Oh God! This hurt! AAAArg! I cradled my hand to my chest. *I broke it.*

He stepped in my path. "Elizabeth, did something happen to you? Let me see!"

I hate you, Fitzwilliam Darcy. I hate you! "DO NOT DARE TO CALL ME ELIZABETH!" I saw him reach for me. "Do not DARE to touch me either!" I drew back. "Is that why you thought you had the right to detain me all this time? Because you thought I was one of those women!?"

"No. No." He rubbed his face hard. "Of course not."

"Really? Do you deny you thought the worst about me when you went to that place? Can you deny it?" Straight in the eyes, I defied him to lie to my face.

He tried first to avoid my stare, and then dropped his head. I could feel his deep unease. *Well deserved Mr. Darcy!* "Yes, I did."

How DARE you! "If I did not need my other hand on the morrow, I swear I would hit you again! No matter the cost."

"I thought you were desperate. You had no money and no friends! You had nothing but your body. You had no way of surviving in that town. I know people do desperate things under desperate circumstances!"

"What do you know about desperate, 'Mr. Silk Cradle?'" GOD! My hand! "I would rather starve to death than sell myself! You should know this better than anyone." *Try to argue with that fact!*

He stared at me a long moment. At length, he dropped his shoulders in defeat and whispered, "Yes, I should have."

"I must get going." I could not handle the pain much longer.

He stepped in my way again. "Wait! I hurt you."

"I HURT MYSELF!" He undoubtedly had stopped loving me. Even before we met here. "I should have found a good bat or stone to hit you!"

"No. I hurt you. I… I am a fool." *Oh yes you are. But I do not have time for that now.*

"Mr. Darcy I must return to my place." I tried to walk past him while he moved to stand in my path, "I am not in the mood for silly games, sir." I attempted to avoid him again, taking another direction.

He would not allow it.

I looked up to find his face of — *pity*? Oh, no. Not that. "Mr. Darcy, could you stop doing that? I need to go. I…" *Who do you think you are!?* "Are you going to impose on me again?"

He retreated but stayed in the way, "No. Of course not. Why do you think I am going to impose?"

Was he playing dumb? "You just did it when you lifted me!"

"No! I lifted you because I have not conquered this!" He was exasperated. "I just want you to act reasonably. Right now I need to get you to a doctor, and you are not even considering… You are not acting rationally."

"RATIONAL! Rational? I am irrational! Who says that?" I dropped on the ground and sat with my thighs close to my chest, hiding my face between my hat and my knees. I needed to deal with this hell in my hand! He was pacing the space behind me. I put my good arm around my head. Do not let him see your tears. He thought I was a courtesan. A COURTESAN! A fallen woman — a whore! With the corner of my eyes, I saw he was crouching and leaning over me. No. No. No. Go away! I hid my head lower.

"I am sorry. I am so very sorry. I do not know how I could ever have… I… I just want to help you. I feel responsible for what is happening to you." The nervous manner in which he was moving was palpable, even concealed as I was. "I know you are without protection, and that you gave up telling the truth about Wickham and Georgiana when you wrote your warning note to your parents." He finally rested his upper body on his knuckles, "This is the least I can do."

I felt his eyes on me. *Are not you tired of my appearance already? I am ugly now. Stop looking at me!* I moved my hand to see it through blurred vision under my legs. My thumb had a decidedly strange angle with respect to the rest of the fingers.

His shadow moved, changing to stand at my front. "Would you please let me take you to a doctor?"

I had to compose myself, someone could come. "I have a condition." I glared at him after drying my face on my trousers. "You will call me 'Ellis' — Michael Ellis. You are going to treat me like a man. Do you understand me?"

He offered a handkerchief (which I rejected). "I promise to behave like that in front of other people."

****

Mr. Darcy took me to the inn where he was staying. The owner had a spare room to lend for a short while, and I asked to be left alone.

Once inside, I heard Mr. Darcy give orders to find, as fast as it could be, a physician he apparently already knew. He surely had studied here in Cambridge. That is why he was so familiar with this place. I looked at my surroundings and compared them with the last place I supposed to be an inn. I was a brainless. How was it that I did not realize the differences?

I caught sight of a comfortable chair and settled in it, to get some rest.

A prostitute. He thought me a prostitute.

****

"Ellis."

"Ellis," someone was shaking my shoulder to wake me up. "Mr. Wheliker is here."

I looked up to see Mr. Darcy and a chubby older man. Half asleep, my first impulse was to make a curtsy.

Luckily, the doctor asked me to keep my seat, "So, this is the young fellow that had the accident during your training?" He looked at his companion with a knowing gaze. "You have not softened with age, son."

He positioned his bag on the bed and asked me to show him my hand.

"It is a dislocation." He signaled with his finger the obvious delocalization of my thumb bones. "It is like the one you had in your shoulder so many years ago."

A panicked expression crossed Mr. Darcy's eyes.

"It has to be dealt with immediately. Otherwise, the risk of a further disruption with the ligaments is probable." Mr. Wheliker pulled out two small bottles from his bag, signaling to each of them. "Laudanum or port?"

I was lost to what was the best choice. "Which one acts faster?"

"Neither is fast. They will only lighten the ache after the short procedure."

"Then I prefer to do it right away." I did not want to lose even a tad of my five senses.

"You should take a drink, Ellis." Mr. Darcy approached to take my good hand, "It will help you."

"No, sir," I gestured discreetly for him to keep his distance. "And I would rather be alone with the physician now. Please."

He walked reluctantly out.

The doctor asked me to approach the window, "Let us then take advantage of this light."

An abrupt agony overtook my left hand, I bit the other one, until a moment afterwards, my thumb felt back to normal, and I could breathe in peace.

Mr. Wheliker also looked relieved. "Everything seems well. Good that you called right away." He inspected the results. "Do you play the piano?"

How could he tell? "Not any more, sir." Were my hands too feminine?

"You should keep it tight like this all the time — until one month has passed." He took scrupulous care of wrapping my wrist and my injured finger. "Are you left handed or right handed."

"Left handed, sir."

"Then, you should ask for help to have this correctly done, once you take this bandage off to change to a clean one. Ask one of your classmates, for example."

I nodded goodbye while he called for Mr. Darcy in the hallway. He appeared to be just behind the door. "The boy is fine. Just make sure he does not get into any trouble in the next month. It is evident he has not had any kind of experience of the sort of fight you wished to teach him. Better take your time. Otherwise, he will get more injuries from the lessons than from the actual confrontations with the older students you are trying to avoid."

Mr. Darcy agreed while asking for the amount of his fees. It was a fortune. Why did I come?

****

He accompanied me in his carriage to Gibb's building. There was silence in the next few uncomfortable minutes — *Get used to the impropriety of being alone with men, Ellis!* — during which we sat facing each other. Until he tried to move beside me.

"Mr. Darcy!" I jumped at his intent.

He pondered his alternatives, and in a flash, was bending down, with one knee supported on the narrow space between the two seats. "Miss Elizabeth," *I told you not to address me that way!* "Sorry, Ellis. I did not really think you would truly become that desperate to... to succumb... I cannot even bring myself to say it." He was going to reach the fabric of my trousers and retreated to rub his nape. "When I heard you had stayed at that place, I did not know what to believe. I did not want to believe you could have been that desperate, because it would have all been my fault." His fault? My running away had nothing to do with him. "I went through hell when I thought some depraved men could have taken you there. That they could have cheated you somehow, and done something you did not know was going to happen. The images of the things they could have done to you have haunted me since the day I was there. I could not help being scared by the repellent scenarios my mind played, in my endeavor to find you." He looked at me for just a second, and it lasted enough for me to ascertain the horror he had gone through. "I was so relieved to find you. I have been heart sick. So sick not knowing what had become of you. What you must have suffered! I can tell that it was severe indeed, as you have lost even more weight. I fear that you have hardly eaten the entire time you have been gone. If there is anything, anything at all that I could do to take away that time you have been alone! I will do everything in my power to help you now! I will not take 'no' for an answer. So do not say it. I know you have starved, and I do not take it lightly that you felt compelled to steal in order to survive. Except, I cannot help feeling relief for knowing you did not have to go through all the horrible things I imagined. When I laughed in the orchard, after the tale of how you met the vicar, it was not at you. It was the result of the happiness from learning you did not suffer the violence I predicted."

Dear God. At the time he finished his confession, I only wanted to erase those dark shadows under his eyes.

When the carriage was coming to a final stop, I tried a pitiful attempt at a joke, "Well, sir. I was determined not to starve, you see... and not to have to earn my living on my back. I was not all that successful, you see... I attempted to steal the hosts."

He smiled weakly and got out from the confined space. Helping me, he asked to accompany me upstairs. "Are you going to be able to do your job under these conditions tomorrow?"

"Yes, I never thought I would appreciate my mother's insistence in teaching me to write with the right hand." *Please, go. Go away.*

"I will see you when you finish your working hours then."

****

Rime XXX, Gustavo Adolfo Becker

Came to her eyes a tear
And to my lips words of regret;
Pride spoke and dried her tears
And the words died on my lips.

I go through one road, she goes through another
But when thinking on our mutual love,
I still say: "Why did I keep silent that day?"
And she may be saying, "Why did I not cry?"

Chapter 14

On Thursday, I woke up frozen like an iceberg. When Mr. Falcon realized I was feeling this way, he resorted to what must be his remedy for everything. He gave me a bottle of port, "Take it to the attic. You will soon find this can be a man's best friend."

He ordered to work as little as possible on the cataloging, and resume yesterday's activities of taking care of the side chapel. I realized he was going through a period of accepting his deteriorating sight, and needed some time alone.

Installed in the same chair as the previous day, I was in a position to overhear some interesting (and some not so interesting) conversations. To my greatest astonishment, I started to understand that, at the majority of the tables where there was no tutor, the central theme was the marriage bed. Apparently, this was the main interest of the boys this age, and I discovered they could not help falling into this subject. No matter what was their intended course of study. Perhaps this was the reason behind the well-established separation of the sexes. Did men speak about this over their cigars and ale?

There was a new group, from another of the local schools, which was distinguished by discussing mathematics' most difficult subjects. Their tutor was with them, a Mr. John Hudson, and they were concentrating on examining their Tripos*, which I understood were the toughest courses in Cambridge. They probably were from Trinity College, then. I listened to their conversation with mixed feelings. I liked the way this man taught them. As a matter of fact, I envied the three students (Peacock, Wright and Blomfield) having such exceptional guidance through the modern** discoveries — other than that I felt they lacked independence. What would you like the best, Ellis: To have an incredible teacher tell you the fastest and safest road in which to understand a subject, or to battle with it and discover things by yourself? Hmm?

Of course, the best time came when the four 'pirates of calculus' came. This time they were having some difficulty finding who was the first to measure the actual radius of the Earth. They had a clue about the time it was done (the Greeks two or three centuries before Christ), and they were lost like a soldier's sock about the author. After some debate as to whether to search Aristotle or Archimedes, they finally gave up and tossed a coin to see which of them would ask me. Starkey was the unfortunate soul that came to seek advice. Poor boys, they thought I was some teenage erudite. If they only knew how far I was from both things.

I pointed them to Eratosthenes, who in the best of my knowledge did it the cleverest way. He measured the distance between Alexandria and Syene, counting the wheel turns traveling from one town to the other; and used the shadows of flagpoles in a summer solstice to know the angle they represent in the Earth's circumference. What I did not expect was that this gained me an invitation to the tavern. What was I getting into?

****

At two o'clock, eager to go to my room, I walked in the direction I had last seen Mr. Falcon. What I found there was far from what I expected.

"Oh, Ellis, here you are." He tried unsuccessfully to stand up from the floor.

"Are you well, sir?" I wanted to help him with his drunken state.

"Oh, yes. Blind like a bat, healthy like a stone." He took a new drink and offered me some. "Did I ever tell you how much you resemble my late wife Barbara?"

I searched to see if anyone had overheard, while taking the bottle and hiding it as far away as I could. Thank God we were alone. "Let me assist you."

"She had the prettiest eyes and the prettiest breasts I could dream of holding," he said with a dreamy look while I blushed, "and her hair... her hair was like a cascade of gold in my hands. My dearest Barb."

I shook my head, trying to lift him up. To no avail, he was too heavy.

"Have I told you about the day I took her to the theater for the first time?" He pulled me down to sit with him on the floor. "You see, I wanted to impress her. We were still courting, and I thought that taking her to such an elegant place would make her appreciate me more."

I nodded for him to follow, as there was nothing else at my disposal.

131

"She came with her best friend (a little mouse who talked so softly, I could not understand a word she said), and I thought I could escape from her chaperone skills. That is why I ventured to take Barbara's hand during the performance. As you can imagine, I was not paying any attention to the play. On the contrary, I was full of her smell, the soft skin of her hands under mine, her beautiful profile, barely visible with the glimmering light from the stage," he looked at me, seemingly comparing the two images, "and lost as I was in her alluring features, I dared to touch her thigh."

Incredulous at this confession, I could not help frowning at him.

"Oh yes, I did it, and I even thought she liked it, because she started to gently stroke my arm until…" and here his eyes shined with something I could not make out, "Until she pinched me hard with a pin she had extracted from nowhere with her other hand!" This woman's bravado was astounding. "She made me what I am — my brave wife," he sobbed. "How I miss her, God!"

Soon enough, the rescue from this awkward situation came from Mrs. Smith. She was looking for the librarian, like a caring sister after her lost sibling, and handled his drunkenness with expert skill.

****

When I left the chapel, an hour later than what I expected, I was surprised to find Beth in the entrance of Gibb's building. I was eager to say hello and hug her tightly, until I approached and saw her scolding face.

"Nice to see you, Mrs. Beth."

"Are you happy to see me here? Honestly? When you have your own issues going backstage."

"I beg your pardon?" Why was she angry at me?

"I came to Cambridge with the task of warning you someone was looking for you." She handed me one of the reward pictures. "Appears that they are deeply concerned about your wellbeing, and look what I find!" She signaled to the top of the stairs, "You are having a man living with you there! Is that why you were so eager to leave Newmarket, to have immoral relationships?"

What! "Mrs. Cochran, I do not know what you are speaking of. I live alone." Why was everyone thinking the worst about me?

"You live alone?" She raised a brow in disbelief, "Then who is that man I saw lifting the bed in the attic?"

"Lifting a bed in my attic? My bed is immovable — so heavy, no one can lift it. Unless..." It was Mr. Darcy, I realized, picturing Goliath. "Why would he do that?" I needed to go stop whatever he was doing right away.

"So, there is a 'he'."

"It is nothing like that, Mrs. Beth. It is not what you are thinking. He is an old friend. He is the one that drew this portrait."

"Just a friend, and he is offering a fortune to anyone that gives information about your whereabouts?" She stopped me from going inside the building, "Tell me what is going on first Eliza... Ellis. I deserve to know the truth."

"Oh, Mrs. Beth," I pulled her to a corner in the small space of the first floor's stairs. "He is a friend of my brother, he is... he is like Euler. He has a gift for drawing from memory. I never posed for him. I..." I was saying incoherently what came first to my mind, not knowing how to explain his presence in my life again. "He found me, but he is not going to say anything to my family. He is only trying to help."

"Trying to help?" She took my left hand and signaled to the bandage on it. "Is he the one that did this to you?"

"No. No. I did this myself. I..." This was so embarrassing! "He was trying to stop me. It is nothing like that. He is honorable and..." *kind, loyal, responsible.*

"Are you sure this is not why you ran from home? Is he not pressing you or threatening you somehow? He has spent some time there, and I am sure those noises are from what he is doing arranging the furniture. Nobody does that for free."

"No, Mrs. Beth. No. My running away from home has nothing to do with him. As a matter of fact, if he knew why I left my home, he would not be here! I am sure he has no designs on me other than helping. He knows I am hurt, and is probably doing this because he knows I cannot use this hand." He was disgusted by me!

"You are telling me *this* man is the one offering the reward. That his search was so successful that he *did* find you — even if you are unrecognizable now — and that he is taking so much care of you, only on behalf of *your family*?" She crossed her arms defiantly. "No man would do such a thing unless you were her royal highness herself."

"I will ask him to remove all the pictures that have been posted. There will not be any danger coming from him." Oh God, what was he doing with my things that was provoking such noise?

"Elizabeth, look at me." She focused my attention from the top of the stairs. "If he is here on behalf of your family, he should tell them where you are. Nobody is this unselfish, unless... unless he is in love with you."

In that moment, we heard a crash coming from the attic, and I decided to climb the steps. Oh, Fitzwilliam, why must I always race up the stairs because of you?

Once in the threshold to my room, I saw him standing back to me, his hands on his hips, his coat off, and a satisfied look directed toward the same bathtub I had spotted the previous days. He had taken away everything from above it and had fixed it! I observed the area surrounding him, spying the way he arranged all that was unnecessary in an old rack I could not reach before either. How did he do it? It was buried deep in a pile of useless parts! I looked at our setting and realized he had also moved my bed to a place next to the wall in front of the window, and the giant wardrobe and rocking chair were at both its sides; like the way they were arranged before, but much more comfortable.

"Elizabeth?" Mrs. Beth took me out of my stupor, asking for an invitation in.

"Yes, I am sorry."

He turned in our direction, his color high from the exercise and some beads of sweat running down his face.

"Ahem," Mrs. Beth cleared her throat. "Elizabeth, would you please introduce us?"

He took his coat from the armchair next to the desk. *Do not. No. Do not put it on. You look gorgeous with those broad shoulders on display,* I wanted to say, and felt defeated for not being able to stop him.

I led Mrs. Beth into the ample space left before the bed, thanks to his thorough work. "Mrs. Elizabeth Cochran, this is Mr. Fitzwilliam Darcy of Pemberley, Derbyshire." I took another step in his direction. "Mr. Darcy, Mrs. Cochran is the friend I told you about yesterday. She is the one who helped me in Newmarket."

"It is an honor to meet you, madam." He bowed elegantly. "I am delighted to make your acquaintance."

Mrs. Beth looked at me and moved her eyes in a way that said 'he is tall' and curtsied in return. "Elizabeth speaks very highly of you." Thank God she was not going to disclose her suspicions.

"Her good opinion is rarely bestowed, and therefore more worth the earning." He directed a small questioning brow in my direction. *Oh, no, no. Do not think I am not angry at you anymore! I just want Beth to have a better attitude toward you.*

"Yes, I am impressed she has such a loyal friend. Would you care to tell me how you found her here?"

And I thought she was not going to embarrass me! I rolled my eyes, exasperated. *Do not tell her about my first night in Newmarket, Mr. Darcy!* I pleaded with a small shake of my head.

"It was a coincidence. I was looking for a friend of her father. A Mr. Isaac Milner***. I was hoping he knew something about her. I am sure you have heard about him, madam." Was not Mr. Milner Papa's old colleague that recommended looking for Lavoisier's works?

"Yes, Isaac Milner — the mathematician," Mrs. Beth nodded knowingly. "He is a friend of my husband, and President of Queens' College. I know him well." Luckily, I never told Beth my last name. What if this fellow made the connection?

"Mrs. Beth, would you tell me what is in the basket?" I pointed to a new parcel she carried, efectively changing the subject.

"Some food for you, my girl. I am sure you have finished what we brought on Monday."

"Thank you." I took the basket from her and peered under the cloth. "But do not think this frees you from my visit tomorrow afternoon or on Saturday." I directed her to sit beside me in the bed while offering a piece of bread in a conspiratorial way. "I still need to see my Michael."

"Yes, I know he is the man of your dreams." She said in return while Mr. Darcy moved to stand in front of the window. *There is nothing to see there, sir.*

"By the way, Mrs. Beth," I finished a small bite, "can I take some of these linens and ask Helen to wash them? They smell like things that were stored for a long time."

"Of course, child." She observed some of the fabrics surrounding us, and the ones we were sitting on, and realized I had more than one set. "What if I take some today, and you pick them up tomorrow? You will have them sooner that way."

"It sounds perfect." I stole a glance at the stiff posture of Mr. Darcy. "Sir, would you like some refreshments too?"

He turned in our direction, seemingly pondering what to do, until he decided to set the rocking-chair in front of us and have some polite conversation. *Well done, Mr. Darcy. This is what I need from you — to make a favourable impression.*

What followed then were some questions and small talk, where I could see both my protectors were taking the measure one of the other, until Beth realized it was late for her ride home. We accompanied her downstairs, and Mr. Darcy offered his carriage, while the servant was called to help Mrs. Beth with the package of linens.

Once again in the attic, I felt not a little uncomfortable with the impropriety of us being alone without a chaperone, and I tried to find a courteous way out while standing on the threshold.

"Mr. Darcy, I thank you for all you have done with my accommodations; except, do you not think you should ask me before intruding in this, my bedchamber?"

"I thought you were too proud to ask, and yet you cannot lift any of this furniture — much less after yesterday's injury. I did not mean to intrude."

"It is a lady's room nevertheless, sir. You should not be here and..." I looked down, a bit ashamed. "We should not be alone."

"I thought we agreed to behave like men, and that you were willing for me to take care of you in exchange of my secrecy? I have a lot of things to discuss with you yet, and there is no other place than my rooms or yours."

He was right, other than the fact, he would reassert his shocking opinions about me if I let him in. "What if we sit by the river, sir?" This was a public site affording enough privacy for conversation.

He expelled a sigh and asked for permission to enter, to secure something before leaving. "I want to ascertain the bathtub is correctly installed," he said while advancing toward that piece of furniture. "You see, I made a kind of repair with a brick to replace the foot here." He showed the new part which was affording a better balance. "I will ask Tom — my valet — to prepare a hot bath while we are outside, if that is all right with you."

"Thank you." *It would be glorious. Still, you should not take so much upon yourself.*

****

Once settled in the grass along the river, Mr. Darcy explained he had written to my family to relate that he had found me, and that I was in good health. He assured the letter was sent from his house in London, and they would not have a way to find out where I was. He also gave me my garnet cross, assuring he had not had to purchase it, as he had proved the owner of the pawn broker was the one to steal my belongings.

I put it on under the shirt, happy to have this back.

"Ellis, I want to ask you to let me treat you as a friend should. I am pleading with your family to trust I will take care of you, and you will lack nothing. You must let me keep my word, and allow to be part of some things that could be considered private."

"I can survive by myself once I have my first payment, tomorrow morning, sir. You do not have to put such a burden upon your shoulders."

"I think you underestimate the danger you are in every day. If it is discovered you are a woman…" He tore a weed forcefully. "I do not want to think what would happen if anyone found that out."

"Neither do I. That is why I cut my hair so short."

"Are you sure this is a safe disguise? Do not you think someone could recognize you or find out somehow?"

Oh, My! Mr. Falcon already did!

He looked at me and recognized my fear, "Then, you agree you must accept my protection?"

I shut my eyes hard. This was so difficult! How could I accept the protection of a man that was unrelated to me?

"Would you do it for your family? I think it is the least they deserve."

I asked him to let me deliberate about this for a minute.

What alternatives do you have, Ellis? I did not want to leave this place, this job, and he was being more than generous while assisting to keep the secret of where I was living. I looked up and saw he was playing with some stones, making them dance over the water. *Let him do it.* There was no danger of him falling in love again. No matter what Mrs. Beth alleged, his good opinion once lost, was lost forever… and I would be safer.

"Mr. Darcy, I have a problem then."

He approached with a questioning stare.

"Would you please ask the servant watching over me to be more discreet? Someone could realize he is taking care of me, and that is not normal. I am just an employee, after all."

He assured he would hire someone that could be taken as a student. "Would you let me take you tomorrow to Mrs. Cochran's house?"

"That is not such a bright idea, sir. You will be bored, and besides, I want to be as discreet as possible in that place. There are too many pictures of me spread."

"That is easy to solve. I have only to order for them to be removed. It can be accomplished this very night if you wish."

Why was he insisting on this? "It is not that easy, Mr. Darcy. People saw me when I went to the mass, and your carriage cannot pass unnoticed in a town that small."

"I can rent a coach. Unless you do not want me to go because of that Michael."

Because of Michael? Nonsense. "No, sir. It is only that Mrs. Beth has a wrong impression about you. I do not want her to be suspicious."

"I will talk with her and explain my motives. She seems a sensible woman. She will understand."

I hope you do. What was the matter with this place that everybody was obsessed with improper behavior?

****

Cambridge, Thursday, 1st October night

A certain warmth spreads through my chest while thinking about all the effort Mr. Darcy is going through, to see to my comfort. After the odyssey he endured to find me, he should be more than tired of taking care of me. And yet, he has arranged this space in a way that I feel it like a homely refuge. My bath was warm (which is a mystery in itself — how could that be achieved if I do not see any kitchen around?) and comforting, whereas I did not have to carry one single bucket of the many needed to have such a delightful luxury.

He has such high moral standards. Why does he accept someone like me? He knows my real father abandoned us. He has been with my family (especially my mother) at their worst. He knows I am the farthest from what is considered an accomplished lady. He has seen me in a disguise repulsive to behold. I have mistreated Georgiana — this list is endless.

Sometimes I feel he can see through me. That my mind is transparent, and he knows what I need to hear. At least, he always chooses the right words to convince me of whatever he wants.

Because your eyes were aflame, José Martí

Because your eyes were aflame,
And a pin was not fastened right,
I thought you had spent the night
Playing forbidden games.

Because you were mean and devious
Such lethal hatred I bore you:
To see you was to loathe you,
So alluring and yet so villainous.

Because a trace came to light,
I do not know where or how,
I knew what you had done unseen —
All the night long you cried for me.

****

After writing this poem, I went to check the first entry in this diary. *Oh, dear! It took place in Derbyshire!* Was he there? Did he see what I did? Recalling the whispers I could not attach an image to, I grasped it was not just about Wickham and Jack anymore. More people knew about this. Yes, there were others there. But who?

Other men were aware of the test. There were more witnesses! WHAT DID I DO? WHAT DID THEY DO TO ME? I started to breathe deeply and sob. Could he be one of them? NO, NO. HE WAS NOT LIKE THAT. NO. He did not attend the wedding. Why should he? My uncle was far below him — they were in trade!

I ran to hide myself under the covers, hugging my legs and muffling my cries. Shut down your mind Elizabeth! Shut it down! HE WAS NOT THERE! HE WAS NOT THERE!

As soon as I managed to calm a tad, I reasoned I could not suspect all the people from Derbyshire. I would ask Mr. Darcy on the morrow. Somehow. Yes, I would find a way to discern if he was there.

---

* Learn more about Cambridge here: http://www.cam.ac.uk/

**The coined phrase for this kind of research nowadays is 'state of the art', but this expression is not used until the middle of IXX century. Mr. John Hudson was actually the tutor of those three outstanding mathematicians Lizzy mentions.

***Who was Isaac Milner? Here is the answer: http://en.wikipedia.org/wiki/Isaac_Milner

Chapter 15

On Friday Mr. Falcon behaved uncommonly circumspectly. I perceived an air of uneasiness, and that he was almost afraid to look me in the eyes. Hence, I only had to work on the cataloging of the library. This job brought a lot of questions, and some answers, to my mind. I managed to translate something of the work by Alexander von Humboldt*, "The Chemical Composition of the Atmosphere," and found he not only wrote about the dependence of air's composition on the altitude, but also about the composition of Earth itself. Surprisingly, finding a relationship between these two subjects was not as rewarding as my other discovery: The Earth was formed during the course of millions and millions of years!

It is strange how much satisfaction this knowledge brought. Maybe it should not have; nonetheless, I could not help feeling immense self-worth from the memories of the day I discussed this subject with Mrs. Parker. I know this brought her enmity, and her hostile treatment during the subsequent lessons in Sunday School; however, I will never repent my bravery. She was so angry at my question, "Are you sure the days in the Bible are the same length as the days in our lives?" What did she expect us to believe? — That the Earth could be formed in seven *literal* days?!

Those days were surely in some other 'God's time scale'. And anyway, even if she were right, why should such a question merit the many humiliations she attempted toward a girl of nine years? Why should this question lead to her accusations that *only I* could have this lack of faith, as she called it? Why did she say my name with disdain? Why did she treat me as if I were stupid?

Yes, I was happy for this discovery. She was wrong! No matter how many years had passed since those difficult days in Meryton.

The second extremely satisfying event was that I received my first salary.

****

Once on the stairs to my attic, I found Mr. Darcy waiting for me in the small space in front of the steps. *What am I going to do with you, Fitzwilliam, when you appear all the time in my daily life and in my dreams?*

I requested some minutes to refresh myself, before getting into the rented carriage heading to Newmarket. "It will not do if people see me being helped by you, sir. Please wait for me inside."

Once on the road, positioned in front of him, I started to think about the best way to inquire into the issue that had been eating at my brain.

Mr. Darcy gave me the opening himself when he offered some apple tart. "I know how much you like sweets."

"Is it from the Michaelmas' dinner, sir?" I tried to pull the conversation toward the holidays.

"Yes, I am sorry for not being able to bring it that day. I had to take care of some business transactions that could not be delayed.**"

I dismissed his unnecessary apology. "In any case, you sent enough food for an entire army, and I understand you have many servants and tenants at your charge, sir." I managed to say after finishing a tasty bite. "By the way, when are the main holidays here in Cambridge?"

"The main holidays? I think the next is All Saints' Day, and then Christmas." He reached for my injured hand cautiously. "I do not remember the ones before Easter though."

"This hand is much better. You see?" I leaned forward moving my fingers. *Stay calm, Elizabeth, this is nothing. He will not notice what you are trying to find out.*

"Yes, it seems so. Would you allow me to wrap it tighter?"

"Thank you." I tried to hide my nervousness while he carefully removed the fabric.

"Do you always spend Easter with your aunt?" There, this would give me some clue. My heart had climbed to my throat. This was the time when the Gardiners' were wed.

"Yes," he answered undoing the knot in the fabric, "since I can remember."

Thank God! HE WAS NOT THERE! I wanted to scream, and rested my head on the walls of the carriage. He knew nothing, and he was not part of it. I closed my eyes, feeling a soothing relief wash over me. *You are so silly, Elizabeth; so much fretting for nothing.*

"Ellis?" He signaled for me not to withdraw my hand.

"Oh, sorry." I had him with the bandage in one hand, and had taken away my left when I relaxed.

"Is anything the matter?"

"No, sir," I laid my hand back in his. "I am exactly where I want to be." *I am glad you found me.*

He lightly squeezed my two smaller fingers for a long moment.

"Please, Mr. Darcy, a skilled nurse would not let this touch the floor," I teased, seeing he had dropped the bandage inadvertently.

He smiled gently and started to wrap my thumb and my wrist, carefully and tightly, alternating his gaze between my hands and my mouth.

****

Once we arrived at Newmarket's church, we met Mrs. Cochran, and she guided us to what I used to call my room. "I would rather receive you in the adjacent one," she signaled with her head to the place the abolitionists had used to have their meeting, "But my husband is having another important conversation there."

I left them comfortably seated (Mr. Darcy on the couch and Mrs. Beth on the chair in front of him) and asked about directions of where to find Michael. I saw a shadow cross Mr. Darcy's demeanor, only to be quickly replaced with a polite straightening of his spine, while Beth informed I could find mother and child in the gardens. He had suggested he would talk with her yesterday himself. Why should he find strange that I wanted to leave them alone?

Helen was trying to fold a paper like a boat when the boy detected me. His face lit up immediately, and he threw open his little arms in my direction. Dearest baby.

Helen was also glad to see me, and I noted a certain air of bliss in her I had not seen before. Poor woman, it had to be terribly hard to have to provide for her son and herself. These few moments of a break were precious to her. "If you let me, I will take him inside so you can rest in this beautiful weather."

She answered a soft "yes," and handed me the folded paper. "In case you can do something cute with it."

When reaching the room where my two friends were waiting for me, Michael threw it to the floor. "Wait until I make a frog and you will think differently, little one."

Crouching to reach the sheet, I could not help overhearing Mrs. Beth's last words. "She is stubborn. You will not be able to take her home easily."

"I am resigned to it. I know better than to scare her or make another proposition for she might run away again. I mean, her family is worried, and her brother is a friend..."

My attention was called to the adjacent door as Mr. Cochran was saying his farewells to a gentleman whom I recognized to be one from the abolitionist group. I did not need to know what they were saying to understand the vicar was giving some final instructions to the younger man. However, what drew my curiosity the most was the strange feeling I had when observing this stranger's demeanor. There was such an air of falsehood. I observed his posture and his eyes looking rightwards***. *He is lying. I do not know why I can tell, other than I am sure he is lying.*

Relieved to see Mrs. Beth and Mr. Darcy were satisfied with the conversation they just had, I entered shaking the previous thoughts and speaking to the boy, "Come Michael, let us listen to a tale."

I sat on the big couch, placing the baby in the middle between the gentleman and me and started to build the promised frog. Then, I arranged it in my right index and thumb to make the movements that should imitate the speaking. "Hello, Master Michael, do you want to listen to what happened to me recently?" I said with a nasally voice.

145

The small boy looked at me with expectation, while the gentleman next to him grinned broadly.

"You do? Let us start then. I was cleaning the entrance to my house yesterday, like I do every rainy day, when I found a coin." I took one from the pocket and showed it to him. "I was very happy, you see, and started to think about what I could buy with it. Perhaps a new dress? — I thought first. But no, no, no. This is not enough money for that." I played with the coin to mimic the reasoning. "I can buy some candies — No, no, no. I will eat them all, and they will be gone in a blink." I pretended to bite his belly with the frog's mouth, "Mmm, let me think, let me think…I KNOW — I will buy some face powder to look handsome!" The little boy giggled, showing that funny empty gum of his.

"I bought it and put it on right away. Then, I went to sit on the bench of the doorway to observe the passersby."

I looked at my two adult companions, to see if they were enjoying this as much as the boy. Yes, they were. "What was my surprise when Mr. Dog neared and said," I changed my voice to a hoarse one, "Miss Martina, how beautiful you look today!" and I answered, "As I am not beautiful, I thank you more." I played the shy damsel batting my eyelashes flirtatiously, "Would you like to marry me?" requested Mr. Dog, and I asked in return, "Would you tell me please what do you do at night?" "I bark like this — WOLF, WOLF, WOLF!" I imitated the sound loudly, "No, no, no. I will get scared."

"So, Mr. Dog went away and Mr. Cat came: "Miss Martina, how beautiful you look today!" I answered, "As I am not beautiful, I thank you more." I looked up at Beth. "Would you like to marry me?" requested Mr. Cat, and I asked in return, "Would you tell me please what do you do at night?" "I meow like this"

"MEEEOW, MEEEOW, MEEEOW," cried Mrs. Cochran cheerfully.

"So, Mr. Cat went away, and Mr. Lizard came, "Miss Martina, how beautiful you look today!" I answered, "As I am not beautiful, I thank you more". I looked to the gentleman now, "Would you like to marry me?" requested Mr. Lizard, and I asked in return, "Would you tell me please what do you do at night?"

"Sleep and be quiet," replied Mr. Darcy.

"I will marry you! I will marry you, Mr. Lizard!****"

****

Once in the carriage back to Cambridge, Mr. Darcy was wearing one of the brightest beams I have ever seen alight his face. "So, *that* is Michael."

"Hey, hey, not just any Michael. That is *my* Michael."

"*Your* Michael? What did he do to earn such a high position?"

"Apart from slobbering and making a mess of my clothes when I lived in the parish?"

"Yes, I have only seen you this way with the Gardiners' children."

I shrugged, thinking how to explain the connection I had with the boy, "I think it is just that we have many things in common."

"Many things in common?"

"Yes, I am sure his and his mother's lives will not be easy in the years to come."

His gaze swept my face, and his smile changed to a sympathetic one, "But that can change if she finds a good father for him."

"Yes, if she is lucky — very lucky — he will have a father like Papa."

The rest of the hours, until late at night, were spent chatting amicably. Mr. Darcy explained more about my family and about the way he found me. It has been almost three weeks since my departure, and I missed them dearly. Thank God he was in touch with them, and I was assured they were well. There was no news from Jane though. He explained this was because Charles had taken her to the very north of the Continent — to avoid the territory at war. He also explained they could conceal my running away, thanks to the coincidence that it occurred before Mary's wedding. He told they alleged that the Sthieve's accompanied me to Bath, to recover my health; and that they were supposed to leave me there during their honeymoon.

My mother, after waiting impatiently at home during that time for me to change my mind, decided to travel alone to Bakewell, and even to Scotland. She was probably that far yet.

Mr. Darcy's path from Longbourn to Newmarket was the same as mine, except that he found himself without clues after visiting the first place I slept. Finding it useless to keep looking randomly at all the places in that town, and considering the possibility I could have asked for help somewhere else, he came to Cambridge in search of Mr. Milner. This was, in his estimation, an unlikely recommendation from Papa. However, it proved to be providential when his carriage stopped near King's College's pit.

Seeing an opportunity to lighten the mood, I asked if I should say "thank you" to the horses for being thirsty, and he followed, trying to tease me about my fear of those animals.

What proceeded were some tales about the origin of my "respect" (not 'fear' I emphasized — feigning being offended) of some animals. The horses — because of the incident in Bakewell where I was almost killed by one horseman atop his stead; and the bees — because one of the boys my mother attended when she was a nurse, had died of stings from those insects (both events Mr. Darcy was oddly familiar with).

At the end, I had a discussion, very difficult to win, when I asked to pay for the servant's wages. He stubbornly refused for a long while, until we came to another bargain. He would let me pay for a half only in exchange for something he would tell me later. He had not yet figured out what it was what he was going to ask.

****

On Saturday, Mr. Darcy came early in the morning, asking if I would like to visit a place he thought I would enjoy. I was intrigued by this quizzical proposition, and climbed into his carriage with enthusiasm. Once seated in the soft cushions, he narrated a story about a nun, St. Etheldreda, who was a Saxon queen in the seventh century before being ordained thus.

She was the daughter of Anna, King of East Anglia, and was born near Newmarket in Suffolk. At an early age, she was married (c.652) to Tondberht, an older man of the South Gyrwas, although she remained a virgin. On his death, she retired to an Isle. In 660, for political reasons, she was married to Egfrith, the young king of Northumbria, who was then only fifteen years old, and several years younger than her. He agreed she should remain a virgin, as in her previous marriage. Twelve years later, he wished their marital relationship to be normal. Etheldreda refused. Egfrith offered bribes in vain. Etheldreda left him, and became a nun at Coldingham and founded a monastery in 673.*****

Mr. Darcy disclosed we were going to visit a Cathedral constructed by the Benedictine monks, after this saint. The place was partially closed and uninhabited, due to the need for restorations, but he was sure I was going to enjoy the architecture nonetheless.

He talked almost the entire trip, showing an incredible knowledge of the history of this place for about two hours; until we stopped in front of the most spectacular building I ever beheld. *And I considered King's College to be huge* — through the window, I observed the Romanesque carvings, the combination of decorating stones and marble, the iron work, the sculptures and the stained glass screens.

Once in the street, he showed me to a less conventional entrance through one of the side chapels and asked me to close my eyes. Guiding me carefully through some rooms with a strong smell of wood and lime. I could not help remembering the last time we were together, holding hands like this. It was in Jane's wedding, just after the ceremony.

He placed me in the position that was our intended destination, and I knew he was standing close behind me as I sensed his breathing close to my neck. "Welcome to Ely Cathedral, Ellis," he whispered with a deep voice.

I opened my eyes and found myself in the most incredible sanctuary — perhaps the largest chamber in existence. I was amazed, immobilized by the beauty before me. It had incredibly high ceiling, which stood resembling a cloud above us. Intrigued how something so magnificent could be supported this way, I looked more carefully and found out it had the form of an octagon.

Mr. Darcy narrated, "The Nave is one of the most inspiring interiors in England. Its architecture has the old Norman's style. The term 'nave' comes from 'ship' — from the belief that the Church is a vessel in which the faithful can journey safely to God. Ely Cathedral is known as the 'Ship of the Fens'.

"Here at Ely, the ceiling decoration and the angel panels represent the heavenly host; the figures in the windows and we ourselves, represent the world of time and space. The Octagon is a symbol linking earth and heaven, time and eternity."

I tried to keep my attention to the ceiling, but at some point, his voice started to sound like a lullaby. I observed the Gothic style of the octagonal roof, with stronger pointed arches and elaborate adornment, while relaxing on some warm pillar behind me. This was so peaceful. As he said, this was the place where earth and heaven joined together. I lowered my sight to the series of small carvings on either side of this chamber. I followed the veins of the marble on the floor.

"When did you learn all this, Fitzwilliam?"

"Yesterday." He touched my ear delicately with his lips.

Yesterday? How come?

I woke up from my daydream and felt how I was supporting part of my weight on his. *Look what you have done Elizabeth!*

"I think I need to sit." I carefully walked toward a bench. He had such a power over me. I could not think clearly.

"Are you all right?"

"Yes, sir. It is just that... that I am sleepy. We went to sleep too late last night."

"That is a pity, as I was planning to tempt you to climb the towers."

I remembered the numerous high ceilings visible from the façade, "I would not miss them for the world!"

****

Saturday, 3rd September, night

I am so happy.

After visiting the chapels, Mr. Darcy took me to the towers and other labyrinthic halls. I must recognize it felt like an adventure. He made me picture myself as one of the conquerors of castles and palaces — like a discoverer.

During the excursion, we talked about everything. He told me about the profound love his mother and his father shared, about the day Georgiana was born and his childish excitement at the time, the way his mother taught him to draw, the sadness of her loss and his father's later death. He confessed he wanted to be a spy when he was a lad (after Sir Francis Walsingham******). He also shared many tales about his stay at Trinity College and described Pemberley in detail.

In exchange, I shared with him the tales about my childhood: How I officiated a wedding ceremony between a frog and a lizard with the boys in Bakewell. How I met my sisters and Papa, and how he taught me the value of books. About the way I met Charlotte, and how her father brought her with him every time he came to visit Papa. How we hid from her grumpy mother in the woods around Meryton. I also explained Sir William had been best man in my parents' marriage, and that they were close friends.

****

On Sunday, Mr. Darcy came later than I expected, with a worried expression hard to match. I received him in the doorway, and tried to convince him of going to the riverbank again.

"No, Ellis, I need to impart something that is private. It cannot be done where other people may see us."

"Is anything the matter with my family? Is Jane well?" I imagined the worst.

"No. It is not that. They are all in good health. Yet, it is something that will upset you greatly, and I do not want to risk another injury."

I searched his mien for an explanation, and only found shame and upset. "I think the orchard where you found me the other day is secluded enough."

"Do you promise not to run?"

"Yes, I do." I rushed to the steps and headed to that place as fast as could be.

Once in the orchard, I reclined my back against one of the apple trees. I waited anxiously for the news.

He alternated between long strides and brief stops a couple of times, until he gave up and stood in front of me. "A letter has arrived from your father this morning, in which he states that he is going to sever all communication with me — with us."

---

*Alexander von Humboldt (1767-1835) was a German naturalist and explorer. His quantitative work on botanical geography laid the foundation for the field of biogeography. Charles Darwin found his work particularly fascinating. The specific article Elizabeth is referring to is: Experiments on the chemical decomposition of the atmosphere.

**According to Regency Encyclopedia: Michaelmas, 29 September, the third quarter (or rent) day of the English year, was traditionally used to transact estate business.

*** In general, a person looks rightwards when making up or imagining something and leftwards when remembering.

****This is a free version of "La Cucarachita Martina".

*****Visit Ely Cathedral here:
http://www.elycathedral.org/visitors/tour.html

******One of the first famous English spies was Francis Walsingham (1532–1590).

Chapter 16

WHY?

"Your family has been influenced by some slanders. I suspect they have received poisonous statements that are being fabricated by Wickham. I am not sure yet."

Dear God help me! My legs began to fail — to shake violently. Please God. Please God. My view clouded with tears. *It must be Wickham has divulged what happened that day.* "He is blackmailing my family," I cried.

"No. No. It is not what you are thinking." He tried to hold me by the arms to talk. My body refused to stand.

"Elizabeth, look at me!" he commanded while I dropped on my knees.

"I do not want to see you. No! My father knows what happened. You know what happened!" *Papa must have told you, for you to be this upset.*

"No, No. Elizabeth what your father is blaming us for is another thing." He inched close, "He thinks I am not letting him know where you are, because he believes you are my mistress!"

"What?" I reacted instantly.

"Yes. Someone has blackened my reputation once more, and your father thinks the entire search was a pretense. He initially thought you had eloped. He now thinks I planned it all, because I would not marry a woman of lower station. He is convinced I took advantage of you, that I offered some juicy monetary benefit, and you agreed to it." He hesitated, "If it was Wickham, I have no idea why he would take that man's word over my own; when he knows his character and what he did to Miss Maria's reputation. He worked with me to find you. It makes no sense!"

This was insane. Papa had misconstrued everything. "I thought he trusted you!"

"I thought the same. I believed he improved his opinion about me the day you disappeared; after I reinforced the warning in your farewell letter with the account of the treatment Georgiana received from Wickham. I am sure someone is truly resentful and trying to inflict on me all the pain he is capable of by questioning my honor. He is seeking revenge. Perhaps it is Wickham, as he has always sought to revenge himself, and maybe he is even more convinced to do so after I broke his tooth when we last met. This has nothing to do with you. This must be his doing."

"You broke his tooth? Why?"

"I ran into him and Denny on the road when I was leaving for town, and they were arriving to Meryton. He greeted me, boasting he was marrying into nobility. I just could not help myself. I am tired of seeing how he injures innocent people!"

"Did he hurt you as well?" I spanned every visible inch of him, to ascertain if there was any evidence of that fight in his appearance.

"No, No. He is too much of a coward to give battle, and he fell unconscious from my blow. Gossip and flattering are his usual weapons. Perhaps these are what he is using to turn Sir Lucas and your father against me. You said they are close friends, are they not?"

"Yes, but that does not explain why father should think something like that about _me_?" Papa perceived I was in love with Mr. Darcy — was this enough reason for doubting me? No. It had to be something else.

"I know you are right to be mad at any person who thinks you would do something like that. I just beg you not to be angry at me for bringing this. Please believe me: I would never have this happen to you. Still, understand many women feel compelled to do it. It is not something they deserve, not something they wish. It is something they are forced to do. For their families, for their children."

"I did not have those strong incentives. I… I only starved… I… Cannot Papa see having intimate relationships with a man would be more hurtful than starving for a couple of days? Why would I trade one pain for another? Why will I subject my body to something like that?" Then, I realized father did not know of my struggles to get a job; _he thought I stole away with Mr. Darcy the day I disappeared — Why?_

Mr. Darcy gazed at me for a long silent moment, with a heartbreaking expression.

154

I looked down, endeavoring to focus on finding an explanation to this. "Why should I choose to be a mistress when I was living among people that cared about me? When I had everything I needed in exchange for nothing? Why should I suffer…"

He reached for my hands and hugged them yearningly to his chest, "You are so naive, sweetheart. So brave and so naïve. You have not seen the things that happen in the *ton*. People do scandalous things to gain material wealth. They will stop at nothing." *Scandalous.* Something scandalous. I had done something scandalous myself once — in exchange for being included — in exchange for nothing! "You are not like them. You are not like anyone I know."

"It must be something I did. But then, I *did* leave my home and I asked you *not to* tell where I am staying. I brought all of this to myself."

"It is not that. I am sure. They just do not understand your motives for running away."

"I did it for them," I confessed, separating a bit. "I still think it was the right decision." This could be so much worst if Wickham remembered.

"I know."

"You know? What do you know?"

"I know how far you can go in defense of your family."

Oh no, he was remembering my rejection at Hunsford. That was why he was so sad. I felt a chill run through my body and embraced my arms to avoid the wind. I needed to find the courage to tell it was not his fault; that his meddling in Jane's affairs was not the actual reason behind my negative speech. *Soon I must.*

We stayed like this for a while, both lost in our inner thoughts, until he saw I was getting cold. "I think we should go now. I have to find a way out of this misunderstanding and find out who is influencing your father. I might have to travel."

****

Once back alone in my attic, I decided to take an early dinner. I grabbed the plate and the bottle of port Mr. Falcon had given me the other day to sit by the window.

After too many glasses, I realized what would be more warming would be a hot bath. That is why I sought the servant and asked him to prepare one.

It took a lot of time to have all the water in the tub, during which I decided to wait on the roof, drinking directly from the container now. It was as cold inside as outside anyway. I started to walk along the edge of the building, just within the stone balustrade, until I felt my equilibrium was failing. Mr. Falcon was right. One could lose all the senses with this thing. I did not even remember what was so upsetting today — to steal away with Fitzwilliam? It would not be so exceedingly bad. As a matter of fact, I would run away from paradise if he would hold me in exchange.

It was better not to get close to the edge, lest I fall. I went to the door connecting the attic and the roof. The servant looked at me with a warning expression. Why was he so worried? I was just waiting for him. I was just having a nice conversation with my new friend booze!

I closed the door firmly behind him the second he finished. *Why do I see two bathtubs here?* "Brrrr". I shook my head to clear it and took off my clothes in a blink, immersing in the hot water with anticipation. "Hey, hey. Be careful, my friend. You do not want to drown here," I put the bottle on the floor and reclined my head on the edge. This was wonderful.

I was playing with the bubbles, making some funny noises with water, when I heard loud knocks on the door. Agrr. Who could that be now?

"Open the door, Ellis! Open it!" It was Fitzwilliam. Why was he in such a rush? TUM TUM TUM, I heard his strong bangs.

"I am coming, I am coming." ...*hic*... Where did I put the towel?

"IF YOU ARE THERE, OPEN IT RIGHT NOW OR I WILL KNOCK THIS DOOR DOWN!"

I shook my head in exasperation, "Shhh, shhh, someone will hear you!" I would have to dress still dripping water like this. Where were my trousers? I tripped over something — here they were.

"Oh, My God, where is he? Go to the street and see if you can find him there." *He must be talking with the servant.* TUM TUM TUM. He was serious about pulling down my door!

"I am not deaf!" I screamed, deciding between wrapping my bosom or not. No. I hated that wrap!

Where was the shirt? ...*hic*...

TUM, TUM, TUM. *Agrrr. If you do not have a compelling reason for me to get dressed in such a hurry, Fitzwilliam Darcy, I will push you down the stairs!* Buttoning the shirt over my wet torso, I was having a hard time managing the fabric stuck to my body. *How many eyelets does this thing have?*

Almost stumbling over the bottle and deciding to take it with me, I reached the entrance and unlatched the bolt. Opening the door slightly, I poked out my head, "What is so urgent, Fitzwilliam?" I saw his face was red. Was it because he was angry, or because he ran all the way here?

"What are you doing? Why were you walking on the roof?" he inquired agitatedly. "Are you well? Let me in!"

That gossiping servant! "It was just a stroll, very refreshing, by the way. Nothing to worry about. Did he not tell you, I was taking a bath now?" I released the door for him to ascertain everything was as it should be.

He stepped in and looked at me from head to toe, widening his eyes like saucers.

"Never been better, as you see." I brandished the bottle, feeling quite lovely indeed.

I saw him gulp and look at me with strange eyes.

"Ah, do not be so stiff and aloof, Fitzwilliam. It is not such a big deal...*hic*... That roof is safe. It has a veranda all around. Come." I took his hand and guided him to the window. "What can be wrong in walking in that path?" I signaled to the place I wandered before.

"Maybe that you are drunk?"

"I am not wrung, ah… drunk… Sorry," I covered my mouth sniggering; "I was, just talking with this fellow. We have become good friends… *hic*… I call it friendship at first sight."

He reached for the beverage.

"Are you jealous, Fitzwilliam?" I hugged it to my bosom. "Why do you want to take it from me? He is my new friend!"

He looked down and shook his head slowly, but I caught him grinning.

"You should not. He is harmless. Come, come, I will share it with you." I led him to the nightstand and placed the port there. I could not find anything with this blurred vision! I nibbled one finger between my teeth to highlight my following statement, "I think we have a problem…*hic*…"

"Really?"

"Yes, we do not have glasses!"

He arched a brow and followed by lifting both hands in a sign of resignation.

"No. No. No. I will have none of it… *hic*… Drink from my bottle! He can be your friend as well," I offered the container. "You are not the haughty Mr. Darcy today."

He seemed a bit reluctant to take a sip and made a gesture of slight disgust, "This is strong."

"Tell that to me. I had never drunk before."

"And you should not do it again."

"Shhh, shhh. Do not scold me — you resemble Papa when you do."

"Your father?"

"Oh, yes. Except that you are handsomer," I winked at him.

I moved to sit on the edge of the bed while he went to do something outside my room. *You are taller today,* I asserted, when he closed the door firmly, observing the smile he could not help showing after my flattery. *Yes, you have dimples like Papa, too.*

I jumped from the bed to approach him, "As a matter of fact, I have an idea."

"An idea?"

"Yes, an experiment of sorts." I looked up at him, to enjoy his puzzled demeanor. "Would you please take off your topcoat, Fitzwilliam?"

"My coat?"

"Yes, yes." I helped him out of it, "do not be missish. ...*hic*..." I hung the cloth with care on the back of the rocking-chair. I extended my hand demanding, "Now your cravat."

He gaped at me, incredulous, undoing the knot and handing it to me. *Oh, yes, you are enjoying this too.*

"Now," I approached and rested my head on his chest. "Yes, this will work. If I do not look up, this will definitely do!"

His heartbeats were strong.

"Papa?"

"Mmm?"

"Would you play my Papa?"

His breathing caressed my scalp with a big intake of air, "Yes."

"Good," I held him by the waist. "Would you hug me like when I was a little girl? Please?"

His arms enveloped me. "This feels heavenly."

"I miss you so much, Papa. I need you so much. This is so difficult. I want to be strong. I am strong — you have always told me to be and I am. But, I am also so tired of it! And you are not proud of me, despite everything I am doing. Being strong without the reward of your prizes is not the same." I inclined my head a bit to look at his neck, "Papa?"

"Yes?" he whispered huskily.

"Would you tell me, I am your good, brave girl? Please, Papa."

He reached to lift my head. I could not oblige — *if I look up, you will not resemble Papa so much* — and he embraced me tighter, "You are the most beautiful, courageous girl I know. What you are doing for your family is the loveliest of presents. I have no words. You are an awesome gift from God. I love you."

"Thank you, Papa." I clung to him tightly, saying, "I love you too," and sensed something was heating my belly. This port was better than a hearth. "I like being here with you."

He reached for my hands at his back and separated slightly, "Should not we sit down?"

"Yes, come." I animatedly guided him to the bed. ...*hic*... He was doing it exactly like Papa did, when I was sad. I waited for him to be comfortable and sat on his thighs. "Would you cradle me like when Mrs. Parker ignored me?" I arranged my sitting position to one in which I could be under his jaw again, "Would you say I am worthy? Please, Papa?"

He seemed to be pondering my suggestion, until he hugged me. "My sweet girl. My child, you are worthy of all the good things. Would that I could give you all the gold in the kingdom, and take away your sorrows. You are unselfish. You are a loving sister and daughter. You are a true friend. You are all that is noble." He struggled to find himself comfortable again, changing slightly the position of his legs. "When you walk into a room, the place brightens. When you speak your mind, I become enchanted by your spark. And when you look at me, Dear Lord, when you look at me, I feel blessed for the incredible miracle is being noticed by you. You are the most precious thing in my life!"

"Thank you, Papa." I was good. I was worthy. I was an obedient daughter. I was... Why was Fitzwilliam's heart bumping like this? As if he had run up the stairs again? I concentrated on his breathing. He was agitated, he was... "Your heart is beating so fast!" Papa never behaved like this. I pressed my ear to listen carefully. "I think a bull has been installed in your chest." I jumped from his lap, kneeling on the bed, to look at him and ascertain that everything was all right. "Your eyes are dilated," I noted as they roamed my body, stopping at my bosom.

He gulped in response.

"I need more port. It is cold without it." I reached for the bottle and had a sip, until he stopped me. "Do you want some?"

He shook his head 'no' and asked, "Do you want to wear my coat?"

"YES!" I went hopping happily to the rocking-chair. Once I put it on, I observed the way my hands were hidden beneath it. "It is huge," I caressed the elegant lapels, "and so warm." I stepped to take the same position in front of him, over the bed. "Why has Charles taken Jane so far? I do not want her to get cold." I hugged myself, better covering my legs with the rich fabric. "I miss her so much!" *Do not cry, Elizabeth! Do not cry!*

My companion reached to grab my shoulders, to embrace me again.

I refused, "You cannot play Jane. I am sorry. She is special, Mr. Darcy."

"Mr. Darcy?" He puckered his brow. "I thought I was Papa now, or at least Fitzwilliam."

"Can I call you Fitzwilliam?"

He nodded with a smile.

"Does that give me some superior rights?"

He nodded with a bigger beam.

"Can I kiss one of your dimples? Just one?" I asked with a mesh of shyness and excitement.

"Yes, you can."

I took his face with one hand and leaned closer, "Just one kiss in the middle of one of your dimples."

I kissed him briefly on the cheek, and observed how the biggest smile in the world transformed into a silly grin.

He looked so gorgeous like this; with that white shirt and dreamy look. Giggling, I visualized how it would be to see him like that every day. *In our own room.*

"Our room?" he asked suddenly.

What? I said that aloud? Oh No!

This was the moment to build my courage. *Remember what you resolved to do today, Elizabeth.* "Mr. Darcy," He tried to protest. "Let me say this now… I think you must know I can never marry… I think… I did something horrible a long time ago, and cannot marry." I could not refrain from the tears spilling this time. "This is unfair, because I need you, and I do not have the strength to push you away anymore… And I… and I…" Sobs were taking my breath. I threw myself face down on the bed. "And I would die if you knew what I did," another loud cry escaped my throat. "You cannot marry me, and I need you so much!"

A hand caressed my head, "I am here. I am not going anywhere. Do not cry, darling. Please. Do not cry. I am here."

"Can you sleep with me as Jane does?"

"How does she do it?"

"She lies with me. I turn around, and she assures all will be well. Can you?"

He reclined over me with an almost imperceptible, "Yes I can".

"Would you keep at bay that bull in your chest? It scares me."

"That bull will be tamed for the whole night. Do not worry about him."

I turned with my back towards where he was, and he snuggled close to me. I took one of his hands and intertwined my fingers with his on my belly. "This feels like home."

"All will be well, Lizzy. All will be well."

Rime XI, Gustavo Adolfo Becker

I am fervent, I am brunet
I am of passion the symbol
My soul is full of anxiousness of delight
Are you looking for me? — No, it is not you.

My forehead is fair; my braid is gold.
I can give you never-ending happiness
I have a treasure of tenderness
Are you calling for me? — No, it is not you.

I am a dream, an impossible
I am an empty ghost, made of mist and light
I am incorporeal, I am untouchable
I cannot love you — Oh, come, you are the one!

Chapter 17

Wake up, Elizabeth. Time to wake up. Get up. Get up. It is late. Time to go to the Library.

This was the part I hated the most about having a job — waking up this early. OHHH. I opened my eyelids slowly — very slowly. How beautiful Fitzwilliam looked asleep. His nose and his soft lips, in an almost smile — *I would so much like to explore the profile of your face, love!*

Reaching to follow my impulse, I noticed my hand was intertwined with his. I leaned on my elbow to follow the path of his arm. This was why the pillow was so inviting: I was resting on his forearm.

He was uncomfortable in this position: sitting in the chair and inclined to keep his head on the bed. Poor dear, he... I looked back to our joined fingers, and then to my wrist covered with his topcoat. This was not a dream. Why was he here? Some flashes of my behavior last night appeared in my mind. *I slept with him!* I unhooked and sprinted to the door.

Escape!

Trying to take off the bolt, I detected I was barefoot. I could not go out this way. I turned around to search my boots. I saw him stretch. He was awakening. Hide! Do not let him see you. I spotted the wardrobe and ran to get inside of it. The tail of the large coat made it more difficult. Hurry up. Hurry up.

I waited, eating my nails and listening to every sound until a vibrant laughter was heard. *Not again!*

His loud steps approached, "Elizabeth, do not be silly, get out of there."

I kept silent to see if he would withdraw.

I felt him sit by the wardrobe instead, leaning his back on one of the wood panels. "Come on, you know this is childish. You know I can open the door, and that you will have to face me sooner or later."

"No. No. No. I cannot look you in the eyes after this. Go," I begged.

"After what?"

"After all I did."

"I do not remember you doing anything shocking."

"Nothing shocking? I hugged you and sat on your lap!"

"No. You hugged and sat on your father's lap, not in mine," he spoke factually. "It is normal between father and daughter. Georgiana does it all the time."

"I slept with you! I did something terribly improper!"

"No, no. You slept with Jane."

He was teasing me! AGGRRR, "Really? And how is it that I woke up with you?"

"Well, we did manage to come to some agreements."

Oh, no. He could not say I agreed to marry him. I did not! "Which ones?"

"Let me see. I remember mainly three: that you think you can never marry," Thank God, "We will call each other by our given names... and... and..."

"AND WHAT?" He liked to exasperate me!

"And that you like my dimples!" How could I flirt like this?!

"Well, it seems everything is taken care of. Why do you not go away now?" *Will I ever win this argument?* It was getting late, and I had to get to work!

"I cannot. You have my overcoat."

I studied my attire, and found out there was only my shirt and trousers under his coat. Inside, my breasts were visible through the fabric, even in this dim light. That was why he was looking at my chest all the time. I was almost naked! I covered my face. "You must be thinking the worst about me."

"On the contrary, I liked <u>everything</u> about you yesterday. Come, come, where is the brave girl we were talking about just a few hours ago? Where is my brave girl now?"

"I was very improper," I repeated. "I behaved like the loose woman you thought I was." Why did I take that bottle? "Go, please."

"You will <u>never, ever</u> be that for me. You will never be improper." He opened one sheet slightly and slipped his hand inside. "Besides, you were drunk," he said while looking for something blindly.

"You must hate me — I did not answer Georgiana's letter," I lamented.

"On the contrary. You protected her." His hand palmed my thigh.

"I ran away from home."

He touched my shoulder. "You did it for your family." He reached for my hand over my face.

"I look like a boy."

"No, you do not." He opened the door widely.

I was helped out of the wardrobe.

"You can stop pushing me away; it is not necessary. I am only asking to be your friend, after all."

I shook my head, trying to refute — *I am not worthy.*

He stopped my actions by lifting my chin. "No, no, no. Do not even think about another self-recrimination. I will not accept one more comment on that subject. What you did yesterday was just being yourself, and no one has the right to ask you to be something you are not. We are friends. Friends do not judge each other."

"But I was drunk!"

"Yes, you were. You were drunk, you were witty, you were daring, you were unselfish, you were caring." He moved his hands to rest near my neck,

"You were breathtaking. You were all that is good — all that you always are. I would not dare to ask you, never in my life, to be any different."

"MR. ELLIS. MICHAEL ELLIS, OPEN THE DOOR!" We were surprised by loud bangs by Mr. Wightwick. "You are thirty minutes late to work. I will not tolerate such behavior. I am most seriously displeased." *Is it possible that no one knows how to knock on a door civilly in this place?!*

Mr. Darcy instructed me to be silent. Yes, better let Mr. Wightwick think I am not here.

Another strident series of bangs were heard. "I will not leave this place until I see you, and you give me an explanation."

"I will deal with him," Mr. Darcy whispered. "Give me my coat."

What? I am naked underneath!

He separated and turned around, reaching for his cravat. "Hide under the bed," he directed while I handed him his cloth. "Where is that telescope?"

I covered my chest with a pillow hurriedly, and pointed in the direction I remembered seeing it last.

He took the shabby instrument, settling many dismantled parts on the top, and walked with a precarious equilibrium toward the entrance. I quickly disappeared under the bed, and saw his feet as he opened the door with some difficulty.

"Would you help me with this?" He closed it with one leg, "Instead of standing like a statue?"

I heard Mr. Wightwick babble something.

"Give it to the servant that is waiting outside," Mr. Darcy ordered.

"Sir, I... I am looking for Ellis. I am not a servant myself."

"Neither am I, yet look at me! Ellis is not here to help me. I sent him to Trinity to get some documents, and he is going to be there for a while."

"To Trinity College? Why?"

"Why? With the provost, of course!" He paused, and I could not help the image of his tall figure hovering over the mole that intruded in my mind. "Do you know who I am, sir? Do you know to whom are you speaking?"

"No... Yes, yes..." Mr. Wightwick lied nervously.

"Go then. Stop interfering and be of some use!" Poor curate; he had to be scared to death.

After listening to their retreating steps down the stairs, I rushed to dress appropriately, and was ready by the time Mr. Darcy came back.

"I think we have earned a two-hour window for you to get to the chapel." He indicated for me to occupy the bed. "Which is less than what I would like, but enough for what is imperative for us to speak."

What can be this urgent? I was still afraid of saying anything after my forward behavior before.

"I know you like Cambridge, but it is not safe anymore. It is clear you are in a highly vulnerable position; even with the man watching after you. I have a plan..."

"I do not see what has made me more vulnerable, Mr. Darcy."

" 'Mr. Darcy'? No, no, miss. That is the single thing I will not let you forget. I am Fitzwilliam now! Besides, we agreed you will oblige me in exchange for letting you pay part of the servant's wages. This is what I want — for us to call each other by our given names!" He sat in the rocking-chair with a roguish mien.

"You cannot be serious!" This was unfair!

"Oh, yes I am," he inched closer. "Or I will take desperate measures."

"Desperate measures?"

"Yes. Any from the many I made up while resting here last night."

"And what could that be?"

"Well, I have a wide range of options, which go from singing a serenade under your window to kidnapping you."

"You are not speaking in earnest. You would not dare!"

"Do you doubt me?" He stood up and went to the window to start in an exquisite baritone The Marriage of Figaro's most famous song, '**Non piu andrai farfallone amoroso…***'

"No, no," I rushed to cover his mouth with my palms. "I believe you, I believe you. I will call you by your name. I promise!"

He spoke through my fingers, "Say it."

"Say what?"

"Say may name, Elizabeth."

"Fitzwilliam," I muttered.

"Louder."

"Fitzwilliam."

"Louder."

"FitzWILLiam, FITZWILLIAM!" I shouted finally.

He took my hands in his and gave me a small kiss in the wrist of each of them. A wave of shivers travelled my spine. "Now, back to our original subject, you must be more careful than ever these few days, while I am gone. I am going to be spending a little time in Hertfordshire."

"You are travelling? When? Why?"

"I must talk with your father about this misunderstanding, and I must… I have other issues to clarify with Wickham."

"With Wickham? Do not do it, please. He is dangerous. I beg you."

"Elizabeth, are you trying to protect me?" He scrutinized my face, "Yes, I can see that you are. You do not need to do anything to protect me; not from

169

other people, nor from myself. You are so wrong if you think I am in need of your protection. So wrong! You should not worry about me. I am a grown man. I know how to take care of myself. If you want to do something for me, take care. I am afraid some people might suspect we have an improper relationship — a very improper relationship between a man and a boy. You would not like to know the kind of scorn that would raise.** You must consider leaving this place and this disguise soon."

"But, Mr. Darcy..." He opened his mouth to protest. "Fitzwilliam. Fitzwilliam... this is a fantastic job that I have here. I would not find anything like this in a million years. This is the place where I can be useful!"

"You do not understand. This situation is untenable. You are in imminent danger of being discovered. If anyone finds out..." he hesitated, seemingly deciding which information to share with me, "This is not a place for a woman."

I shook my head, gazing down. There was no way out of this, I had considered it many times.

"What if I get you something with the Lunar Society's*** industrialists? Something where you would not need to disguise yourself like a man? Would you not like to live in a house with a hearth, warm food, and all the things you have given up — and on top of that, have an interesting job?" He bent his knees to find my eyes, "Hmmm?"

I nodded.

"Then, come with me to London. I promise to contact those men."

To London? My uncle lived there. "Would you give me a couple of days to consider it?"

"Yes, I would. Except," he wore that teasing beam again, "do not take too much time, or I will have to take those measures I told you about."

I nodded. What was this man up to?

"Good bye. Take care," a fast kiss landed on my cheek unexpectedly. "This comes with the bargain, remember?"

My hand went to the moist spot on my skin. I had opened Pandora's box.

When I thought he was gone, peering through the door, he breathed, "Elizabeth."

****

That morning, after arriving late and apologizing to a decidedly unsatisfied Mr. Wightwick, I spent a while with Mr. Falcon. We spoke about many aspects of his life while cataloging the books. The poor man was so tormented with the memories of his late wife, I spent half the time patting his back, and the other half blocking the sad feelings his tales produced in me. That, however, was easily accomplished, taking into account my mind was full of the memory of Fitzwilliam's happy demeanor during the earliest hours of the day.

One of his tales impacted me the most: the tale of the day he was momentarily blinded when seeing 'his Barb' escorted by another man. He was at some assembly, and they were not yet engaged. The friend attending with him spotted the girl dancing with a gentleman who was considered the most eligible bachelor. He said, "I asked if the lights were turned off, and was categorically contradicted by my companion, who took me outside until I regained my vision. Can you picture that? I was so jealous my brain blocked the image!"

Could this be what was happening to me — the reason behind the fact I could not see the faces of the boys participating in the game? Could it be that my brain was blocking an image that was particularly disgusting?

At the end of my working hours, I found my new friends eagerly waiting for me in the other side chapel. They had had a difficult day studying statistics, and alleged finding themselves lost without any guidance. "Please Ellis, you cannot go now. We are totally out of clues in this." Consequently, I spent the afternoon talking about averages and expected values.

I discovered excellent resource in which to show those concepts in the readers surrounding us, as they inadvertently licked their fingers to turn the pages. We estimated how many times a book could have been borrowed each year (for example Newton's were probably exceeding fifty times) and according with the publication date, how many varieties of human saliva it could contain. This calculation yielded two different outcomes: that they swore to follow my example and <u>never</u> to turn the pages this way again, and that it was essential for me to go to the tavern with them.

"Yes, Ellis, you owe us. You gave us your word last week, and tonight we need your help to win the gambling games!" Mr. McCartney insisted.

I tried to avoid going, with all the resources I had at my disposal, but to no avail. They dragged me, arguing a man must be faithful to his word.

In the end, the only promise I could extract from them was that we would not play — only observe in order to have a fair sample to study afterwards; and that they would not make me drink a single sip of ale.

****

Monday, 5th October, midnight

Oh Lord, I have made a big mistake. I have gone with the boys to the tavern, and the result is horrible. I am so afraid! Please, God, please, do not let him know who I am! Do not!

It all started when we met with another student who was an old Lennon's acquaintance. It happened that two sailors, as well as the man I had seen with Mr. Cochran the other day accompanied him. This man's name was Churchill. He was sitting straight in front of me at the table, and he was the most perverse person I have ever met.

I tried to behave cautiously, to be invisible during the encounter, but to no avail. There was an unknown man staring at me from another table all night, and the boys forgot about the gambling and dedicated the night to showing off their amorous feats. They shared tales about their prostitutes and how they liked a large manhood. About the way they cried their names when making love. I so much wanted to disappear, to run from there. My friends would not let me.

The tales drifted to other subjects I found even more repulsive; about disgusting jokes to some younger students and disabled men, which I noticed, were partially fabricated. Harrison would not do something like that!

Finally, the sailors spoke about the cargo of negroes they usually carried, and that the women were almost naked before being delivered into American ports. They referred to them as if they were any merchandise, as if they were dispensable, and Churchill described with morbid detail how they fought and screamed when he took advantage of them.

"So they are considered merchandise, as if they were not human. And yet, they are human enough to be raped!" I shouted, standing up and hitting the table, "You are the one that is not a man! YOU ARE A PITIABLE PRETEXT OF A MALE!" I lost my patience at last, calling the attention of all the people present.

In an instant, the abuser was standing in a hostile pose, with nothing separating us. He reached for something at his back while saying he knew me from somewhere else. Lennon reacted fast, and with McCartney and Starkey, stopped him from stabbing a blade into my belly. A general uproar was heard, and Harrison removed me swiftly from the bar. I do not know what happened after our departure; I can only remember this man's last words: "I KNOW WHO YOU ARE! I AM GOING TO FIND YOU AND KILL YOU!"

Please, Fitzwilliam, come back soon. I am terrified.

****

The following couple of days were spent in a state of utter fear. I tried to avoid being seen. However, I could not help feeling observed, especially when walking from one building to the other.

I worked diligently in the catalogue, to finish it as fast as possible. Today was Friday, and I would leave Cambridge.

"Why does this place smell so strange, Barb?" Mr. Falcon approached.

His habit of calling me by a woman's name annoyed me further. I wanted to say, *"Other than your odor of cheap port, I do not notice anything different,"* but restrained myself in order to be left alone.

It was not to be.

Mr. Falcon started another confession. This time, an acutely painful one. He took my hand, and stood on his knees, imploring, "Please, forgive me. I was a fool for being with her. I am so sorry! I should not have done that. I should not have had another woman. I am nothing without you. Come back."

I tried to disentangle myself, yet, his grip was too tight, too desperate.

"Barb, you know she did not mean anything to me. She was just a pastime. She was nothing compared to you. You must see that. You must understand you are the only one in my life. Please say I am forgiven."

What should I do? "I forgive you, husband. I forgive you," I took his hands in mine and helped him up.

"Really? You do?"

"I do, with one condition." I waved a finger to emphasize my point. "You have to quit drinking. No more port." He tried to kiss me, and I pushed him away. "When you are sober — only then."

Mrs. Smith helped me to get rid of him, and I resumed my job. He was right, there was something strange here. Something did not smell right. Better hurry up.

Where would I go? Where was Fitzwilliam?

Could it be that something has happened to you, love? Did you have another fight with Wickham? Have you had an accident in the road? It was more than fifty miles, after all. If he had arrived at Hertfordshire on Monday, he should be here already. I pictured neighing horses and the carriage overturned; a wheel spinning off its axis. *And nobody knows I am here. Nobody would tell me if you, if you... Oh no.* I pictured his body broken, his beautiful eyes staring without life. No, NO!

I started to cry, miserably. *Come to me soon, love. Come. Please God, keep him safe. Do not let Wickham harm him. Do not let anything happen to him.* I prayed over and over while writing in the catalogue. My hands — an extensive stain of ink. Nothing could dry these tears. The notes would be unreadable after this.

****

At the end of the working hours, my face was itching. Men do not cry! I should have been able to control myself.

I climbed the stairs to the attic. The door to my room was open.

"Thank you, Lord," I saw Fitzwilliam inclined over the telescope next to the window. "You fixed it!"

He turned around and rushed toward me, "I missed you so much!" He lifted me and turned us around merrily. "That road was twice the length I remembered." He looked at me lovingly. He stopped his spin suddenly. Carefully placing me on my feet, he moved his hands to my cheeks, "What has happened to your eyes? What has happened to your face?"

I hooked around his neck. "Nothing, Fitzwilliam. Nothing. I was just scared about your delay."

He extracted me from our embrace and gazed at me again, "They are red and swollen; this is not normal." He touched my eyelashes with the utmost delicacy.

"These are just some silly tears I spent at work." My face was stained as well; I should look a fright.

"No, Elizabeth. Your skin is red all over. You have a rash, and the inflammation around your eyes is making them look smaller. There is no way this can be produced by only tears," he affirmed alarmed. "This is some strange reaction or something like that. I will call the doctor right away."

I wanted to argue, except he was faster than light. I had barely seen him, and he had left me again!

It had to be the ink. I moved to watch myself on the mirror of the wardrobe. Some cleaning water was what was needed here.

Good Lord. How could this have happened? There were odd spots covering my whole face — my eyes red and my eyelids so frightfully big with irritation. I reached to touch the marks. They felt sore. This had never happened to me before. I wetted a towel and was going to try if it helped somehow.

"Let me do it." Fitzwilliam reached for the fabric. He started patting my skin cautiously. "I have never seen something like this. What do you feel?"

"I feel an increasing itch, nothing else."

"Do you feel any pain?"

I shook my head.

"Does it hurt when I do this?" He pressed a bit harder on a place in my brow.

"No."

"What have you been doing today?"

"I only went to the library to finish the cataloguing. I have not spent a single hour out of it. I wanted to have it done when you arrived."

"This is not helping. What have you eaten these days?"

"Mostly eggs and lots, lots of potatoes," I licked my lips, pretending it was the most exquisite dish. "Did you know potatoes were imported from South America and saved Europe from a great famine in the last century?" I tried to distract him. "It is a crop that can survive the hardest of winters."

"I do not understand why these dots are so crowded around your eyes. I would expect them to be around your lips instead, if they were from some food." He kept rubbing my face, and I noticed I was having some difficulty keeping my eyes open.

We heard someone knocking. A very tired Dr. Wheliker appeared.

"What have you gotten yourself into this time, boy?"

"Good afternoon, sir. I do not know."

He guided me to sit on the bed, and observed my face attentively, "This is some eruption you have here. Where have you being playing?"

I looked at Fitzwilliam to ascertain which version he prepared today.

"He has only been to the library. He has eaten eggs and potatoes, and he has cried a bit."

Mr. Wheliker asked me to lie, "I must see if you have any other manifestation in your body, let us undress you." *Oh No!*

"Is it absolutely necessary?" Fitzwilliam inquired.

"If you want to cure him — YES."

Mr. Darcy asked him to speak outside. The door shut after them, and I rested my eyes too. What could be happening to my face?

"A WOMAN?" The doctor's voice could be heard utterly exacerbated. "YOU HAVE BEEN KEEPING A WOMAN HERE? ARE YOU OUT OF YOUR SENSES?"

I could not discern Fitzwilliam's long reply though, only his earnest tone.

"I did not expect this from you! You have always behaved like a principled man." Mr. Wheliker came inside with the severest of demeanors.

"This is most unconventional, Miss. I do not like to be taken for a fool." He ordered for me to take off my coat and my shirt only.

I obliged and laid like a stone on the bed.

After a throughout inspection of my body, he went to examine my face again and asked more questions about my day. It was getting more difficult to see. Why?

"Come in, Darcy," he called, as I covered my wrapped bosom, and said gentleman approached from outside. "This is strange. This has many similar symptoms to early poisoning. But, I cannot explain why the eruption is focused on her eyes. It should be all over her body, if it is the effect of a life threat. I need to check the things she has been in contact with today, in the last hours. This is something that is spreading fast."

I looked at Fitzwilliam for an explanation to this odd speech. His body gave up to an invisible power that forced him to slide down the nearby wall to a crouching position. "Poisoned," he whispered with a quivering voice, "Poison."

I reached for the doctor's hand, to divert him from the scene of grief developing in front of us. "Mr. Wheliker, you can ask the servant to guide you to the library. I have spent the last six hours there. Perhaps some of the books are the source of this infection."

"Yes. I will go right away."

---

*Listen and watch Non piu andrai farfallone amoroso, here:
http://www.youtube.com/watch?v=v_iW4Coo2rI&feature=related

**According to Regency Encyclopedia and Harvey, A. D. *Sex in Georgian England*, Phoenix Press (1994):
"In 1806 six men were hanged for sodomy as compared to only five for murder. Executions for sodomy averaged two a year thereafter till 1835."

***The original Lunarmen gathered together for lively dinner conversations, the journey back from their Birmingham meeting place lit by the full moon. They were led by the physician Erasmus Darwin, a man of extraordinary intellectual insight with his own pioneering ideas on evolution. Others included the flamboyant entrepreneur Matthew Boulton, the brilliantly perceptive engineer James Watt whose inventions harnessed the power of steam, the radical polymath Joseph Priestley who, among his wide-ranging achievements discovered oxygen, and the innovative potter and social reformer Josiah Wedgwood. Their debates brought together philosophy, arts, science and commerce, and as well as debating and discovering, the 'Lunarticks' also built canals and factories, managed world-class businesses and changed the face of Birmingham.
http://www.lunarsociety.org.uk/3
and http://en.wikipedia.org/wiki/Lunar_Society_of_Birmingham

Chapter 18

"Fitzwilliam, listen to me."

He hung his head, rubbing his fists against his scalp.

"Fitzwilliam, this is nothing. Stop tormenting yourself."

"This is all my fault. I should have stayed here. I should not have left you."

I finished dressing, cleaned my likely-poisoned hands, and went to kneel in front of him. "This is not what you are imagining. This is just a passing thing. I will be well soon, I am sure."

He remained in the same position, and I stroke his back comfortingly, letting my eyes rest a bit from the increasing effort keeping them open required. "You should not punish yourself like this. There is no way you could have made sure this would not have happened. It must be something that was in the books. I must have wiped my eyes too many times while arranging them."

"I should have taken you with me."

"To Hertfordshire? That cannot be! I cannot go back there!"

"No, I should have proposed the day of Bingley's wedding and taken you to Pemberley right away."

"Oh dear." His long legs prevented me from getting close enough. "You are blaming yourself for not figuring out so long ago something that is unpredictable! How could you imagine back then I would work in a library? You are not to blame for anything. You have done all in your power to protect me. You have done the impossible — finding me, and taking care of me in a way even my family cannot understand. Through your unselfish guardianship, you have become my best friend — the most important person in my life. Why do not you see that?"

"I am always late. I came too late today. I found you too late here. I reacted too late to the absence of letters. I proposed too late in Kent. I confronted Wickham too late."

"Stop. Stop. Stop! I am the one that has brought this upon myself. This has nothing to do with you. I am paying for my own mistakes. Being here is the consequence of an event that occurred even before meeting you." Oh my, I could barely see!

He peeked at me with those agonizing eyes that break my heart. "Yes, even there I was late."

"This is too much! How can you say such a thing? How can you blame yourself for something as random as meeting another person?" I took his face in my hands to prevent him from hiding it again, anticipating these were the final few minutes I would have this luxury, before coming back to health. "Fitzwilliam Darcy, there is nothing you could have done to prevent this, and you should not have those pessimistic thoughts you are having right now. I am going to heal soon, and we will remember this as a long blink." I gave myself leave to rest my eyelids a tad.

"Well, this is not going to happen again." He rose abruptly and took me securely by the shoulders to help me up. "We are leaving this place right now. You are not going to spend one single day without protection again." I heard him walk in the direction of the bed and come back. "We are going to London, then to Pemberley when you get better." He placed my coat over my shoulders. "Come," he took my hand and pulled me toward the door.

"Wait, wait. We have to wait for Mr. Wheliker. He is in the library, searching for the source of this malady. We cannot leave like this." *This is crazy.* "I have a lot of items to pack. I have to say goodbye to Mr. Falcon. I have to inform my friends. I…"

"You do not need those male robes in my house. I will give you some of Georgiana's dresses. I will take care of everything."

"I am barefoot, Fitzwilliam! Stop!" I managed to say something coherent at last.

It was not to be. He grabbed me in his arms and cradled me as he always does. "You do not need any shoes this way," he said, walking awkwardly through the narrow door.

"Please, let me take my diary. Let me get the book you gave me. I cannot depart without them."

Incapacitated, I could not read his reaction, but I did feel him hug me so very tenderly. "Where are they?"

"They are in the desk, in the first drawer." I remembered putting the diary there to dry after writing about the incident at the tavern. "The notebook is on top."

He walked with me a few strides and sat in the chair adjacent to the table, with me on his lap. I heard him open the compartment and extract the diary first. I waited for him to reach for the book. What was taking him so much time? I felt his chest rise a couple of times. What was he doing?

He hit the table forcefully instead. "WHY?"

Oh God, he found the record about the scene in the pub! I felt an excruciating need to know what his features said, and touched his face. "You read that!" his joined brows confirmed. "Why did you do it?"

"It was an impulse, a natural thing. I am used to studying everything that has your handwriting. I cannot help it," he said in a voice that, instead of showing repentance, demonstrated his belief that he had the right to read my personal things.

"You should not have. You are angry at me now."

"I am not angry at you. I feel powerless. I have tried... I did everything to prevent you from being involved in anything dangerous." He pressed the diary in my hand. "And see what has happened. You not only went to a place unfit for a lady. You had to risk your life too."

"I did not do it on purpose. I gave my word to the boys more than a week ago!" *You must see I had no choice.*

"Yes. And you almost got killed for keeping your word! Wait, when was the last time you touched this?" he snatched the notebook back.

"No, sir," I hid it within my coat. "There is no way you are going to see it again."

"What if it is poisoned?"

"It is not. I have not used it since Monday." *There is no way you are going to read anything else that is written here!*

He muttered something under his breath.

Someone was climbing the stairs, and tried to get off.

"No!" Fitzwilliam demanded.

"But..." I bubbled, "Mr. Wheliker..."

"What do you need other than the book?" He stood up and placed me carefully back on the chair.

"My boots, of course."

He must have reached for them, and I extended my arms to put them on. "Here they are," he grabbed my leg and worked to insert my foot himself. AGRR. I could do that by myself!

The steps approached. "Smell this," he directed to Mr. Darcy. What did he find? What did he bring? "It is Prussian Blue."*

Prussian Blue? It could not be.

Fitzwilliam groaned aloud.

"This is only one of the catalogues she has been working with. They are all impregnated like this. It is a miracle the books were not the same. Whoever did this was diligent with the job," the doctor said factually. "She was the only target of this."

"We are out of here right now." Fitzwilliam voice could only be confused with a thunder. The drawer squeaked back — *he must be extracting the poems* — and I was lifted once again. "We are heading home, Elizabeth."

"Yes, you should, Darcy. I am afraid there is very little to do but wait. I recommend keeping a cloth around her eyes with sweet almond oil. Her eyes may itch a great deal. Do not let her scratch her face. Make her rest and drink a lot of water…" The instructions were barely heard while we descended the stairs.

"You should put me down when we arrive at the bottom."

"No." He grabbed me closer, and I heard the wrinkle of my diary between our bodies.

"Someone will see us! They will think we are improper. They will think you are…" I could not say that word!

"I do not care!" He reached for the doorknob.

I put my arms around his neck to help in his intent, and felt him slide out. Why was he limping? He walked with the same long strides typical of him, a slight linger in the left foot. "Are you well? Has anything happened to your leg?"

"Just a scratch," he answered while someone rushed to open the door of the carriage, and I was positioned on the step.

Touching the framework and the walls to ascertain my position, I got in as Fitzwilliam climbed in by the opposite side. I sat straight, as being handled like a toy was quite irritating. He grabbed my foot. "What are you doing?"

"Taking them off," he said resolutely, although he was being delicate whilst removing my boots.

"Whatever for?"

He stood and sat me on his lap again. "For this."

The carriage started the journey.

"You are being rude. You are angry, and you are imposing on me again."

"I am not. You do this with your father. You sat here yourself the other night."

"Yes. Because I was drunk!"

A long silence ensued until his lips spoke to my brow. "It is just that it is so frustrating to not have any right over you. You say I am the most important person in your life, yet, I do not have even the right to protect you as I ought."

"You are doing that remarkably well now."

"I am sorry. I do not mean to impose. Last time we saw each other gave me such delight, I dared to hope next time would be better. I dreamed of showing you some places in Cambridge; to relate what I know about the origin of the bridges and schools; to show you some of the constellations with the telescope at night. And now, you cannot even <u>see</u>. I need…I need to recover some peace. Holding you is the only way I might."

"Fitzwilliam, if you want me to sit here, I am willing." Well, if no one was watching. "You only have to ask."

"Do you want to stay here, or you would rather sit alone?"

"Of course, I would rather stay. It is warmer here!" I slid an arm behind his waist. With the other, I touched his face to gather my feelings. He was more relaxed now. "Was it difficult? Asking, I mean."

"No. It was not." He covered my hand with his. "It was not."

We sensed my diary crackling between our bodies for a second time. I extracted it from inside the coat. Where should I put it?

He took it from me with an 'allow me' and store it somewhere. "By the way, how did you preserve the book if you were robbed in Newmarket?"

"I did not pack it with the rest of my belongings. I…" I intended to remove my hand from his face, but he did not let me. "I had to decide between my diaries and the poems. They were dear to me, though dangerous to travel with. It was a difficult decision. It was the only thing that had my true name, and I was afraid it could be seen by accident. I wrapped it in the middle of my chest with the same cloth as my bosom. I have become addicted to those poems. They…"

He moved both arms abruptly to squeeze my body to his. "My love, I swear," he embraced harder, "I swear I will find that man from the tavern, and kill him!"

"Fitzwilliam, NO!" In vain, I tried to separate, to make him see reason,

"How can you know it was him? How can you be sure he tried to take my life? You might get injured or worse!"

"The coward thought you would lick your fingers to move among pages. It is a trusted way to murder, and he dared to inflict it on <u>you</u>."

"That is too elaborate for that imbecile."

"Describe him to me. Tell me more about what happened on Monday night!"

"I will not!" *I will not give you any details for you to search him. That is not what I want!*

"Well. You have described him clearly enough in your notes. From what I just read I know he is a rapist and that he has threatened you. I will ask about a description of his looks in that bar. Everyone must remember him."

"Do not do it. Think about Georgiana." I argued to his chest, listening to the trapped beast that was taking possession of it.

"No."

"Please, Fitzwilliam, do not."

"No."

"I will marry you if you agree not to go after him," I beseeched impulsively.

"Not this way. No. I want you to <u>choose</u> to marry me. Not to do it to avoid a risk. You must <u>want</u> me as much as I want you. This is not something we can bargain about. I love you too much for that."

Oh God, how was I to prevent this?

"Lord, do not take her eyes from me. Not that."

****

We fell asleep in this position, I realized when awoke at a slight dip of the carriage. I listened carefully, to ascertain if my companion was still slumbering. I removed myself carefully from his lap, and sat close to one of the walls. I palmed his clothes softly, to find out how to help him lay his head on my thighs now. Dearest Fitzwilliam. I cradled him to avoid his body from sliding down.

How long would this last? I touched my face and verified the state of the sore skin. It was quite swollen. That was why he was mad.

The image of his dead body intruded in my mind once again. Eager to find a solution out of his headstrong resolve, I considered asking him to take me to Pemberley right away — it was far enough — then I realized he could leave me there and go back to his previous task. I could pretend I was still blind after healing. He would not leave me alone under such circumstances. However, I rejected the idea; it was repulsive to manipulate him this way. He would only get more inconsolable.

I could distract him somehow. I could do like Scheherazade and keep him close to me while he forgot about this wretched business. Do you think you can make up enough stories for one thousand nights? — the naughty thought was tempting. *No, Elizabeth. The days should suffice.*

"What are you thinking about?"

"Nothing noteworthy. I am just looking forward to this stay in London. Is Ana there?"

"No, she is in Derbyshire; a bit upset, but it will pass soon. She is not the kind of person to hold on to angry feelings toward a friend for an extended time."

"I should write her again as soon as I can," I started to fondle his hair, "and to my family too. Would you tell me what transpired during your stay in Hertfordshire? How did Papa react to your visit?"

"Your father…" He rose to a sitting position and then kept silent.

"Fitzwilliam, tell me. I need to know."

"He would not receive me. I could only talk with the housekeeper. He would not even let me enter the foyer." There was a controlled ire underneath this words. "I could only gather from Mrs. Hill that a man had come to warn him about me, a man brought by Wickham, who had not been seen before. Your father prohibited all your sisters and your mother to write back to you after that incident. Although, it does appear your mother has not arrived from Scotland as of yet."

"You could not speak with him?" Why would Papa do such a thing? "Do you have any idea as to whom that man could be?"

I could not discern his response until he said, "Sorry. No." He must have shaken his head.

This was strange. "What took you so long then?"

"I had to attend to other business. I had to arrange the issue of Wickham."

"With Wickham?" *Tell me, he did not remember.*

"I just made sure he would not fabricate another slander against any of us; not against your family, not against mine, nor against you or me. I made him retract from all his vicious statements in front of Sir William Lucas. He will never do you any harm again."

"You did that in front of Sir William? Did you just burst into their lodge and break another of his teeth?" This made no sense. Maria and Wickham should be living in another house. "Was he not married already?"

"Yes he is. I do not think the groom looked too joyful in that wedding though." He pulled me into his lap again. "He does not show his smile as often as before. He looks whiter than a cloud from so much hiding indoors."

Like the snake he was, the rascal was hiding underground now.

Fitzwilliam grazed almost imperceptibly the place where my cravat was missing. *Stay calm. You are going to distract him for a couple of days.* "I have missed looking at this part of you. I look forward seeing you wearing a dress."

"Ah, about that." I strove for composure. "I do not think Georgiana will appreciate me wearing her clothes. Why not give me a dress from someone else? There must be someone my size in your household. Or maybe you still have one of your mother's dresses?"

"What? That is absurd. Better buy you something new. I can call one of my sister's seamstresses to take your measurements tomorrow morning. They can have at least one or two dresses fitted for the next day, and some others for our travel to Pemberley."

"Fitzwilliam, what have we just agreed to?"

"Do you object to that, too?"

"No. Except, we agreed that you would ask. Should you not ask if I am willing to go there?"

"I have not said when. I am not imposing. I just know you will go with me someday. Someday. The day I break your prejudices (the way miners break the rock). The day you love me."

****

Arriving late at night, Mr. Darcy (I could not help but revert to calling him thus after the deference his staff showed toward him) followed the same procedure. He entered his townhouse with me in his arms. He introduced his housekeeper, Mrs. Robson, and climbed the stairs to the room I supposed was intended for guests. He ordered her to find almond oil, while sitting me on the softest of beds. "I will be back in a second."

It was so strange to only imagine this place, to only listen to the voices of these loyal servants. I waited impatiently for someone to talk to me or give some indication of what was happening. Realizing I had been left alone, I reached for the pillow. It had the sweetest smell — his smell. They used the same soap for his clothes and the linens. I extended my hands in all directions to gather the dimensions of the bed. It was mammoth in proportion.

"I know it is late to have a hot bath for her. Do what you can to see to her comfort, and dress her with these robes," he was giving directions from what I supposed was the hall.

"These robes, sir? Are you sure?" The housekeeper inquired with — *awkwardness?* "I can get some of Georgiana's from her room."

"No. Do not worry; I will have the seamstress come tomorrow morning. She will have new dresses and everything else soon. These should do for tonight."

"Yes, sir. I guess you expect the utmost discretion in this situation. Everything will be taken care right away."

"Good. Needless is to say how important her wellbeing is, Mrs. Robson. She has been through a lot. I want her to recuperate her health as soon as may be, and ascertain she feels welcomed here."

"Of course, sir," answered the lady with an intonation that only a loving mother would use.

"Go and bring me a cloth to bind her eyes. Get that almond oil too. Please. I do not know why it is taking Cook so much time to get it." *Be patient, Fitzwilliam, this is an enormous house from what I gathered when you brought me here.*

His long strides approached. "How do you feel?" He grabbed my hand to hold it on his face with his. He had bent for me to sense his expressions, my sweet protector.

"Except that I hate being disabled, I would say I have missed being in a homey and warm house, enough to be grateful for this malady now."

"And your eyes, your skin? How does it feel?"

"It itches. Only that. And, if the itching grows worse, I will not scratch it. Even if you should declare me truly stubborn."

"I can invoke some other examples if you fail at this particular test," he jested straightening, and pulled my head to rest on his abdomen. "I would ask you to concentrate your energies on sleeping though."

"There is no almond oil in the kitchen," it was Mrs. Robson's melodic tone. "Do you want me to ask one of the boys to go buy it right away, sir?"

"No," he separated, "I will get it myself. Ask the stable boy to prepare a horse."

"Immediately." The lighter steps of the woman were lost.

"You do not have to go. I can wait until tomorrow. It should not make any difference after such a long journey."

"Of course I must." The mattress yielded under his weight.

"Please, do not lift me to your lap in front of the servants. It is improper enough the way it is."

"I will not. Do not worry."

****

I fell asleep directly after being cleaned with care. I was also dressed in a long shirt, and a gigantic and warm nightgown. I was scarcely conscious when Fitzwilliam wrapped a cloth around my eyes and kissed my hair. What I do remember well, were the images my worst nightmare brought.

"DO NOT LEAVE ME, JACK! PLEASE... DO NOT LEAVE ME ALONE!" I awoke sweating profusely. They blinded me — I established at last. That was why I could not see their faces. That was why I was paralyzed with fear. Jack left me in the woods sightless. With strangers.

---

*Prussian Blue is called cyanide nowadays.

Chapter 19

I came in and out of sleep many times during the night. I was sure, now, I had agreed to be blindfolded by Jack and Wickham. I had expected them to ask me to be 'It' in a game of Blind man's bluff, after they had put a cravat very tightly around my eyes. I was afraid of getting lost in the unknown woods, and asked Jack to give me his hand. Then, I heard the voices of other boys. I was preoccupied, thinking it would be difficult to catch them all. I waited for instructions in vain — they never came. There was a long, frightening pause; with only whispers to be heard and strange actions around my lower body. Someone pulled at my dress, and there were some light touches around my waist and legs, until an insult and an uproar diverted everyone's attention. At some moment, Jack broke loose despite my desperate plea, and I struggled to take off the cravat. What happened next was extremely confusing. I only know I saw Mama at the end.

A maid came to see if I needed help with my morning toilet. I was grateful, as I could not discern a single thing in this unknown bath chamber. "This nightgown is very concealing, I am sure, but due to the length of it and my inability to see, it makes it difficult discerning my way around the room." I tried to build some camaraderie with this girl. "Is it at least beautiful, the gown I mean?" There was nothing to fear. She could not read my thoughts. This was uncomfortable enough for all of them.

"I do not know, miss. I think Miss Darcy's would be more fitting," she retired to wait outside the room.

This was my fault then — do not complain, Elizabeth. "What is your name?" I kept speaking through the door.

"Vivian, miss."

"Mine is Elizabeth." I finished arranging my underwear and putting the large shirt in place, glad for not having to wrap my bosom any more.

"Would you help me with this?" I asked her to do the bandage around my left, once we were back in the bedroom.

"I will do it," Fitzwilliam appeared from behind us.

I heard the maid retire from the room, and a sound indicating something was laid on a nearby table. I smelled the aroma of coffee. Detecting he was approaching, I turned to face the master of the house. Remember to smile; he will be less sure about going after that man if he sees you are well.

"How are you doing today, my love?" He put a small kiss on my cheek.

He was taking advantage of this situation to do all he wants! "I am well now. What did you bring there?"

"Our breakfast: coffee, bread and a very special treat, solid chocolate*," he guided me to the bed. "Would you like me to wrap your hand before or after we eat?"

"It depends. What is this 'solid' chocolate we are having?"

"A surprise." He hid my legs under the covers, "This should be warmer."

"A surprise?"

"I will only tell you in advance that it is Italian — from Turin, actually."

He brought what I supposed was the tray with our food.

"From Turin?" I crossed the legs to keep my balance when he climbed in front of me. "I thought chocolate was brought by the Spaniards from Mexico."

"Yes, but not this particular dish." I waited for him to arrange the things in the space between us, and extended a hand to take a cup. "With milk and sugar, is it not?"

I nodded yes. He remembered <u>everything</u>.

He took my right hand and guided it to take the coffee cup by myself. "Take it here whenever you want a sip; however, let me show you where the other things are." He placed my left over the bread and then, on a sticky bar. "This is the surprise."

I took a first bite. "Mmm, delicious. This is exquisite. It is sweet. It melts on my tongue. From Turin, you say? Can we move there?"

"When the war ends, yes," he chuckled, "because you would betray His Majesty's Army, if the enemy offered anything with sugar in exchange for information."

You like easy bantering with me, do you not, Mr. Darcy? "Are not you eating it too?"

"Yes, I am. However, you should have seen your face when you tried it."

"Really? And how is it that you have this foreign luxury here? Someone else in this house must like it for you to have it early in the morning. I do not think you could have traveled to the Continent since I last saw you."

He did not respond instantly. Wrong word, I should not have used anything related to seeing.

"Georgiana likes it a lot, and Bingley has been investing in a business that imports it from Italy. It gives him the ability to procure some of the delights from that country."

"So, this is another thing I have in common with your sister, besides being the same height and climbing trees?" I started to search unsuccessfully for a napkin on the tray.

"I think she is bit taller, but not much." He grabbed the hand that was surely making something ridiculous and mocked, "Are you after my chocolate, miss?"

Good. His sad musings did not last long. "No, sir, just for the napkin to clean my fingers like the spoiled child I am becoming now."

"Oh, no. Not that," he feigned the grumpy father. "My trousers are not to be used that way." He took my hand and moved it up close to his face. "Besides, I have a better method to clean these little troublemakers."

God, he was sucking them! His tongue first traveled up and down my little finger, then did the same with all the others.

"I think I will ask you to feed me this way every morning. Who needs sweets and coffee when there are these delightful meat snacks to nibble upon?"

I will melt myself if you insert them into your mouth like that again, I wanted to say.

"Do not you think the same?"

"About meat and chocolate, sir?"

"No. About waking up this way every morning?"

What was I supposed to say to that? "It depends, I have not tried the bread and coffee yet. It would be intolerable, if they do not have the right amount of sugar." Ugh, a safe way out.

"God help us in such a case."

We spoke about some other trivial matters for a while. I asked to send a letter to Mrs. Beth on my behalf, in order for her not to despair about my whereabouts and to ask her to give the news of my indisposition to my employers. He proposed he would better send an express messenger with the news to Mr. Cochran, explaining the true nature of Mr. Churchill as it was revealed in the tavern. For, if they believed that man was a part of their movement, it was dangerous not to inform he was a spy.

When we finished our breakfast, Mr. Darcy asked to remain in my room until the dressmaker arrived. Sitting on a couch, what followed was an awkward conversation in which he asked about Jack. He had heard me calling him in the night and was fast to step in his defense. Mortified, I explained I cannot help speaking when asleep and apologized for disturbing the house. Nevertheless, he should not believe he knows him, just because they met in Hertfordshire. Of course, Jack's betrayal so long ago was not something I could talk about, and we ended up making each other wary.

****

The modiste came and took all the measurements that can be taken on a woman. She only missed measuring my volume by drowning me in some immense test tube. She promised to have two dresses, as well as corsets, chemises, and pantaloons available for tomorrow. Stocking and shoes, and the rest — in a couple of days.

What could she be referring to by 'the rest'? I would warn Mr. Darcy that I was not staying here forever.

Staying here. Forever.

It had been my dream to be with him so many times, and it got further and further away with each revelation.

"Have you seen her without the bandage, Vivian?" I heard two maids walking in and entering the toilet, where they were to arrange a bath for me. "Can she be the one in his drawings? The one that caused him to be so isolated after he returned from Kent? Can she be the reason behind what Amelie told us, that the last time he arrived at Pemberley he drank every day?"

"Hush, Lillian, hush! She will hear you!"

"I am not saying he did so over her. I just want the same. I want someone who would look after me like that, who would roam half of London at night to get a remedy for me; someone who would not take his eyes from me as he does with her."

"You had better be careful with that tongue. You know how much Master appreciates discretion. I am sure she will be the mistress. Better keep those thoughts to yourself."

"I know. He could have stayed here during the night, without being noticed by her, and yet he went to sleep in the next room. He is mindful about respecting her privacy."

"Is it ready, girls?" the chat was interrupted by the familiar step of the housekeeper. "Lunch is almost set."

"Yes, madam."

"Stay here and wait for us, then."

Once I was guided into the bathing room, they allowed me to touch the tub in order to gain my bearings. The water was welcoming.

"Girls, let us take off the lower undergarments before the chemisette. This way, she will not get cold before entering into the tub."

I sat in a nearby chair, and the stockings were stripped off first. I stood up. I hated being helped this way, being useless! One of the maids held both my arms to aid in my balance, while the other reached under the skirt, to unfasten the ribbon that kept my drawers in place. *This is what Wickham did in my dream. He lifts my skirt and he... and he... he unties my... GOD, I WANT TO DIE!* The underwear fell to my ankles, and the girl touched the back of my knee to help me lift my leg. *Dear God, he touched my knee too.*

I started to tremble.

"Put her legs inside the tub before taking the rest off." Mrs. Robson helped them to set me. "She must be freezing."

A pair of hands aimed to lift the hem of the long shirt. "Please, do not do it," I begged, lowering into the water. "I can bathe by myself. Please, do not undress me more." I grabbed my robes to keep them clutched to my body. "I want to bathe with this cloth on, please."

"Miss, what is the matter? Why are you shaking like this?" the housekeeper exclaimed. "Pour the bucket at once, she is very cold."

I felt six hands rubbing my body. The same as that day.

Others saw me. They inspected me <u>there</u>! "DO NOT TOUCH ME. PLEASE. DO NOT TOUCH ME. LEAVE ME ALONE. PLEASE." I cried this time. *I want to die.*

"Girls, let us take her out of here. This is not working." The maids lifted me up and sat me back on the chair. They inserted my legs in a dry set of pantaloons and tied it to my waist quickly. One of them tried to take off the wet shirt. Mrs. Robson stopped her hands on my thighs. "No."

"What is going on here? Why is Elizabeth screaming?" Mr. Darcy's voice emerged from nowhere.

"She started screaming when we tried to bathe her, sir. She would not let us take her clothe off."

"She is freezing, sir. That is all."

Fitzwilliam rushed to wrap a heavy quilt around my body. "Get out of here. I will take care of her."

A pair of strong arms enfolded me and stroked my back while a sweet voice whispered, "All is well, Lizzy. I am here. All is well."

"I want to die," I wailed. Wickham did it. He undressed me. And those boys handled me.

"No, Lizzy. No." He moved us to sit in a warm place on the floor. "Do not say that, love. All is well. Do not think such a thing. I cannot live without you."

"They blinded me, Fitzwilliam. They blinded me and they…"

"You can tell me. I can help you deal with this. You can tell me." He cradled me to him, wrapping the quilt tightly around my feet.

"No. Nobody can. I brought this on myself. I let them blindfold me," I sobbed.

"No, it was not your fault. I am sure it was not."

"They know. There are many boys that know. They witnessed all. He encouraged them to do it… " Jack let them do it.

"It does not matter. A long time has passed. No one remembers. No one will harm you. You are safe. It does not matter now."

"It does. They blinded me, and Jack remembers. I am sure." *I cannot marry you. Never.*

He kissed the top of my head first, "I do not care, love," and then my forehead, "I do not care."

Wickham saw me. Others touched my waist, my legs and between my thighs. Their fingers… I let them do that. I let them touch me. I let them see me. Fitzwilliam could not know. If he knew, he would go after him. I let them blind me. I let them blind me! — I repeated while I was rocked.

"All is well, Lizzy. All is well."

****

We sat like that for a long while until I regained my equanimity and dressed alone. There was no point in making Fitzwilliam miserable too.

He asked for our lunch to be brought and fed me himself. When finished, he feigned a playful tone. "I have a proposition for you: what if we spend the afternoon with a good book? I have two kinds of subject that could tempt you. I think you could enjoy a classic, like 'Romeo and Juliet' for example, or," *no, no, too similar to real life.* He arranged the quilt around and under my legs to keep me warm, "I have some intelligence that says you could enjoy a book by an important scientist. A book about nature, about the elements in nature particularly, written by a remarkable man; a book considered revolutionary, a work that is published in many languages, and is only a couple of decades old. A book which I have the first edition, the one in its original tongue…"

"Fitzwilliam, you are talking in circles like Mr. Collins!"

He chuckled 'yes' and followed, "By the way, are you interested in those journals about fashion that Miss Bingley is always perusing? I think Georgiana has some in her room. I could describe those dresses instead."

"You wish to spend an afternoon describing dresses? Are you trying to annoy me, Mr. Darcy?"

"No," I felt his respiration close to my nose. "I just want something in exchange for my skilled services."

Oh, no, "You are going to blackmail an innocent blind person now?" I pouted childishly.

"Yes! This is a very special service and requires payment in advance."

"What would be the service, and what would be the prize, sir?"

"Translating from French in exchange for," he took my right hand and laid it on his cheek, "one kiss here."

"One kiss on this cheek?"

"Yes. That cheek has been jealous of the other one for almost a week now."

I took his head with both hands — *naughty Fitzwilliam* — I turned it to have his dimple in front of my lips — *I hope that book is an extremely long one* — and gave him a lingering kiss. "Would you tell me now, who the author is?"

"Lavoisier, Antoine-Laurent de Lavoisier, mademoiselle."

****

I spent the afternoon and night comfortably nestled with Fitzwilliam. He found it especially fitting to lean on the headboard (in the same place I had occupied before) with my back reclined on his chest, his long legs around mine. He translated fluidly Lavoisier's 'Traité élémentaire de chimie', which is considered to be the best modern chemistry textbook. I discovered this volume presented a unified view of new theories of chemistry and contained a clear statement on the law of conservation of mass — that had to be the same law I read in Lomonosov's manuscript. He also denied the existence of phlogiston***.

This text clarified a fundamental concept, the concept of an element as a substance that could not be broken down by any known method of chemical analysis. It finally presented a new theory of the formation of chemical compounds from elements.

The best of it? I learned all this without a glance toward a dictionary, with a delightful voice crowding my senses, and two mischievous lips brushing my nape from time to time. "To distract you from the itching," Fitzwilliam justified.

"Do you think the elements were created by God at the same time?" I asked when his translation ended.

"Mmmm?"

"I want to know if you think the chemical elements were created by God at the same time. If, in one moment, there was nothing, and the next moment, they were all made. Do you think that possible?"

A low snore was the only response.

He had fallen asleep — the logical consequence of searching for my medicine all night.

What should I do? To find the door and call for a maid? No. That would wake him. I remembered the cozy couch we sat on at the beginning of the day. That place was suitable for sleeping.

I straightened my spine slowly, for him not to notice my movements. I crawled forward to escape the circle of his legs. I reached the end of the long bed, and finally, got off.

I walked with my palms up, trying to prevent a crash. My fingers sensed something hard. Now to the right. I trusted the settee was closer this way. My foot hit a chair unexpectedly. "Blast," I caught it just in time to prevent the hit. Those boys were a bad influence, Elizabeth; you should not talk like a man. I found a discontinuity and supposed it to be the entrance of the bathing room. I should have called for the maid. There will be servants' talk if he stays. I walked slowly and nearly slipped on some water on the floor. I found the frame to stabilize myself just in time, *almost*. Until I touched soft furniture at last.

I sat on the arm of the couch with a liberating sigh, and reached to take the cushions. I palmed the fabric until my hands distinguished a different texture. *It is warm* — was my last thought before being unceremoniously pulled to lie over the man I was trying not to wake up. "Where were you going, Frog Martina?"

"Fitzwilliam! What are you doing here?"

"Waiting to learn some useful words you might have recently discovered."

"Oh. You heard that."

"Yes. And they never sounded so funny before."

I tried to stand up.

"Wait," he pulled me back, "would you let me sleep here? I promise not to bark, not to meow, not to neigh, not to even chirp."

"No. Let me down!"

"All right." He opened his arms and stood with me, to help find the way back to bed. "Would you let me sleep on this couch you considered for yourself before?"

"How am I to let you spend the night there? You need to rest in a comfortable bed. You are tired."

"You know that is not important."

"Please, do not ask me that. Do not make me feel guilty about this. You know it would be highly improper."

"Yes, I know that is a handy word. But if it were not for 'propriety,'" he spoke the last word as if it were a curse, "we would be married by now. Besides, there is nothing improper in two people being in love."

I shook my head vehemently. *You should not harbor so many false expectations, Fitzwilliam.*

****

I could not find restful sleep that night either. The faces of Churchill and Wickham were bound to play the worst trick in my mind. In this nightmare, Fitzwilliam went after them in revenge. It was a trap. In Lambton church, Jack, Wickham, Churchill and a mysterious adult — the one present when I was freed at the wedding — were waiting for him. Jack put a blind on <u>his</u> eyes. HIS EYES. Churchill and the stranger were holding his arms while Wickham prepares to hit him. "NO GOD, NOT THAT, NOT TO HIM."

When awakened, I tore the bandage from my head. I hated it! I did not want to wear it anymore! I did not want to know any more!

****

The next morning, Mrs. Robson came to help me with the morning routine. She bound, with the utmost care, a new bandage over my eyes, although I suspected maybe I would be able to open them today. Yes, my skin was not that swollen anymore. She was cautious to give me privacy in which to change my pantaloons. She informed two new dresses were already here, and I asked her help in dressing.

I ascertained the type of fabric with my fingers (cotton, my favorite) and ran

201

my fingers through the décolletage. "Would you describe to me how I look, please?"

"Like an angel and a temptress at the same time," the object of all my thoughts replied from the direction of the door.

I heard the footsteps of the housekeeper retire and the heavy ones approach. He took my hand and turned me around, like in a dance. I felt his eyes observing my body and moved with all the intention of provoking a pleasant sensation in him. His arms grabbed me abruptly to lean my back onto his body. "If you keep doing that, I will not be able to keep my resolution of spending the morning in the garden."

My skin became gooseflesh. *Fitzwilliam, how do you do this? How can you stir these reactions?* "The garden? Are we going to take apples and plums directly from the tree again?" I took his hands from my waist and turned to face him. I touched his cheek to collect his smile at the remembrance, "Like the day you climbed a tree to get the refreshments for Ana and me? You are a good climber yourself 'Mr. I have a garden at my town house.' I must have been quite the rascal when you were a boy, and those trees must have some marks from your adventures to prove I am right."

"That is true, but I was thinking of something more tranquil today. Planning we might have a picnic. It is a bit late, and we could take our breakfast and lunch as one in a less formal manner there," he said as he escorted me downstairs and out to the backyard.

We sat on the grass to take a meal worthy of a Roman emperor. The sun rays were crucial for me to ascertain, by the many shadows that could be distinguished, I indeed was recovering my vision.

He served many of the fruits himself, and asked to give him "his meat" in return. "You should be thanking me for not using this same method to clean those candy lips of yours," he threatened. "They are the most exquisite dish in this place, and you are not sharing them as I do with all this food."

This was getting dangerous. Think of something different fast! "By the way, speaking of giving thanks, do you have any news from Mrs. Beth? Has she written back?"

"Yes, the express messenger has brought a note from Mr. Cochran." He withdrew from my side. Was he standing up? "He has some news about Churchill. He has embarked to America after attempting your murder. He will be at sea for a couple of months at least." *You are trying to hide your frustration, are you not, love?* "I hope he drowns there," he said very low. *And I am happy that man is lost to you.*

"Well I think I can cheer you up. I have good news." I raised myself on all fours and reached for any part of his body with one arm. My fingers touched the fabric covering his calf. "Come."

I followed the movements of the silhouette outlined though the wrap. He hesitated a moment but assumed a more or less a similar position as mine, in front of me. "Better than this view?"

"It is the best news: I think I am almost healthy. Would you let me try removing this bandage?"

"Of course I will help you." I felt his fingers working. "You do not have to ask permission for that. How clumsy I am! Inviting you to enjoy the weather, and not removing this thing!"

A blaze intruded into my eyes, and I covered them with both hands. I could open my eyelids. Yes, at least one half. I tried seeing my fingers. I could distinguish them too.

"Are you all right?"

I touched him to stop his worrying while making a shade. "I am." I looked at him at last, "I can see your beloved eyes as well."

---

* The history of chocolate can be found here:
 http://en.wikipedia.org/wiki/History_of_chocolate

**Lavosier original text can be found online in 'Google books'.

*** The history of science is plagued with mistakes, like the one about the existence of Phlogiston — a firelike element, which was contained within combustible bodies and released during combustion.

Chapter 20

I had never seen Fitzwilliam as happy as the moment I had regained my sight. He kissed my forehead and eyes chastely and what appeared to be unendingly, thanking God.

"Peeling skin will be the only consequence by tomorrow morning. If I can open my eyelids half as much by this point in the day, by evening hopefully my sight will be totally restored."

The next few minutes were spent preparing to give me a tour of the house. I inspected my dress. It was a classic design — yet exquisite; the cotton was dyed to a dark blue, with tiny white flowers and birds embroidered all over the upper bodice, with white a ribbon around the top of my décolletage, as well as at the sleeves and the waist.

My observation of my wardrobe complete, the excursion began. Mr. Darcy's townhouse was constructed around a beautiful garden: practical in the arrangement of the rooms, expansive in the large magnitude of the spaces, and simple and inviting in the decoration. He showed me every single corner of it (with the exception of his bedroom — *thank you, love, it would have been too much trespassing*), presented all the servants, dogs and even horses. Mrs. Robson was the way I had imagined — a kind person whose bosom invites you to be cradled like a baby, cleverness shining in her eyes. Vivian was a young maid with spark too. The other girl, the one that had helped her yesterday, was her younger sister Lillian. They had another sibling, Amelie, who worked at Pemberley, and they had all been born in Scotland.

The rest of the servants were especially polite and mirrored their master's broad smile at every salutation.

Fitzwilliam's office was the last place he showed me. It was part workplace, but mostly library; with a big desk, three comfortable chairs, and a cozy couch next to the shelves and facing the fireplace. It easily held as many volumes as some of the big shelves in the side chapels in King's College.

"I know you already started cataloging them, but would you please let me show you something without letters?"

I nodded 'yes,' not taking my eyes from the books, until he led me to sit in the chair in front of his desk.

"These are not sketches by Leonardo da Vinci, and the subject might be too familiar, yet I want you to see them." He pushed a big notebook in my direction and opened it to the first page.

There I was, almost alive in the accuracy of the resemblance, with my hair untidy and blowsy, my petticoat six inches deep in mud and my cheeks highlighted as if I were wearing cosmetics. "How can you depict eyes that light like this?"

He walked in the direction of the sofa. "There is nothing there that is the product of my imagination. You are like that." He took off his shoes and coat and tumbled comfortably on the nearby couch to rest. "Wake me up to dress for dinner."

****

I do not know how many hours I spent gazing at his sketches. There were at least a dozen that had been completed, and ten times that many that only showed some part of my body. I saw myself playing the pianoforte, dancing at Netherfield's ball, rambling in the path to Rosings Park, praying in my abandoned church, walking in the direction of the altar at Jane's wedding, Oh my — crying with my hair so very short, playing with Michael, opening a door with wet shirt and trousers, sleeping with his topcoat on, curled in the huge bed. I saw only my eyes uncountable times, my hands on the pianoforte or embroidering or resting on a chair, my lips pouting, smiling or biting the lower. So many.

This is how he sees me. I ventured to imagine all he was communicating through these drawings. He found me beautiful. He observed me and he liked what he saw. He was enchanted with me as much as I was with him. I was in his thoughts and in his dreams, too.

I stood up and walked in the direction of the couch. I crouched in front of his sleeping form, to delight in his features. I started by his feet — *so large*. I observed the place where his trousers gave a glimpse of his calf. One leg was covered with a stocking, but the other... had a recent wound? I became alarmed. Was that why he was limping when he lifted me? It was not a minor scrape at all! It was at least four inches in length. It merited the work of a surgeon! How could it have happened?

I continued to look for what I had missed in my blindness. The muscles of his thighs were well defined. He spent many hours traveling by horseback. I took pleasure in his informal attire today; no cravat, no waistcoat, his left hand resting on his belly — long and thin. His veins were so highlighted on this part, I focused on his forearm. He had dark hair here too, the same as in the small window usually covered by the cravat. I walked the collarbone with my eyes and followed to study the arm that made up part of his current pillow. Even his armpits were attractive…

I suddenly found his merry face looking at me.

"You always fall into my trap."

I dropped onto the floor. *He saw me doing that.* I started to crawl back like a crab, when he followed me to crouch on the floor too, like a feline. I retreated, with his close pace following mine, until the shelves stopped my progress and I had to sit, with my legs bent in an unladylike position. I was trapped here. I closed my eyes.

"Look at me, Elizabeth," his breath was as near as an inch.

I shook my head. *I do not want you to see how much I _desire_ you! It is not done!*

"All right," he placed his arms at each side of my head, leaning close, his thighs between mine on the floor, "if you do not want to see me, you will feel me." He kissed the sensitive spot under my ear. "I think there are two individuals in you: Elizabeth and Lizzy." He placed a kiss on the opposite side of my neck. This was slow torture. "Elizabeth is daring, restless, curious, inquisitive — the scientist. She likes nature and everything related with it. She is good at finding ingenious arguments and experiencing the world around her. Elizabeth is well liked and admired by everyone. She is fond of sweets and bites her lip when she worries about something." He kissed the edge of my jaw. "Lizzy is a scared girl, who has learned the world is not as she would like it to be. She is the one forgotten by her real father. Lizzy is the cautious child that stops Elizabeth, when the last one is going to get them both into trouble. She is also the braver of the two, because she does what is necessary for the people she loves, no matter if it would hurt her to protect them. She is the one that takes care of not letting herself be guided by sentiments alone — the one always attentive to the consequences of actions. Lizzy is also who sent me to sleep in the next room yesterday."

I wanted to protest and opened my eyes to start my application. He would not let me.

"Wait. I mean to make something clear: I am in love with both. I love my impish Elizabeth." He caressed the right corner of my lips with his. "And I love my mindful Lizzy." He brushed the left corner. "Yes. They are both mine, and I am going to cherish them all my life."

I delighted in the seas that were his eyes. I observed his chest rising, and our breath become one. *How I adore this man!* His thumb caressed my hairline. He stared at my lips for a long moment, and I could not help but do the same.

Our eyes returned to look one at the other.

He leaned into my chest. "I want to hear from your heart that what you do not dare."

****

My companion's stomach was the one to wake us up from our heaven. We decided it was time to change, and started to ascend the stairs toward our rooms.

Holding his hand securely, I remembered the injury to his leg I had noticed before. I asked about it.

The change in Fitzwilliam's features took less than a second. I saw his jaw become tense, the muscles of his shoulders contract, his hands loose the grip of mine and the rail.

I climbed one step over him. What could lead to such a strong reaction? What could be the cause of this wound? He started limping after coming from Hertfordshire. He… I remembered his words about Wickham in the carriage to London, *"I just made sure he would not fabricate another slander against any of us; not against your family, not against mine, nor against you or me. I made him retract from all his vicious statements in front of Sir William Lucas. He will never do you any harm again."*

"You fought with him in Hertfordshire, did you not? You fought with him with swords!" All my attempts to protect him were in vain!

"I <u>had</u> to do it. I <u>had</u> to call him out to duel!"

"Why?"

"WHY? Because Wickham defamed us! He contributed in turning your father against us. He questioned your honor! He harmed you."

"My honor!" I stopped his argument, "You risked your life for my <u>honor</u>!" I could not believe this. "Did not you bear in mind what would have happened if you were killed? If you were dead, no one would have come to impart the news to me. I would have waited day after day for you in that attic, thinking the worst and knowing nothing. Nothing! I would have been blind and alone! ALONE!"

"I had to stop the spread of the lies!"

"At the expense of your <u>life</u>?" I lifted a hand in denial of his next words. "You must forgive me, but my reputation is a trifle when faced with the pain I would have suffered, that WE would have suffered (because I remind you there is Ana too) had Wickham killed you." I turned my back to him and climbed the stairs on my own. "He is a soldier, for God's sake!"

"Wickham is no rival for me!"

"That is not what the cut in your leg reveals," I stated while reaching the next floor. Which of these doors was the one to my room? I looked back and saw his wounded expression.

"Wickham is nothing. This injury is nothing!" He took my hand and guided me to the first entrance. "And this is certainly the last time he provokes a quarrel between us."

He opened the door for me, and I stepped in. There was the massive bed where I had been sleeping... and the couch under the window. I turned to see the wall that was next to the door. What was this bookshelf doing here? I walked over to examine the titles. They were all about philosophy and astronomy. I walked past his figure in the threshold and entered the dressing room. I saw a woman's garment and many masculine robes. His robes.

"You had me in your room! You dressed me with your clothes!" I grabbed the nightgown that was laid on a chair. "And I thought you respected me."

"There is nothing disrespectful about it. This is the only room that is always ready — warm and with clean linens." He stepped in front of me. "Besides, this is where you belong!"

"What about giving me an option? What about our agreement about asking? This is why the maids were sure I was going to be the mistress soon. You did not want for me to have any other choice but to stay here. You did not want me to have a job!" I accused him, disappointed. "Was it a lie, too, when you talked about speaking to the Lunar Society's men?"

"Of course not. I did not act with premeditation."

"Well, let me tell you, Mr. Fitzwilliam Darcy, things are not like this. I am not a doll from the *ton* — one of those women that only think about getting a rich husband and will sell themselves for a couple of jewels. I want to study, and I want to work."

"I never tried to buy you. If I had attempted that, I would have chosen books! Do you really think you would be able to study at Cambridge? Do you think any of those tutors would accept you? Do you think they would permit you to prove a woman can best them in mathematics? That they would allow a single woman to be in their venerated chapels, revealing you are not just Adam's rib? You are the proof against all they say and do about the inferiority of the fair sex. No, they will burn their schools before letting you in. They will flay you alive as they did with Hypatia*."

"Then, I will become a nun, like St. Etheldreda or Sor Juana. They were not a threat, and could do what they wanted."

"Over my dead body!" he swore — indomitable — and walked out.

****

This was wrong — very wrong. He called Wickham to duel for such a paltry thing as my honor! I remembered the wound on his leg; the flesh whose perfection was profaned by Wickham's sword and a surgeon's needle. It could not happen again! What would he do if he knew what happened in

209

Derbyshire? I moved to stand by the window. Thankfully Churchill had left for America; there was no danger in that score — at least for now.

But it was not enough. Not enough! I had to do something.

"Mrs. Robson told me, you asked for a tray with your dinner." He was a few strides behind me. "I suppose it means tonight I will have to hear you, and will have to stay on the other side of that door while you cry... until morning comes and I am left to pick up the pieces."

There was a combination of sadness and ire in his voice difficult to bear. *Do not turn around, Elizabeth.* He would read your thoughts if I did.

I heard a maid enter almost noiselessly and place the food on the table. I waited.

"I see you prefer to be silent."

A long pause issued until his strides indicated he was gone.

Disgusting. You are disgusting Elizabeth. He would go after Wickham again if he heard my memories while I slept. I pictured the villain firing at him in a duel with swords. He was the kind of scum that would draw a hidden pistol when he was threatened. Fitzwilliam would be surprised by a discharge into his abdomen. He would look down to ascertain the source of the pain. He would see he has been shot. He would look up, astonished. He would fall to the grass in agony. He would die in someone else's arms.

Do not cry, Elizabeth. Do not cry. Find a solution. Do not cry! I walked in the direction of the dressing room. Here was where the connecting door was. The other room had to be the mistress'. I listened. He was restless. He stopped several times in front of my door. I locked it soundlessly when I thought he was farthest from it. I perceived he sometimes reclined in the same place. I imagined his forehead close to mine and slid down to snuggle on the floor. I could not stay here. He would find out sooner or later if I did. I saw my old male robes on a ledge and decided to put them on. *Think, think, think!* I took off my dress and started to wrap my bosom. First priority: he could not know it happened in Derbyshire. I grabbed the shirt and inserted my arms in it. Second: he could not know it was Wickham. I began buttoning the cloth. Third: He could not run into Jack. He suspected something about him already. I put the trousers on. Fourth: Marrying me would have been a discredit for him. This rupture was unavoidable.

Where was the looking glass? It was in the bathing room. What was I doing? I looked at the boy who was staring at me with revulsion. This was cowardice. *At least tell you are going to leave!* I went back to the main room. I would write a letter. To leave something for him to be in peace. I searched for ink and paper. He did nothing wrong. *At least tell him that!* I found the scissors instead. I WAS A COWARD! COWARD! COWARD! *TELL HIM TO HIS FACE!* I went back to the dresser. Where was that coat? I sat on the floor and started to cut the outfit mercilessly. "I hate you, Elizabeth!" I cried as I shredded it. "I hate you, Lizzy!" I did a large incision into the fabric. "I hate you, Ellis!" I attempted to tear at the extremities. It did not rip. It only made my injured hand sore. I stabbed with the sharpest blade; handling the scissors like a knife, "I hate you!" My vision was blurry, "I hate you! I HATE YOU!"

"You are going to hurt yourself." Fitzwilliam's hand extracted the weapon from mine.

I was dumbfounded by his presence, "By which door did you enter?"

"By the main one. The one in the hall."

"You should not have." I dried the dampness on my face with the sleeves of the coat. Oh my God, look how I was dressed.

He kneeled in front of me. "You were going to run away? Because of one argument, you were going to flee without telling me? You were going to leave me?!"

"No. I lacked the courage. I did not have the courage to even finish dressing!" I kicked one boot with rage, "I am a coward!"

"Do not any of the moments we shared here mean anything to you?"

"Because they mean the world to me, I have to go."

"You were going to do it because of Wickham. Because of what he did to you in Lambton. The same thing you attempted to do for your family."

"How do you know about Lambton? HOW DID YOU FIND OUT?"

"I was there. I was there the day he abused you." His voice cracked as his gaze hid downcast.

"No. You were not. I confirmed…"

"I was not in time. I have regretted all my life not paying attention when I was told George and the others were playing with a servant. I accompanied Richard to the church, where he stayed to chat with some teen girl, until this boy came. Jack — he was the one to ask for help. I followed him into the part of the wood where some lads were barricaded around Wickham. I could barely make out… I did not understand what was happening. They wanted to lay someone on the ground — they had paid money for this. After I pushed my way forward, I finally saw him clutching a small girl to a tree — almost asphyxiating you. The others were peering underneath your skirt. When I glimpsed your scared face, how you clang to the trunk behind, I pounced on Wickham and initiated the fight that would change our friendship forever."

"Wickham was strangling me?" My hands went to my neck. "That is why my throat constricts when I remember any of it. He was not handling me like the other boys!"

"Yes. You had your eyes covered that day, and I did not realize it was you. On the contrary, I have been bewitched by your eyes since the party at Lucas Lodge. Only when I met Jack Sthieve at Bingley's wedding breakfast, I found out it was you. When I understood why you fell ill after the ceremony in the church, the hurt I had caused when you were a child. I was too late getting there, in preventing Wickham from tricking you, and you have suffered the consequences of that negligence all your life. I implore you to forgive me. Forgive me, please. Forgive me." A single tear streamed down his cheek.

He has been through this nightmare too. "Fitzwilliam, look at me. I have something to tell you."

He obliged, showing the accumulated angst and remorse that crowded his heart.

All my resolutions broke in that instant. "You saved me that day. You saved me in Lambton, when you were a teen yourself, from an even worse public humiliation. You arrived at Cambridge before I was blind. You watched after me when I was there, and if it were not for you, I would have starved to death by now. You helped me make a home from that attic, and you filled my lonely days with joy. You have always been with me when I needed you." I pulled him towards me to say the next words, "You are my friend, and you are my love."

He closed his eyes as my words were soothing his tormented soul.

I looked at his inviting mouth, and back at his sealed eyelids. "I will kiss you now." I brushed his lips with mine.

I was separating, to ascertain if he liked my caress, when he took my head and pressed into me — capturing my lips with all of his mouth. I felt his lips enveloping me, how he moved from my lower lip to my upper lip, how he caressed them, massaged them, tasted them, pulled at them. His tongue invited me to let him in. His tongue — so wet and soft — explored mine, wrestled with mine, licked, examined, toyed, stroked everything in his reach; while his hands rubbed my head.

Slowly, I mirrored his movements. I lifted my hands and inserted my fingers in his hair. His assault brought a reaction that called to join the battle, to sip from his soul. I started to cradle, smooth, play and envelop him. I thrust my tongue into his mouth, I brushed his teeth, I savored his saliva — so sweet, so exquisite.

He aimed to catch his breath. I wanted more. I climbed on top of him and pressed him down onto the floor. I kissed him on the mouth. I nibbled at his lips. I caressed his cheeks with mine, "I love you." I kissed his eyes, "I love you." I kissed his nose, "I love you." I sampled all of his face, dampening it, "I love you. I love you. I love you."

He tried to do the same, most likely wishing to turn the tables on me, but the space was too narrow. We chuckled at a small "uh" after he scratched his hand on something on the floor, then he swiftly lifted me into his arms. We walked into the alcove, and I saw him ponder where to settle: the bed or the couch? He chose the latter. Again on his lap, he returned to kissing me.

Oh, how he kissed me! He alternated between hugging me, and caressing my back. He kissed my neck. He assaulted my mouth once and again. Coveting all of him, I rubbed his neck, his shoulder blades, his arms, his head. We persisted in our battle, our clothes a mesh of sweat and wrinkles, our tongues becoming one. I heard our agitated breathing. Our minds were losing the war against an unknown enemy. This was too much. I felt him hesitate. *You have to stop, Elizabeth.* He supported his forehead against mine, "Marry me."

"Hmm?" my senses were clouded.

"Marry me. Let us go to Scotland. Marry me!" his voice was, at the same time, supplicant and demanding.

"What about all those boys — men — from Derbyshire?"

"What about them?"

"You are not calling them out to duel, right?"

"It did not cross my mind."

"Thank God," I sighed. "And Wickham?"

"I already did that. I think once is enough. Do you not think so?"

"More than enough. Yes. Still, I need some more time to think. I... How you can accept someone that has kept so many secrets from you? Someone that is soiled like me?"

"You are not soiled. Not to me. And besides, I know all of your secrets. I have your diaries."

What? "You have my diaries? You read them?" I grabbed my head with both arms, shielding behind my elbows.

"I found them in your church. I went searching for you there the day you disappeared. I..." He pulled me back into his chest, "That part of the building was in precarious conditions, but something called me to climb the tower. I do not know. I just... It is... I was seeking clues of your destination. Any clues. The diaries made me understand you. I wept many times. It is compelling reading, and I am a weak being when confronted with tales of your past."

He had my diaries! With thoughts I would never dare say even to my shadow. "You still love me? Despite the awful things I wrote while in Hunsford, and the way I distrusted you when the Lucases accused you?"

"If I remember well, you wrote, 'His proposal was insulting: to speak of Mother and Father as if he knew anything about them! About all they had been through! No, it was well done. And if he knew the real me, he should be disgusted by me. I did him a service'." He kissed my shoulder, "I only see you judged me rightfully — I slighted your family without knowing

214

them — and you tried to protect me. You did the same when you decided not to write back to Georgiana; the same as when the Lucases threatened to marry me to their daughter."

"I doubted you! I lied! I kept secrets from you! I…"

"We all have a skeleton or two in the closet. Your diaries — they only made me love you more. You were a lovely child. All the tales from your childhood are endearing. I just hope someday you will give me a daughter to enjoy the same things your father must have done with you." He gently removed my limbs. "The things you went through made you this guarded. It is not your fault."

"Then, why did not you tell me before that you had them? Why did you not tell me, you were there?"

"Why? I almost did, but then I pondered how much pain those memories bring to you. When you saw Jack at the wedding, you hid. When you remembered Wickham was there, you ran away. When you thought your father wrote about it, you trembled like a leaf. When you were drunk, you said you would die if I knew." He took my head in his hands firmly, his eyes full of agony again, "And when you remembered yesterday you were blinded — please, Elizabeth, swear you will never think about dying again!"

"I have no reason for that anymore. I am still a maiden, thanks to you."

"Yes. About that. About 'You have to be brave and it will be finished soon'. You know I would not harm you. Do you not?"

"I know. I know." I kissed him fast on the mouth and returned my gaze to my thighs. *Just do not touch my lower body.*

"Is that a yes?"

I nodded.

"A yes?!"

"Yes," I whispered, and dared to look up. He was <u>so</u> handsome when he shone like that. I felt a blush spreading up from my bosom at the same time as a grin burst forth, "My William."

"My Elizabeth." He inclined his head to lean slowly, "My wife."

We shared the sweetest of kisses, and he asked if he could sleep on the couch during the night. I agreed for him to stay if he promised not to mistake his bed with mine.

"Yes. I know my Lizzy is afraid I may allow a bull in this room."

---

*Hypatia (AD 350–370–March 415) was a Greek mathematician who was brutally murdered in Alexandria by a mob of Christians led by "Peter the Reader". She was also a prestigious astronomer and philosopher.

Chapter 21

"Would you let me change then? Please?" I moved off of his lap.

He went to the connecting door. Once there, he stopped and turned around.

He grabbed the scissors that had been carelessly dropped on the floor, and approached again. "Can I do something I have dreamed of — a vagary of sorts?" He looked at me with those eyes so difficult to refuse. "I promise it is harmless, it will not go far beyond what we have already sampled."

I looked at him intrigued, while he reached for the quilt on the bed.

He placed the enormous counterpane over my shoulders, arranging it to cover my breasts. "This is for you to feel confident I will not do anything to observe you without your permission." He placed a chaste kiss on my forehead and started to unbutton the front of my shirt. "You are not going to dress like this ever again. Right?"

I could only nod, as I did not dare answer with words. Trust him, Lizzy. He undid the last button holes.

Two fingers slipped underneath the fabric that wrapped my bosom, from where it ended close to my belly, and a cold blade slid between my skin and the offending garment. He was cutting it.

The tattered wrap fell open. He pulled the severed pieces from around me and dropped them to the floor.

Two fingers traveled the valley in the center of my bosom with a gentle touch. "I never thought I could be jealous of a book, until you mentioned it remained here for a couple of days. You are beautiful. I cannot wait to show you off as my bride."

"I do not think that is such a good idea, unless I wear a bonnet," I teased, to ease the tension.

"It is hard to behave like a gentleman at times. Like today. Like that day in the attic. Only today I inflicted this on myself," he lifted my chin, bestowing a soft kiss on my lips. His pupils were so full of — *bliss?*

"We had better change as planned. It will not do to wake up with dark circles under our eyes if you are planning to show me off," *which I hope you are not.*

"Yes, I will be back soon. Tomorrow will be a busy day."

****

This day had been such a chaotic flush of news, successes and revelations, that I found myself quite overwhelmed. I had recovered my eyesight; I had met many of Fitzwilliam's staff; I had been relieved of the fear Mr. Churchill could do us more harm; I had seen Fitzwilliam's drawings; I had discovered that he had been wounded in a duel with Mr. Wickham; I had almost run away again; and I had learned he was able to prevent the worst from happening, many years ago.

Most importantly, I had agreed to marry Fitzwilliam.

Mrs. Darcy. I was the future Mrs. Fitzwilliam Darcy. I was his betrothed. I was going to be <u>his</u>.

Why did he read my diaries? Because he was searching desperately for me, or because he wanted to own me? I never planned to get married! How was I ever to risk my body, my dreams, my heart, to belong to someone else? How? The familiar taste of doubt was threatening to pervade my guts. It was more destructive than anything else. It ought to be pushed far away. At any cost. For the reason that this 'someone' was Fitzwilliam!

****

Having dressed in new night clothes, I went to lie in the bed that had become mine. The one that would likely be our marriage bed. I looked at the couch he would use for the night. Poor dear, he was so eager to share these hours, he was going to try to fit on that sofa.

Remembering the kisses we had just shared there, I felt my heart rise and a blush spread up from my torso to my face. I turned around and hid under the pillow, to hide my shame. The picture of his hungry kisses intruding. He was like a mad man after months of starving.

I asked myself why I had permitted all that. The truth, Elizabeth, the truth!

I had the purpose of distracting him from the search of Mr. Churchill — a purpose built in the despair of finding myself blind with him in the carriage from Cambridge. Yes, that was one incentive... and that I had enjoyed his proximity since the day he trapped me on those stairs to the attic. Why?

Because of the feelings — the unexpected feelings — his touch brought.

And here is where I lost track of my own reasoning. How to explain the contradiction between what I thought it should have been, and what it truly was? How was I to solve the puzzle between the information ingrained in my brain from the teachings received — the disgust and pain connected to marital relations — and the actual longing his lips and fingers provoked in me? How?

****

On Monday, I woke up early, with a strange mesh of exhilaration and alarm. I was happy to find Fitzwilliam's hand and mine intertwined by my pillow (he must have moved the sofa when I was asleep); yet, I was worried about the consequences if any of the servants discovered us like this. I inspected his beloved features. I had to ask him how he earned the small scar in his cheek. It was well-healed. Was it from some adventure in his childhood. Or maybe from his years in Cambridge?

Today I should write to my family and tell them the news. Mama would be happy — and Papa — I did not know about Papa. I pictured the wedding. It could not be in Scotland. I had to make Fitzwilliam understand I could not do that to them. I needed to clear the issue of my escape, and restore my reputation and the Bennet name. Although, it was better to have a quiet ceremony, I wished Jane could accompany me at the altar.

I was overwhelmed with the change my life was going to undertake; also aware of the shock my appearance would raise in the circle I was going to enter now. The *ton* would not like that I had stolen the most eligible bachelor from them. And I would have to live a significant part of the year in Derbyshire. I knew how reticent people were to receive new inhabitants.

"What are you thinking about that is bringing such a frown?" Fitzwilliam dragged our hands toward my forehead to erase the lines there.

Apprehensive he could read my craven thoughts, I smiled timidly. "Nothing important. I was just considering you should go to your room, before one of the maids sees us this way. You would not like for the mistress of Pemberley to be known by the brazen behavior of letting a man…"

Before I could say more, Fitzwilliam pulled my body, together with the quilt that was wrapped around me, to lie on top of him on the couch. He captured my mouth in that hungry way of his and spoke between kisses, "You said we had to be brazen." He secured my head to command it, "And I am unwilling to disappoint the mistress of the house." He placed his legs over my calves, "I would rather be called bold than risk being removed, because the lady is bored in the morning."

Oh my, from where was I going to draw strength to make him leave? "We should not…" He nibbled my lower lip, "do this…" He dragged the upper into his mouth, "now…" He stroked my teeth to let him in, "when a servant…"

He won the precise moment I could no longer resist the urge to taste his tongue.

I felt his soft strokes, the sweet flavor, and all the rational thoughts ran away.

He repeated a pattern from my mouth to my neck — a chill invading my body; from my mouth to my earlobe — another wave claiming my senses; from my mouth to the hollow between my collarbones. *Oh God!*

Falling into an unknown dimension, my body started to be possessed by an energy that dragged me toward him. *Fitzwilliam.* His name filling all my thoughts. *Fitzwilliam.* I immersed my left hand in his hair. *Fitzwilliam.* I immersed my right into the back of his shirt. *Fitzwilliam.* I crushed him to me. *Fitzwilliam.*

"What were you saying?" he asked in one of his travels to my earlobes.

I love you.

He licked the valley of my ear. "Are you certain this is an inappropriate position?" he mocked.

I want you.

"Or would you rather rest a bit here?" He positioned my head to look me in the eyes.

I yearn for you.

He read my thoughts, "Oh, Lizzy," and rested my head on his heart, loosening the grip over my legs. We stayed like that for several minutes until our minds cooled down. "You do not know what you do to me."

"I?"

"You."

"You started this."

"Yes. But you are the one that can drive a man to bedlam with a gaze."

****

When he went out, I resumed the previous ideas that were crowding my brain. There were many questions yet to solve regarding the events of the day of the Gardiners' wedding. To understand how it was that he was at Pemberley during Easter, and who was the adult that had appeared at the end were the most critical ones. Ahhh. Could not that issue be postponed a bit? It could drive him to be more explicit about a subject I was not ready to approach.

During breakfast, we shared the meal in the dining room for the first time. And, although my companion was all politeness, and the epitome of propriety, I was aloof and shy.

I did manage to clarify my wishes to wed in the presence of my most beloved family members. Fitzwilliam suggested it could be in the small chapel of Pemberley, and that we could travel the moment I wished for it. I could not answer with an immediate "yes," as he would have liked, but I did begin to consider the idea.

An uncomfortable moment passed when we finished our meals and headed to his office.

"Elizabeth," he asked for my full attention while closing the door behind us, "I have to spend the morning with a friend, as I need to attend to some urgent business. I must leave you alone for a short period of time. Would you promise not to do anything reckless during my absence? Do you promise to wait for me here, without venturing into the street, or doing some other dangerous activity?"

"You are scared I might run away again," I removed an errant curl from his forehead. "Is it not true, love?"

"I cannot chain you to me as I would like, in order to be sure of your wellbeing. I must trust you know how much you mean to me, and that you would not hurt me with your absence again."

"This is not necessary, dearest. I know how much my safety means to you. I have experienced the sting of despair from your absence. I know how it feels picturing the worst, too. I will wait here, writing a couple of letters: one to Charlotte and the other for Longbourn. You will never have another reason to be afraid. I have learned the promise of our moments together is the best incentive for me to keep you safe."

"I look forward to a quiet afternoon in your company then."

"Would you lend me my diaries?"

He signaled for us to approach the desk. In a drawer with a key, were my three old diaries and a braid — *my* braid and a ribbon from the broken dress binding it. So, this was where it went the day in the garden.

He also showed where I could find anything necessary to write my letters and the many pencils he used for his drawings.

When he left, with a demeanor that expressed clearly his reluctance to do so, I sketched a rational plan to clarify my motives for running away, and the happy news about my wedding. I spent quite a while discerning what they already knew about that day in Lambton. After perusing my own notes and picturing Fitzwilliam's tale yesterday, I confirmed Mama did not know about the presence of Jack in the game those boys had played on me. No one saw Wickham — that was why his face was not familiar to her. The only source my parents had of what happened in the wood, was the version given by the adult I remembered at the end.

They could have been totally misinformed by that man. Mama could have had other motives for...

Misinformed. Like I about intimate relations. The thought triggered the subject that would not give me peace. Could any of the books surrounding the room help clarify my doubts? No, Lizzy, NO. It would be too much trespassing. I remembered the strong admonishment received from Mama, when she found me taking some of Papa's without consent. *Do not even think about that!*

****

It was hard to write the letters to my parents and Charlotte. It was useless without a clear idea of when and where the wedding was going to take place. What about taking my time? What about making those decisions tonight and writing afterwards? They knew I was not on the run anymore. They knew I was safe. Better to ponder my alternatives while spending more time with the household employees.

I found Mrs. Robson and the maids in the kitchen, and asked to stay with them for tea. Vivian was taking care of her two beautiful girls, one of them, a three-month newborn. She gave me the opportunity to cradle her for a while. The housekeepers from Pemberley and London kept a close correspondence. I asked the maids which of them would like to accompany us to that state, in the event of traveling soon, and found Lillian was more than pleased to be a part of the expedition. "She is in love with one of the drivers," Mrs. Robson shared in my ear.

The homely atmosphere gave me pleasure. I enjoyed a couple of sweets Cook offered, and forgot the outside world for a time. The baby in my arms, her tiny nose, her little fingers and snowflake nails, her light hair, were strong incentives for forcing further away some of my doubts.

"I do not know if women are chosen by God to be mothers because they are the most lovely sight to behold, or if they are the most lovely sight to behold because they are mothers," an unknown voice startled us.

At the door, a man of tanned complexion was looking at me with inquiring eyes. My fiancée was peering proudly from behind the gentleman. *Oh, my. He was serious about showing me off.*

I stood up and curtsied, trying not to wake up the warm bundle in my charge.

"This is my friend Adam Sedgwick*, Elizabeth." Fitzwilliam strongly patted the back of his companion and pushed him aside to walk in my direction. "We studied together at Cambridge. He is like a brother to me."

"It is an honor to meet you, sir."

"He came here under the incentive of a good lunch and a worthy opponent in the subject of the origin of the Continents**," Fitzwilliam opened his eyes in my direction as someone that is communicating some clandestine message.

I do not know what you are trying to say, love.

"You have studied Alexander von Humboldt's articles," the newcomer explained.

You read my new diary too! "I think he is the only worthy opponent in that subject, sir. I only managed to read a small part of his work." *You sly thing!*

"Yes, but be aware of her questions, my friend." Fitzwilliam signaled for Vivian to take her child from my hands and guided us to the hall. "She will make you see the weaknesses in your theories as if she were an expert."

****

Lunch was a quiet affair; taking into account how uncomfortable I felt with the idea that Mr. Sedgwick could think I was something more than Fitzwilliam's fiancée. Our guest was familiar with everything related to the Darcys as this was a sincere and long friendship. He related about his new work in the subject of 'The Superposition of Strata,' and about how much he looked forward to the many excursions he planned ahead.

He had investigated many of the caves in Derbyshire, and they were both skilled in the sport of climbing mountains and exploring the interiors of the

Earth. Pemberley was their headquarters while exploring The Peaks, and during all those other adventures they described.

Fitzwilliam explained, although his favorite subject was astronomy, he found geology matters to be useful in his own study of the universe. "Under the hypothesis that the other planets have a similar origin, of course."

The reunion ended with an invitation for him to visit again, and for me to accompany them on their next exploration.

****

After the departure of the gentleman, Mrs. Robson informed us there were letters waiting for the master in his work room, and some new clothes waiting for me upstairs.

My fiancée sent an apologetic look, while I went to take a warm bath and see the prettiest clothes I have ever imagined.

He was spoiling me. He was spoiling me, and I was enjoying it unabashedly.

"Elizabeth, I have good news," I heard Fitzwilliam say through the closed door to the hall.

The sisters interchanged an amused look, and I asked for them to help me put on one of the day dresses. "I will come to your study if you give me just a few moments."

"I think you would not like to wait if you knew what the news is."

"Well then, tell me now." I started to slip into the new gown.

"The Bingleys are in England. They are asking for an invitation to spend a couple of days at Pemberley."

What? I ran to the door (without paying attention to the fact that my state of undress exposed my upper back) and opened it to snatch the letter from his hands. I tried to read the illegible handwriting, and understood they were in Scarborough, that they were supremely happy with the trip. Charles seemed as cheerful as ever, and described his time with Jane as one of the most memorable… *I should not be reading this*. I returned the paper self-conscious.

"Is anything the matter?" I asked, when observing his gaze was directed at my shoulders.

"Can I help you with the hooks?"

"Which hooks?" I reached to touch my back. Would I ever manage not to embarrass myself in front of him?

"Please."

I turned around. It was most unfair I could not say 'no' to him.

He secured the first hook and placed a lingering kiss on my nape. A shiver covered my left arm. He fastened another and mirrored the previous caress at my right. Another frisson took possession of me. I was going to lose my wits before he finished clasping them all.

"AHEM!" Mrs. Robson startled us with a light cough. "Mr. Darcy."

Fitzwilliam released the fabric abruptly and moved one step backwards. "Yes, madam."

I heard the giggles of the maids on the other side of the door, and became conscious they <u>all</u> knew we were doing something too forward.

"A Mr. Cochran and his wife are requesting to see you, sir."

"Beth is here?" I glanced at Fitzwilliam, surprised.

He linked his hands in his 'Master of Pemberley' posture, "Ask them to wait in the drawing room. We will join them right away."

Mrs. Robson curtsied, and my companion followed her to the stairs with secure strides. Once the housekeeper was out of sight, he turned to wink at me. *Oh, love, you have perfected that mask exceedingly well.*

Shifting my gaze to the door of <u>his</u> room, I reasoned for the hundredth time this was developing too quickly. Living together was inevitably throwing us into uncomfortable situations!

****

When I reached the drawing room, it was evident in the faces of all those present that some grave news was to be imparted. Fitzwilliam's demeanor reminded me of the moment he thought I had broken my hand. Mrs. Beth was looking at her lap and Mr. Cochran was showing discomfiture and grief (much more than I would have expected from such a strong man).

Greeting, I sat next to Beth. She took my hands in hers and her husband imparted with the saddest of voices, "Mr. Falcon was assassinated yesterday. Someone stole the catalogues, and the rest of the evidence of your poisoning, and shot him. We do not know who can be the perpetrator of these incidents."

---

*Adam Sedgwick was a prominent geologist and was the tutor of Charles Darwin. These two men shared a close friendship, although Sedgwick was not inclined to believe in the Theory of the Evolution of Species. The scenes where he appears in this book are all fictional.

**The process of the evolution of the Earth (the formation of the continents and the composition of the land) has been described with detail by different theories over the years:

- There was one theory which stated all the rocks are the result of sea sediments (no volcanic activity). The limestones (minerals based on Calcium) were in the bottom of the ocean, deposited from 1000 million years ago to about 116 million years ago. These waters retired when, around 50 million years later, the internal forces of the Earth produced compressions, foldings, brakes and lifts of the sedimentary rocks.

- Another theory stated he origin of the dry earth is in the volcanoes. They were the driving force for the existence of the mountains and islands around. The last eruptions occurred around 60 million years ago.

- James Hutton unified these theories. What we have is a mesh of both processes, as a result of cyclic movements of ups and downs. Many times what we see is that the sedimentary rocks have incrustations of volcanic rocks. At the same time, the volcanic rocks are silicates that have intrusions of metals.

Chapter 22

I looked at my friend for confirmation. Tears were impeding her speech. Mr. Falcon had been murdered.

"He was killed during the hours the church is always empty. He should not have been there on a Sunday afternoon. This could have been prevented if we had not advised you to take that job," the reverend affirmed.

This was my fault then. I dug my nails into the palm of my hand. He had been killed in my place!

Fitzwilliam came to kneel in front of me and stopped my nervous movements. "You are not to blame for this, Elizabeth. Do not do this to yourself."

Beth embraced me. "At least he is with his Barbara now."

I was too shocked to say anything rational, too overwhelmed to think clearly. "He was a good man. He was… He did not deserve such a death."

My betrothed looked at me apologetically and signaled to the vicar to leave the room as Mrs. Cochran and I comforted each other.

Why would someone hurt Mr. Falcon? He was harmless. He was just a lonely man. "The person who poisoned me is determined." Mr. Churchill was at sea. It meant someone else was behind all of these attacks. Someone else was after me. We were still in danger. "How else can we explain he killed a harmless person like a librarian? I do not think this has anything to do with my job." Who could be so angry at me? What had I done to deserve such hatred? "I should do something to prevent more deaths."

"You are not thinking of running away again. You cannot!"

"No. No. That would make Fitzwilliam miserable. That would drive him crazy."

"I am glad you are taking him into account. Mr. Darcy seems to me a righteous man. And you have only to observe him a couple of minutes to ascertain he is deeply in love with you."

"You were right about that, when you told me in King's College. I have been blind in more than one sense."

"Has he proposed?"

I nodded.

"And did you agree to marry him?"

"Yes. I did."

"I am very happy for you. There is nothing in the world more wonderful than being with the man you love."

"Yes, but this decision puts him in danger as well."

"You should not be thinking about that. You are not responsible for everything that happens around you. You must have faith. You must stop attempting to control the future — it shows lack of trust in our Lord, and a bit of arrogance, too."

"Arrogance?" I asked, feeling scolded again, like when we were planning my moving into Cambridge.

"Believe it or not, it is what lies under all those self-protecting layers you have constructed around yourself. You think it is in your capacity to prevent all the events in your path." She released me to lighten her speech with a smile. "I know you are trying to protect the people you care about, but you cannot. No one can bear so much weight on their shoulders. You must release some of it, and be willing to travel this life with God at your side."

Male voices were in the hall. The men entered, and an invitation for the Cochrans to stay for the night was issued and accepted. According to my betrothed, there was a lot to plan.

****

My friends were guided to the guest wing, and Fitzwilliam and I headed to his study.

"Elizabeth," he eased onto the couch and sat me on his thighs, "I have to advance the report of the business I attended in the morning. I wanted it to be on another occasion — a more romantic one. After the news we just received, it cannot be. It was not my intention to use this document yet. I went to see my friend Sedgwick, because he has close connections in the clergy, and I thought he could advise me as to how best to obtain a special license* dated a few weeks ago. We ended up in the archiepiscopate's offices here in Town, and it is most probable the permit will be ready as soon as tomorrow, early in the morning."

"I do not see any problem with you accomplishing that particular errand. I agreed to marry you, after all."

"Yes, but what I need to tell you is why we should marry right away after I get it, and why the official date of our wedding must be around the days you were in Newmarket."

"What do you mean by right away?"

"Tomorrow. I want us to marry tomorrow. I have spoken with Mr. Cochran and he has agreed to marry us, once I get the license. Although, I would like to speak with Mrs. Robson today and cut the gossip between the servants, by informing we are already married."

"You want us to appear as a married couple before even announcing our engagement!? I thought you abhorred lies, Fitzwilliam."

"I do. But it is what will help the most in our relationship with your family, and more decisive: to do it soon will ensure your safety, as I want to travel right away to Pemberley after we marry."

Despair precipitated this. "You are scared, are you not, love? You are doing this out of fear."

"I am not marrying you out of fear. You know for certain I have been decided since Hunsford. If I am frank, this has been my dream for more than a year now. I would have liked to give you some time to become accustomed to the idea of our marriage — it is something you only decided yesterday, after all."

"Fitzwilliam, everything that one does has consequences. Every lie, every incorrect decision, has its punishment. Are you sure you are not going to repent doing something so very final in a rush?"

"Why would I repent?" he frowned.

"I have nothing to contribute — not even beauty. I am ugly without my long hair."

"Nothing to contribute? Ugly? Are we speaking of the same person? The Lizzy I know is much more than all those so called accomplished ladies. No, no, no. You are grossly mistaken. You are better than any women I know: you are authentic. Besides, if you are thinking about the things considered fashionable, let me tell you: you only lack the certain air. And I am willing to provide it in case of emergency," he added, blowing on my neck in a clear attempt to light things up.

I rubbed my arms. "I am afraid."

"Afraid of what, Lizzy?"

"I am afraid of everything. I am afraid of the man that is after me. I am afraid of disappointing my father even more, and of never having his love and acceptance again. I am afraid of encountering the people that know about my mistakes in Derbyshire — all those neighbors that whispered under their fans when I was a girl. I am afraid of not being good enough for you in the eyes of those who matter to you… I am afraid of… I am afraid of…"

"Making love?" he completed the thought I could not bring myself to say. "Let us look at all of those fears one by one, shall we? We should go to Derbyshire because it is far enough away for us to feel confident we are not in danger. Not you, not me, not any other person we care about. It is in order to safeguard us all, that we should go. Would you let me protect you, night and day, as I wish to do? Would you let me do the same as you have been doing for me since Hunsford?"

Traveling that far should prevent another attack. I nodded against his shirt, remembering his desperation when he had found out I had been poisoned.

"Good. Now, about your family. I do understand you would have liked to walk to the altar with your father. It is a tradition, and I respect your wish to be able to have the man that means so much to you, escort you. Yet, you are already one and twenty, and it is not a requisite you must fulfill in the eyes of the law. We are only considering not taking his opinion into account in this matter, because of the hazard your life is under now. You must agree it is too risky to wait until he consents to accept me, under the present circumstances. On the other hand, if I know your mother well, I think she will have a different reaction from your father's. She will be supremely happy to have another of her girls married. Am I right?"

I nodded another time, picturing the proud exclamations of my mother when she heard the news. It would be quite the comedy act when she found out.

"By the way, if we invite the Bingleys, we will have your sister's support to intercede with your parents. They are close enough to Pemberley to join us within a week of our arrival." He paused to ponder his next words. "About those people that could identify you — which I consider highly unlikely — my only fear is what will happen if you learn something else, something new to both of us that could hurt you even more. I just beg you to love me still if you find out that, because of my actions, you were further harmed that day."

"I will never blame you. You rescued me. And, I would not be able to fall out of love, even if you were one of the boys that…" I took a deep breath, "played with me."

"I am happy you are realizing it was just a game for them. That they were not necessarily bad. Some of them were too young. They just overlooked the consequences. They lacked the foresight to see this was going to leave scars. You were just an unknown girl, after all. People care little about those they have not met before. This is part of human nature. I would like you to understand they were not concerned for you, because you mattered little to them — as it matters little to me what anyone but Georgiana and Richard think about you."

"Would you tell me about them? About how to please your sister and your cousin in order to gain their esteem?"

"You do not have to do anything except to be yourself. They both like you. It is impossible not to like you. That is why I must rush to marry you before someone else offers for you."

"You are making fun of me. You know no one in his right senses would do such a thing."

"Are you saying I am not in my right senses, Miss? Are you saying that I am a crazy man?"

"Yes, you are."

"Yes. So much more after tasting these soft lips. However, do not think you can distract me from our last topic with temptation, petite fairy. I know you spent all night thinking about lovemaking."

I was confused about the source of his knowledge.

"You know you speak while sleeping," he placed a warm hand over my belly. "And I was able to discover a couple of things while you were dreaming." *Oh my God.* "It served to confirm how much you enjoyed my caresses and how eager you are to have our children."

I CANNOT HIDE EVEN MY MOST PERSONAL FEELINGS FROM HIM! "Fitzwilliam, is it not enough for you to read all my diaries?! You have to know this too!" I wanted to stomp the floor with my foot, but it was impossible while seated on his lap. "You will have to sleep in your own room tonight."

"What? You are…" He separated to scrutinize my face. "You are throwing me out of your room because I received the gift of knowing I have managed to raise, even a tiny inch, your fears about intimate relationships? Because I have learned you are starting to fantasize about me, the way I have done with you for so many months? Is that a sin? Is it a sin that I desire to be with you, and make love each night until we die? Is it a sin to want to awaken the same sentiments in you? You think I should be punished for that?"

He had experienced this yearning for months?! I opened my mouth a couple of times, amazed. He wanted to have intimate relations every night?! Was this his idea of not harming me? I focused on the eyes that were a strange tangle of sadness and incomprehension.

And then, the strangest recognition came: I grasped what passion brings. It makes a mess of your life. It destroys everything in its path. It takes away any peace you could have had. There were only two roads to be taken in front of such formidable forces: to control this threat and surrender to an empty life, or to take the chance and expose our helplessness.

The awareness that this was why he had hesitated about offering for me before Hunsford struck me — the battle he must have gone through! Now, I was the one hurting him. *Let him do with your body anything he wants. It cannot be worse than what he is suffering by your rejection, Lizzy!*

"I am sorry," I moaned. "I do not know why I say these things. I…" I prepared to kiss him with the same ardor he had taught me, but stopped and said, "I made the resolution of trusting you today. I have belonged to you since the first time I saw you from a tree on Oakham Mount. You are the owner of my thoughts and my dreams." I inserted my fingers in his hair to drag him towards my mouth. "I will marry you the moment you want me. I will be yours the moment you come to take me. I swear I will never injure you again with my doubts."

"Do not be afraid of me, Lizzy. Please. I just want to love you. I will not take anything from you until you are ready."

****

While Fitzwilliam spoke with Mrs. Robson, I went to attend the guests. I do not know the specifics of the information he shared with her. Nevertheless, I could clearly see the changes in the household's deferential treatment during dinner.

Startled, the first time one of the servants called me Mrs. Darcy, I could not take the eyes from my plate during the conversations. Once the uncomfortable affair was concluded, we moved to a private sitting room, to discuss the plans for the morrow. I was informed the vicar has agreed to perform the ceremony in his own chapel. It was decided we would travel with the Cochrans to Newmarket right away (as soon as Fitzwilliam concluded his business in the Archbishop's office) and for us to start the trip to Pemberley the same day.

I excused myself to write to my family, and Charlotte, to invite them to the reception Fitzwilliam and I had agreed to have in Derbyshire (to belatedly celebrate our marriage). I hoped they would come, and not be too grieved that we married without their knowledge. I could not tell them the truth of it, at least not by letter, as it would undo all the detailed work William had accomplished to protect me. I wished Jane arrived soon.

While I was engrossed in the last letter, the maids were packing my clothes.

Lillian was so proud to be, "the one chosen by Mrs. Darcy to be her abigail," I could not help feeling her enthusiasm was contagious. I was so silly! Why did not I see tomorrow was one of the most transcendental days of my life? I was going to be Fitzwilliam's wife! Yes! I would have the privilege to hold him and kiss him freely. I was going to be with him all the time.

****

The man of my dreams was examining a document on his escritoire, when I went downstairs. I closed the door, seeing an opportunity to lighten the solemn mood his face revealed.

"What is taking you so much time?" I asked while standing behind his chair. *Say something to erase the worries of the last conversation, Elizabeth.* "I thought you were eager to spend the night with me." I bent to tease his neck. "You are not behaving as expected of a husband during the first days of his marriage."

He pushed the papers away and turned around, tugging me to lie awkwardly on his outsized desk. "You know I cannot stand disappointing you, my lady."

I wanted to move to a sitting position. He placed his hands over my shoulders to stop my intent.

"Everything that falls onto this table must be thoroughly inspected by me," he stated with an academic expression whilst reaching for a cushion on his chair. "Let me see what we have here." He inserted the pillow under my head and moved to take off my slippers. "This is apparently a very interesting piece of art." He traveled with his eyes from my toes, to my thighs, my hips, my belly, my bosom, my neck, my lips. He was doing it again — a strange pull was developing under my navel. "Although it lacks some few touches." He pretended to be pondering his next actions, toying with an imaginary beard. "Where was that paintbrush?"

His arm immersed in the depths of a drawer that was full to the top.

"Here it is." He blandished the long instrument in front of my eyes, "Where were we?"

What was he up to? I aligned my hands along my body and crossed my legs.

Think of something, Elizabeth. Do not let him win! Tease him back. "By the way, Fitzwilliam, when were you going to tell me about that special license?"

He grabbed the stick, close to the brush, as I wondered about that snide smile that meant I was in trouble. "At your first sign of weakness or indecision," he grazed the top of my forehead with the drawing tool. "This part is too smooth."

"And what could be a sign of weakness?"

"A sign of weakness?" He followed to sweep my right ear. "It could be an involuntary shiver." He traced the line of my jaw, "A small groan." He swept the other earlobe, "A drop of chocolate on your luscious lips." He brushed the path from my chin to my throat and below my neck, "Another glimpse of your spine." He traveled the lane of my clavicles, "An invitation to sleep in your bed." He arched a quizzical brow while repeating the last road once and again, "This part is too soft, you know?" He pretended he was doing a meticulous job of fixing them. "And this small cleavage is just too inviting." He leaned to replace the instrument with his tongue in the middle between my bones. "Too sweet." He traced the previous path backwards. "Too delicious." He nibbled beneath my ear. "Too beautiful." He kissed my brows. "Too perfect." He rested his gaze on my mouth.

I closed my eyes. *Kiss me.*

"Yes. This could have been the ideal moment to show you that permit." He chuckled. "I am sorry to inform it is not ready yet, wife."

I opened my eyelids to discover he was standing upright, and presenting his right hand to help me rise from the desk. *You are not going to kiss me?! You cannot be serious!* "You are becoming quite proficient in detaching yourself from the object of your study, sir." I sat, annoyed. He wanted for me to boil just in front of him!

"Far from that, madam — I only realized this was the precise moment to show you our marriage agreement." He leaned closer as he reached for the document behind me. "This is what was keeping me busy when you knocked at my door. I hope you approve. Or I will have to find other weak spots to win this bargain."

I looked at the title and could not help the thought that this was undeserved.

I did not even have a dowry, for heaven's sake! I looked up to protest. "This is not nec…"

He placed a finger on my lips. "Read it first."

I lowered my gaze to start again, and was stopped in my intention when I had a glimpse of the prominent object, a few inches from the paper I had in my hands. Those pants were going to explode any minute. I giggled, "You are right."

"I am always right," he spoke with his haughty voice while I perused the agreement. "However, enlighten me, what is the particular subject that has provoked your approbation and your mirth at the same time?"

I played the part of the unconcerned reader. "It is evident you are quite affected by the *current* subject of your study." And I did not understand a single word of what was written here.

His gaze studied me questioningly. "You naughty girl!" He stole the papers and lifted me skillfully in his arms. "I think I can tell you all that is written there on the trip to our room." He walked in the direction of the door.

I saw how he battled with the key, to get out of his study, and laughed aloud at the uncomfortable position he was keeping — half kneeling with both arms supporting my weight. "I am not the only one to make a fool of myself now and then."

"You are laughing at my expense, ah? Let us see who has the final laugh." He transferred my weight to bend me over his shoulder. Wow!** He managed me as easily as a sack of potatoes. "Much more now that I have this fantastic view of your assets."

"Fitzwilliam!" I threw several punches to his back at the same time as he climbed the steps two by two. "Put me down!"

"Oh, no, Mrs. Darcy, I will show you now who holds the upper hand here."

We reached the second floor and were in the bedchamber in a blink. He laid me on the soft mattress, ejected my shoes with a fast move, and pressed his entire body to mine. *Do not open your legs, Elizabeth!*

"I think you will have to agree to all my terms now." He took both my hands in one of his and placed them atop my head, the other supporting part of him in order to avoid crushing me altogether. "Which are actually very few." He slid up over my body to trace kisses from my fingers to my armpits, from one arm to the other. He was all over me. His smell was so delicious! It was like immersing inside of him.

"I agree. I agree!" I exclaimed out of breath. "You do not have to explain them. I am sure they are flawless. They are natural and just. They are perfect. They are…"

"Natural and just? Are you insisting on teasing me, Lizzy? I would not do it if I were you." He started to bite all my fingers one by one. "I know of another place where this technique would be much more effective, if you insist on your endeavor to mock the master of this house."

"No. No. No," I beseeched when I realized his eyes were directed to my décolletage. "I found those words to be appropriate because they always jump into my head when I see you are right… I agree… I will do whatever you want."

He crept down till his eyes were at the same level as mine. He was burning inside. "Let me undo the hooks of your dress, and I promise to behave for the rest of the night."

"Allow me to turn around, then."

He removed himself from above my body to lie beside me, and I could see the silent combat that was being held within his heart.

I looked at the many wrinkles his attire had. "You should remove your coat too. Your valet will hate me after this mess." I pulled at the remains of his cravat and opened the first buttons of his shirt. He stood up while folding his outerwear onto the couch. "You can also sleep in my bed."

He took off his boots and returned to be with me. I laid with my stomach to the mattress to gather all the new sensations I knew were to come.

"I should have bought a nightgown with the opening at the back. I adore the line of your spine… I…" His fingers worked with the many hooks that were impeding his access to my skin. "I think I would rather ask you to stay with this dress on for the night. Just keep this opened, because I do not think I can hold back if you are clothed in anything else now."

"Only if you do the same. Although my mother would <u>kill</u> me if she knew I was sleeping in the same dress I wore during dinner."

"Not because you are sleeping with a man?"

"No. She will only make us marry for that."

"Why did I not figure that out when you stayed at Netherfield!"

****

I fell asleep with Fitzwilliam's caresses, and was awakened by a shake of my shoulders.

"Wake up, Elizabeth, wake up!"

I found myself seated on the bed with agitated breathing. *It was a dream.*

"Why were you screaming like that? Who is the man staring at you?"

"The man staring at me?" Where was I?

"Yes. Was it Churchill? Were you screaming because of <u>him</u>?"

"Churchill? No. He was not watching me."

Fitzwilliam went to find my last diary in the drawer, while I tried to replay the scene in the tavern in my mind's eye. "I am sure you mentioned something about an... Here, look." He signaled for me to read the lines: *"I tried to behave cautiously, to be invisible during the encounter, but to no avail. There was an unknown man staring at me..."* "Is this last unknown man Churchill? Is he one of the sailors? One of the students?"

"Wait dearest. One question at a time."

"You are afraid of him in your nightmares, Elizabeth."

"This last sentence... I do remember one gentleman scrutinizing all my movements. No. No. It was not only one man. All the three men that were on that adjacent table were pointing at us. And now that I think of it, those gentlemen were not drinking. I wondered why were they there, and if they knew I was not a boy. I had never met them before, though. The only face I was familiar with in that tavern, apart from my four friends, was the one of Mr. Churchill. During the introductions, I had remembered seeing him speaking with Mr. Cochran in Newmarket, and concealing something. We must ask tomorrow for the particulars of the relationship they had." An image from my nightmare intruded again, and I could not help the sharp pain of having provoked a man's death. "I should have left the pub that very moment. I am sorry for having gone. I thought it was harmless if I did not drink, and now… Mr. Falcon has been killed."

"Shhh. Shhh. We cannot change our past, and we all make mistakes. I have made enough mistakes to occupy your beloved King's Library, actually. You are correct. It is strange that the vicar had a friendship with such a despicable man. We can speak about this in the morning. Go back to sleep now. There will be plenty of time to discuss this issue in the carriage to Newmarket."

---

*According to "Regency Lore"
http://hibiscus-sinensis.com/regency/lore.htm:
"In the Regency the only place to obtain a Special License was from the office of the Bishop of Canterbury at Doctor's Common in London. Only the Archbishop had the privilege to issue such dispensations, which allowed a couple to marry at any place and any time, although still officiated over by a member of the clergy. A regular license could be obtained from any bishop, and they allowed dispensation from the reading of banns, yet the marriage had to take place in the morning and at the parish church of either the bride or groom. Both types of licenses were personal and nontransferable, needing the sworn statement by the obtainer that the couple was either of age or had their legal guardian's permission to wed. For most situations, a regular license would suffice."

**According to the Online Etymology Dictionary: 'wow' is a Scottish interjection from 1510.

Chapter 23

The next day I awoke alone as Fitzwilliam had gone to get the special license. I hurried through my morning routine, and went downstairs to share breakfast with our guests. Only Mrs. Beth was at the dining table. Mr. Cochran had accompanied my fiancée on his errand.

"Are you nervous, Elizabeth?"

"Yes."

"It is a normal reaction. Do not worry. This is the best decision," she reached for my hand and squeezed it lightly. "If you agree, we can have some private conversation before the men arrive. It was particularly useful in my case, when my Mama reassured me."

I smiled shyly at her and nodded in agreement. It was in vain, however. The gentlemen appeared just as we were finishing our meal, and the rush for the long journey began.

****

Mrs. Robson had everything ready for our departure before I had awoken. Hence, we were out of the house and seated inside the carriage in no time: the ladies on one bench, the men in front of us. It was a convenient arrangement, for them because they came in a rented coach, and for me, because my friend's closeness reminded me this was the correct choice. Look at your groom, Lizzy. He had never been so satisfied, so eager to…

"Miss Willoughby," I was startled by Mr. Cochran's strong voice; addressing me with a name I had almost forgotten*. *It must be because he read it on the official permit.* "Mr. Darcy has explained to me there are other suspects, apart from Mr. Churchill, in the attacks perpetrated in King's College. I would like you to relate what you remember, of any and all the men you met the day you were out with the students. I would like you to do it as meticulously as possible. It is imperative that we find the assassin."

Mr. Falcon was the one responsible for keeping the catalogues. He knew they were contaminated. They would ask the boys for a description too, as there were some other students they knew prior to that day.

"It is better to write those descriptions down." Fitzwilliam reminded me of the pencils I carried.

I started the onerous task immediately on blank pages of my diary as Mr. Cochran discussed his relationship with Mr. Churchill. He had met him through one of his colleagues. They were not close relations, save for the misguided idea that he could be useful to the abolitionist's cause. He explained he had believed him to be a functionary of the Glasgow Chamber of Commerce**, and said false information had urged him to use his services in order to learn about the slave trade.

"It was a colossal error. I cannot apologize enough for the injuries, and the loss, I have inflicted through my ignorance. The fight against human traffic is not something that can be done with the same weapons as spreading the word of our Lord. It must be done with cleverness, discretion and suspicion. We have to work together with the rest of the movement," he concluded as we were reaching the outskirts of Newmarket.

****

Come, come, Lizzy. I resembled mother before a fit of nerves. *There is no danger*, I tried to reason when the horses were stopping. *And you are marrying Fitzwilliam!*

Your Fitzwilliam.

My betrothed was the first one to step out of the carriage. He was making sure it was safe, regardless of the distance from Cambridge, I guessed, seeing the way he searched the land. This was the right thing to do. There was no way to have this ceremony in the house in London when, in the eyes of the servants, we were already married. The other passengers left their seats. *You see, all is well.* And, if the marriage certificate was backdated to the time I was living here, it was better to have the actual service as close to the official setting as possible. A cheerful spirit was the best way to start any endeavor.

Fitzwilliam helped me out of the coach with a bright smile. "I have the loveliest bride this church has seen."

I mirrored his expression, "And I have the silliest groom — too handsome and too silly," turning to see if the Cochrans were within hearing distance. "Did you bring the paintbrush for me to fix those...?"

I could not finish the thought. There it was, in the entrance to the vicarage, the reminder of my last mistake — a black mourning bow. *Mr. Falcon was their best friend. You have no right to be joyful, Elizabeth!*

Fitzwilliam followed my stare. He straightened his posture and took my hand to guide me inside. The two servants responsible for our protection took posts at the two entrances of the chapel. This was the farthest scenario from a happy wedding. I looked at the familiar benches and the place where I had been found by the vicar and his wife about a month ago. It all started here.

"Remember I love you," he said in my ear, as we had to separate at the altar.

Mrs. Beth took my hand and explained her husband was going to be back in a minute.

"Thank you for always being there for me, my friend."

"It has been an honor. My brave girl." She fixed the lapels of my pelisse and brushed lint from my shoulder. "I would have liked to have a child with your strength and good heart."

"I would not change the moments with you for anything."

"Now, smile. Only we, old ladies, are allowed to cry at weddings."

"You are not old!" I spotted the reverend approaching. Moment of truth.

****

The wedding came in a blur of warm and guilty feelings. Fitzwilliam was at my side, handsome as ever while reciting our vows, although I just had brief glimpses of the glow he radiated. My thoughts varied from: "You are putting him in danger" to "You are making him happy." Everything would be right when we were back on the road.

The Cochrans insisted that we stay for dinner. As it was the closest thing to a celebration, and our friends had done so much for us, we could not refuse.

"Where would you like to spend the night, Mrs. Darcy?" Fitzwilliam asked when we were having dessert.

How can you ask me such a thing in front of other people? They will find out we are sleeping together!

He reached for my hand over the table and played with my new ring. "Elizabeth?"

It slowly dawned on me, there was nothing improper in his question. "Oh, sorry. I did not realize it was this late." I gazed at the window, to pretend I had just noticed how dark it already was. "I do not know. The only beautiful memories I have from this town happened in this chapel. I would better rely on your knowledge." I turned to look at our hosts, "or yours."

"There is a cottage, about ten miles to the North, which have been leasing until recently. Mrs. Dashwood maintained it clean and cozy. I am almost sure Helen can have it ready in less than a couple of hours," Mrs. Beth's suggested.

We all agreed this was much more appealing than some inn, especially after my mishap in one of them. It was ten miles in the opposite direction from Cambridge; we were more than twenty miles from danger.

****

Save for the welcome opportunity to be with my Michael and his mother, the separation of sexes had to be time-consuming (Fitzwilliam had to do some extra arrangements). However, the voyage to the new accommodations was not actually long. And, with the fatigue the previous activities had brought, I dozed during that time.

"We have arrived, Sleeping Beauty. You will rest much more comfortably in a bed than here."

He promised to join us promptly as I walked with two armed footmen, Helen and Lillian, from the carriage to the house.

Opening the door, the cottage transmitted a personality that spoke about love and family. There was a small garden next to the main room infusing a cozy smell to the whole house. And, apart from beginning to take off the white cloths from the furniture, there was little my maids allowed me to do.

After enjoying a bath, I sat on the window frame. I looked at the expensive jewel I was wearing now — a pure gold band with three stones — and asked myself if it had an inscription inside. I took it off and read.

"I will cherish you forever." The devotion with which he has followed this oath impacted me. *I will cherish you too. My husband.*

****

We fell asleep between confessions, and woke up similarly: I was resting my head on his arm; one of his legs resting over my thigh. He wore a peaceful mien. Was it wrong that I felt happy? Was it wrong that I was enjoying this moment?

"Lizzy?" he called me with his eyes still closed.

"Yes, William?"

"I need a kiss to liven me up." He disentangled himself to lie on his back.

"Why do you move away from me then?"

"Because I am deceased until you give me that kiss." He dropped his head in the opposite direction and poked out his tongue.

Adorable. "Then, you will only come to life when I kiss you on your mouth. Agreed?"

He nodded.

Where should I start? I tried to lift his hand, and he made it look like a heavy, dead limb. *You should perform on a stage, love.* I took the quilt from

245

atop of us and placed it under his naked feet. *Mmmm. Let us see if you are ticklish.*

I went to take a feather that was on the writing table, while he followed my movements through half-opened eyelids.

I neared the bed from the end where I could do my mischief, as close as possible to his legs. I looked up at his face and saw him trying to suppress a smile. *You do not know what an expert I am in this art, Fitzwilliam!*

Using the writing implement I teased him on the arch of the sole of his left foot, for just a tiny fraction of a second. He suppressed the natural reaction of bending his limb. I repeated the same move on the other target, and he could not help a chuckle. "Remember you are dead, Mr. Darcy."

I brushed the left sole from bottom to top twice. This time he could not avoid inserting his foot under the discarded linens. *Got you!* I chortled.

I will not let you do the same with the other! I climbed on the bed and sat on top his right thigh, facing his feet I knelt with my legs at each side of his. I leaned to hold his calf firmly with one hand and started to torment him mercilessly. This time, his actor's skills failed him completely: he started to shake, laughing and moving randomly, provoking an earthquake in the whole furniture.

"I see you are determined not to kiss me, wife." He reached to take my feet and stretched them out, pulling me to slide over his body upside down. "Let us see how you react to the same practice."

Now I could not tease him any more! I unsuccessfully tried to turn around. It only served for him to snatch the feather I had used. "This is unfair. You said you were going to be still until I kissed you!"

"In love and war, all is fair." He held my legs firmly on his torso and tantalized me in return with his ability to tickle.

"Oh, no. Oh, no… Fitzwilliam stop! Fitz…Fitz…Fitz…STOOOOOP!" Why did I attempt this game, ahhhh.

I tried everything. I struggled to get loose. I kicked him. I pushed to get off his body. I even bit him lightly. It was useless. His gentle, but iron grip would not let me release even one foot. "Pleeeeease… This is too much!" I cackled like mad. "Pleeeeease…. My stomach… aches… from laughing!"

"You know I will only let you go when I come up with a good bargain," he said with a devilish voice, not slowing even a tad of his tortuous maneuvers.

"I will kiss you! I will kiss you!"

"The stakes are higher now."

"Pleeease?"

"I will stop, if you promise to stay immobile." He placed both hands around my ankles to indicate where he wanted them to keep at rest.

"No problem. I will do it."

He covered my soles with his long hands gently. "Your feet are so small."

I started to slow my giggles. "Yes, I think I could use your gloves as shoes."

He caressed my calves gently: from my knees to my heels. He stroked them several times, keeping them warm and allowing for me to calm my breath. What can he be up to?

He accommodated my nightgown and robe for me to be more comfortable. "Relax, Elizabeth. Relax. You do not need to do anything."

I placed my forearms over his knees to make the part of a pillow in this same funny position.

"Have you ever been to Bath?"

"Yes." This felt gooood.

"Imagine then, you are there on a sunny day. Picture yourself resting on the sand. Imagine that the only thing you can hear is the murmur of the waves and the sea birds."

Mmmm.

He started a massage at the bottom of my left foot, sliding his thumbs toward my heel a couple of times. He then placed his hands at both sides and started to squeeze in opposite directions. He repeated that mild squeeze several times in my toes and my heels. He pressed each thumb individually from base to top. He commenced to put pressure on my arch in circular movements, and ended back at the heel. He finalized that foot with loops around the ankle. Never have I felt anything so delightfully soothing.

He used the same procedure with the right limb, and I ended up perfectly sedated — purring like a cat. "My love, do we absolutely have to leave this cottage today?"

"Sadly, yes. We have to cover as much distance as possible. I only agreed with Mr. Cochran to have the ceremony here knowing it was impossible to do so in town. Particularly since he needed to be back soon." He readjusted us to lean together with his back against the head board.

His arms surrounded my waist. I could not help looking at the picture we presented in the mirror in front of us on the table. I observed his manly forearms in our reflection. I delighted in the contrast of our skins and forms. "I like the simplicity of this cottage a great deal. It has such a homey feel to it."

"It is truly inviting. Nevertheless, I have been barely able to sleep tonight with the fear of being found. I am sorry to do this to you on our first day of marriage."

"It does not matter, dearest husband. You have awakened me in the sweetest of ways. I never had such an interesting experience with my feet before. Would you teach me later?"

"Are you a devoted student, wife? Pensez-vous que vous pouvez apprendre l'art du massage?" he asked with his perfect French.

"I do not know, but I was told practice is the key to becoming truly proficient. By the way, Fitzwilliam, where did you learn that? I do not think this is taught in any of the books stored in Cambridge — not even in the Great Trinity College."

His playful visage changed instantly. "Where indeed?" He deposited me on the mattress, away from his body, and shifted to stand.

"William, is anything the matter? Did I do something wrong?"

"No. <u>You</u> did nothing wrong."

---

*According to MacDonagh, Oliver — Jane Austen, Real and Imagined Worlds. Yale University Press (1991) (taken from the Regency encyclopedia): "Adoption was not yet recognized in English law." This is why Elizabeth is still a Willoughby in any official document. People call her "Miss Elizabeth Bennet" in Meryton, just because it is what she has become for them after so many years.

** The oldest known existing commerce chamber in the English-speaking world with continuous records is the "Glasgow Chamber of Commerce", which was founded in 1783. The Regency Encyclopedia also speaks about the "House of Commerce".

Chapter 24

We dressed in separate rooms and packed hurriedly.

When I stepped out of the cottage, he was standing with four unknown men at the entrance — giving them some money. I looked in the direction of the two servants that were waiting to escort us, and understood the reason behind everyone's tousled appearance. *They probably spent the night awake, each in some corner near the house.* Those were guardians recommended by Mr. Cochran, when I missed Fitzwilliam last night.

We traveled to the vicarage, to return to the main road.

We found Mrs. Beth with open arms and a basket of food prepared for our trip. Her husband was already on his way to King's College, in order to arrange the funeral for Mr. Falcon. Attempting to look happier than she was feeling at present, she hugged me and declared not liking farewells. "Besides, you owe me a tour of your new home. We are going to see each other soon."

"I look forward to it."

"This is why you wanted to look for a job in the North. You were trying to be closer to your handsome beau."

This made me feel a bit self-conscious. Thankfully, I was saved by Fitzwilliam's approach. "Come, wife, we have taken advantage of our hosts long enough."

****

Once in the carriage, I waited for my husband to enter and arrange me on his lap. Strangely, he just sat beside me.

"Are you eager to see Georgiana? Is she expecting us?"

"No. Do you want me to send an express?"

"I do not know. Does she like surprises? Do you think she would like to be informed in advance, or would you rather appear at her door when we are not expected?"

"Appearing at her door might be better."

Where was the merry man that played dead in the earliest hours of the morning? "Is there the possibility of encountering some of your family? Does anyone live close to Pemberley? Does Colonel Fitzwilliam visit frequently? Can I meet some of my new relatives?"

"Maybe."

Aggrrr. "If you do not tell me what is the matter with you, I will have to use my own store of desperate measures." I kissed him on the mouth, hard.

"I have something to tell you. I have been thinking about this all night, and I will do it now." He inserted a leg behind my rear and rotated me to rest with my back toward him. "I just want you to listen to me until the end, and not look at me until I say so. I have asked you to trust me several times. However, it is obvious we will not reach a solid relationship before I can relate to you my own most intimate secrets."

Why was he sad? I arranged his arms around my waist.

"About eight years ago, my father contracted a muscular disease that started to consume him slowly and steadily. I was in my last years at Cambridge, and he would not let me neglect my studies. So each time I came to Pemberley, his deterioration was more and more evident — more painful to witness. The strong man that had been my father was now only capable of travelling any distance via carriage, his robust complexion became lean, and his tanned skin became pale. I visited during the holidays, and asked him to allow me to stay at his side. He would not let me. Several months afterwards, I found even a short trip was a strain to his deteriorated body. I would beg him to accompany me to London every time, for me to see him more often, and to be able to take care of him. He would say it was impossible to journey that far, and that he had too many things to attend on our land. I returned again and saw him struggling to walk. This scenario awaited every time I came, although Georgiana, a child less than ten years old, was the one to watch this process of misery closely, and witness the worst moments."

That must have been a terribly difficult experience for both of them. My mind depicted an old gentleman with my beloved's nature turning into a skinny and gray shade.

"At the end, it was evident he was incapable of doing anything by himself, not even his most basic needs, and I decided to take matters into my own hands. I sent my sister to live at a nearby estate, and I left college. Yes, I never graduated, if that is what you are asking yourself." He breathed in, like someone that had lost a precious thing. *To have to choose between his family and his vocation!* "My dear parent was exceedingly angry at me; however, I still think that was the right decision. He threatened to disown me. He stated I was betraying him. He told me in the hardest words I have ever heard… He even withdrew from my presence and stopped speaking to me — all out of his love and his desire for me to finish my studies. I did not relent. I adopted the duties of master, and attended business matters that had been neglected and were urgent due to his unavoidable decline. I also visited Georgiana. Although my neighbor, the general, was in the war on the Continent — the territory he always returns to." Fitzwilliam fastened the hold about my ribs in a gesture that spoke aloud of inner struggle. "Mrs. Deborah Mullen was my late mother's friend — one of her closest confidants — and a caring companion for my teen sibling. She was French, and about fifteen years younger than her absent husband."

I think Ana talked about her too. I thanked the Almighty for the small relief in having a trusted woman to watch after her.

"I went to her house every day, sometimes late after work, sometimes to find Georgiana already asleep. That is how it happened. That is how Deborah and I became lovers. That was the moment I forgot my father's teachings about the consequences of my actions, and I failed."

Oh My God, he has been with other women! He has loved someone else! HE HAS BEEN WITH OTHER WOMEN! I pictured Fitzwilliam covering a sophisticated beauty with kisses. AHHH. I was so stupid! Of course, he had been with other women! Like everyone else. Like all the students in Cambridge. Like all men! My mind was full of incoherent thoughts. I detached from his proximity. She was French. That was why he spoke that tongue so well.

"It was partially innocent at the beginning. I was totally inexperienced and was lost in the sensations and adventure. The relief from my responsibilities. The allure of encounters that seemed not to have side effects. I could not have been wronger. After a few weeks, Deborah received a letter with news about the imminent arrival of her husband. She started to behave in a strange way."

Deborah. He even called her by her given name! I felt a strange feeling of hollowness take control of my heart. He loved that woman.

"She asked me to remove Georgiana from her house. Afterwards, she begged me to escape with her. I could not comply, because of the circumstances of my family. In the end, she became hysterical with the thought that we would be discovered, and she would be prosecuted with the charge of adultery. She transformed from the consummate flirt to the depressed victim of terror. She started to talk about death. And finally, just the day when her husband was expected, I was told she killed herself*."

"She killed herself?" I was stunned with the way this wretched affair ended.

"Yes. I do not know how."

She killed herself? She took her own life? Why would someone do such a thing? I remembered the moments when I had had the same thought. Yes, but I never tried. A lot of resolve is needed to do something like that. I gazed at Fitzwilliam, not being able to construct a coherent speech. A lot of resolve and fear.

"So, here is the real man you thought to be without fault, the man you supposed to have the highest moral standards."

I moved to the bench across from him. "I need time to think." This ached too much. I pulled up my legs on the cushions. He had loved that woman, and maybe many others. That was something I could not change. He had kissed them, he had caressed them, he had received from them much more than what I had given him. I could not help the intrusion of scenes of my William having intimate relations with someone else. *She died, and now he has those memories of her.* I took off my big pelisse, to cover myself with it and cuddle. He surely remembered her touch, her lips, her body. He could not forget something like that. "Was she the first one?" I controlled my voice in an effort not to betray my feelings.

"The first, and the last. Before you."

"What happened when her husband arrived?"

"He called me out. He must have been informed by a servant."

"To a duel?" Was that the only way men had to solve their problems?

"It was a shameful fight. My father became livid at me when I came home with a cut on my face. It was a death match (not like the one with Wickham); however, I was unable to finish Mullen when he fell unconscious."

"Why are you so regretful? Are you still mourning <u>her</u>? She was the one to seduce you, if I understood well."

"Because adultery is a shameful thing. Because the punishment could be hanging the woman in public, and because I did not care for her as she deserved. I used her to get out of my grief. I was in <u>lust</u> with her, not in <u>love</u> with her. She was lonely, she was… She needed me and I did not protect her."

"Was she beautiful?"

"Yes. She was attractive."

"Is that why you said I was not handsome enough to tempt you, in the assembly when we met?"

"No!" he answered with fervor. "She was different. She was older."

She was attractive. Surely some tall striking blond. "Then, why did you say <u>that</u>?"

"Why did I? — because you looked like a girl. Because you resembled my sister in age, and at the same time you had an angelic halo around your features. You were a vision of loveliness. How could I dare approach you? I thought you were younger than your sisters. I thought it was sinful to think about you as a woman."

He thought me younger than my sisters, I acknowledged desperate, clinging to anything that would serve to heal this wound. *He believed me too young to be out.*

I was startled by a tug at my pelisse and peered at him. It turned up he has moved to bend awkwardly between the benches while I was hiding. "Lizzy, please, tell me what you are thinking. Do not withdraw from me."

I observed for a second time the dark circles that were the product of his restless night. I perceived his shoulders down. Defeated. He looked defeated. "I am not withdrawing from you. I am trying to put my thoughts in order. I am struggling to make this out."

"I understand if you are angry at me. I should have told you this before you decided to marry me. I accept if you are disgusted by my selfish actions."

"What selfish actions, William? When have you ever been selfish?"

"When I considered Deborah's feelings with disdain. When I was inconsiderate of her fear. When I disregarded the consequences of an affair with a married woman."

"It is easy to see you have repented heartily, and that you have carried that guilt as a penance for many years. I am not mad at you. You were just a young man, with all the responsibility of your family and Pemberley on your shoulders; a lad giving up all his dreams for his duty. You were the same age I am now, the same as all the students in Cambridge, taking the job of your experienced father. You were having a tremendously difficult fight against your parent's wishes, risking his good opinion, craving to do what was right."

"Why are you troubled then? What are you struggling with?"

"I? I am devilishly jealous of that woman, Deborah, who dared to touch you. She took from me that which I sought to be the only one to provide." I saw him open his mouth to say something. I silenced him, "I know this is a naïve thought, yet, I am entitled to it."

"Lizzy, she is dead! How can you be jealous of a person that does not exist anymore? That cannot threaten you in any way?"

"She lives in your mind. She has a lot of power over you still. On top of that, she has made you feel regret because of <u>her actions,</u> for more than six years! She should be the one begging forgiveness!"

"I am not doing a good job explaining myself. She was a victim herself. That is the only remorse I have: the awareness of her fragility and my indifference. It is a painful thought. I have not evoked her in any other way since long ago." The aisle was too small for him to be in that position, he seemed to ponder how to be closer. "Besides, thoughts of you have thoroughly occupied my mind since I met you."

"How can you say that, Fitzwilliam? She kept you awake all night!"

"No. I was awake because of the proximity to Cambridge." He sat next to me. "She was not you. She could not give me what only you have. What do I have to do, to make you see what you mean to me? She is not even a shadow of what you are!"

"If you are referring to taking my innocence, I do not see any merit in giving you that. There is no work, no effort, no dedication in keeping some flesh unharmed!" I declared, although repented instantly from saying aloud something so very unconventional.

"I do not know what you are referring to exactly. I..." He gazed at my eyes, then at my feet and back at my face. I had truly scandalized him now. "Sometimes it seems to me, you are completely inexperienced, and sometimes... sometimes you speak about this as if it were some scientific knowledge you have already thoroughly studied."

Hide, hide! If only I had somewhere to run to. How did I dare speak about this subject?! This was not done! I covered by head with the pelisse once again. Stupid! Stupid!

"Lizzy, we must learn to speak openly. We must learn to share our problems. We could have avoided a lot of misunderstandings if we had just talked about what troubles us. No one is judging you." His arms slipped under my body and lifted me into his lap. "I only wanted to point out I do not follow your reasoning. I am not saying anything else. It is difficult to rationalize something so personal, so intimate and so puzzling as one's feelings regarding coupling. Nonetheless, it is something we must talk about. Would you please tell me what is in this beautiful mind of yours?"

No. No. No! I kept my knees close to my chest.

"Well. Let me guess, then. You are jealous of Deborah because you think she means something to me still. Is that it?"

I nodded silently.

"Are you angry at me because I had that relationship in the past?"

I shook my head 'no'.

"Then, you are disgusted because I met a woman before you, and you are not angry at me."

I nodded 'yes'.

"Is that the conclusion to your thoughts?"

I shook my head 'no' once more.

"No? What else then? I must confess, I do not understand even the first part."

I shrugged my shoulders.

"Why do not you write it down? I think those pencils and your diary are near." I felt him strain to take my traveling bag from the seat in front of us. "Here."

After opening the notebook, I wrote under the covers. *"I am not angry at you. I am angry at her. I want to be the only one to give you love. I want to be the only one to make you that happy."* I poked the diary out.

"Oh, Lizzy. You are giving me a precious thing already. No one… No one ever has opened up to me as you do. No one has ever cared for me the way you do. No one has ever sacrificed for me the way you have done. The devotion with which you have tried to protect me, is something more precious that all the gold in this world. It is not in your innocence where your allurement resides. That is something fleeting. It resides in the fact that, in spite of all that has happened in your life and in spite of the mistakes I have made, you still have faith in me."

I gestured for him to give the diary back. *"Would you have loved me the same if I were not an innocent? Truly? What would you think of Wickham, or anyone else, if you knew I had…?"*

He read my question and buried his face in my pelisse. I felt the rise of his ribs a couple of times. "I would have loved you still. I would have loved you, but the images of any man worshiping you would have been unbearable."

"Worshiping! That is what I am going to do!" the obvious solution came to

257

my mind. "I will do it tonight. I will erase that woman from your mind this night!" There was no way I was going to let her usurp my place any longer!

He tried to argue this was not the right reason for us to be together. Not the right reason to make love. I refuted him with everything at my disposal, almost furious that he would disavow me this right. I did not know why it was so very necessary to be this way with him now. After the many times that I had thought the opposite. I only knew there was this hole in the middle of my chest. A hole that ached so much, that was so deep, and, at the same time, so imposing. I had to do this! I would go as far as necessary!

****

Late that night, we arrived at the estate where Mr. Sedgwick was a usual guest. Fitzwilliam explained he had sent several teams of horses and servants to Northampton. Lillian and her beau, the young driver, departed before us with that mission. He was giving the young couple an opportunity to travel together. This was a long trip for one day, and we wanted to be as far away as possible. His friend had a cousin that lived there, who was currently in London. He had arranged for us to stay for the night. The park would be all for us.

Treated with the utmost politeness by the housekeeper, I was relieved to find the rooms and our baths were prepared in advance. The house was a splendid residence of large spaces, tall windows and clear colors on the walls.

I dismissed my abigail in the hall, and her relieve could not have been more playfully sincere.

Fitzwilliam and I entered our cozy bedchamber. This was a beautiful place to consummate our marriage. I disentangled our fingers to approach the mattress and take off the quilt. I removed my pelisse and blew all the candles off, leaving only the hearth to illuminate the place. I sat, took off my shoes, my stockings, my pantaloons and lay on my stomach — turning my head so that I could observe him.

My beloved was still leaning on the door. This invitation should be more explicit. "Come." I lifted my skirts to leave my lower body exposed.

He wavered for a moment, traveling my legs with his gaze, and then, lifted his shoulders in a sign of agreement.

Just shut down your mind and do not think! My eyes half-closed, I heard his topcoat, waistcoat, smaller clothes and boots being tossed to some corner of the room. I sensed the yield of the bed under his weight. I felt his hands caress my backside, and contracted my muscles in expectation. He would be gentle.

And then, the most unexpected thing happened: his lips brushed my exposed flesh. He was kissing my cheeks!

He could not do that! I turned around abruptly and covered my thighs. "What are you doing?"

"Loving you." He reclined over me. His limbs at my sides. "You are utterly delectable."

"But… but… you cannot! You will see me there. You will see my…"

"Shhh. Shhh. It is dark enough."

"You are not going to… do… not do… that again. It might…" He was distracting me with caresses. "Look at me, Fitzwilliam!"

The pools of his eyes were darker than ever, and I was afraid he would not obey my plea. "What is the matter, Lizzy? Did we not agree to speak openly today?"

"Yes, but… You do not need to kiss me there to be inside me. It might smell." I whispered as low as I could.

"You always smell irresistible. There is nothing to fear on that score."

"It does not matter. You do not need to do that."

"I do not want to hurt you. I want you to enjoy it as much as I do. I like arousing you. It is part of what makes me happy."

"You cannot avoid hurting me. Do not think about that. It is supposed to hurt."

"What?" He removed himself from atop me and rubbed his face hard. "Where have you heard that, Elizabeth? Who has told you those things?"

"You do not have to gild the pill, sweetheart. Mrs. Parker, my Sunday School teacher, told me how much one bleeds, and I have read it. I studied 'Philosophy in the Bedroom' a long time ago."

"Marquis de Sade's 'Philosophy in the Bedroom'**? When? Where?"

I felt scolded like when Mama discovered me, "When I was ten."

"Ten!" he shut. "TEN! How the hell did you run into that book?"

I should not have told him. Why did I do it? "The teacher threatened Jane and me that we must not be rambling through the country or making bonfires; that some men were going to run into us and take advantage. She spoke with that scary tone she always used to frighten me. I decided to do my own research. I was tired of her intrigue, of not knowing. I only wanted to have a clear idea in order to defend myself. I thought it was a harmless book when I found it in my father's library. I... It had the word 'philosophy' in the title, William. That is believed to be the mother of science. I did not know it was going to get me into trouble!"

He turned his back to me. "Sometimes I am amazed by your cleverness. I find it challenging and exciting to see the world with your eyes. Except that, I never imagined curiosity could get a person into so much of a mess as you have." He stood up and walked around the bed to be by my side. "Come. Let me erase that man from your mind too." He offered his hand to help me up. "We are going to take a warm bath and start again on the right foot."

---

*England, by the late 18th century, became known as the center of suicide in the civilized world and self-murder was known as the English disease. This was partly derived from the 1774 (1779 first English) publication of The Sorrows of Werther, which inspired copycat suicides.
Regency Encyclopedia also states that the sentence for bigamy was capital punishment. http://www.capitalpunishmentuk.org/bcode.html.

** "Philosophy in the bedroom" is a disturbing reading. You can read about the plot here: http://en.wikipedia.org/wiki/Philosophy_in_the_Bedroom

Chapter 25

"We?" I hesitated when he signaled he was going to accompany me.

"Yes. I think the tub can accommodate us both."

I pulled at his hand, "Please, Fitzwilliam, I cannot…" *do not make me say it.*

He neared to stand an inch apart. "What about bathing with our undergarments on? I will wear my drawers, and you will wear your pantaloons and chemise. What about that?"

His masculinity impregnated the air. I gazed at his expansive shoulders and his eager expression. I picked up the garment that was previously discarded and inserted my legs into it. He opened the door to the other chamber for me to enter.

I took off my clothes at the same time as he. His naked torso was beautiful. I followed the line of the hair that went from his navel to his pectorals: a path that called to be touched. When he immersed into the water, I calculated it was going to be inevitable to spill some when I did the same.

He extended his arm in invitation, and I stepped in between his legs. "Do you think you can kneel in this space?"

My pants were wet within a second, and the warmth started to spread through my chest. I looked at my barely covered breasts and went deeper under the foam.

He moved me to lie on his upper body. "I have dreamed of doing this since your stay in Netherfield."

"I had no idea at the time."

"Yes. I was a fool trying to impress you with my knowledge — trying to show I was smarter and more knowledgeable about the world — unaware of your marvelous nature. Did I at least make you uncomfortable during that half hour alone, at the end of your stay?"

"Mmm?"

"Do not say you do not remember." He lifted my chin and the tender way in which he looked at me, made me want to engulf in his eyes forever.

"On Saturday, you mean?"

"Yes. I must confess I was somewhat enchanted by that curl you played with while reading. I almost reached for it — twice."

"It would have been quite the shock, Mr. Darcy."

"I would have reached for it, kissed it slowly, following the path to your neck. I would have nibbled at your ear, and then, I would have followed to your arms and waist. I would have made you mine if you had let me. Although, the position you suggested some minutes ago is not my favorite." He extended his hand over my cheek. "Lizzy, we are not sheep or horses. Humans mate in a different way. I want you to understand making love has nothing to do with what you read in that book. Nothing. Making love is giving pleasure to your partner. It is not a sacrifice for either of the parties involved. It is a journey, one of discovery and adventure. It is an interchange of caresses and kisses. It is finding a new world inside of us. It is completing one another. Do you understand me?"

I nodded, relishing in his smooth skin, figuring out what he was telling me.

He took the soap and started to travel my back with it. "You will see that this is a gift from God; that there is nothing to fear. It is something immensely enjoyable, actually." He reached for my toes under the water and rubbed them one by one. "If it were not like that, do you think there would be so many people in the world? Do you think couples would mate so often if it were not something unique, something in which both members feel pleasure? Do you think men in love would do something hurtful to their wives? Bingley would do that to your sister? Your father to your mother? Or I to you?" he asked while washing my feet and legs. "What you read from Sade, and what you were told by that teacher, are aberrant behaviors. Men do not usually possess that violent disposition."

"What about the stallion, the stampede, I hear in your chest when we are this way?"

"A stallion?" he laughed quietly, "that is a very nice compliment, madam, but I do not think there is anything animalistic in our lovemaking."

"Why is there so much secrecy around it, then? Why is not something people talk about openly?"

"I do not know, honestly. It is something intimate. However, at the same time, it is as normal as eating." He stroked the sides of my thighs, "…for people married at least."

"So, no one does what is written in that book?"

He placed the bar on the side table and lifted me to sit astride his lap. I rested my hands on his chest, still rejoicing in the discovery of its silky nature. "There are people that do that, yes." He took the soap again and traveled my arms reverently. "Following the parallelism with eating habits, I would say that, for me, it seems like consumption by the nostrils." He soaped my belly and the middle of my bosom slowly. "It does not seem something enjoyable or desirable."

"What are we going to do, then?"

"We will undress. Completely. Get under the covers. And slowly, very slowly, I will caress every single inch of you."

"The lights will be off, right?"

"For tonight. Yes."

"Is that all?"

"Mostly, although I will caress the insides of you at the end." He pressed my buttocks and pushed me to him. "Do not worry. Your only occupation will be to close your eyes and feeeel, Lizzy. Feel."

****

I was lying on a cloud, surrounded by the wonderland that was Fitzwilliam's body, meditating on what had just happened. *How can this be so overwhelming?* My mind refused to acknowledge the closeness and tenderness that had transpired.

I was his wife now. Truly his wife. I reveled in the sensation of my lover's flesh against mine. I replayed the incredible intimacy of our union — the soft touch, the kisses, and finally, the ecstasy when he filled me. How could he transport me to that waterfall?

"William, how could you provoke that..." how to say it? "...discharge?" I buried my face in his chest, a bit embarrassed.

"Because I know you. Because I had planned this many times. Did you like it?"

"Like? I do not think that is the right word. If I were to use a word for this, it can only be a synonym for 'infinite' and 'incredible,'" What a fool I was when believing the opposite!

"Did it hurt?"

"Not at all," I looked up for him to see the sincerity of my declaration. "Was it this glorious for you too?"

"Lizzy." He slipped me up his abdomen, his impassioned eyes leveled with mine. "It was divine. You are a goddess. I never felt anything like this." He took hold of my head to approach our grinning faces. "I never *discharged* inside a woman before. This is better than all my fantasies and dreams."

"I love you, William. Thank you for this gift." *

****

I was awakened lying on my stomach, with the bed linen covering my derriere, my husband's naughty tongue outlining the path of my bones.

"Good morning, Mrs. Darcy."

"Do we have to travel today?"

"We do. But we can take breakfast in the carriage and enjoy other sweets before departing." He resumed his path over my shoulders, leaving a delightful moisture behind. "Would you like me to show you the direction of travel at present?"

"Yeees."

"This is our destination today: Nottingham." He bit the middle of my nape lightly. "We will have to spend the night there." He started a zigzag down my spine. "Lunch can be in Leicester," he kissed the middle of the 'map', "which is exactly half way from here," he brushed my skin downwards. "Do you want me to explain the land that is to the Southeast — the part we already covered yesterday?"

"If you promise to close your eyes." The light was already intruding trough the curtains.

"Your wish is my command, my lady."

****

Once in the carriage, after disrobing of our outerwear, the first thing I did was take off his cravat and my shoes. "Love, would you tell me who was the adult that appeared at the end of your fight in Lambton woods?"

"The adult?" He lifted my legs to rest on the cushions. "You mean the man who separated Wickham and me?"

I nodded.

"It was his father, the late Mr. Wickham — the manager of all the Pemberley estates while my parents were alive."

"Describe him to me, please."

"He died shortly after my father, and I did not know him well. He was respected in my family, though."

"In one of my nightmares, Churchill and he are holding your arms while Wickham hits you. I cannot make anything out, though. I am sure many of those scenes are fabricated, because you are grown up in them. No. No. I should not be paying attention to those thoughts. The man is dead, after all. He is not a threat to us."

"Speaking of which, Lizzy, we need to contemplate the suspects of these attacks. We cannot just hide. We must find out who it is."

"You are not going after that man, Fitzwilliam! Do not even think about that."

"I understand. I am just trying to inventory those that might wish to harm you. Tell me, is there anyone that could have been holding something against you for a long time? Someone like that teacher, Mrs. Parker, someone that might have a propensity to hurt you?"

"No. I do not think so. Mrs. Parker is deceased, and the majority of her friends too. As a matter of fact, I only remember Lady Lucas as someone that has shown any resentment recently, and I am sure she was in Hertfordshire when I was poisoned. Was she not?"

"Yes. Well, Wickham is also off of our list for the same reason." He stretched for my bag, subtracting the notebook and the pencil inside. "Let us write this down. You think the people from Meryton are excluded?"

I nodded.

"And from Bakewell?"

"I do not remember anyone except Jack and my Uncle Gardiner from that time; at least not their names."

He wrote:
"Suspects:
"Jack Sthieve"

I stopped his hand and pleaded. "No, love, I do not think you should include him. He is Mary's husband."

"Elizabeth, he has motives to try to hide what he witnessed. He can…" Fitzwilliam looked at me, trying to read my thoughts. "Do you have other feelings for him? Is that why you are trying to dismiss…"

"I do have feelings for him — fraternal feelings — nothing else."

"Well, then we will write his name in this list. It is only a precaution. Are there any other places we should consider before Newmarket? Any other secret admirers?"

"Mr. Collins is the only one that dared to approach before you. There is no one else silly enough to do such a thing."

"Ha! I bet you gave that look that says 'not interesting enough' to any boy who approached you with a poem. All dismissed with a 'I wonder who first discovered the efficacy of poetry in driving away love!' and an elegant wave of your hand."

"I do not think that was the reception you received, Mr. Darcy. You looked so handsome at Jane's wedding!"

"I was sweating as if I were to present my Tripos**." He wrote another name. *"Churchill and the sailors"*

"He is abroad, William. He could not have murdered Mr. Falcon."

"Yes, I only want to keep in mind the possibility. Besides, he could have sent someone to do the job." He looked for the notes of the day in the tavern. "Tell me about this man, and the other two accompanying him. What did they look like?"

"They looked like gentlemen, although..." How could I describe their attitude? "They did not belong there. The man with a stump was better dressed than the others — that is why I say he was a gentleman — but they were not enjoying themselves. They..."

"You say he had a stump? Where?"

"An arm. He was without one arm. Do you know someone with that description?"

"No. But Mrs. Hill described the man who went to visit your father with Wickham. She told me *that* man had only one hand. This could be a coincidence, but more than likely — not. It could be the same man that convinced your father you were my mistress."

"The same man? A man related to Wickham? Do you think he remembered?"

"Do not be afraid, Lizzy. No one believes in Wickham's lies in all of

Derbyshire. Do not worry that his deeds will spread or that he will blackmail your family. There are more offended fathers and jealous husbands there, than trees on this road."

Jealousy. That was a strong sentiment for sure.

He wrote down the portrayal of the new suspects. *"A gentleman without an arm."*

"Jealousy. Jealousy!" I shouted. "That is it, Fitzwilliam! There must be some jealous woman from the *ton* who wants to eliminate the competition."

"I do not think that could be the incentive. You were dressed like a boy those days. Besides, I am not as acclaimed as you think. Remember, I hate balls, and I am unsocial and taciturn." He pretended an angry glare. "The only one that has seriously attempted marrying her daughter to me is my aunt, and she is not capable of such a thing."

"Mmm, I think you do not have a clear idea of the impression you make on women. Remember how Caroline behaves around you. She cannot be more explicit in her pursuit." I took his discarded cravat and arranged it around my head. "You write uncommonly fast, Mr. Darcy. Do you think you can sign a bank note in my name with that even handwriting?" I batted my eyelashes flirtatiously.

He chuckled loudly and arranged one of my legs, to put me astride his thighs. "Well, here is one *impression* I want to make on you, my jealous wife." He pulled my hips onto his.

"If I am not mistaken, you had that particular wish many days ago too, my self-confident husband. When I was drunk."

"Self-confident? I wish I were. If you only knew the hell I went through the night before meeting Michael."

"Michael? The boy?"

"Yes, the one you proclaimed to be the man of your dreams," he pouted.

"That is why you were so happy to know him. You are so silly, William."

"Silly, eh?" He inserted his hands beneath my skirt and climbed from my knees to my belly, "I think this is the third time you call me *that* in a matter

268

of only a couple of days of marriage, madam." He unfastened the ribbon that held my underclothes. "It deserves an exemplary punishment."

****

Intertwined on his lap, I concluded this was the happiest day of my life. I rested my head on his shoulder, not giving in to the temptation of opening my eyes. *Yes, it is timeless here.*

My lover asked softly in my ear, "What are you thinking about, my dear?"

"Thinking? I am not thinking much. It was more like flying over a hill."

"That far?"

"Yes. I intend to be like that for half an hour at least. And you?"

"I was thinking about Miss Lydia."

"What?"

"Yes. I was thinking about the erroneous statement she used to discourage Georgiana and me from going out with you. Do you remember?"

"No. I can barely recall my name now."

"Well, the fact is she was grossly mistaken when she proclaimed you never ride. I will have to clarify to her that you are quite an accomplished equestrian."

"FITZWILLIAM!" I pushed away to scold him.

"Mrs. Darcy!" He impeded my intended move. "You cannot deny the facts!"

"Where is the reserved man I married? Who is this saucy scoundrel that is taking advantage of me?"

"Where is the frightened butterfly that traveled with me yesterday?"

Mmm, "She is drinking all the nectar of her favorite flower."

269

"She is the personification of temptation. I eagerly anticipate the next time she offers to take it from me."

"Anticipation? That is certainly an instance where Lydia was right — anticipating getting married." I pictured how she used to flirt with the militia men. My spirited sister, fortunately she did not know about this.

****

While writing in my notebook, I ventured a new subject. "By the way, love, I remembered something a while ago. Would you explain to me what fraternity initiations are about? I think the boys talked about that in the tavern and the library. I could not grasp their meaning."

"There are many kinds: some are simply playful fights or nasty jokes. Some are competitions. Some are traps to put the initiate into uncomfortable situations. Some are, frankly, abusive games. In my case, it was not dreadful at all. I was already pretty tall at that age. I suppose that was why I was lucky. They only left me in an isolated place during the night, and I had to return by myself." *The same as what my friends were planning to do.* "It was easy. It was not cloudy, and the North Star was visible all the time. You are never lost when you can see <u>him</u>."

"Did you participate in them later? When you were older?"

"Oh, yes, I did. I once took the soap from one of the youngest students and shaped it with the form of a manhood. He wore quite an offended visage next day when he discovered it," my companion whistled playfully, "and I played the unconcerned roommate, of course."

"You never witnessed an abusive game, then? They do not actually happen that often, do they?"

"They are not *that* common, but I would rather they never happened. Because I managed to extract him from one of them, Bingley and I are such friends. We have the kind of friendship only the camaraderie of sharing day after day struggles in a hostile place can build; the kind you can only have in College (like with Sedgwick). You see, the problem with those games is that the abuser never remembers as much as the abused. The abused drags that weight throughout life. That is why he takes my judgment to heart. He thinks I am always right just due to the foresight I showed that day."

"Would you tell me more about that fellow, Mr. Sedgwick?"

"He is a researcher. He has not enjoyed the luxury we saw yesterday often — that is only a place he inhabits infrequently. He is the son of a vicar. He has strong religious convictions. I used to compare him with Galileo***, just to annoy him, by means of the argument that *his* theories are as heretical and truthful as the ones of the astronomer. You see, his idea that the Earth was formed in the course of millions of years seems to me as revolutionary as the Heliocentric Theory, in the seventeenth century. I hope he does not get into any argument with the Inquisition, though."

"Sadly, too many morbid things have been done in the name of God."

"However, there is more good that has been done in His name. Those episodes have more to do with power than to religion probably."

"And why do you call the North Star 'him?' Why a 'he' and not a 'she'?" I played the offended female, determined to only have cheerful thoughts. "Because women are not admitted in Cambridge?"

He laughed at my childish joke and retorted, "No, Mrs. 'I can beat anyone in King's College.' I call it a 'he' because of an Indian Legend**** I heard once. Do you want to listen to it?"

---

*Opposite to what is common knowledge, *not* having pain during the first intercourse is a usual occurrence.

** The University of Cambridge, England, divides the different kinds of honors bachelor's degree by Tripos.

***Many advances in science are due to Galileo. Read about his life here: http://en.wikipedia.org/wiki/Galileo_Galilei

**** This legend can be read in the webpage: http://www.firstpeople.us/FP-Html-Legends/WhytheNorthStarStandsStill-Paiute.html

Chapter 26

Nottingham, Wednesday, 15 October, midnight

After two nights, I realize how much I have discovered. The many emotions I can arise in William. Amazement. Ecstasy. Devotion. Longing.

I am the happiest creature in the world. Perhaps others have said this before, but not with such justice.

We are in a road inn, traveling to Pemberley. We are on the run, as if Death itself were trying to catch up with us. And yet, I feel blessed.

****

We had to hurry when we woke up late in the morning, a little sleepy in my case, although my husband was already dressing. We were planning to arrive at Pemberley today, on Thursday. He did not send any servants before us, to be able to give Georgiana the surprise. The majority of them were staying here one more night. They had had tough days rushing around in the elements.

Fitzwilliam had arranged for two drivers (Lillian's beau, Albert, and an older one), a guard and my maid to travel with us the rest of the journey: the girl next to the coachman, the other two men on horseback. We were traveling in only one carriage now. I handed a heavy quilt to them and climbed hurriedly inside, to avoid the freezing air.

When we were having the meats and cheese that were going to substitute our meals, Fitzwilliam asked me to speak about my fathers.

Mama used to call the first one 'the handsomest man of her acquaintance,' of course, before meeting Mr. Bennet. They had been married in Scotland. I related how sad she was the many years spent alone in Bakewell, after my birth and his abandonment. "Papa, on the contrary, dedicated many hours to my instruction — even when he was courting Mother. He was the one to teach me to use mathematics as an escape when my mind was in turmoil," I related, whilst avoiding speaking about Mrs. Parker. "I think that was the way I gained his favoritism — by finding new prime numbers* and seeking and not finding a general equation for them." I brought to my mind the way my parents avoided proper chaperonage with my company. "He taught me to laugh and to be brave when someone disdained me."

"That was a good strategy, except that you learned you had to earn his love by being courageous."

"Well, he also helped me understand, when Lady Lucas and her friends called me a bastard, 'as long as what they say is not true, it does not matter if they say it.'"

"That is a behavior pretty close to the one your parents showed the day you were slapped. They never defend you in front of others," my companion expressed factually (without the resentment that could be expected to be associated by such a speech) while taking the jam I was offering.

"They did not defend me, but they educated me to defend myself. Nobody can hurt me if I do not let them. It is more beneficial to teach your children to fight than to fight for them."

"That is true. Nonetheless, I have always thought your mother was afraid of Lady Lucas. Do you know why? Why should she be afraid of the wife of the best man of her own wedding?"

"My mother, afraid of Lady Lucas? Why do you say that?"

"Is that not why she is always in competition with her and, at the same time, trying to ingratiate herself with her?"

"I do not know. Now that you say that, I do remember a change of attitude in Mama when we arrived in Hertfordshire. She was easier to scare, like in a state of permanent fear. It was then when she started to have fits of nerves."

"Let us go back to the time when you arrived to Meryton, then. Would you describe to me Mrs. Parker's mistreatment?"

I curled to hide my face in his shoulder. "You can read it in my diaries."

"I know those tales by heart. You need to talk about them. It will help to speak it and let it go." *To talk about that?* "I love to see you like the merry jingle bell you were in the morning. You need to share those things with someone, though. You did not disclose this to your mother, or to your father, at that age."

"I did not want to make Mama cry. She was very vulnerable."

"I will not cry," he promised with a bit of impertinence. "Relate them to me."

We spent more than an hour with my narration about the way I felt when going to Sunday School. It was the first time I went to one of those. It was impossible for me to stay quiet and still for more than an hour, particularly sitting on a stiff chair. How could I do that, after being used to an unsupervised life in Bakewell?

"The lady had no patience for a child like me — for a girl asking questions about how time is measured in the Bible; or for one who liked climbing trees with the boys. She started to try to discipline me — first with insults about my seemingly unknown origin; or, hiding my shoes; at times forcing me to write hundreds of times that I am a sinner and that I am not worthy; and at the end, ignoring me as if I did not exist. She ended not answering my questions, and following her lessons as if I were not there, when I lifted my arm to answer. In truth, that was one of the most painful reprimands."

"How did your parents behave when you returned home without your shoes?"

"My mother was nervous. My father just tried to reassure her nothing dreadful was going to happen because of the teacher's attitude; the woman was crazy, and no one in the neighborhood took her opinion into account."

"Again, they did not defend you. Is that not so, Lizzy?"

"No, *they* did not. They knew little because of my own tight lips. But Charlotte and Jane did! My friends plotted to share many of those punishments just to contradict Mrs. Parker. They both have neat handwriting thanks to me. Although, Papa must have known at least something about those cruelties. As a matter of fact, I suspect Charlotte's and Jane's meddling was something our fathers devised to counteract the teacher belatedly — that sounds just like the kind of plot Sir William Lucas and my cunning parent could have made up, to make the woman reconsider her strategy."

"Elizabeth, have you ever pondered all that resentment could have been directed at your mother, instead of you? Is there a better way to hurt a woman than abusing her child? Was it not effective? By the descriptions I have learned from you, the attributes your mother still shows, and your own, I dare say she was uncommonly beautiful. If I had to make a guess, I would say those women were envious."

"So, you think that Mama was not angry at me, but frightened? Her comments about ladylike behavior are directed to shelter me, and that my parents' lack of defense was an attempt to protect me instead? Do you think that is what is behind the secrecy of what happened in Lambton?" I remembered the knowing glances my father showed my mother on those occasions, "And behind her uncharacteristic self-control, in some instances, when her natural reaction would have been to protect me from those women?"

"Yes. Like when Lady Lucas slapped you. You wrote Mrs. Bennet was going to react violently before Mr. Bennet entered the room. I find that was a particularly timely reaction, most likely based on their previous agreements. Your father is an intelligent man. He cares for you deeply. Why would he react that way, if it were not because he had decided before this was the best course of action?"

"If he loves me so much — which I am certain is true — why would he now be suspicious? Why does he trust the man that went with Wickham to slander us? Why does he even suggest I could become someone's mistress?"

"I do not have an answer for that, love. That is something I truthfully cannot fathom."

****

After the last change of horses, Fitzwilliam explained Lady Catherine had spent every Easter at Pemberley before his father's death. He always thought she was a bad influence on Georgiana, and decided to travel to Rosings instead when he gained her custody. That is why he said every year he spent those weeks with his aunt.

Not wanting to rely on the fact that he only cares for Colonel Fitzwilliam's and Ana's opinions, I tried to encourage him to talk about the rest of his family. "Love, you cannot deny they are important to you, and that your sister might be relinquishing a marriage to a good prospect because we are together now. No one would choose to be related to someone like me. This marriage was selfish on our part, if you think of her."

"Do not give a chance for those thoughts to intrude into your mind, Lizzy. You are the best thing that could have happened to us. Think of it this way: what kind of man is she renouncing to, if the subject does not see her virtues and disdains her because of her connections? What benefit will do her a husband like that?"

"Sweetheart, that kind of man is you. She can be resigning love and happiness. A wonderful husband is not the perfect one, it is the one that accepts..."

We could not finish our conversation because we were pushed to the floor by an abrupt stop of the carriage.

We looked at each other, and I sat up slowly. Fitzwilliam exited on to the road. I peered through the window and watched Lillian's beau helping her up from the ground. She seemed well, and the other two servants approached their master to explain the circumstances. I could not discern all that was said, because they moved to inspect the junction between the carriage and the horses' harnesses. I discerned the word 'linchpin,' and by the concerned mien of all of the men, concluded something difficult to repair was broken or lost.

Some minutes passed while my husband gave orders, and the men took the luggage from the carriage. I also stepped out, donning my outerwear to keep as warm as possible. There was no way to link the horses with the vehicle without this piece. The animals were cleared from the main road, and the coach was pushed separately by William and the armed man escorting us.

He looked at the horizon and calculated it was still two hours until twilight. He regretted having left the other carriage and help behind. "The guard will stay here watching over our belongings, while one of the coachmen rides to Lambton to acquire the part. I will take one of the guns. We are at the same distance to the house as to the village, so, it is better if we take the horses that are saddled. They are less tired," he signaled to my maid and her beau. "I can take one with Mrs. Darcy, and you can take the other. We will arrive safely at Pemberley in little more than an hour and a half."

Not on horseback! I separated from the group and asked him to approach. "William, cannot we go on foot? I am an excellent walker, as you know."

He looked at me questioningly for a second, until he realized my predicament. He took the reins of the beast the servant brought. "Go ahead," he commanded to the other couple. "Notify the staff we are underway, and bring aid to repair the carriage. My wife and I are going to enjoy the scenery during our ride."

He placed my hand in the crook of his arm and guided me across the open field ahead, with the steed following us obediently.

After about a mile of cold weather and muddy trails, my beloved suggested, "Sweetling, it is getting late and you are freezing," He signaled to the mountains far away, where the Sun was almost down. "I know this land as I know the palm of my hand, and this horse has traveled with me over half of England. What danger could there be in riding it together?"

"We might fall."

"I swear to hold you very tightly and to guide him at a very slow canter."

"Canter?"

"Well, if you do not want to go cantering, we can trot or even walk on it. Come. I am sure you will take pleasure in the proximity that position affords. I am going to do my best to warrant you will be well attended, and that it will not be boring. Mmm?" He stopped to look under my bonnet. "Besides, if one horseman pounced on you, it does not mean the animal is evil. It is the man who was careless," he reminded the incident where Jack saved my life in Bakewell. "It was a long time ago. You must overcome that irrational fear!"

Agreeing, I waited for him to lift me over the gigantic animal. I hated to be called irrational!

He placed me across the saddle, following to sit astride in a blink. "You see? This is not so horrible."

I started to think of a puzzle that could divert my thoughts. Summing the numbers from one to one hundred proved to be the easier one. *$1+2=3$; $3+3=6$; $6+4=10$; $10+5=15$...***

"There is much more land you can watch from here," he suggested with a hint of mischief in his tone, "and it is plain, clear and deserted, so that I can kiss you at my volition without witnesses."

I slid one arm behind his back and grabbed him rigidly. He secured me firmly while pushing the horse forward. I contracted all my muscles to prepare for a potential tumble. *15+6=21; 21+7=28; 28+8=36...*

We toured slowly for half an hour, through dry streams and yellow grass. William amused me with tales of his youth and sightseeing. We speculated about Ana and her shock when learning we were arriving soon.

Still, I could not help the sense of dread. "Are you not afraid of the dark and not seeing the path?"

"No," he affirmed at the same time as galloping horses were heard from the distance.

My companion turned the mount to see who they were. I felt him gnash his teeth. "It is Deborah's husband. The man in the center is General Mullen."

"They are the men from the tavern. The general is the man with the stump!"

"Close your eyes!" William ordered, while starting a frantic gallop toward the hills.

---

*Looking for prime numbers is a historical hunt:
http://www-history.mcs.st-and.ac.uk/HistTopics/Prime_numbers.html

**Summing the numbers from one to one hundred is a puzzle solved in a clever and fast way by Carl Friedrich Gauss at an early age:
According to the legend, Gauss's method was to realize that if he added the terms in pairs from opposite ends of the list, it yielded identical sums: $1 + 100 = 101$, $2 + 99 = 101$, $3 + 98 = 101$, $4 + 97 = 101$ and so on, for a total of 50 pairs. Thus, the total is $50 \times 101 = 5050$.

Chapter 27

It has been many days since I wrote in the carriage from Nottingham. Much has happened. After leaving our belongings behind, our life took a turn of one hundred and eighty degrees. But I must go back to where I left off, to complete it. My memories are so vivid. The terror so recent still, I sometimes feel it as if it were happening right now. In present tense.

The sound of the horsemen approaches. The speed. The instability of the land. The high slope. My heart pounds in my ears. I clutch tightly to my husband. I hear a gunshot. I start to pray. The steed stands on his hind legs as a second blast rings through the trees. We are thrown. Fitzwilliam absorbs the fall. The horse gallops away. We are on foot. The gun was in the saddle. "Follow me." He takes my hand tightly. "I am sure there is a cave." I lift my skirt and pelisse. I notice them on their beasts. They come after us up the cliff. We run. We sweat. We hide. His first attempt is unsuccessful. That hole is too small. William curses. What would they do? Would they kill him? Would they harm me? Would they break his limbs? Would they rape me? This chase is my fault. I lament having delayed us. Another gun shot. Closer this time. We keep running. Jumping. Surrounding. We cross a cleft. Our breath is short. They dismount. We are trapped. There are no caves in this place. No trees. No way out. They are circling us. Five men. I see their faces. The diabolic miens. The chase is over. My husband turns around. He steps before me. "DO NOT HARM HER. IT IS ME THAT YOU WANT!" They laugh. Fitzwilliam signals the general. "This issue is between you and me! Let her go. I will come with you peacefully." He encircles me backwards. Squeezes me to his body. Like a giant shield.

The general shakes his head. He wears a disgusting smile. "You should know better than that." He signals for the men to separate us. "This is about justice." Eight hands pull at us. "My wife is dead. Yours shall be as well."

I am forced to the ground, lying on my back. A man immobilizes me with his weight. "What should I do with her, sir?" He smells like barns.

Mullen lifts his hand. "Wait."

I manage to shift my head. I see my other half. He is fighting fiercely. *Do not harm him!*

The general approaches. He crouches. He pushes the gun into my neck. "It is up to you when and where."

Fitzwilliam realizes the threat. He stops his struggle. Two men are holding his arms. The third is behind him, strangling him. The other hand points at his forehead with a pistol.

"Now we understand each other." Mullen stands up. He takes a rope from his saddle. He throws it to the servant holding me. "Tie her hands and legs."

The minion moves to constrain me. He passes a tight band around my wrists. He ties my ankles. "Ready." He turns me to lie on my belly.

The general gazes satisfactorily at the result. He lowers and pins me with his knees on my back.

Fitzwilliam's eyes are full of wrath. *What are they going to do you?*

"Bring him to me," Mullen orders. The men force my husband to move forward. They make him stoop. This is the same scene I had in my dream — just different players. "You have healed well." He touches the scar on his cheek with his whip.

"I cannot say the same about you." William stares at the stump. Oh my! He lost that arm in their duel!

The coward that tied me strikes my husband in the stomach. I blink. *Please, do not do that. Not to him!*

"Easy, easy. I have better plans for them." The general signals to the same man to bring something from the horses. My hands are aching. "Do not boast too much. This is the work of gangrene. The wound you inflicted was not a deep one." That was why Fitzwilliam did not suspect <u>him</u>! He has been secluded in the Continent since the duel. He did not know the consequence of the wound he inflicted. Did not realize this man was handicapped.

The flunkey approaches with two small shovels collected from the saddles. What are they going to do with that at night?

"I do not want you to be weaker than she. I saw Deborah die. It is only right that you see *her*." The cripple points with his gun to my temple.

He saw his wife die?! He killed her! It was not suicide! I look at my spouse. He has the same realization. The desperation of not having a way to extract us from this predicament is written all over his face. *I am sorry, sweetheart.*

"But it would be too easy to just shoot her. I would rather you watch her die slowly." Mullen follows with a speech that seems rehearsed. "Killing is an art. And revenge is a plate that is best served cold." He stands and makes a show of looking to excavate something. "My previous attempts to ruin your life through Wickham have failed for a reason. I see that now." *He was behind Georgiana's seduction!* "Now the long wait bears fruit." He stops a few steps from us. He stamps his foot, proving the consistency of the soil. "Here. This is the right place. Bring him here."

They drag Fitzwilliam. The general kneels back on me. "What are you waiting for? Help him dig the crypt. Their crypt," he mocks. "I cannot wait to see Bennet's face when I tell him how his dear daughter died — buried alive with her lover."

At the realization of what was this man's intent, I work harder than ever to block the present from my mind. I cannot watch my husband's humiliation! I CANNOT!

While the servants alternate digging next to Fitzwilliam, the monologue goes on. Only a few things intrude into my head during this horrible hour.

The general was Papa's best friend in Cambridge. He was the one my father looked to as an example. That is why the name 'Mullen' was familiar to me. He was the one that had saved him from a nasty fraternity initiation, like William had done for Charles. That is why he was successful in his encouragement to have Father sever his bonds with us.

My father trusts him blindly, although he was not easy to convince this time. "I had to expose all my dealings with you," he points Fitzwilliam with his gun. He had to narrate how his wife betrayed him, then. "But it was worth it!" He sneers at my father's naïveté. "Bennet has not changed over all these years. The idiot!"

The general and his men were already in the workshop at Lambton, buying a part for his mill, when our old driver arrived looking for the linchpin. The later explained Mr. and Mrs. Darcy were stranded on the road. They offered to help and were instructed where to find our path by our own people.

He confesses he killed Mr. Falcon because the clerk became suspicious. He also brags about poisoning his wife. He had tried the same with me in Cambridge. He was glad he was unsuccessful. He follows by explaining how he will make our death slower, by leaving a small aperture for air. The heaviness of the stones would not let us dig our way out.

"I wonder if you will have the guts to kill her yourself, with your own hands. Or if she will be the bravest and do you the favor."

Never! William will not die this way. He will survive until we are found by our family. Even if I have to feed him with my own blood!

Whilst my husband is left shoveling alone, he is salivating like a mad dog. "This is the best of my strategies. Not even ammunition is necessary, only a full moon and the prisoner."

After big piles of gravel and sand are accumulated around, my beloved climbs out of the big opening in the ground. His shirt and outwear dirty and in disarray, his boots muddy. He tosses the offending tool into the grave. His expression shows a determination I cannot understand. He cleans his hands on his topcoat.

The time has come. The realization that he had finished dawns on me. Why should we lose everything now that we are at last united? Now that we have found happiness? I feel as if someone were tearing my heart.

The general stands up. He nears the opposite side of the cavity. "You certainly are used to luxuries," he scoffs, observing the amount of gritty soil extracted. "I could bury a gang here. Are you planning to decorate your last home?"

My husband stares at him. His fists contract. His jaw tightens. His posture is like a trapped wolf. My mouth is arid. I panic. The torture nears. Mullen signals to me. I turn around on the ground. One of his men walks in my direction. I crawl in retreat. I do not want to be in that hole. I do not want to be thirsty. Not with William! I do not want to see him starve! It is going to be lightless. Oppressive. Airless. Yes, airless, what am I thinking — we are going to die! I can almost feel the heaviness of the earth they are going to throw on us. I feel asphyxiated. The monster nears. He shows his teeth. There is no escape. I try to get invisible. I hug my legs. I compact. I cannot breathe. He snatches my foot. I scream.

"DO NOT TOUCH HER! I WILL DO IT!" William pushes the men apart. I look at him bewildered. Why are you assisting them?

The general nods. They observe thrilled. This is insane.

William lifts me. "I will protect you." I recall his oath. I crave the security of his embrace. They can kill us. Yet, they cannot make us stop loving each other. He walks to the tomb. He stands in front of it. He arranges me to face him. He is defiant. My limbs are between our chests. He fixes me in a ball. I hide my head against my knees. He has chosen a strange position to cuddle me. He jumps in. I hear a loud crack. The ground is brittle. It relents. He makes a case with his body. An abysm opens before us. We fall together down a natural slope. The fall is irregular. We hit several stones. We crash in a muddy vault. Muffled voices curse outside. We are many feet underground. Alive. They cannot reach us.

It is pitch black. The air is musty. We are in a cavern. Fitzwilliam's embrace is still taut. I realize he planned this. This is why he dug deep. He is breathing hard. I am sitting on his stretched legs. Only an elbow aches. He has sheltered me. He received all the strikes. He must be injured. I cannot see him. I want to touch him. To ascertain the damage he suffered. I try to unfasten the ropes on my legs. I cannot. "William? Are you well?" I wiggle out of his hold. "Does it hurt too much?"

"I am well. Just disoriented. You?"

Relief washes over me. He is not unconscious. My God, I thank you. I kneel between his thighs and reach his temple with my lips. "I am fine." I caress his face with mine: his forehead, his eyes, his cheekbones, his nose, his chin. All seems dry. I take his arms between my tied hands. I explore them thoroughly. His topcoat is ripped in one place.

"Please... Elizabeth... Leave that for the morrow," he asks between low gasps. "All my bones are whole. I only hit my head and my rear. The first is too hard, and the second does not contain any vital organs."

He is as stubborn as ever — there are no major injuries. I breathe at last. Please, My Lord, keep him healthy. "Yes." I bend to listen to his heart. "What do you need?" He must be scraped all over.

"To rest."

Of course. I sit on my buttocks and extend my arms to determine if I can move outside his legs. The ground is irregular, however, flat enough. The space is wide. I change, trying not to lean on him. He reclines on his right side. I hate not seeing again! I travel the contour of his body with my knuckles carefully. He is curled facing the wall. His coat has many damp spots. Is it blood?

"Lizzy, come here with me," he tugs at my sleeve to indicate how. "I need to lie with you."

I obey and snuggle in his body. "I thought I was not going to feel this joy again."

His leg encircles mine. "I am glad this thick pelisse covers you so well. I could not forgive myself if that man harmed you. It did not cross my mind Deborah's husband could be the one that wanted to kill you. I thought him abroad. I underestimated him. Tomorrow will be another day. We will have some light. We will find water and a way out. All is well."

We are together. We are alive.

****

Now that I am laying here on our bed in Pemberley, after Mrs. Reynolds interrupted my previous intense memories with the menu choices, I can leave them behind and keep writing idly.

That night, William's plans to forget our circumstances until the next day were not to be. What actually happened was that I remained motionless, until I heard his low snores.

He was sleeping. Thank you. Thank you. Thank you, God. He was my love. My friend. My husband. My owner. My life. My everything. Please, God. Keep him away from harm. Keep him safe. Keep him alive. Help us survive. Help us find a safe exit.

I wondered what the general and his men were doing. They were too cowardly to come for us. They would like to close the entrance. I listened for any indication of movement outside. I could not discern any. Why have not they started already? The lack of light made me feel helpless. If only I could see William, and ascertain he was not badly injured.

When he tried to turn in his sleep, his moans were louder. I pictured his body bruised. I recollected the frightening hours that preceded this blind peace. He knew there were caves underground*. That was why he strove to work on his own. My protector.

I saw in my mind's eye the spectators of the previous hour astonished at our escape, the general swearing. I remembered his brusque tone when speaking about my father, and his self-satisfied mien when watching my husband dig. Someday God would punish him for this. The assassin. The butcher. The madman. I recalled his heaviness when he knelt on my spine. He did that to denigrate us. Now he was the laughingstock of his own people. I was pleased with William's cleverness in using our joined weights to break the soil. 'His best strategy'? Ha! The depraved-twisted-sadist degenerate!

"Elizabeth?"

"Yes, dear?"

"Would you take off my coat?"

"Yes." I shifted to face him and searched if I had to unhook the buttons. He had his chest exposed. "It is warmer here. Is it not?" I voiced, pretending to be unconcerned, while pulling the left sleeve out.

"Aggr," I heard a low protest when separating the fabric from his shoulder. "It is glued there."

"Sorry." So, it <u>was</u> blood, I stopped in my intent. How could I remove it without hurting him? "It would be easier if I could untie these ropes."

"WHAT?" He sat. "Why haven't you asked to help you before, Lizzy?"

I mirrored his position as his hands explored my arms. "You were too confounded, and I did not need that. I was as tired as you, love."

"Those savages! They tied you as if you were an animal. I will kill them! When we are out I will extract my revenge!"

"No more duels, Fitzwilliam, please! It is what brought us here."

He finished undoing the tight binding and moved to do the same with my legs. "I will find a way. I will not leave loose ends this time. I should have inquired about his condition after I wounded him that day. If I had only been aware that he lost the arm after the duel, I would have known he was the one behind the attacks!"

"Do not let that hate install itself into your soul. Odium only hurts the one feeling it. That man has built his own hell by nursing it for so many years."

"How can you ask me not to hate him?" He leveled so that his face was close to mine. "That man knelt on you! He tried to bury us alive! He poisoned you! He killed…"

I immersed my hands in his hair and pulled him closer to me. "I would also hate him, but I want us to forget what has happened." I kissed him, silencing his speech. I took advantage of this moment and explored his head with my fingers. It was dry.

"Lizzy, what are you doing?" He separated me forcefully.

"Proving you have already won this war. He cannot take this from us. We can be happy regardless of whether that man lives or not. <u>I</u> am happy if I know <u>you</u> are safe. We only need to place guards around Pemberley, when we find out how to escape from here. I cannot go through the horror of being afraid for your life."

"Guards around Pemberley? We would need an army for that." His arms went to touch my head and encountered the dilapidated bonnet. "Can I take this off?"

"Are you feeling better?"

"Yes," he tossed it aside and brushed the dirt from my hair. "You are the victim of my past mistakes, and you are still protecting me. My love, you should at least be mad for putting you in danger. You should be angry because I brought your family disruption, your blindness, Mr. Falcon's death and placed you at the threshold of the worst possible of deaths. All you have suffered is because of me."

"All that is worth living for is in you."

"You are too good. You should be cursing the moment you met me. If I had not gone to Netherfield with Bingley, you would not have met Wickham, and your life could be as peaceful as ever. You would not have those nightmares about the incident in Lambton."

Well, that is something you will have to teach me do. I am not proficient yet. Lady Catherine would say I lack practice once again." I tried to drag him out of this self-recriminating mood.

"What? … To teach you? What do you mean by practice?"

"Would you like to sleep more comfortably?" Sensing the moisture of the sweaty shirt I did not finish taking of, I sat behind him. "I was saying I need to practice the cursing words. I do not want to be clumsy at *that*."

"Practice cursing?" The fabric of the coat separated slowly from his shoulder — *he must have some scab there*. "Blast!" He shifted at my tearing. "It is easy with the right encouragement."

"Blast!" I imitated his masculine voice, extracting the sleeve from his right arm. "Damn it!" What else did I know? "God's teeth!" I finished taking his topcoat off. "Shit!"

"Bullshit!...Crap!...Merde!" he growled.

Well, if he could still speak French, his brain had to be intact. Better keep him focused on this subject. I lay the outerwear on the ground. "Mierda!" I remembered from Spanish. "Hell's teeth!"

"I see you took to heart the advice from my aunt. I should ask her to counsel you to keep me entertained at nights when I see her next."

"Are you bored in the nights, Mr. Darcy?" I commanded him to rest with a small push. "Are you complaining about my performance?"

"Not at all, dearest. It is just to guarantee you will not change your mind about *practicing* with me."

"I think you have extraordinarily weapons at your disposal, sweetheart. And Lady Catherine would be a hindrance if she were in my mind while we make love."

"Too true. I would put her on my blasphemy list next time."

---

*According to http://www.thepeakdistrict.info/peak-district-geology.php:
Several glaciations (during 2 of the 3 main episodes of the Pleistocene Ice Age, ending about 10,000 million years ago) affected the Peak District. Ice and melted water removed material and carved the valleys that visitors to the Peak District so enjoy. Sir Arthur Conan Doyle suggested, in his story 'The Terror of Blue John gap', that the area around Castleton was so hollow that if you hit it with a gigantic hammer, it would "boom like a drum or may even cave in completely".

Caverns are created by glacial melt waters travelling as underground rivers through the limestone. The detailed process is as follows:

- When the sea waters slowly retire, the groundwater level lowers (which is technically called phreatic level). The liquid coexists with the soil that is a mesh of rocks. The water, which is rich in oxygen, filtrates and dissolves the volcanic stones. This volcanic rocks have many sulfates. This reaction produces sulfuric acid.

- The sulfuric acid attacks the limestone and slowly, but constantly, opens cavities that are soft and round.

- The beautiful drapery is produced much later (around 3 million years ago) when the phreatic level is lower than the caverns. Now the rain, rich in carbon dioxide, is the one that is going to filtrate and react; giving carbonic acid. It results in a liquid saturated in calcium bicarbonate. This dissolved limestone is the one that builds the columns and decorations seen in the caves.

Chapter 28

After interminable hours, not many of actual sleep due to the fear of whether the assassins were still outside, a small light filtered in. At first, it was barely perceivable, but it gradually became clearer. The sun's rays were scattering through two sources: a bigger one from the entrance where Fitzwilliam and I had fallen, and a smaller one from a far corner, close to the ground. I distinguished the walls through the gloom*. This was about the size of my room in Longbourn.

The ceiling was not high, only enough for us to stand in the majority of it. The stones were all kinds of shapes, from sharp ones to smooth ones. Several reminded me of trees, others of wild animals and the hugest, of the columns in King's College. The shades also permitted us to see that there were many irregular formations on the ground, some of them looking like piles of sand and others as little gnomes. We were lucky not to hit those.

The darkness transformed slowly into a picture in black and white, and I could distinguish the top of the cavern better. There were parts where towering columns of conic-like rocks were almost floating. Some, on the contrary, seemed weightless: they looked like ice drops and flowed in directions that defied gravity. The most incredible ones were stones that appeared to be reaching one for the other — two lovers who would come together after centuries of longing. I guessed that they all had different colors, that with enough candles this place could look like a shop with enormous candies. I regretted not being able to decipher further the many sculpts and the dyes of the minerals that should be part of these walls, until I realized that the lack of illumination was the source of our protection as well. The general had not attempted to reach us because from outside they saw nothing. As long as there was more light outside than inside**, this place was safe.

The thought made me bend to observe the adorable head resting on my lap. He wanted me to believe he was asleep, to tease me again with this trick. He did not have any injury on his face; a bump on one side of his scalp was the only reminder. I traveled down his back and legs. He was covered all over with mud. I would observe him closely later, to determine if a severe wound was disguised under those stains.

I returned to delight in his profile. I pictured a boy around five years old, with black curly hair and large bones, coming home after many hours of adventures in the trees. "I want you to give me at least one like that," I whispered in his ear, to confirm he was awake.

"What do you want me to give you, Lizzy?"

Little rascal, I knew it! "A son that looks like you — you may give me many more, but at least one must resemble you."

"And what if I want only girls?"

"Oh, believe me, you do not want that."

"Why? I have always pictured myself like a monarch, being attended by my charming daughters when old."

"Ask Papa and you will see it is the opposite." I brushed his nose with my finger, happy to see that he was not disoriented any longer. "It is more likely that you will become the slave of all their whims."

"Like I am yours now?"

"Worse. They are going to bewitch you with 'I love you' and 'You are the best father in the whole world' while climbing into your lap."

"I can get used to that." He extracted his arms from behind me and moved to sit carefully. "Why do we not practice?"

"I promise to oblige you as soon as you are able to receive me," I promised, seeing him wince when leaning on his left cheek. "Come. We need to stretch our legs, and this seems like the place where one could find a pirate's treasure." I was determined not to let him get depressed, no matter the circumstances, "Our boy will want you to bring him here."

He made his best imitation of a smile and stood up. The still semi-dark stones projected a strange shadow on his face, and I had the sensation of having an elderly man in front of me.

He made a small tour around the room and concluded there were not many places to hide and no water. We needed to choose between two alternatives: climbing back or trying the other small entrance.

Fitzwilliam walked a few strides in the direction of the cavity we descended from. He tossed aside the shovel that had landed with us the night before. He gazed up and reached with his right arm, to explore the ceiling and slope of what looked like a long tube. I approached and touched the hard mineral above us. The conic-like passage was irregular more than fifteen feet from where we were standing (which could serve as a protection if it was attempted to fire down from the exterior). However, the stone closer to us was slippery and even. We fell more than twenty yards in total.

I looked for imperfections that could serve as a step to scale up the high angle. There were none. I asked if it was safe trying to go to the surface now. My companion inspected the stones that were farther away. He answered he would attempt to approach silently, if there was a way to stretch to the part that was uneven enough to climb.

"Do you want me to try climbing on your shoulders and seeing where I can reach that way?"

"Only if you promise you will take the rope they used to immobilize you, and fasten it somewhere, for me to scale past you and explore the upper part."

He intertwined his fingers to lift me. With my hands on his shoulders I took impulse to step on them. I saw a flash of pain cross his eyes. I backed up. "Let me do some knots with my skirt," I explained, thinking of a way to alleviate his suffering without making him confess what he obviously wanted to conceal from me. "Would you put on your topcoat, William? I think the fabric is less smooth and easier for me to feel secure, this way." I took off my boots. "My father says I am a little monkey, but even a monkey needs a place to grab." We repeated the previous operation. I was over his head in no time. We leaned together on the wall, and I inspected the tube. I touched the stones that were around me. On my hands and knees, I searched every inch, for an irregularity robust enough for me to cling to. Nothing! This was an impossible task. "Sorry, love, we must think of some other method." I descended. I looked at his unaffected eyes and shifted my gaze to his arms. The sun's rays coming from the outside were brighter in this spot, and I could discern that many of the stains I considered to be dirt, were dry blood trails instead. I fixed my gaze on his face again. Resolve was written all over him. Scoop in hand, I directed to a corner where some medium sized rocks were scattered. "Maybe we can make a mountain and ascend it."

Fitzwilliam made the gesture to peek again through the gap, and retreated briskly when some noises were heard outside. He pushed me away from the entrance and stole the tool from me. He ordered to go to a far spot while he stood alert for anyone to intrude. I gathered some loud voices, one of them from the general, but could not discern the words. Interminable minutes passed in awe, until an avalanche of black particles came from the hole. "It is gunpowder***. We have to find another way out," he signaled to the small aperture that provided an additional source of illumination. I put on my boots, and grabbed the pelisse and the rope. I hurried to the other route of escape. When kneeling to crawl through it, I was pulled by one leg. "If there is an abyss, I want to be sure you will not fall," he stated while tying my ankle to his wrist.

He ushered me back inside the passage. Guided by the light at the other end of it, I was on the other side after a few moves. I pulled at the cord, and my beloved appeared from the dark. He gave a short glimpse to the surroundings and took me to the opposite extreme of the new chamber. He turned me against the ground, disentangled the rope from his wrist hurriedly, covering me with his body, enveloping my head in his arms.

BANG!

A loud roar shook the earth. They had blown up the entrance.

****

We observed the cloud of dust that replaced the corner we had come from. No noise or ray of light come from it. Fitzwilliam took the shovel again and waited to hear any voice or clue about the activity in the outer chamber. There was none. This was now a blind end.

We looked up and saw a dome with an unreachable opening at the top. This new room was much bigger, but still dim.

"Will they try to close this access too?"

"No. They believe us dead. What they are most likely to see, should they search, will be a dark void. And even that is difficult to find without a guide. This is a safe place."*** He walked to a faraway part where the few rays of sunshine were making beautiful reflections. He said with more enthusiasm than I would have expected, "Water!"

It was amazingly abundant. I touched it. "It is not cold. The whole chamber is warm."

"Yes," he kneeled besides me. He sipped, tasting it slowly, "It is clean." He followed the stream with his eyes and found out this was a small underground river. "We can survive here as long as necessary."

I looked at him quizzically, and he reached for my hand and squeezed it.

"These mountains are crowded with caves, but not all of them are connected one with the other." He looked at the ceiling, "This orifice could be the only communication with the outside world."

"That means we cannot escape from this cavern?"

"We will, Lizzy, just not right now. We will explore it in detail, and we will either find a new passage to the surface or be rescued by our families. I am sure there are many teams of Pemberley's tenants searching for us already."

This was as large as a small palace; there had to be many other similar caves next to it. "I will not give up, William! I will search until I have a solution."

"My love, you must prepare for a stay of a few days. We were lucky to have found a connection out of that grave. If you had been able to escape up the entrance, you would now be dead."

"I...I...I do not want to starve again."

"A person can survive several weeks with only water, but we will find food too. Give it some time. We could not go out anyway now. Those men may still be waiting for us to emerge."

"William, you must let me take off your clothes, then. You cannot stay with all this mud glued to the injuries you received during our fall." After he resignedly accepted, I took off his topcoat carefully. I noted the many trails of dark color that crowded it inside and undid his waistcoat. It was disturbingly attached to his shirt and skin in some parts. "Sweetheart, would you let me wet it before removing it — to make the process less painful?"

He nodded once more, and I tore a part of my petticoat to soak it in the water. I worked slowly to detach the fabric with the soothing liquid. I managed to extract his upper garments without much agony while he remained in a kneeling position.

I observed his naked back carefully. A chill ran down my body at the hurtful image of his former velvet skin. He had scrapes, blisters and bruises in many parts. His left side was showing a profound cut, that started at his middle region and was hidden under his trousers; blood covering the entire area.

I pictured the jagged rocks ripping his flesh. He did not even release a scream when it happened. I made the resolution to not show the fear of having an infection spread on his many wounds. I looked at his stained buttocks. I hesitated for a moment, out of modesty, but reasoned instantly there was no space for that sentiment here — that I must clean all his wounds, no matter where they were.

I unfastened his lower clothes and slid them down to his thighs. This flesh was wet because he was still bleeding! I pressed the damp rag to the wound carefully to see how deep it was. My God! I could not help a sob escaping. My finger could immerse almost an inch into the incision in his cheek.

"I need to relieve myself. I will be right back." I ran to the farthest corner and hid beside a big rock. I sat on the black floor and hugged my knees to my chest. Why? Why did this have to happen to you? Why must you suffer like this? A low cry broke from my throat.

"Lizzy?" I felt a pair of strong arms around me. "This is nothing, sweetling. This is nothing. I heal very fast. I will be well in no time."

"I…You…How did you?... I am well. I was just…"

"Any sound in this kind of place can be heard for more than a mile. You cannot hide from me here."

"I… This is silly. It will not happen again."

"Elizabeth, there is nothing wrong with crying. Any other woman would be wailing desperately if trapped here. Do it. Let it flow. Cry. I know you need it."

"Crying is wrong. It is a weapon that wives use to manipulate their husbands. I should not do it in front of you."

"Where have you learned such a falsehood?" He pulled at my hand to make us rise. "I have never seen you cry without a good reason."

"It does not resolve anything."

He dragged me to a somewhat brighter spot and looked at me straight. I could not suppress the shame for being the one weeping. He sat me on a smooth and tall rock that permitted us to have our eyes at the same level. "You are used to suppressing your thoughts when you think things are 'bad feelings' and <u>that</u> is exactly what is wrong. You did it yesterday — you withheld your hate against the general, and you are doing it now. You did it when you were jealous of Deborah, and it worked to my advantage that night, except that I should not have done that, without convincing you properly. There are no bad feelings. You can be sad, you can be frightened, you can hate, you can feel whatever you choose," he kissed my nose to lighten the mood, "as long as you still love me."

****

We neared the stream again, and I cleaned his skin. I enfolded his rear with lace, distracting both of us with the tale about the first time I sat on his lap — when he came to my attic while I was drunk. I admitted how handsome I found him without his cravat and coat that day, and we laughed together at the remembrance of my clumsiness. He explained how that image of me in the doorway had stayed in his mind. How he fantasized about opening my shirt and staring at my breasts unabashedly. He confessed he stole a kiss when I was sleeping. We ended inventing scenarios of what would have happened if we had been both inebriated.

When my stomach produced a shabby sound, Fitzwilliam went to find the food in the funniest of attires, with only one of my underskirts and his boots on. I stayed to wash his clothes in the small river.

What could he be referring to by food? Not a snake or a rat I hoped. I could not ingest those animals. At least not without cooking them. I inspected our surroundings carefully. Yes, this place had the structure of a cathedral. The cascade of pipe-like stones could be associated with an organ. The marble-like walls reminded me of St. Etheldreda. The irregular rounded stones could be angel sculptures. The cupola had a framework of interlaced white rocks that could be mistaken with the picture of the façade of St Mark's

Basilica**** I saw in my father's library. That corner was an altar. God had not abandoned us.

After a couple of hours cleaning, rinsing and squeezing, a familiar hand blinded me from behind. "Try this. It is surprisingly tasteful."

I caught his arm and stopped him before taking a bite, "Are you not going to tell me what it is?"

"No."

I drew out my tongue and touched the offered snack with the edge. Not bad. I took it inside. It cracked under my teeth and tasted a salty chicken-like texture. "Shrimp?"

He withdrew his fingers from my face, and I observed the remaining four morsels he was offering. "They are cave crickets. I just took off their paws."

"They are almost translucent. How could you find them?"

"Oh, believe me, it was quite tricky. It required infinite patience." He moved to kneel beside me. "Come, have more."

"Did you find another chamber during your excursion?" Resolute not to starve, I finished eating in a blink.

"No. I only went to the farthest and darkest nook and waited for my vision to accustom to the shadows."

No way out yet. "And how do you feel?" His knees had to be aching from keeping this position all that time. "Are you not tired, dear?"

"I just need some sleep. I am going to take your pelisse and find a tranquil and flat spot. Do not embark on any adventure before I wake up."

****

I gave up cleaning the most difficult stains in my husband's attire after an hour more. Why was blood so difficult to remove!?***** I gathered the many ropes to scatter them on stones and dry them up. One was missing: his shirt. I found it hooked on a rock in the stream; luckily it did not swim away.

296

A slimy and restless surprise awaited me while extending the garment to dry: "A fish! A fish, William! A FISH!" I ran to his side, brandishing the three-inch animal. "We fished it!" I brushed his lips with it.

"What?" he rubbed his eyes, "Let me see it." He captured it and took it away in the direction of the light. "It is transparent too."

"Yes. I think it is blind. Look at the membranes it has over the orbits."

"Take it. I am sure you are hungry still."

"No, love. It is your turn. I am sure you have not eaten enough either."

"No, Lizzy. You are the one that has been ill recently."

I walked away backwards. "You need it more than I."

He straightened too, and followed me. "Remember you promised to obey, Wife."

"Do not try to compete with me in stubbornness, Mr. Darcy. The masseter muscle is the strongest in the body; you will not be able to open my mouth if I do not want it."

I had to stop on the shore. He hovered over me, trying to look hostile, and I replied by tightening my jaw. He grabbed my waist and slowly put us together to lie on the moist ground. He impressed his weight on me strongly, "Elizabeth!"

I kissed him fast, nevertheless I did not relent. He waited for a change of attitude until he tired of my teasing demeanor. He moved his weight to rest on his good side and placed the food on my forehead. What a funny picture this must be.

He squeezed the bridge of his nose until he took the fish into his mouth and leaned to kiss me too. I observed him vigilantly while he nibbled at my lips and pushed his tongue against my teeth. His Adam's apple had not moved. He thought he could trick me this way — by pushing the animal inside. No. No. No, Mr. Darcy.

He insisted for a little more, exercising his mastery in the business of giving me pleasure, in a way that I almost fell to the temptation, until he (thankfully) believed this was a lost battle. "Madam, you are really unnerving sometimes!" he affirmed after a grimace that indicated he had swallowed.

I laughed at his offended expression and promised him in return, "I will find a way to cook it next time. You must be missing your French cook."

"Really?"

"Yes. I am an expert in making bonfires."

"And how exactly are you planning to catch another fish?"

I pushed him and took my dress off. "This way."

"With your arts and allurements?" he mocked, pulling at the hem of my pantaloons.

I removed his hand aside and covered my thighs with it the best I could. Afterwards, I went to stand with one leg at each side of the flow, immersing my gown across it. I stretched to pull two heavy stones to hold the fabric in place. "You see? Now we have a web to trap them all."

"I see."

"Come. Now we must find some flint before the daylight is over."

****

"Would you remind me why we need flint, Lizzy?" William asked, exasperated, after I inspected closely half of the walls of the chamber we were in.

I directed to one of the obscure corners where we had not been yet. "We obviously need it to have a spark to start a blaze."

"What do we need a bonfire for? It could be dangerous and it is warm."

"Yes, love, but in a couple of minutes, it is going to be as dark as the bottom of a well. We could build it in a secure corner."

"It does not matter to me," he grabbed my hand to command my attention. "I am going to fall slumbering like one of those stones at any minute."

****

Five new bites were caught in our improvised web, before Fitzwilliam rested his head on my lap to sleep.

Thanks to the full moon's rays that peered inside, somehow, our surroundings and the slow movement of the waters were distinguished.

My thoughts drifted to our family, and I mulled over what Ana might be thinking. She had to be inconsolable — overwhelmed with grief. I threw into the stream the small stones that I could reach in the semi-darkness. *And Papa does not even know that we are here! That his friend wanted to kill us.* I observed how waves were formed in the flow with each splash. In that instant, one of the stones I was playing with hit a rock, making a thud and extracting a spark.

A SPARK!

I mined another sample from the same pile the previous gravel laid. I surveyed it in my hand. It was white. I took a bigger stone, rubbing it against the previous one.

Nothing happened.

I disentangled cautiously from Fitzwilliam's weight. I approached the place where the shovel laid. I rubbed this unique stone against it. Nothing either. I hit the metal with force. A new spark was produced.

IT WAS CHERT******! Now we truly could survive as long as necessary!

---

*In the caves occurs an interesting effect with the way the human eye perceives light. The rhodopsin (the molecule responsible for vision) can distinguish when a single photon interacts with it. So we can normally see (at least in black and white) in an almost black place.

** This effect of not being able to look inside a cave from the outside, is the same that you can encounter every day when you are in a street during daylight, and you try to and CANNOT look inside a house that has no inner illumination (even though inside said room, people CAN see every detail clearly).

*** Gunpowder was invented by the Chinese a long time ago, and it was the best that humanity could afford before Alfred Nobel invented dynamite. Nowadays this last explosive is considered the ideal to blow holes in caves. In Regency times however, gunpowder would have had to do (sadly it had much limited and unpredictable capabilities).

****Saint Mark's Basilica in one of the greatest symbols of Venetia.

***** Have you ever asked yourself *"Why is blood so difficult to remove?"* The short answer is that the proteins responsible for coagulation are not dissolved by water. The long one is here:
http://en.wikipedia.org/wiki/Coagulation

******Chert is a mineral that has the same properties as flint. It makes a spark when it is pressed in some way. It has the same properties as the quartz stones that make the spark in gas kitchens — **piezoelectricity** — which is, that it creates an electric field when it is subject to a tension.

WARNING: Never drink water in a cave that has been inhabited before you. Human stool possesses a bacteria cold Escherichia Coli which can cause serious poisoning.

Chapter 29

What could I burn to make a fire? I was thrilled with the prospect of cooking. Our clothes would serve to start the process, but they would not last long and they were moist. If we had a branch or a root... If we could reach them, we would be outside already. I closed my eyes trying to remember anything that could have been made with wood at our reach: The shovel handle would not last long either. Aaggrr.

Do not despair, Lizzy. Think...think about what you have learned about combustion*. I pictured the reaction:

Fuel + Oxygen = Heat + Water + Carbonic gas

I tried to reason slowly, step by step. I kept my eyelids shut. The reactant that was missing was the fuel, which necessarily must contain carbon**...the oxygen was in the air...carbon was part of all the living creatures...it was also present in the composition of some rocks*** ...or...there were minerals like coal that were almost pure...

"What are you doing, Lizzy?"

I opened my eyes to find Fitzwilliam hovering over me with his fists on his hips. "I have fantastic news. I found chert. I am only pondering how to find charcoal in such a dark place."

"Making a bonfire here is too hazardous. Besides, what dark place are you speaking about?" he turned to show the walls behind him. "Look at those stones that are shining like green flowers****."

An breathtaking picture awaited me: it looked like fireflies all over, contrasting brightly in the blackness. "It is beautiful," I could not believe my eyes. "What are those lights in the rocks, William? Where do they come from?"

"It is phosphorous I believe."

"Wow. It is as if we were living in the middle of the skies." I approached the mineral and touched it. "It feels like any other. How can this be?"

"I do not know. The stars in the Universe are the ones I have researched — not these. I am only speculating it is phosphorous because Sedgwick told me about it on one of our excursions."

"You are still exhausted. Are you not?" I realized when he returned to his previous spot, not uttering another word (glancing at me as though resigned to my adventurous spirit). "I think I would rather listen to a tale about the real stars. Would you speak to me about them?"

This time his enthusiasm was genuine, "That would be a challenge I am very pleased to take," he patted my pelisse next to him. "You do not care if I cannot actually show you the constellations, do you?"

I helped him arrange himself, and he extended his arm for me to snuggle with my back next to him — our legs intertwined in a favorite position.

"Do you remember when I told you that Galileo Galilei was the first one to actually see the rings of Saturn? Well, he drew them as if the planet had two moons. He could not figure out those moons were actually rings."

"I only knew he was an inventor of telescopes, like the one you repaired for me. Why could he not discern the actual rings?"

"Because Galileo died before Antonie van Leeuwenhoek***** was born. It was impossible to have a clear image without the lenses that van Leeuwenhoek developed much later. The lenses are the key for any optic instrument. Be it telescopes or microscopes, the quality of the glass is everything."

"That is an instrument I will be thrilled to use one day — a microscope. Can you imagine studying the many small animals that must live here? Can you imagine watching the organisms responsible for Smallpox, like Edward Jenner******, and finding a vaccine?"

"No, but I must acknowledge some other *organisms* are pretty interesting to watch with a telescope," he declared with a mischievous tone.

"Really? Like what?"

"Like wood nymphs rambling through Rosings Park."

"What?" I strained my neck to see his face.

"Do not try to deny it. You know I was observing you. Why else would you turn around so often?"

"It could also be your cousin," I teased.

"He would have, if you were only in your underwear, but alas, you were not."

"In my underwear? How shocking!"

"Oh yes. You see, he convinced me to take the telescope to my townhouse, when we were teenagers, and he installed it strategically in <u>his</u> room. I could not understand this sudden interest in astronomy, until I caught him pointing the tube in the direction of the house of one of our female neighbors."

"What did you do?"

"What can one do with Richard? He is incorrigible! I took the instrument to my chambers. But that did not dissuade him — I found him in my room when I awoke from my sleep. I ended up arming and disarming it every time I used it."

"What did you need it for in town, if the nearby lights would not allow you to see a clear sky there?" I was curious if Fitzwilliam spied on his neighbors too.

"Observe the moon, of course. No matter if you can only see one face, it is a beautiful landscape."

"Do not worry, dearest, I would not think ill of you if you followed his steps at that age."

This time my companion was the one to turn me to lie on my back in order to look me in the eyes. "Are you speaking in earnest?"

"Yes. I am starting to understand what happened *that* day. I am starting to accept that I should forgive those boys, and that lust and curiosity are part of being human. I should not be so hard on any of them."

"When are you going to forgive <u>yourself</u>?"

"Forgive myself? I cannot do that. I provoked my mother's hysterical crying. I caused us to have to leave our home in Bakewell. I made her miserable for many years because of my mistake. I…" Oh, God, it was difficult to speak about this.

"You should, Lizzy. No matter the outcome of what you did, you should see that you did nothing wrong. That you only agreed to play out of an innocent desire to be part of a group. There is nothing wrong in the game you thought you were going to play — Blind man's bluff. There is nothing of which you should feel shame."

"Yes, there is! I should have listened to Jack's warning. I should have seen he was right when he told me to go away; that I should not play with boys."

"I do not agree with you. You were used to playing with boys and there can be many other reasons why your mother decided to remove you from Derbyshire. It could have been something the late Mr. Wickham told her. I do not know. She might have been afraid of something else — something that Mr. Bennet and she did. Still, the price you have paid for wanting to be included is too high. It is disproportionate. It truly makes no sense. I would like you to internalize that — to cry it out of yourself and forgive the girl who was lonely and in need of friends and affection. You ought to picture her as the fragile little child you were, and recognize that nothing is your fault. Nothing."

Could he be right about this? Was it that easy? Just forgive myself and go on as if nothing had happened that day? How could I do that? How could this guilt be erased? How could I not be responsible for what I did?*******

"Lizzy, I believe there are millions of stars," he continued in a soothing storytelling-like way. "I even believe there could be other civilizations like ours. There is only one thing that is impossible to find — someone like you. You are my most precious gift from The Creator. I have meditated about this since I read your diaries. I know that Mrs. Parker, your Sunday School teacher, took from you something everyone needs in his childhood. She stole from you the belief that you could be loved unconditionally. She used the highest ideals to impregnate the conviction that you did not deserve to be cared for, that you were unworthy and had to change. She told you that you were undeserving of God's love. I think that if your parents knew the burden you carry, they would reassure you. The same as I am doing now. They love you, and were proud of you as a child. As they are not here right now, let me tell you this in their name and in my name. We adore you without bounds, the same as He, no matter what you do. We love you without conditions. I have found you flawless since the day you stepped into Netherfield with your petticoats six inches in mud. I will be by your side no matter what."

"Would you tell me about that day? Would you tell me why you changed your mind (about me being too young for you), when I visited the Bingleys?"

"I was surprised by your appearance, which was certainly quite tempting after the exercise. Nevertheless, what struck me the most was your gesture towards your sister. Georgiana would need a strong encouragement to walk by herself for three miles. You see, I love her dearly, but she is by no means that unselfish. That was the moment I really grasped the woman you were, a woman worth loving. When I saw you with Mrs. Bingley, I so lamented not being the recipient of your devoted love!"

The warmth emanating from his body and his tale were addictively comforting. I craved more, "And how is it that you did not change your mind when you saw me dressed like a boy?"

"In Cambridge you say? I was frightened to death that I could not find you; and then, when I did, that people would realize you were a girl. It was very difficult to abide by your wishes, when you asked if I would force you to leave. I was convinced everybody saw how beautiful you were. I was terrified — that was the prevailing sentiment."

"I am so sorry, love. I am so sorry for having run away from home. I should have talked to Papa when he asked me to unburden my soul following Jane's wedding. He begged me to talk to him, and I did not oblige. On the contrary, I hid behind my anemia. I see now I was very stupid, very irresponsible when I ran away. I am sorry it took this experience for me to realize how much I grieved my family. And, many years before, when I was ten, I should have spoken to my father too, instead of searching that forbidden book. I should not have kept any secrets from him from that day on. He and my mother have been the best of parents. They have always fought for our family. They have been so very caring!"

He pushed one of my legs between his. He encircled me with his thigh and enveloped me like a warm quilt. "I am glad you are doing this, Lizzy. I would only ask you not to be so harsh on yourself. Being curious is part of your scientific personality. You were much younger than Georgiana when you read Sade, and even she struggled to tell me about the arrangement to elope with Wickham. It is not easy to talk about this with a man. In fact, it is quite difficult to speak of these to anyone. "

****

The floor we were sleeping on was hard and irregular; the breeze that intruded once in a while was cold. Our clothes were dirty and inadequate. Still, when we awoke, the second day of our stay in the cave, I could not help the recurrent thought that Fitzwilliam's grip was heavenly. *It will be this incredibly cozy until we are old and waning*, I pictured my beloved with gray hair and surrounded by noisy grandchildren, trying to get him to read stories late at night. Will he put on his severe mask to send them off to their governesses, or will he just be the compliant grandfather who cannot say 'no'?

"It is snowing outside," my companion stated. "We should better stay like this all day long."

"What about eating, my dear?"

"I am not hungry. You eat fish. I will wait here."

"I will go and bring some. Do not move."

I disentangled myself and went to collect our food. *There may be a route of escape if I follow the course of this stream.* I drank some water and carried another portion in my mouth.

He opened his eyes merrily when he felt the soothing liquid enter his teeth. "Mmmm."

"I wish I had some coffee to offer, but this is at least warm," I placed some snacks in his hand. "I wonder why this cave is so hot when it is cold outside."

"I do not know. I think Sedgwick told me once that lava from the former volcanoes gave rise to the dry land. That could be the source of heat in this cavern. We can ask him some day."

"You resemble Robinson Crusoe before meeting Friday," I pointed at his growing whiskers. "Do you miss your valet?"

He chuckled surprised at my change of subject, and taunted me back, rubbing his face against my shoulder. "Who would you be in that case? The siren that guards the island?"

"No. I can only be Cinderella now. I do not think these soiled pantaloons and chemise can belong to any sophisticated character."

"Are you sure? I think you can play that role remarkably well if you sing with only your pantaloons on."

"Do you want me to sing? Do you want me to sing and make love afterwards?"

His stare returned at me longingly, "I am sorry, I am too tired. Resting seems more appealing."

I saw the many scrapes that were visible on his skin even from this angle. I thought of the annoyance he must feel, not being able to sit properly. "You are right. I would better enjoy this peace."

We needed to get out of here soon. He needed a doctor. I lamented for the hundredth time.

****

After a while, we approached the stream to clean Fitzwilliam's wounds. He was not improving. He had developed an infection instead. I wrapped him again with the few clean fabric strips that remained and dressed him in his dry trousers. I waited for him to fall asleep, to undergo the challenge I planned during this time. *I must explore in the direction the water flows.*

Clad in his long shirt, I kept my pantaloons and boots. The long sleeves would protect my arms better than my blouse. I wrapped the hand that was dislocated in Cambridge the tightest I could. This was just a precaution. I was virtually healed. I studied the opening. It was not deep at all, and I could try to kneel in it and follow the route of the river. I could dive under occasionally — if I was careful with the time needed to breathe from one immersion to the other. I stooped in the passage and studied the rocks all around the irregular tube as long as my hand could reach. I whispered a small prayer. The water was welcoming and the floor muddy. The only problem was the absolute darkness of the passage, like when I was poisoned — I could do it!

With my head out, I moved cautiously many yards. Eventually, a rock from the ceiling blocked my path. It grazed the surface of the stream, but I still had enough space to advance. Using my hands as eyes, I realized there was room for me to catch some air after submerging for the first time. *Do it for William*, I reminded myself, pushing away the phobia of getting trapped. I took a mouthful of air and followed my resolution.

The same routine ensued for a long hour: I explored with my fingers blindly, before immersing, and then I crawled just the distance that I was sure to be prudent. Every time I felt intimidated by the challenge, I brought the images of Fitzwilliam's wounds to my mind to raise my courage. It worked, until the rocks became closer and closer together, and the thought that I might not find my way back overtook me. There were moments, whilst the water filled the upper limit, when I was not sure if there was sufficient distance for me to draw out my head. *Oh Lord, please, I beg you. Don't let me lose myself here.*

Striving for rationality, I tried measuring the distance required to have enough oxygen in my lungs, in case of needing to retreat. At the end, it was impossible to move forward safely. I crept back, trembling and beaten.

When I reached the wider part of this long route, I found enough room to sit in the stream and recline on a wall to rest.

I wept for lost hopes freely, taking refuge in the notion that, thanks to the water, the sound would not propagate into the chamber my beloved was sleeping in. When were we going to find an exit, My Lord? When?

I found it cathartic. I found that crying was the best I could do under these circumstances. I took advantage of the intimacy this place afforded to whimper, wail, hit the water and kick with rage the stones around me. The solution was in God's hands. Like Mrs. Beth told me. I had to stop attempting to control the future.

Last night's conversation intruded in my mind. The line between abuse and a game was difficult to discern. William said the abuser never remembered as much as the abused. If they did not carry all the weight of their mistakes under their shoulders, why should I?

There could be some relationship between the fraternity initiations and lust, as well. That was almost a tradition in Cambridge. It resembled what had happened to me in my childhood. It could not be so very unforgivable to participate in them. Another of our dialogues stroke me. He said, "People care little about those they have not met before." This probably was one of the many causes of slavery. And slavery was as old as humanity.

There was some difficulty in matching my rational thoughts with my feelings, nonetheless. Where can he have learned to be this insightful? Where does all this knowledge come from? This intelligence was not something he came upon easily. There was a veiled suffering behind it. He was quieting his own remorse and his own need for forgiveness.

****

I crawled out of the river to find William pacing restlessly. "What is the matter?"

"Dear God, Elizabeth, where have you been? I have searched everywhere for you." He bent his upper body to rest on a big stone. "Why did you leave me without notice? You scared me to death."

I ran to the corner where he has chosen to lean. "I am well. I just went to explore a passage that seemed a logical route of escape. I did not mean to frighten you."

"You were looking for an escape through the water?" he shouted. "Are you out of your mind?"

"Do not be irate, I was extremely cautious not to do anything too reckless. I am here now."

He set his forehead on the rock; his stance the one of a castaway drained of his physical force. I hugged him from behind to placate his wrath. He had a fever!

"You need to lie down again, sweetheart. I will not leave you alone. I will be by your side." I guided him to our improvised bed. "I will take care of you." I wetted several rags to cool him. With the resolution to keep his spirits high, I distracted us with remembrances of the many moments we had shared together. He liked the most, the part when I enacted the dialogues with his aunt. The way I made up suggestions about, how to cross his legs, take the spoon, sip the soup and clean his teeth covertly (if a piece of meat was misplaced between two grinders) were his favorites. I also recalled our wedding night and the trips in his carriage, as well as our naughty behavior.

I used all the weapons at my disposal.

"You said that you fantasized about opening my shirt and staring at my breasts when I was drunk, is that right Mr. Darcy?" I went to dress in his great topcoat, to resemble my appearance on that afternoon as closely as I possible. "What about playing with that idea a little more?" I arranged myself alongside him. Would he take the hint?

His reaction was slow and timid. However, the way he crossed his ankles showed he was not immune to this game.

Seeing that he was too subdued by the high temperature, I proceeded to unbutton the garment myself. I relaxed on my back, putting my arms as a pillow behind my head.

He extracted one hand and traveled the contour from my armpits to my hips with his knuckles.

The melancholic manner of this caress and the wetness in his eyes was unexpected. "Do not be sad. This is a gift, a present to make you happier."

His answer was to lie over my thighs, his head against my diaphragm, holding me unyieldingly. "I will make this up to you, Lizzy. I will make this up to you!"

"I know. I know we will be out soon. I know we are not lost. You told me this yourself. We are not lost, because the North Star is visible through the opening of the roof."

****

That night and next day were the worst of my life; my beloved's deteriorating health and the drain of our energies from exhaustion and fear were taking their toll on us.

In the afternoon of our third day, a strange noise was heard.

"AAAHHHYYYYY," it came from nowhere. "AAYYYY OOOODYYY TEEERR". I looked in the direction of the hole in the ceiling. It was not from there.

"AAAHHHYYYyyy."

"Did you hear that?"

"Yes!" I put on my boots speedily and ran instinctively. *The noise must come from a remote corner. I feel a breeze.*

"WAIT!"

I did not obey until the light was so slim I had to accustom my eyesight to the shadows. I stood impatiently until I could establish my surroundings. I discerned a barely visible vertical fissure in the black stones. I reached for it and inserted my head to look inside. It was narrow and dark. I followed the contour down. The tube widened in one direction.

A light approached fast from behind me. It was Fitzwilliam that had managed to build a torch with the opposite extreme of the shovel and a few fabrics. He dropped on his knees close to me. He pointed to the orifice with it, breathing heavily. He looked at me with a silent question.

"Yes, I can do it!" I took the lantern from him.

"Please, please, Lizzy, be careful. It could be our salvation, but I cannot lose you…"

I disappeared in the blackness.

---

* In 1812, the Carbon dioxide (CO_2), we are so well used to consider part of life, was called "Carbonic gas". Lizzy is stating in this text the simplest equation for combustion.

** Carbon is present in all living organisms and is an indispensable part of the reactants, in the type of combustion Lizzy is trying to achieve here. Let's see what she has. 1) She has the chert stones that are scattered in some parts, which would serve to make a spark. The spark must be converted into fire by a material that combusts easily/rapidly: 2) their cotton clothes can serve for that (any fiber in general could), although the best would be hay. Once the fire is started, she needs to make it last. The rapidly combusting materials will not serve: 3) she needs minerals like charcoal (as she will not find any wood in a cave). Charcoal is easy to extract from a wall if you have adequate instruments — like the shovel — it is not a hard mineral and

England is known to have a lot of charcoal depositions (thanks to swamps that were buried millions of years before). So, in her case, this is not an impossibility, she just will have to find it between the limestone strata.

BUT, the extraction of coal is a dangerous adventure, as it involves the emanation of gases which also combust easily. Many accidents have happened in mines due to these gases; that is why the author is not forcing our heroes to build a fire. They are in a warm cave, which is a likely event, as part of England was formed by volcanoes and (although they will not erupt) the lava can heat the groundwater.

*** The composition of rocks is a knowledge that has changed with time, as it is explained here:
http://en.wikipedia.org/wiki/Discoveries_of_the_chemical_elements

****Fluorescence in rocks is a spectacular effect that can be found at night in a cave, if there is full moon.

The origin indeed can be from phosphorous or other elements that show this interesting characteristic cold "fluorescence". The short explanation for this process is as follows.

Fluorescence is explained taking into account the levels in which the electrons are located inside an atom or molecule. The different levels have different energies. For example, if an electron is in the orbital 1s (the lowest) it has the energy associated with being in the level 1. If an electron is in the orbital 2s, it has a bigger energy associated with being in level 2 — and so on with the rest of the orbitals 2p, 3s, 3p, 3d, 4s, 4p, 4d, 4f, etc. They all have the energy associated with the number written in the name of the orbital (for example, 4s, 4p, 4d, 4f, all have the same energy associated to being in the 4th floor).

When a photon (a quantum of light) hits an atom it can excite the electron and push it from, for example, level 1 to level 4. The bigger the energy of the photon (which is proportional to the frequency of the wave light) — the farther away the electron jumps.

So, lets us suppose that the light coming from the moon has some rays that have a lot of energy, like the ultraviolet rays (which is not visible). When it hits our mineral atom, it will push the electron to a high level, like the 4th. Then, the electron moved there (in level 4) needs to come back to his previous more stable position in 1s. He could go directly back, expelling a photon in the ultraviolet region, BUT, there are materials like phosphorous that don't like this direct road and prefer relaxing a little bit by the so called "internal conversion" mechanisms into a level like the 3rd, and then, only then, they expel a photon themselves to go back to level 1s.

The result is that, in this more troublesome road, the quantum of light resulting in the "fall" of the electron from the 3rd to the 1st floor has less energy than the one (the invisible ray) that started all the process. This new photon has a lesser energy and a lesser frequency, which is in the visible region. That is why we can see more in these caves, than if we didn't had a fluorescent mineral. Isn't it surprising?

There is another intriguing thing that Darcy cannot know yet in 1812: phosphorous is a remarkably peculiar fluorescent element that "stores" the energy given during daylight. The phenomenon that occurs in phosphorous is actually cold phosphorescence, and is distinguished from the previous mechanism only in that the time for the "internal conversion" process is much longer in this element. This has as a consequence, that you can see a phosphorescent object even in absolute darkness!

*****Antonie van Leeuwenhoek was a remarkable lens builder.
http://en.wikipedia.org/wiki/Antonie_van_Leeuwenhoek

******Edward Jenner was the one to develop smallpox vaccine.
http://www.jennermuseum.com/edwardjenner.html

******* The feeling Lizzy is experiencing is described in a very clever way in a poem by *Leo Booth and John Bradshaw. Toxic Shame:*
http://www.goddirect.org/mindemtn/writings/january/toxshame.html

Chapter 30

DARCY

It seems my Lizzy never quite finished our tale. Her time has not been her own of late. So, my love, in case you are reading this know you can add your own version in the future, should you wish.

I, however, feel a need to end our story.

I ran with the improvised torch in the direction I had last seen her. I dropped on my knees, breathless, the moment I neared her. I pointed with the lantern to a crack in the wall. This was the place the sound came from. It was very narrow, I glanced into the opening she was exploring.

Resolution was written on her countenance. "Yes, I can do it!" She took the lantern from me.

"Please, please, Lizzy, be careful. It could be our salvation, but I cannot lose you."

While she disappeared in the blackness, I rested my head on my fists and prayed. Do not run into any danger. Come back to me unharmed. God, do not let her get trapped in that passage! Let her find the way out, and friends, not enemies, on the other side. Keep her whole.

After an interminable wait, a low scream was heard. I rushed to the aperture. "ELIZABETH."

The answer was her muffled voice. Papa? Was she calling her Papa?

Masculine tones were heard distantly. I inserted my head as far as I could. Yes. I distinguished a familiar timbre. It was Richard. We were saved!

A short eternity passed before I could distinguish a movement at the top of the cavern, and my cousin's profile was outlined in the hole. "Darcy?"

"I am here!" I approached the light.

He descended through a rope. "Could you not have sent an express rider signaling your location?" He landed in front of me with a relieved smile.

"And make it easier for you?" I hugged him, "No way!"

We were in that position until he remembered he had to admonish me. He grabbed my shoulders and held me at arm's length, telling me how damn angry he was for scaring Georgiana as I had. "The next time you make us believe you are dead, I swear I will kill you!"

"How is she?"

"She is much affected. Only the distraction of those crazy Bennet misses convinced her to stop wailing like a mad woman."

"They are here?"

"Yes. Miss Elizabeth's parents are outside, and all the girls are at Pemberley."

"Mrs. Darcy," I corrected, walking to pick up our topcoats. "Is she well?"

"She has a cut on her knee; nothing that someone with her resolve cannot stand."

This stopped me in my tracks. "What do you mean by a cut on her knee!? She was fine when she disappeared through the rock!"

"You are lucky she could make it, man. It was nearly an impossible challenge to fit into that wall!"

Discarded the idea of covering against the elements, I went to ascend the rope slowly. I was helped by two servants to exit the opening (which I found to be surrounded by bushes), and crawled out into the snowy landscape. They offered water; I refused mutedly, knowing it would take several minutes for my eyes to adjust to the brightness of daylight.

"Where is she?"

One of them pointed in the direction of a cart where three people were clustered. As I approached, I began to distinguish the profiles — Mr. Bennet, Mrs. Bennet and the maid Lillian — Where was Elizabeth? I wanted to run, and the wound in my rear would not let me.

She was lying between them. Why? I heard a lamenting scold. What was her mother saying? Why was she howling like that? I got close enough to discern the faces of her parents. The gentleman was silent — in a way that spoke of the grief they had been through. The lady was doing something with Lizzy's leg. The quilt she was wrapped in obstructed seeing her expression.

I climbed onto the wooden platform, to be able to determine what was taking place. She had her eyes closed and was being cradled by her father in the same manner she likes from me, her expression one of peace. I observed the movements of her mother. Elizabeth was bleeding. A bandage was being arranged and could not stop the flow.

"Why did you have to run from home child? You could have married at Longbourn instead of some forgotten place. Do you have any idea how was it like not knowing about you for so long? Do you know the nightmare we have been through, until your letter arrived? We have been searching for you across the entire Kingdom! First, your father receives this *friend* when I am absent, and then, the mad man comes across you and buries you here! How could this happen to you? My poor child. You are so smart, so good. How could you do this to us? So skinny, so pale... with this hemorrhage..."

"Darcy, you do want to catch a cold!" Richard came from behind me and taking his jacket off. "Put this on!"

My wife opened her eyes at the mention of my name. "We made it." She pulled one arm out of the cover and strained to reach me.

I saw a tangle of sentiments on her face — relief, hope, happiness and an unexpected physical pain. "Yes," I bent and covered her fingers. "But you are hurt."

"It is nothing. We are alive. That is what matters,"

How could I have let her go through that passage? I turned to see if my cousin had something else to cover her. My in-laws were scrutinizing my movements closely. I had not the slightest inclination to pay any mind to them now. The housekeeper would know what to do to alleviate her pain.

****

Georgiana's welcome at the entrance to the mansion was full of happy tears and heartfelt embraces. My dearest poppet had had the scare of her life, in the three days we were lost, and she could not get enough reassurance from my presence. I did my best to restore her confidence regarding our safety, diverting my eyes with difficulty from the scene of family reunion and siblings' love the three other sisters near us were sharing. Why was Mrs. Bennet was so scared? This deeply concerned me. Was it because of Lizzy's injury?

We were all guided into the small drawing room on the first floor. I jealously allowed Elizabeth to remain in her father's arms. Mr. Bennet was particularly careful not bend her legs as she was laid on a big sofa.

Mrs. Reynolds beheld the regiment entering the room and with her expertise of years as officer of the manor, assessed the damage of the troops. She put in motion the entire household in order to take care of us. Blankets, clean water and bread were delivered (the later devoured instantly). Elizabeth and I were separated by the incessant simpering and stalking of close relatives around us — my new family, with their characteristic effusiveness; and my quiet Ana, with her possessive command of my attention.

Few minutes later, a servant came to inform us that the doctor was on his way, and that the master's and the mistress's rooms were ready. Lizzy insisted she needed to have a conversation with her parents alone, that I was feverish and it would do us no good if I got worst, and that she was going to be well taken care of. Thus, I asked to be helped to mine. It was understandable she wanted to fix the rift with her family.

Too tired to attempt to preserve my dignity, I scaled the stairs with the help of Richard and my loyal valet, Mr. Olson — secure in the knowledge that my heroine would join me for a most cherished homely sleep soon.

****

I was cleaned, shaved and dressed, while my cousin narrated the happenings of the last days.

He had been at Matlock when an express from Georgiana arrived, stating that we were missing. He departed immediately, and upon reaching Pemberley, was told of the gravity of the situation. We had been expected to have reached the estate the evening before, but according to the testimony of the young driver, Albert, we had been buried alive by General Mullen and his men.

He had interviewed said servant. The boy had received a head injury that had him prostrated since the explosion, but he was able to find out what had happened.

Apparently, Lillian and Albert had been distracted by the scenery (or by each other) on their journey on the other horse, and were not far ahead from us. They had been on the same trail when they had heard a gunshot and had followed the sound. Realizing Elizabeth and I were being chased by armed men, they separated. The maid took the animal, with the intention of alerting the people at Pemberley as soon as possible; while the young man stayed behind to follow us.

Sadly, the Scottish girl had not been able to find her way in the darkness as swiftly as she wished. She had gotten lost several times alone in the unknown woods, and news about the danger we had been in, only arrived at dawn.

When the teams of servants and tenants were guided to the place where Lillian had seen us last, a detonation was heard from one of the mountains nearby. Following the noise, they arrived at the crest, to find devastation of broken rocks, and men covered with soil. The five bodies, including the general and his henchmen, were found after a day of excavations. The loyal Albert miraculously escaped this fate as he had been further away from the blast attempting to avoid exposure; he was unconscious.

Late at night, his almost incoherent testimony made Richard hope that my wife and I could still be alive underground. He had dedicated uncountable hours to finding the entrance we had escaped through. It was for naught; the energies dedicated in the cold had only served to ascertain no one could have survived.

The third morning, he had almost been resigned to our loss. He had spent the first hours to supervising the works of what seemed an unfruitful digging in the hill, and the rest to consoling Georgiana.

At noon, the unexpected arrival of the Bennets had changed the bleak atmosphere.

After informing Mr. and Mrs. Bennet of the state of affairs (far away from the ears of the girls, due to a strong argument about the lies spread by Mullen the couple had), Elizabeth's parents had insisted on coming to the place where the excavations were occurring. The necessity of using a cart in order to transport the stubborn lady — as using a carriage was unthinkable due to the irregularity of the terrain — had made them travel by a different path.

That had been when they spotted an opening in the ground. The snow had melted around it, and it was easy to explore inside. Both gentlemen entered it looking for an alternative passage inside the earth.

"You know the rest. *Mrs. Darcy* came from a wall in that obscure hell. Her father found her curled on the ground, when she injured her knee. She promptly informed us where you were, and I could finally find you. The only thing I do not understand is how she is still alive considering the sad state of her health." He moved a chair to sit in front of me and demanded, "Would you care to enlighten how the attractive Miss Elizabeth Bennet came to be the shattered shell that is in the next room?"

In the meantime, Georgiana came into my chamber and sat on the mattress, reaching for my hand. I perceived her eagerness to know all that had happened since we saw each other last. *They will support me;* I solved, and shared with them the events since I had met a Michael Ellis in Cambridge to the moment we were found today.

My sister ended up weeping silently as my cousin paced the floor, deep in meditation. He was connecting the dots and filling the parts I did not want to unveil in front of my sister. I prayed she never found out about my affair.

"So, her family does not know that you were married last week. Instead, they think you kidnapped her in Hertfordshire. That certainly explains why that man is so angry with you."

"He should not be," my sister interjected. "William is as injured from the inexplicable hate the general harbored toward him, as she. As a matter of fact, you have suffered more than she — you have a fever!"

"Well, it is not your fault that Mrs. Darcy ran away from home. They should see that," Richard inferred.

"Yes," Georgiana patted my hand. "Why did she not answer my letter and abandon her family like that?"

Resentment was still apparent in my sibling's attitude. "Poppet, I am sure she will tell you soon. Please, do not be judgmental. You have no idea what she went through at Wickham's hands."

Richard approached with alarmed steps. "Did the coward abuse her?"

"Not the way you are imagining," I avoided divulging too much. "Calm down."

"Do you know why her mother is so afraid of being in Derbyshire? Why does she want to remove her from here as soon as may be?"

"What?" I got rid of the quilt that was impeding me to stand up. "Why do you say that?"

"She said on the way to the caves, that she knew this was a cursed land for her; that was why they came immediately, once they knew her daughter's whereabouts."

"They are not going to take her anywhere. It is not going to happen!" I directed to the connecting door.

I opened it to find the old physician storing his implements. He was wrapping the tools: scissors, needles… *a scalpel?* Lillian rushed out of the room with linens stained with blood. I distinguished my darling girl lying behind the bed curtains and neared. Her parents were seated on each side, grabbing her hands tightly. She was squeezing her eyes shut; her forehead was damp with perspiration, her lips were set in a tight line, her exposed leg was showing a wound with many stitches.

Mrs. Reynolds approached from behind and looked at me apologetically. She asked Mr. Bennet to give her some space to complete the curing protocol. She painted my wife's knee with the green concoction I remembered from my childhood. She bandaged the limb carefully, whereas Elizabeth was immersed in her own world of agony.

"You were very brave, little monkey," her father was saying with cracked voice. "I am so sorry."

Her mother must have had the same contraction as I in her guts, because she only nodded whilst lovingly brushing the sweat from her brows.

I turned in the direction of Dr. Roberts. Why did she need to go through this?

He seemed to recognize my silent question, and explained in a low voice, "She had a part of the cartilage detached inside the junction, and I had to dig in her flesh in order to extract it."

The pillars of the bed cracked under my nails.

"It would have been worse if I had just closed the wound, leaving it there. That is why I <u>had</u> to open the skin a little further, sir." Good Lord, it was worse than I had assumed.

Mrs. Bennet sniffed at this description, and Elizabeth, drawing strength from I do not know where, pulled her to her chest for a supportive embrace. "It is over, Mama," she declared, not opening her teary eyes yet. "It is over."

Long minutes passed until the muscles of her face relaxed, as the sting was slowly diminishing. When the lady disentangled, Lizzy's gaze connected with mine. Her appearance brightened in that instant, smiling at me lovingly.

"Why did not you call me to be here when you went through that surgery, sweetling?" I surrounded the furniture to comb her moist hair. "I could have comforted you."

"I was in good company. There was no need for you to go through this twice." She signaled in the direction of the physician. "It is your turn now, and I do not think I have the capacity to be at your side when the same is done to you. Why would I ask for you to watch that which I am not able to watch myself?"

I shook my head, thinking about the unselfish feelings she always had. "I do not deserve you."

"Do not be silly." She poked her tongue out in that childish way I adore. "Who else will stand up to my impertinent self, other than you?"

"Sir, I think your wife is right," the doctor interrupted. "We should be working with you before the blood in your wounds gets too cool."

****

The truth was there was little that could be done with the cuts in my back. "This one is infected," Dr. Roberts declared, "which is not unexpected under the circumstances. With the medication, you are out of danger. So much time has passed, the skin should not be sewn. It is better to abide by Mrs. Reynolds's remedies for you to scar swiftly and to lower your temperature. Remain in bed for a week — that is all I can recommend in your case."

Richard guided the gentleman to the hall, as my valet wrapped me in clean compresses.

"Does the master need me to attend him during the night?" he asked in a strange tone of respect and fatherly affection. "I could sleep on the couch and do what is necessary to keep you comfortable, Mr. Darcy."

I remembered Elizabeth's mocking statement yesterday, that I required my Friday. I rubbed my shaved jaw with satisfaction. "No. I feel like a new man, Mr. Olson. Besides, I am not going to sleep alone a single night ever again."

With a secret grin, he helped me into the nightshirt and trousers, and opened the door to the mistress's room.

Mrs. Bennet was occupying the sofa, the same way my valet intended to do with me. She stirred when she heard my approach and opened her eyes. "Where is Lizzy?"

"She is safe, madam. I am going to lay with her and make sure that she is well attended. You can go to rest now. You have nothing to worry about."

She stood up and studied my face with an expression I could not make out until she declared, "Yes. The laudanum helped her with the discomfort, and you are right. She is safe at your side. Thank you for all you have done, my boy," she reached to touch my cheek as my mother used to do. "She has recounted to us all you did this past month. I have no words to say to you, how indebted I am for the devotion with which you have protected her. You are truly the best of men."

I guided her toward the door. "I will keep doing it, my lady." This woman had to be really fatigued to speak to me like this.

She disentangled from me and ran to her daughter's bedside to kiss her goodnight. I waited at the door, amazed at the turn the day had made in a few hours.

"Good night, Mr. Darcy. Take care."

I could not help feeling better because of the warmth that Mrs. Bennet showed. Now I knew where Elizabeth learned to be so kind. I climbed into the bed that already had her delightful perfume.

I observed her frame silhouetted under the linens. Her pose, lying on her back, was not as relaxed as it used to be when sleeping. A small foot was peering out of it, and a line was drawn between her lovely brows. I covered the leg and inserted my fingers under her hand, trying not to wake her up. The lights made a beautiful rainbow on her ring. I delighted in the fact that she was now my wife, in our bed, here at Pemberley. To think I thought her a mere slip of a girl when I first saw her — what a woman was hidden inside — a genuine, loyal, strong, passionate woman. I submerged under the bedclothes to feel her body. And she was mine.

Chapter 31

A few days after our rescue, while the dawn began to intrude through the curtains, I refused to wake from the dream world. Fantasies of the time I had wanted her, collided with the reality of having her as my wife and wove into a tapestry. Her smell was so real — I savored the feeling of genuine peace that resting on my 'pillow' offered.

Slowly, rational thought entered my mind as I felt her stir under the covers. Elizabeth was opening her dazzling orbs lazily. She was truly here. She was hurt.

She patted the contour of my shoulders up to my nape and crown, then to my forehead. "Your fever broke, William." She bent to pull my head up. "You were right — you truly heal with dispatch…"

We were surprised to hear someone giggle next to our feet. Elizabeth diverted her gaze toward the extreme end of the bed. She stammered a complaint, identifying the source.

"Kitty! Lydia! What are you doing here?" She admonished them in her most severe tone.

I could not believe this! I extracted my hand as discreetly as I could, feeling for the counterpane to assure we were concealed.

"We came to see how you were recovering. We were sent to sleep too early last night," the younger explained, trying to hide her mirth.

"Girls, but you should not intrude into someone's rooms; even less so when you are guests."

"We have missed you a great deal, Lizzy," the other one circled the bedstead to be in front of her. "We want to be your nurses today."

I pulled Lizzy more firmly into my arms, in order to convey my reluctance for such a scheme. *Do not speak, Darcy, or they will realize you are not the master of yourself at this moment.*

Elizabeth reached for her sister and spoke in a gentler voice, "Thank you very much, my dear, but I do not think you would enjoy changing bandages and helping a cripple with her morning toilette. You would be of much greater assistance if you could cheer up Ana. Ask her to show you the house and gardens. I was told they are amongst the loveliest in all of England."

Miss Lydia seemed to be fond of the suggestion and signaled Miss Catherine to a corner, whispering into her ear. With apparent mutual agreement, they both disappeared behind the door, in a mist of whispers and light steps.

"Good God! If we were not ensconced by the quilt, I do not know what would have happened." I kneeled on the mattress, to show my evidently unfit state.

Lizzy looked down my figure and disguised a chuckle, "Luckily, they do not suspect the danger they have just escaped."

"Danger?" I feigned being insulted.

She strove to sit up and encircled my middle region, pulling me towards her. "The danger of witnessing the brazen behavior of their sister."

She detected how my pulse quickened, and smiled at me with that bewitching way of hers. My Lord! I cautiously drew her away, disentangling her arms from me. "Lizzy, we should be wiser than this. Your health is too delicate yet."

She dropped her head back on the linens and grimaced in what seemed — *shame?* Why would she feel shame?

"What is it? Why are you sad?" What had I said? I reviewed the previous scene in my mind, and one word jumped immediately. Cripple. She pictured herself as a cripple. She thought I was rejecting her.

I uncovered her injured leg and started to massage her small foot in a circular motion, up her calf, until I touched the strap. I bent to kiss the same path and lingered around the fabric. "I love you, Elizabeth Darcy," I stroked my lips against the border. "I love all of you," I grazed my cheek with the part that was swollen on her knee. "I do not like you less because you cannot walk today. You are perfection to me."

"Are not you repulsed by my worn appearance? By my wraps and my emaciated condition?"

I looked up at her left hand — it was almost restored from the luxation — and took it. "No. You are as beautiful as ever."

"Why are you unwilling to make love to me?"

I bordered her with my legs, wary not to touch her wound, "I am as impatient as you, my pretty one, but you should not take that risk yet. I cannot allow you getting worse. And honestly, I am not in shape either."

"Is it not because I am not attractive anymore?"

I pressed my hips against hers, demonstrating exactly how gorgeous she was. "How would you describe my body's reaction to you? Do you sense an answer to your questions?"

She nodded a shy 'yes'.

"You have faith in me, then?"

"Yes," she breathed, showing her fatigue unintentionally. "I think you are right. I should not have doubted you."

I observed the dark circles under her eyes. She was inclined to have marital relations out of a wish to indulge me. It was good that I had learned to read her moods.

****

Once assured of my continuing affections, Lillian came to our room, and I asked our housekeeper to arrange some comfortable furniture to be placed on the balcony next to our chambers. It was not to be. I was planning to show Lizzy the park and distract her from our illness when her mother barged into the alcove, claiming the right to be the one to tend her. I could not share that responsibility as Georgiana eyed me suspiciously from the door to my room. She discreetly signaled for me to join her.

I followed my sibling to my quarters. I asked her for a chance to get dressed, and she entered immediately after Olson's departure, with a breakfast tray for two.

She started complaining about having spent little time with me, and no time at all at what she perceived to be her nursing duties. Overwhelmed with being the hostess, as Mrs. Bennet was driving the entire household crazy usurping the Mistress's role and supervising everything related to Elizabeth.

I could not but acknowledge that she was right (although most likely she was exaggerating). We agreed to make an extra effort to divide our schedule between entertaining our visitors, patient care and being together. *How am I going to manage to do all this from here?* I wondered blithely.

She was more tranquil when she finished her meal, and excused herself to use my washroom in order to clean rapidly a fresh stain, while I ate lying on my stomach.

****

I was distracted with images from the previous hour when my valet informed Mr. Bennet was in the hall, asking for an interview. I stood up and invited him in. I offered some tea, in order to start on the right foot. I knew this conversation could get ugly, so, for Lizzy's sake, I did my best to avoid a confrontation.

"It is unnecessary, Sir," he avowed. "I would rather have this dialogue alone and without the interruption of third parties."

I waited for the caller to make himself comfortable. He demonstrated the most bizarre behavior, sitting and standing a couple of times, until he asked, "Why do not you sit here with me? I think it can accommodate us both without making either of us wary."

There was a bit of sarcasm in the old man's intonation. I decided against any kind of argument over trivialities, "I cannot sit. I am… I have a strapping around my rear that forbids that at present."

He shifted uneasily, making the same gesture as Lizzy does, when she makes up her mind about something, "I should start with an apology then."

This show of civility from someone that knew about my many failings surprised me, and I listened attentively. He started relating, with more detail than I deserved, his long friendship with the general.

Consistent with the monologue of our attacker, he relayed that they had met in Cambridge, after the latter had extracted a young Bennet from a trap in a basement. He had been left there as a part of some nefarious game, in which he was expected to survive without provisions through a whole weekend. Maybe it was Mullen who orchestrated that trap too.

"In those early days, we shared countless pleasant and unpleasant moments. He was my mentor in many things. Apart from his guidance in academic matters, we went to brothels together, and I learned from him how to avoid diseases. After graduating, we kept a close relationship by correspondence — only to be interrupted when Mullen parted to campaign on the Continent. He helped me with my finances on several occasions, and he came to lend his support after my first wife died."

By this part of the tale, I was too tired already. This was going to be long. I had to excuse my rude behavior, interrupting, in order to arrange myself back on the mattress.

He conceded nonchalantly, "I must admit that I had not heard of him until a few weeks ago. I am convinced now, the War twisted Mullen into the depraved man, capable of using my trust in order to endanger the life of my own child. I was misguided by the conviction that he was the same friend I confided in so many years ago. I have no other excuse for the way I wronged you and Lizzy. Fanny was right to argue with me when she returned from her difficult search. I should not have believed in his lies. As she says, I should have thrown him out of the house as soon as he disparaged our daughter. I should have noted that he was not the same. That he was full of resentments and hate. I bet he used a disproportionate amount of gunpowder in the attempt to close the hole you were in. I am glad he died this way — because of his own mistakes. If not, I am not sure what I would be capable of after finding out his deeds."

There was certain parallelism between the blind confidence between these two men, and the unmerited admiration I evoked in Bingley. I studied the gentleman in front of me. War could certainly change someone. I thought about his past experiences; they could justify his suspicion about my behavior — but not about Elizabeth's. No matter that her family rushed to come after her as soon as they knew where she was, I would not forgive Mr. Bennet as easily as she had. I could not!

He followed with telling me how insulting he had found my recent letter, where I had written that I would not reveal the whereabouts of his offspring, whilst arguing that I did so to safeguard her. "Which is exactly the opposite of what has happened." He glared at me. "It breaks my heart to see the condition she is in: thinner than when she was a teenager, and with straps on her limbs."

"I was not with her when the events that unleashed the attempts to murder us were put into place, Sir. I could not have envisioned this when I went to visit you. When you denied an audience!" I justified, compelled by the same sorrow as he.

He dismissed my reasoning, stood up, and looked at me sternly, "And I cannot come to terms with why she left her family in the first place! Longbourn is where she has always been safe!"

"Is that the reason why you came up with the idea that she could have had eloped with me? Is that why you thought she was my mistress? Someone as special as Elizabeth?!"

"That and the fact that you had had a scandalous affair with a married woman! That and your lack of honor in a duel where you were expected to fight to the death!" affirmed an increasingly discomposed Mr. Bennet.

There was no way I was going to explain the circumstances of my affair with Deborah. "You would have preferred that I take a life!" I shouted, unable to control my temper any longer.

He shook his head in the negative. "Still, I deserve to understand why my daughter did that!"

She is the only person in all these incidents that has acted impeccably! I should have replied. Instead, "That is something you should be familiar with better than me," was my evasive response, as the door flung open and a determined Elizabeth appeared.

Standing on one leg and leaning on her mother, she said with a menacing growl, "Are you fighting over General Mullen's lies!? Is that man going to contaminate our happiness further!?"

What was she doing here? Why was she permitted to walk? I stood up and lifted her.

This last move was done too hastily, and I struggled against the sting in my backside. I had intended to restore her to her own chamber. She pierced me with a stare that said 'Do not even think about it' and I had to lay her on my bed.

I barely registered how Mrs. Bennet alleged that she had no choice but to abide Lizzy's wishes. I had to guarantee that no added harm would come to my precious cargo.

"No. I have already given your husband an apology for confiding in that man," her father answered unrelenting. "What I am striving to elucidate is <u>why</u> you ran away from Longbourn. <u>Why</u> you risked your family's reputation? <u>Why</u> you neglected the consequences that your acts would have in yours and your unmarried sisters' lives? I do not think that is something you have explained thus far."

With the same harsh temperament, my beloved rebutted, "And you presume <u>that man</u> had nothing to do with that. Do you not?"

For God's sake, she was injured! I wanted to scream to her parent, at the same time as I adjusted some cushions on the headboard. Yet he kept questioning.

I focused on alleviating the pain that showed due to the strain she put upon her body. I accommodated her and asked not to bend her injured limb.

She heard me and took a deep breath that seemed to calm her. She closed her eyes, in a sign of meditation. "I will not let these secrets separate us. I will… I have learned that they only served our enemies. I will… I will relate my motives," she decided at last.

The couple nodded, satisfied.

"I was escaping from Wickham's presence. I was evading a worse family outcome."

"What does Wickham have to do with anything?" her interrogator interrupted.

"Was he not the one to bring *your friend* to our house a couple of weeks ago? Was not Wickham the first to slander my husband? Was he not sent to Hertfordshire by the general, a year ago, in the first place?"

"But you were not married then, my girl. At that time, what was Mr. Wickham to you?" her mother inquired.

Meanwhile, her father seemed to be digesting some thoughts, until he sprang from his position to hover over the women, "What did that scoundrel do to you, Lizzy?"

She became surprised by this alarming attitude. I took her hand in both of mine, "I am here, my love. I will support any decision you make."

She covered her forehead with her free arm — unaware of the resemblance with the way she looked that day. She asked for us to listen patiently.

She narrated her tale bravely, avoiding the mention of my name. All the while, her parents listened astonished — stricken with the knowledge of her childhood trauma. Silent moans and low curses were uttered from time to time.

Untamed tears traveled Lizzy's cheeks until the end. "After being left alone by the boys that were distracted by a fight — when I was battling with the tight cravat that was knotted to my hair — Wickham came with an adult that seemingly was his father. One of them snatched the band from my head. I cried, and the man demanded an explanation of why was I there alone. He asked my name, and his fury elevated higher. He dismissed his son, who had the face covered with blood, and grabbed me by one ear — pulling me while searching for someone. Someone I cannot recall."

What? MR. WICKHAM PULLED HER BY THE EAR! Why? This was why she asked me about who separated Wickham and me.

Gathering the change in the disposition of her spectators, she finished, "That is all I have managed to remember thus far."

I guided her to rest her brow on my belly. I smoothed her shoulders and short curls, to communicate how proud I was of her.

Mr. Bennet was speaking in a low voice with his companion. From the phrases that reached us, I surmised they had absorbed the motives behind Lizzy's escape.

In the interim, my beloved was undergoing a healing process, repeating to herself that they had understood her; that they had forgiven her; that they no longer thought her irresponsible.

I tore my gaze from her when Mrs. Bennet started to wail in a discomposed manner. Her husband soothed her in an embrace that spoke volumes about their torment and regret. He whispered some words in her ear, and followed with a story that was unknown to Lizzy and me.

"We knew something dreadful had happened that day, but it was not what you have related this far. It is another matter. This morning you just recounted for us — the day of the Gardiners' wedding more than a decade ago — Fanny, after seven years of absence, ran into her husband, John Willoughby. We did not know what had happened in that wood, because the man that delivered Lizzy to her was not a stranger; it was Elizabeth's true father. He accused his seven-year-old child of provoking others with her disgraceful behavior. I reckon he must have been connected with the man you are speaking about and must have brought her to him. This scoundrel dared to terrorize his own spouse with kidnapping their daughter, if he ever saw her again! This man was the reason why they both had to move hurriedly from Derbyshire. He is the actual culprit of us having to conceal from our own family the illegal nature of our marriage."

This made no sense. "Are we speaking of the same day? Are you sure Willoughby was the one to deliver Lizzy to her mother?" It was not the late Mr. Wickham? Lizzy surely had not remembered it all. She was still unaware of part of what happened.

"Yes. That is the reason behind our secrecy. That is why we live with the fear of being discovered, being accused of bigamy or being deprived of Elizabeth since then."

"But, I never knew of a Willoughby around here."

The girl in my arms set her neck to stare at me. "It is the same day."

Mrs. Bennet straightened and alleged categorically, "He was here. I saw him with my own eyes. He said to me the worst invectives and threats, and he appeared to know the place well."

A heavy stone was placed over my shoulders. I did not protect her that day! I left her with George's father, and it happened to be worse. He behaved abominably. He brought her to her natural father. Why did I not go after them?!

Yet, how could I have known this was going to happen? Even now, it seemed implausible.

Well, this at least shed some light into the question of why they did not defend her from Mrs. Lucas and Mrs. Parker — they must have been afraid of being discovered, or were indebted to Sir William, for his support in having this illegal wedding.

Apparently, there was a battle going on inside every player or spectator of this episode.

"Perhaps he also left," the old man ventured. "A long period has passed. Not having heard of him could be good news."

"I am sorry, my child. I was so afraid! A-afraid of being hanged. A-afraid of running into Willoughby. But overwhelmingly afraid of losing you." Her mother apologized nervously. She explained that she could not reveal to Lizzy they had met her father that day, the many times she had demanded it, because she was terrified of being prosecuted. With acute regret, she confessed that she thought Elizabeth could blunder something when she talks in her sleep.

"All this time, your parents were trying to protect you. Do you see, sweetheart, that we were right in our speculations?"

Elizabeth did not pay attention to my last question.

The couple approached us. I perceived their need to hold her. I drew away, letting them have her for themselves.

Her Papa embraced her, her Mama cried. They spoke of how repentant they were. They comforted each other for a long hour.

I only watched Elizabeth's expression. It was neutral. Mrs. Bennet's whimpers did not stop, and she needed to rest. I signaled to the gentleman to take his wife outside. He agreed and guided her to their chambers.

When I was closing the door behind them, a new sound coming from inside my apartment was heard. I approached the washroom and listened to a mouselike moaning. I knocked and entered, to find my sister sitting on the floor and blowing her nose. All the redness in her cheeks and lips evidenced that she had eavesdropped the entire conversation. Damn it! How could I forget that she was here?

"Poppet, what are you doing?" I bid her stand up. "Why did you not make your presence known?" So much discretion over the years, to have her come to this intelligence this way!

"I am... I am," she sniffed. "I was embarrassed of coming out when Mr. Bennet started his speech about the General... and... and I... The courage was lacking to tell that I listened to his confessions about his youth. It only got worse when the subject involved Deborah. I was waiting for an explanation from you. And then, it was crowded... Fear of being found out kept me hidden... I..."

"Shhh. Shhh," I offered her a handkerchief. This was too much information for her to bear.

"And... Oh, brother, poor Lizzy! I never imagined George was capable of such things. I have been so mistaken. My behavior was abhorrent. You told me not to judge her, and I did not listen. I did not answer her last letter. I..."

I pulled her to me, "She is not mad at you. She understands why you did not reply."

"She does?"

"Yes. She cares for you. She has no claims toward your behavior. There is nothing to fear in that quarter."

"Do you think she will forgive me?"

"Of course, Georgie. Come, you must regain your composure and get out of this hiding place."

I consoled her a couple minutes more, aware of our need to talk about all the news she had come upon. Nevertheless — drained and abashed — I decided to postpone this discussion. Elizabeth was there, dealing with a much more unbearable heartache.

My sister agreed with me. "Yet, I had proofs of her friendship and the strong motives behind her escape. You see, I did not pay attention to the letter she sent from Cambridge. I should have known, by the sensible way in which she addressed my affair with Wickham and by the way she understood my regrets, that it could only come from tough past experiences. Lizzy needed me, and I turned my back on her."

"She does not think that of you, my dear. It was impossible for you to foresee all this. She was as worried, perhaps more so, that you would not understand why she did not answer your letter," I murmured, stepping out to discover a bundle hidden under the covers.

"She must be asleep." Georgiana tiptoed toward the door to the hall (not before I extracted the promise from her that she would search for Richard right away).

Lizzy's was compacted in a small ball, except for her broken leg — still awake. Why did not she talk with Georgiana when she overheard us just now?

I got inside the linens and huddled against her back. She shifted to look at me and scrutinized my expression. I could almost see how she worked the following statement in her mind: "Mama was not ashamed of me that day. For more than a decade, they were only caring for the safety of our home."

"Then, it is <u>my time</u> to do so with you, wife. You need to rest and to heal. No rambling from one bedchamber to another."

"Yes, husband. We need to abide by the doctor's recommendations — both of us. Let us forget about this."

I used our intertwined fingers to pull her closer. An inexplicable feeling that something was wrong (although unable to determine the nature of it at present) distracted me, until exhaustion took us both into the arms of Morpheus.

Chapter 32

The next morning, I asked how she felt regarding yesterday's findings. I helped to rest her back on the headboard, whilst expecting her to berate her natural father and lament about her mother's long standing lack of trust.

Lizzy's reply was unforeseen, and the conversation that followed was full of incoherencies, the origin of which I could only discern much later.

"There is nothing to say, Fitzwilliam. Apart from the illegal nature of my parents' marriage — in essence — I have learned nothing new, and have remembered nothing new either. The facts are that my father Willoughby did not love my mother, or me. I have been lying to myself all these years, as it is obvious from his abandonment, that I was not the product of love. He hated me, and it should mean nothing at this point. I have used the Bennets' name without having any right to it — so has my mother. In fact, from the circumstances of impoverishment under which my mother was when we lived in Bakewell, I would not be surprised to find out that I am truly illegitimate, as all those matrons from Hertfordshire proclaim."

"What? What have those circumstances to do with being illegitimate, Lizzy? Being poor has nothing to do with this. Your mother would not have behaved in the manner you are suggesting. You are not illegitimate!"

"Oh, no," she protested with cynicism. "She thinks she is married to that man! She believes she was wed in Scotland, no matter if there is no marriage certificate to account for it. The same happened with that aunt, the one that tempted her with being her heiress, right before she met Soldier Willoughby. She is so easy to manipulate!"

"Your mother inherited from an aunt? How come?"

"No, no. She took care of one distant cousin when she was single, the late Mrs. Weevil. The old witch made her believe she was to inherit her mansion, in order to have her nurse her for free. This, of course, did not happen as the lady had a son that appeared in a timely manner upon her death."

"You are saying that she met Willoughby when she was taking care of this woman? Was he from Bakewell?"

"I do not know. According to mother, he came to that village accidentally. But now that I think of it, he could have been interested in my mother due to the inheritance. He left soon after the determination of the will. As I said, he did not love my mother, nor did he want me."

I pondered that her analysis had some logic. Nonetheless, it was very painful. I did not know how I would feel if my father had not cared for me. It was better to evaluate other alternatives, "Lizzy, you cannot affirm that. You know men have other reasons to marry. There is attraction, loneliness, progeny, among many others."

She conceded grudgingly, and I followed with a speech I deemed to be somehow reassuring.

"Besides jealousy, there are many other reasons why marriage was instituted. We, men, have no guaranty of our parenthood, other than watching over the woman we pair with. You must see the logic in that we need to be sure our heirs are our own blood. From ancient times, it is all about blood." How could I explain the Gordian knot a bachelor was in? Having to choose between widows and prostitutes? "You see, the way things are perceived by society is a double-edged sword, as we also have needs — biological needs — which are very difficult to fulfill within the bounds of morality and expectations; very difficult to fulfill without hurting someone else."

"Yes, it is all about blood."

Well, this was not the course I wanted this conversation to take, or my point exactly, yet it was opportune to establish this too. "Yes, my love. For me, as your husband, it is a legitimate wish. I would like for our children to have those sparkling eyes of yours, and your lips, and your nose, and your hands, and, well, everything. However, you must agree that something borrowed from me will be desirable — at least the hair."

"In that light, I should be happy that Papa had the courage to do something illegal, and even immoral, in order to be with my mother." She crossed her arms on her chest.

"Do not blame them, Lizzy. Under the circumstances they were in, they did their best. The people to blame are the late Wickham and Willoughby." They must have been intimate friends. Which entailed that they were both of the worst kind — as George was. "Like father, like son," I blurted, and messed up my own attempt for reassurance.

She immediately became more argumentative. "If you consider bigamy 'the right thing to do,' you might as well approve sexual relationships outside of the marriage bed."

I realized the thought behind her reaction: 'Like father, like daughter'. "No, that is not what I meant. I know that what I did was wrong. I should not have had that affair. " From the way Father trusted him, Mr. Wickham must have been quite artful in the craft of deceiving as well. In contrast with Elizabeth, George was raised by an evil man. I strove to find the right words this time.

Lizzy, in turn, rushed to amend. "I should not have spoken to you in that way. You are right, William. I am sorry. As you say, my parents did the right thing considering the situation they were in. And, yes, Willoughby might have had many other motives. I do not know. Maybe he wanted a boy."

"Silly man!" I teased, seeing an opportunity to lighten her mood. "It is far cleverer to have girls."

"Perhaps it is better to have this conversation another day, as I need some more time to accept my parents' silence. It is not easy to come to terms with the idea that legally, my mother is only his mistress."

It was not easy to accept her wishes either, as I had the conviction this conversation had gone badly. So, this was what was behind her errant thoughts. Her mother was Mr. Bennet's mistress. Was this why this man thought Lizzy could agree to be mine?

****

The following days were more or less routine. I shared my time between my steward, Georgiana and Lizzy — while the parents of the latter alternated taking care of her injuries and soothing her. They had a series of conversations concerning the day of the Gardiners' wedding. In the end, they served to help her see things in a different light.

Elizabeth's Papa related to her that he had had an innocent game with a servant girl, when he was around six years old. "Something like 'you show me yours, and I will show you mine'," my wife explained one of those nights. They also came to the conclusion that Jack Sthieve had not wanted anything violent to occur. The boy was younger than George Wickham, and thus, more susceptible to his manipulations. Actually, her cousin was protective of her. The other lads had acted out of curiosity, and my childhood friend was the only one with deviance in mind.

Seeing she was making good progress I worked, to the best of my ability, on lessening Lizzy's remorse. When my sister was a baby, I happened to see her naked, accidentally, once or twice. There was no malice in that. Likewise, we talked of other rules of society: things that were exaggerated and considered improper. For example, a year ago, after Wickham broke her heart, I went as far as accompanying her until she fell asleep. I had to play her father better than ever those days.

What I found exceedingly abusive in the game in Lambton, was the lie and the collective manipulation. The deception of blindfolding a girl (a tiny thing) and exposing her to those boys without her consent. "You were truly unaware, and scared of what they were doing to you, Lizzy. Your face reflected a terror I cannot forget."

Georgiana and my wife restored their camaraderie soon after the Bennets' revelation as well. It was apparent that the former had a strong preference for staying in the mistress' room, sharing confidences, rather than touring the park with the younger misses.

I admit, I was somewhat perplexed by the blatant way in which I was thrown out of the bed by my sibling. Until I saw the giggles and conspiratorial glances that brightened their countenances, each time I intruded to check if it was safe for me to come back. Only Lizzy could transform a sick room into a happy place. She had saved me from having to explain the matter of Deborah to Georgiana.

These hours served to take care of the most urgent estate business too. It allowed me to visit the young Albert. The driver's swift recuperation and pride for my visits was worth the effort of using a cane to navigate from one place to another.

On days, when the weather was warm enough, I arranged to have the sofa taken to the balcony, and carried Elizabeth to recuperate outside. I had the opportunity to show her the park from this vantage point, and pointed out the many paths she would enjoy rambling. She had a spectrum of feelings about it: from admiration to apprehension about the vastness of the land, from interest to worry about the tenants' hard life, from eager expectation to anxiety about the duties she was expected to perform as mistress. Elizabeth had to be the only woman in the world that, instead of thinking about the riches she would enjoy, thought about her responsibilities.

We also had glimpses of a pattern followed by Richard, Miss Lydia and Miss Kitty. The trio would start the day with the design of avoiding each other, until one of the girls found my cousin unguarded, and pulled him into some mischief. Performing host duties with the utmost diligence, he would take any role — from showing the winter landscape, to being the carrier for a picnic — until the other sibling would catch up, ending the happy excursion with a fight or a fall into the muddy snow by any of the three involved.

"Those girls are shamelessly in competition for Colonel Fitzwilliam's affections," Lizzy protested, when she watched this a couple of times. "Papa should do something before it goes too far."

"I do not see Richard complaining," I interjected, while arranging for us to go back to her bed one night. "They are just having a good time, pretty one."

"Yes, but at the end, he cannot indulge them both. He will necessarily hurt one of them."

"Do you want me to speak with my cousin?" I asked while placing a small wooden panel on the mattress, to be able to write a letter to my friend Sedgwick.

"No. It is my family that is acting without regard for propriety. I am the one who must stop this."

"They are my relatives as well, Lizzy. Do you not think I care for their wellbeing?"

"Of course, William. However, you should not have to take the burden that is Papa's."

"I think Richard is not an innocent in this. He is well aware of the consequences that can come from his behavior. He is not as young as your sisters."

"We must not quarrel for the greater share of blame. The conduct of neither, if strictly examined, is irreproachable. We should agree to speak to those who are inclined to listen to us. I will speak to my parents as soon as they visit me on the morrow."

****

Lizzy was half asleep, with a textbook on her lap. I was finishing the letter, conveying many questions about geology and cavern formation to my former classmate, when a knock was heard upon our door.

It was Mrs. Reynolds.

"Master, I am sorry to wake you up this late, but Mr. Bingley and his wife have just arrived. Should I place them in Mr. Bingley's usual rooms in the guest wing?"

"No, madam. Mrs. Bingley and Miss Bennet is the same woman. They should be with the family. The wedding was a few months ago. That is why many of us still call her by her maiden name. I am sure you have heard a 'Jane' being mentioned several times these days."

"Jane is here?" Lizzy jumped from her slumbering. "Where?"

"On the first floor, Mrs. Darcy," the longtime housekeeper was startled by my companion's sudden disposition. "I can solicit her to come to you, should you wish it."

A huge grin spread over Lizzy's countenance, and I nodded for Mrs. Reynolds to follow through with her suggestion. "It seems someone has forgotten that she is an invalid, and wants to run to meet a favorite person."

"Tease away, Fitzwilliam, but forget about sleeping tonight. My sister and I have a lot to discuss."

****

The encounter between the sisters was as warm and as emotional as we all expected. It was held in Lizzy's room, and after exchanging the greetings that protocol demanded with my sister-in-law, I left the women alone.

341

I received my old friend in my own chamber. He related with enthusiasm their travels through the North Sea and the Norwegian Sea. Apparently, he had planned to travel as far as St. Petersburg; however, the cold weather and the fear that the war could extend that far, impeded to fulfill those schemes. The last town they visited was Bergen, in Norway, although they spent some days between the icebergs near the Arctic.

That was the place they enjoyed the most, regardless of the freezing waters, as they could spy some exotic animals from the ship. Mrs. Bingley was especially fascinated by the polar bears, whales, walruses and seals.

Seeing that our wives truly intended to extend their reunion till dawn, we retired to my study in order to sample the vodka Bingley brought from his trip. He had many new opinions about the invasion of the French troops in the Russian territory, and that made the wait more entertaining.

He expounded how that army was being defeated by the Tsar's, together with the upcoming winter; and how the people burned Moscow, before leaving it foodless and deserted, for the foreign invaders to starve. We ended up celebrating the victory over Napoleon that was soon to come, and reliving the memories of the old times, as drunks always do*.

****

Mr. Olson's voice awakened me. "Sir, I do not want to disturb you, but Mrs. Darcy wants to know where you are. What should I say to her?"

I opened one eye to gather my surroundings. The light that was straight on Bingley's somnolent face indicated that it was almost noon. I leaned on my knuckles to stand up from the couch.

I SPENT ALL NIGHT SITTING ON MY BUTTOCKS! I realized at this moment, "Woohoo!" I stood up and sat. Stood up and sat. Stood up and sat. "I do not feel any pain. This is fantastic!" I cried, while my astonished audience interchanged unbelieving stares.

I went to the window to inspect my back in the reflection. I removed my shirt and pulled the trousers down. It had scarred nicely.

"Mr. Darcy, what should I inform the mistress? She is…"

"Nothing," I arranged my pants back. "I will tell her myself!"

I rushed out, finding the stairs shorter this time. She was being attended by her abigail. Standing on one leg in front of the mirror, she was getting dressed in a new gown.

"Elizabeth, I have good news." I went to sit on the chair nearest to her. "Look."

She tilted her head, trying to guess what I was referring to, until a sweet smile signaled her recognition.

"I will help her with the hooks of her attire, Lillian. You can leave us alone." I stood up and guided my wife toward a comfortable window seat. I arranged myself there and pulled her to cozy up on my lap. *Oh, Lord, how I missed having her thus!* "How do you like this news, Mrs. Darcy?"

"Excellent recovery, William. When did you find out?"

"A few minutes ago," I replied, lifting her skirt to inspect how the cut in her knee was progressing.

"It looks much better. Does it not?" She waggled her leg from one side to the other.

"Yes. Almost ready to ride."

"You are not suggesting I climb onto one of those beasts!" She stared at me, half fearful, until she realized what my meaning was. Her face and neck turned a pretty shade of pink. "You are tantalizing me."

"I am." I nibbled her transparent ear. "But I think we will be doing our favorite exercise before long."

****

My wife and I made our way to my study, to be part of the talk Lizzy's parents needed to have with the newcomers, about the nature of their own marriage. They detailed the events after leaving the Gardiners' wedding so many years ago.

According to the gentleman, he had escorted mother and child from Lambton to Bakewell. However, they had decided against traveling together to Hertfordshire, as they had understood that the former Mrs. Willoughby needed to be with her siblings. Once they were safe and far from Derbyshire, they did not know what to do to solve their problems. They had seen it was risky for the females to remain without protection, and that Longbourn would benefit greatly with having a new mistress. Beside the absurdity of it, the impossibility of their union had compelled them to fall further in love.

Sir William Lucas was the one to suggest that, as no one knew Willoughby in Hertfordshire. He could spread the gossip that he had met him a long time ago — that he understood the soldier was dead. This is why they had finally married, by the same Mr. Parker that had performed the ceremony for my friend and my sister-in-law a few months ago.

"It could have been easier if we had come to Hertfordshire with Fanny pretending to be already married to me, as no one could have alleged that she was not, if I had just presented her as the new Mrs. Bennet. However, understandably, she had a lot of objections against living with a man without the blessing of God," Elizabeth's Papa explained.

"I was afraid that Lizzy could have remembered her father from Lambton, and might disclose our secret," the lady added. "I see now, that she never realized who the man that delivered her to me was."

"We also had the fortune that Mr. Parker wrote to his colleague in Bakewell, and that the good reverend from that village had confirmed that my wife's husband had not been seen for many years."

After these confessions, I felt comfortable enough to approach the subject of the motives John Willoughby had for marrying the former Fanny Gardiner. My father-in-law, while relating to the Bingleys the circumstances previous to Lizzy's birth, agreed with us that the rogue could have been after the presumed inheritance from Mrs. Weevil.

The sisters held each other's hands reassuringly during this conversation. With the exception of Charles's expressions of skepticism, it ended amicably with the Bennets planning their trip back home within the next two weeks.

"I hope we can make that voyage leisurely. I do not want to repeat the Crusade my wife made us suffer on our way to Derbyshire," Mr. Bennet teased.

****

One unexpected outcome was Elizabeth's silence the remainder of that day. I still suspected that she could be troubled with hurt, due to her parents' lack of trust in her, and their unwillingness to tell her of the meeting with Willoughby for so many years. After spending the evening trying to extract her from her melancholy, she disclosed in the privacy of her bedroom that night, she was indeed troubled by anger against her parents, which became more intense every time they approached the subject of this afternoon. She explained that she did not want to speak, in order to avoid unveiling this sentiment in public.

"Finally! I thought you would never say that they <u>had</u> to confide in you, instead of having you think you did something awful for so many years."

"Yes, William, but wrath is a horrible sin. I would have been sinful if I had expressed it."

"Lizzy, there is no sin in feeling betrayed as you do now. It was unwise for them to hide this secret all this time. I know you could have said it accidentally in your sleep. Nevertheless, this preventive measure they took was unnecessary, as you had your own room since you were a teen. Who would have heard you before you married?"

She just looked at me, and I could easily read that she still did not permit herself to have negative feelings.

"I see you do not agree. Why do we not analyze this from another point of view? You say you are a sinner because you are angry at them now. Do you think they are sinners too because they got married knowing that Willoughby was still alive?"

She shook her head 'no'. "We are hypocrites if we judge them, after the many improprieties in which we partook while in Cambridge."

"There was no sin even in that, Lizzy. It is in the motives where sin resides. Do not you see it? You are angry with them since, with their secrecy, they made you lonely. They even made you not trust them, as you would have needed. They unknowingly isolated you! No, there is no sin in your anger. At the same time, there was no sin in their marriage either, as they did not wed for lust. At least in my eyes, whether in the eyes of society as a whole or not."

"Do you think I should talk with them about it? Do you think I should claim or demand an explanation from them?"

"Yes. I think you should tell them how they let you down — make your point about their distrust. The sooner you do it, the better."

****

The remaining couple of weeks of the Bennets' stay, seeing Lizzy recuperating swiftly under Mrs. Bingley's care, I immersed myself in the search for clues as to the whereabouts of Willoughby. I started by asking my manager to inquire discreetly in the village to determine if anyone remembered him. I studied all the notebooks and journals my father recorded with every detail of the estate's financial affairs. I even went as far as reading his personal diaries.

Nothing divulged the truth. Not even on the day of the Gardiners' wedding was that name mentioned. The only entrance was related to the late Mr. Wickham:

"My steward came today with more concern than necessary, to disclose that George and Fitzwilliam had a dispute. I am glad that he had decided to be open with me and relate even those matters that make him uncomfortable. The mistake he committed, so many years ago, had served him well. I had not had any reason to repine from my forgiveness of his abandonment.

About the boys, there is really no reason to fret. It is of little consequence. Our sons are both too young to merit taking this seriously."

I knew what my old man was referring to by 'his abandonment,' because I was already eight years old when Mr. Wickham disappeared and left his family alone. I remembered Father saying that, at his return, the latter apologized profusely and explained he had tried his luck in America. As he appeared to be sincerely repentant from his adventure, and abashed by the longing for his wife and son, my father decided to give him a second chance.

346

Regardless of remembering this quite clearly, I validated these memories with the oldest journals I had in my study. I corroborated that there was no additional information from that time. Our family had no news of his estate manager for many months. My father tested him at his return and, at the end, decided to trust him again. It was as if Willoughby was swallowed by the Earth!

****

Elizabeth had busy days as hostess (together with family dinners that compelled calling each other by our given names). For instance, it seemed that half of the good people of Derbyshire paraded through our drawing room, wanting to meet the woman that not only married the Master of Pemberley, but saved him from death.

She thought her appearance was going to be the target of all kind of scorn, and was pleasantly surprised to find out that it was the opposite, as the legends of our rescue grew disproportionally by the spiciness every gossiper added about the origin of her shortened curls. Theories went, from needing to cut it in order to make a long rope to extract me from the cave, to the insane idea that it was the only food in the cavern.

"I think Lillian is making up all these tales out of pure boredom," she ventured when the last visitor left the parlor and my friends, and I dared to enter.

Bingley and I sat next to our wives, and Richard arranged himself at the card table in the corner.

"Luckily, Jane and Georgiana are helping you. I know how much you hate feeling like a dress in a shop window."

"That is unavoidable, William. They cannot stop staring at her," my sister intervened. "Lizzy is so beautiful, that some of the young women in the village are starting to imitate her style, to see if they can catch a rich husband with that trick."

"No. If they were paying attention to beauty, they should be staring at you and at Jane instead. I am sure it is only curiosity," Elizabeth declared.

We were interrupted by the entrance of the Bennet misses. They came in uncharacteristically quiet and surveyed the room. There were two comfortable spots on each sofa, but Miss Kitty seemed to find the chair next to my cousin more appealing.

I shot him a warning look, and he straightened his spine. Meanwhile, Miss Lydia seemed to be pondering her alternatives. She wandered in circles, surveyed the books that were resting on the window seat, made a show of studying the night outside, until, making up her mind, she opened one of the ladies' magazines and approached the table.

"Colonel Fitzwilliam, which of these gowns do you think is more appropriate for a ball?" I heard her say with her back toward us.

Richard, trying to look indifferent, shrugged his shoulders and attempted to stand.

"No, Sir, it is not necessary. I am tired of sitting all day," she pushed the sketches closer to him. "As a man who has traveled the world and has seen the fashionable ladies in Paris, would you advise me in this matter?" she insisted, highlighting her request by reclining on the table with her face at the same level as his.

From my position on the couch, I could not discern Lydia's exact expression, but I could see Kitty's and Richard's. The first one frowned most severely, and the later stuck his gaze on a point around the low part of Lydia's neck.

"Lydia!" Lizzy, called indignantly. "What are you doing?"

The girl turned around abruptly, and I caught the source of my wife's scolding, as the revealing décolleté the girl was wearing was visible to the rest of the audience. Ah, Richard was having a feast with that view.

"Sweetheart," Jane turned to look at her husband. "Have you offered the good Colonel a sample of the vodka we brought from our wedding trip?"

Bingley, reacting to his wife's timely intervention, proposed, "Would you invite us to your study to have some, Darcy?"

"Yes, of course." I answered, although silently cursing the young girls.

****

That night, on top of having my plans frustrated — as Lizzy and I had had very little intimacy during the Bennets' stay — I endured an inebriated Charles's vulgar comments.

"Darcy, you must find great pleasure in your chambers, with the differences in your size in comparison with your petite wife. Hopefully she can accommodate all of you by this point in your marriage?"

"Bingley! I will not pretend that I do not know to what you refer. Suffice it to say that I am happy with our sizes. Yes," I replied, annoyed at the thought that he was picturing my Lizzy this way. "Because of one main reason: it allowed us to escape alive from the general's designs. I could protect her from the fall in the cave, and she could fit in the narrow passage to the other chamber, when people were looking for us. Our marital felicity has nothing to do with sizes!"

"Oh yes. Here is before you, Bingley, a man obsessed with his wife's perfection. Do not try to argue with him this point," my cousin mocked. "Any disrespect toward her or her family will find you at the sharp end of his steel."

"Humph!" Charles spilled part of his drink. "He will not. That would leave him alone at the mercy of the Bennets, and I am sure that is a heavy burden for only one man."

"Which reminds me, I should leave this place tomorrow morning." Richard filled his cup to the top. "I had better call it an evening, gentlemen. Just let me take some of this vodka… in case I get thirsty on the trip up the stairs."

Bingley winked at me, following my cousin's actions. "Yes. We can safely leave this study now. Those Bennet girls must have retired already, and my wife waits to enjoy the night."

Dismissing them, the journals secured within a drawer, I reached to turn out the lights as a long-forgotten voice startled me.

"Darcy!"

---

* Napoleon will start his retreat from Russia this very winter (1812), but Waterloo is still 3 years off (1815).

Chapter 33

It was Uncle Fitzwilliam, with Richard in tow.

"Matlock." I refrained from bowing.

"I see that you, Darcys, are determined to tarnish the family name!"

"What?"

"First your father, and now you! Have you no shame? Is it not enough my sister married a Darcy — an untitled man? Now you have chosen this country nobody, with no manners nor idea of how to show deference to her peers?"

Unable to listen to this antiquated nonsense about why Mother should not have fallen in love with Father, I stopped him. "What are you doing here? Did you not swear that you would never set a step on this land after she died? Should not you be with your mistresses and gambler friends, trying to leave your heirs penniless? Who invited you to come?"

"Ha!" he uttered a cynical snort. "I see your wife is not only the most impertinent woman, she keeps secrets as well," he brandished a letter emblazoned with Lizzy's handwriting. "She has invited my wife."

"I gave Mrs. Darcy the address," Richard clarified apologetically.

"If my wife invited your wife, then what are you doing here?"

"What? This is ridiculous Darcy. Why as soon as I became aware of the invitation, I instantly resolved on setting off, that I might make my sentiments known to you. You ought to know that I am not to be trifled with. However insincere you may choose to be, you shall not find me so. My character has ever been celebrated for its sincerity and frankness, and in a cause such as this, I shall certainly not depart from it. I have been proven right by this same woman you call your wife. She is the most obstinate, headstrong girl! I demand to have her apology this instant!"

"Really? What has she to apologize for?" What a fool he was, thinking he could demand anything in my house.

"She must apologize for her disrespect!" He approached to stare at me, but was apparently dissuaded by the change our respective statures had experienced over the years, and retreated. "Do you know what she did? Do you? I will relate the conversation I had in your parlor over the last hour. I explained that my niece, Anne, and you were formed for each other; that you are descended, on the maternal side, from the same noble line. Your fortunes on both sides are splendid. You were destined for each other by the de Bourgh and Fitzwilliam houses; and what is to divide you? The upstart pretensions of a young woman without family, connections or fortune?"

"Father, she is a gentleman's daughter," my cousin interrupted.

Not giving his son even a glance, Lord Matlock went on, "Then I asked, who was her mother? Who are her uncles and aunts? Do you know what she did? She refused to answer my questions! She refused to answer ALL my questions! She even refused the generous offer I extended to her in exchange for annulling your marriage!"

"YOU OFFERED HER TO DO WHAT!?" This could not be true. It was impossible to annul a marriage.

"On top of all this, her hair is shorter than yours. What do you have to say to that?"

By this time, I was not sure of being able to restrain from asphyxiating this man. "If her short hair is the worst thing you can argue against her, it means that she is the best woman of my acquaintance. Do what you must with your father, Richard, but I do not want to see him ever again!"

****

Leaving my uncle berating me, I climbed the stairs to find Georgiana weeping silently outside our apartments.

"Oh, brother," she rushed to cling at my neck, "That is the most evil man I have ever seen! He said the most insulting things to us… He is… Oh, brother, how could he abuse us so?"

"What did he do?"

"He entered the room unannounced and scolded Jane and me for helping Lizzy stand, as if Lizzy were no one at all. He spoke to Jane as if Jane were the one to be Mrs. Darcy... saying that her low breeding was showing, doing the job of a servant. He was so cruel, so... He recognized me and told me, I should know better than seconding you, and that I should set the example and behave according to my station. Lizzy was most courageous and stopped him, clarifying who *she* was. She invited us all to sit and asked who *he* was. He extracted the letter in which she had extended to our aunt, saying that she had no right to write to a person with whom she was not acquainted. He said such disgusting things, William, so many insulting questions. I just cannot repeat them."

"I know, Poppet. Do not worry. He already told me what he said to her." *Blast!* "I wish I could have prevented it."

"Fitzwilliam, why do not you come inside? I imagine it is quite a bit warmer here," I heard Elizabeth say, opening the door. "I would not mind sharing the hearth with you both."

Georgiana shifted her gaze toward Lizzy, declaring, "I do not want to intrude."

"You would not be intruding, even if you sleep with us."

Elizabeth need not have insisted that Georgie comply. "I will be right back, then. I will change and come right away."

This was all my poppet was after. I rolled my eyes. Little scalawag.

Seeing the younger girl enter her chamber, I took my wife's hand and guided her back to rest on the couch. "Why did you write to my aunt? Why did not you tell me?"

"It was just a polite invitation, William. There was no secrecy in it. I just wanted to fix any rift our marriage could have brought."

"Did I not tell you that Richard and Georgiana were the only ones that matter to me, and that we would not worry about the rest?"

"Yes, Fitzwilliam. But they are your family. They must love you. Ana told me Lady Matlock was nice. They should accept me, if they love you as they must," I heard her say, while I was looking for my nightclothes in the other room.

"They do not love me, Elizabeth. They did not even accept my mother's choice of my father. I do not care for their friendship, or for their support. This only served my uncle..."

"They cannot be so very bad. They are Richard's parents. Besides, what did he say that was not true?"

"What do you mean he said the truth?!"

"Nothing."

I scrutinized her stance from the connecting door, while undressing myself. Her lower lip was a bit shaky, and she was doing her best to avoid my stare. "Why do I have the impression there is something you are not telling me?"

"I am sorry. When I saw your uncle, I just could not stop asking questions about myself. I remembered you told me Richard was here the day of the Gardiners' wedding, and I was afraid he could have been as well. What if Lord Matlock was one of the adults that scorned my mother and me that day, before we left? What if he also remembers? What if he is...?" she groaned. "My wish to conquer this does not seem to come. I wish I were stronger. I wish I were another person."

Matlock and John Wickham knew each other well, and my uncle was here at Pemberley that day. Was she suspecting he could be her father? So what? Maybe he was, but why did she feel unworthy again? Why did this idea resurface? "You are my wife, no other will do. Your heart is so big that you break all the dictates of propriety by inviting Georgiana into our room."

"William, please do not be mad at me for spoiling her. She needs our reassurance after so many insults."

Well, that was something I would rather Elizabeth had not suggested. "You are forgiven for that. She has missed having a friend and a mother-figure for too many years. It has affected her confidence in her self-worth." Although it was understandable that Elizabeth was, the same as I, wondering who were the men that could have been around Lambton that day. To whom Wickham's father delivered her? Who was Willoughby? Where was he?

Except that, we could not suspect <u>all</u> of them. My own father was here. If we allowed that hypothesis, we could even be siblings.

Sitting on the bed, I took off my shoes. Our bed. No. No. No. Siblings? That was unthinkable!

Could she be scared by the idea that we were <u>thus</u> related? I noticed she was surreptitiously surveying me. No, the only thing we had in common was curly hair. Like Matlock. Yes. This was one hypothesis. As good as any other.

I kept rationalizing Lizzy's behavior while taking off my shirt. It had to be that something that was instilled in your consciousness when you were a small child, never really goes away. That was why she felt unworthy...

Georgiana knocked.

"Wait for us in your chambers, my dear. We will be right there," I instructed her loudly.

Consequently, my sister's steps indicated her retreat, and Elizabeth interrogated me by widening her eyes.

"We will accompany her until she falls asleep and return afterwards," I gathered the discarded clothes and went to place them where the others were.

My wife was standing in front of the window when I came back. Turned from me, she brought up a subject I had not anticipated: the motives behind my affair with Deborah. She started relating to me a discussion she had with my sister about this same topic (trying to smooth the contradictions that plagued them both). "I had delved into your circumstances at that time — your father's ill health, the difficulties you had with the tenants, as well as the friendship with your former lover. I talked with Papa, and had theorized that lust was not your motive to succumb to that immoral relationship — you were lonely instead."

What? She had been talking with Mr. Bennet about my personal life!? "How dare you? I thought you were helping my sister when you were talking to her, not gossiping like some bloody harridan of the *ton*. Who are you to be gossiping about this? Who gave you the right to research this matter with your family? HOW DARE YOU!"

"William, I have received a great deal of wisdom in discussing issues with my parents. I have been meditating about their situation, about the loneliness my own mother suffered before meeting Papa, about their right to be happy. I have realized that things can be illegal and yet not immoral. I did not mean to do you or your sister any harm. It is only that I now see the situation that you and Deborah confronted was not dissimilar to my parents'. You both were lonely, and she was married to an evil man. Why should I see my parents' behavior as one I should approve, and not yours? Why could you not act out of loneliness, as they did, and find refuge in the care of someone else? I only want to give you my support."

"Support!" Interrupting her speech, I grabbed her by the shoulders and spun her around to look at me. "You are trying to give ME support by gossiping about my relationship with Deborah!"

"Yes. Why not? You are only human and she..."

"Because I am a <u>Darcy</u>, Elizabeth! I am expected to act better! I am a DARCY!"

"'Because you are a *Darcy*?' What kind of explanation is that?" She looked like someone who has been slapped in the face.

"Many people look at us as an example. We are supposed to be the family our tenants look up to as a model. They depend on us. We must *earn* their trust in order for them to follow us. We must behave according to our station, be it moral or economical. It is our family pride that is in stake." I let her go, adding through greeted teeth, "If you have not learned this already, it is time for you to do so!"

"So, according to you, a Willoughby can behave immorally and can be forgiven, and yet a Darcy cannot? I had better avoided the Bennets then, and the Bingleys, and the Matlocks. After all, they are ordinary mortals needing guidance. Let us not forget that what they have is contagious."

"I will not let you ridicule me, Elizabeth. I have no patience for this. We have more important matters to attend to. Georgiana is expecting us."

"Yes. I see. She is a Darcy." She shifted to be closer to the cold glass and rested her brow on it.

As you are, my dear. I moved to take her shawl and offered it to her. "Let us go."

"No. You are right. I am not only improper but inappropriate, as well. I will go with Ana alone. It is better if we do not share the bed tonight. Deborah and your cousin Anne Fitzwilliam were more fit. You could have been much happier with a more appropriate partner than a Bennet, or whatever I am. It would do you good to consider your uncle's proposition."

"What proposition?! What are you talking about? Annulment?" This could not be happening!

She straightened and wrapped herself in the shawl, signaling for me to stay. "Yes. Think of what would have happened if you and Deborah had escaped. Think of what you have sacrificed by marrying an illegitimate woman."

****

The next morning, after a night that can only be described as the most infernal purgatory, I left the house with the knowledge that I should not have been so hard on my wife. Still, I was angry, convinced that her actions were most certainly shocking and uncalled for.

"Follow me, Bingley. We have one last errand to do before our in-laws depart on the morrow." I led us in the direction of the Wickhams' former abode.

After a few minutes, we entered the abandoned cottage and my companion, dumbfounded at the unusual way in which I broke the padlock with a pistol shot, asked, "What are you looking for here, Darcy?"

"For any evidence about the friendship between Wickham senior and Willoughby. Anything that can tell me where to find that rat." I cleaned one table from the dust.

"Here? Why here? Why was this house abandoned like this?"

"This place is where Mr. Wickham spent his last years. He died from something resembling leprosy, and no one has ventured to enter since his death. We are here due to the fact that he was the only person, besides Mrs.

Bennet, to have seen Lizzy's natural father in Derbyshire as far as can be determined. I have inquired everywhere, and there is no other soul to account for his presence that day."

"Apart from Elizabeth, herself."

We started by looking in the places that seemed to be straightforward — like drawers, closets and shelves — and ended looking in the more bizarre ones. We chatted about yesterday's visit and about how Richard had to take his father to Lambton's Inn during the night. Charles questioned the way in which the general was buried, and I expounded that my cousin did not go into any details concerning the matter. He just assured me that no one would ever find his grave. Not having a place to be honored and not being remembered was the worst that might happen to the highest rank officers. Glory was everything they were after at this age.

The many hours seemed to be unfruitful, though, as there was nothing of interest to be found.

When it was past the hour for lunch, I decided it was time to concede defeat. Looking at my reflection in the old mirror, dusting off my clothes, I noticed a strange object between the glass and the wooden frame. A worn yellow piece of paper had been folded and stuck in the narrow crack. I extracted it carefully to find the most amazing proof. It was the marriage certificate of Fanny Gardiner and John Willoughby.

It seemed to be a genuine document. It was dated twenty-two years ago in Scotland, and had all the formality and pomposity of a legal certificate. The signatures at the bottom also appeared to be authentic.

"Is that what I think it is?" Bingley startled me from behind.

"It seems so." I handed it to my brother for him to study. "Why do you think this document is here, Charles? Could the late Wickham and Willoughby be family?"

"Only God knows. I am afraid *that* will make you related to George Wickham."

"Not even in his dreams!" I rose, satisfied to at least have found evidence that Lizzy was not illegitimate.

****

Upon our arrival, I was informed by Georgiana our family had already had their meal, and Lizzy was alone in her room. It was evident from my sister's demeanor Elizabeth was not pleased with my long absence. Bingley suggested I ought to have left a note before venturing into the search that had consumed half of the day.

Well, I am not going to need an apology when I show her this. I parted from them and entered her apartments. *It might even help her forget all this absurdity of my need to consider other women.*

Lillian was waiting outside the washing room, and she told me my wife was taking a bath. Dismissing the servant girl, I placed the document on the table next to the bed. I opened the door, careful not to make a sound, and entered.

All the reasons behind my annoyance were forgotten then, dazzled by the sleeping figure in the foam. Most likely she did not get any sleep last night, as I did not. She probably tried to apologize to me in the morning. Only to find me gone. Poor dear. She had to be as tired as I was of this fight.

I surveyed her relaxed features: her arms on the edge of the tub, her head resting on a folded towel. I delighted in the gleam of her breasts, impeccably symmetric as the circular waves a stone makes in crystalline water.

Bending to observe her closer, I was tempted to lift her and place her on the bed, soaked, to kiss her all over — until I could distill entirely the elixir that emanated from her skin.

"It is the same man," she bellowed, waking up.

Her voice should have distracted me from my musings, but it did not, until she studied her surroundings and focused on me. Her visage transformed into one of alarm. She stood up brusquely. I helped her to get out of the bathtub as she reached for her bathrobe. I could see that she was still irritated at me, and was slightly amused by her curt movements when dressing. "What were you doing, Fitzwilliam? Attempting to spy inside my head yet again?"

"What do you mean spying inside your head? I just came in."

"Were not you listening and guessing my thoughts as is your wont?"

"No. I have learned that lesson well. I know you do not like that." I reached for the band she was tying around her waist and pulled her to me, smiling rascally. "I was much better entertained with your body and was bringing news. Do you want to know what I found?"

She looked down to the place my hand touched her, seeming to study it for a couple of seconds. "No. I have a question of my own, then. Tell me the precise position Wickham was in when you stopped him in Lambton woods. I want you to do the same *he* did."

"You want me to do <u>what</u>?" I detached from her, wounded by her rude manners. "What kind of morbid game is this, Elizabeth?"

"There is nothing morbid in this. I only want to know. I have the right to know!"

"You want me to…? No. No. NO! You do not need that! That will do you no good!"

"Fitzwilliam, I have remembered! I have remembered <u>everything</u>!" She stomped her foot in that typical way of hers. "I need to know if what I have just seen is the truth. I deserve to know the truth! You owe me this much!"

Her determination was so strong that I had no other choice. I stood in front of her — *this is wrong* — pushed her to have her back against the wall and made the gesture of sustaining her by the neck with one hand, the other touching her navel under the robe.

"He was not only strangling me. He was speaking in my ear. He was pinching me with a stick or something spiny and saying that now was <u>his</u> turn. That is why I feel needles in my belly every time I picture this."

It was not just his hand then. He was hurting her! "Damn it!"

"His father came. He said something about having betrayed too hard."

An old entry from Lizzy's diaries was associated with these words — '*The sound of broken bones and an excruciating scream culminates the unsettling memory…*' — "John Wickham must have beaten George hard until his violence took another direction." Her direction.

I stormed out of the bathroom. The conflict experienced from want of her, after being intoxicated with her smell, and the melancholy of all that had transpired, was too much. The longing from the many nights of waiting for her to be healthy was drawing me into taking action. Begging her see that all these could be solved together, or demanding that she obey as a wife should, was what I wanted to do. I wanted so to make her drop this subject, and once and for all make love to her.

She does not want to see you, Darcy! I felt used. Dirty. Disloyal. Frustrated. I could not understand why Elizabeth had this obsession with the past. Why did she need to know everything? Why did she have to research every single thing? Why could she not leave that day behind? WHY?!

****

In the evening, I decided to give the marriage certificate to my father-in-law. The Bennets had spent many hours with us this month, which led to a favorable change in our relationship, and it seemed to me indispensable to relate this news. So, I called him for an interview in my study, in order to discuss the matter of my inquiries about Willoughby and this unexpected finding.

After perusing the document, he folded it meticulously and gave it back to me. "You say Willoughby has not been seen in many years. It should remain that way. Do not tell Fanny that you saw this. It would only add to her fears. Tomorrow we will be gone, and it is better for her to think that Lizzy is safe — which I am sure she is. For us, this man is dead, and my mission is accomplished once I give you this letter in return." He sat in the chair across from me, reaching for a paper in the pocket inside his coat. "Before you read it, let me assure you that the author of this correspondence is a discreet man. He has had this information for years, and he has not divulged it, as opposed to the general who dropped in and out of my life according to his whim, I now see. Watson and I have been in contact uninterruptedly and, as he lives in London, we visit each other often. I am convinced that his description is factual, and that Lizzy was right to ask me to write him about this subject. I have not given it to her for reading, because I respect your privacy, yet I feel you should. She has been troubled by many questions about bigamy and marriage these weeks, and I think, it will benefit her to see that your wedding, although too hasty, was the right decision in this case."

Intrigued by this accounts, and seeing the gentleman was leaving the room, I opened the missive. Even without reading it, my name and Deborah's jumped in front of my eyes repeatedly, and I was compelled to burn it right away. "What had she requested you to do?"

"I told her that Watson, the friend whose letter you hold, arrived with Mullen the day his wife was killed. She wants to know what he witnessed and how much he knew about her death. That is what you are going to find there."

How could Elizabeth have gone this far?! I dropped the paper on the desk. My next step was not reading anything, but giving Elizabeth a piece of my mind. Was all of England going to gossip about this affair? I hurried up the stairs. MADDENING, OBSTINATE WOMAN! I HAD TO STOP HER NOW!

I arrived at her door and was surprised to overhear Jane's voice behind it. I paused to check my appearance and knocked, when a strange cry from my wife broke through the walls, "I cannot be a Darcy, Jane. I am Elizabeth Wickham. William will hate me!"

What the hell! Elizabeth Wickham? — the thought reverberated in my mind. She was Elizabeth WICKHAM? How? What? It was not possible! The ground was disappearing under my feet, and I fumbled to the entrance of my room. Blinding suspicion was infecting my vision as I saw the grown up George Wickham in my mind's eye, holding <u>my</u> wife, the same as I had an hour ago, the same as he had in the woods. I dropped on the bed and rebuilt the many dialogues about bigamy we had these days, about the easiness with which one could evade justice. The fact that Elizabeth was asking to dissolve our marriage, as well as her distress when finding out I was observing her sleep, was understood at last. I considered the way her thoughts about the immorality of her parents' marriage evolved with the passing of this month. I replayed the argument about why it was justifiable for me to have had the affair with Deborah.

She was hiding this from me! All this time she had been lying! My fantasies grew disproportionally as I visualized George's contemptuous laugh in the road to Meryton. He was mocking <u>me</u> — he was setting a trap for me! He must have forced Elizabeth to marry him by threatening her. He might have blackmailed her with the game in Lambton. Yes. She did not remember all of it then. He had married Maria Lucas and Elizabeth! The general helped him!

I stood up and tried to remember what was in Lizzy's diaries. Where did I put them? When could this have happened? When were they together? I asked myself while searching frenetically through all the drawers.

The echo of this day and the torment of the doubt, were clouding my wits, as I could not erase the images of Wickham enjoying MY WIFE. I was afraid it would drive me to Bedlam, until one coherent memory imposed. I recalled our wedding night. I evoked her blossoming under my body and the timid way with which she parted her legs. I brought to my mind that treasured moment when my manhood broke through her barrier and she smiled reassuringly at me. *No! No man was before me!*

Thanks to the Lord, the last fact made me reason the previous deliberations were insane. New pieces started to fit into the puzzle. Could I have heard wrongly and what she said to Jane was Elizabeth Willoughby, instead? I took off my cravat and dwelled on what had happened in the bathtub. She had remembered something new. She woke up after shouting that it was the same man — The same man? Elizabeth Wickham? Elizabeth Willoughby? WILLOUGHBY AND WICKHAM WERE THE SAME MAN! That was what was tormenting her! How did I not decipher this before?! Wickham senior did not disappear to America. He was here, in Bakewell, when my family assumed him missing! The scoundrel that was Lizzy's father was Mr. Wickham! She was Wickham's sister! SHE WAS ABUSED BY HER OWN BROTHER!

All the previous emptiness was replaced by an iron chain that drew me from my room into hers.

She was nowhere to be found. The candles were lit. Everything was in place, except that there was no one inside. I sensed the wind intrude through the open balcony and a flash of white outside. I took of my coat and approached her. I covered her with it.

"I have something to tell you, Fitzwilliam. We need to talk."

"I know. You do not need to tell me anything. I know."

Even in the dim illumination from the celestial vault, the soreness of her eyes was visible. "You know? You hate me, then, do you not? You are disgusted by me — a WICKHAM! You want me far away from Ana."

"Never." I lifted her up and strode back inside her bedchamber. "No matter if what we are presuming is true or not, I cannot stop loving you."

Seeing that she was too cold, I tugged at the blankets, taking them off, to place us together in front of the fireplace. I laid her at a safe distance from it and removed my clothes too. I settled, resting against her. "Let your body become accustomed to my heat."

"Fitzwilliam, what are you doing? He is your worst enemy. Your blood will be soiled with the Wickhams'! I cannot be your wife! I can never be a proper Darcy! You do not want that! I am Elizabeth Wi…"

I covered her mouth fast. "No! You are Elizabeth Darcy! You were never Elizabeth Wickham! Those men are not your family. Your family is Mrs. and Mr. Bennet — the loving couple that has taken care of you for so many years. Remember? Those girls that came to nurse you and Ana and me. There is not a speck of the Wickhams in you."

She gazed at me, bewildered, and I relaxed my hand for her to speak. "And what about all that you told me yesterday?"

"That does not matter. Not anymore."

"But… but. I am totally unfit. I…"

"You should forget that. I was wrong." She still considered George took something from me. I was going to show her there was so much more. "I know a very good method to exorcise all those ideas about you being a Wickham." I leaned to stare at her succulent lips closer. "Elizabeth Darcy." I kissed her cheek first, then, petted her eyes. "Elizabeth Darcy." I separated a bit to memorize her passionate expression. "Elizabeth Darcy." I bent to slowly brush her jaw. "Elizabeth Darcy." I rubbed her lower lip with my thumb. "Elizabeth Darcy." I nibbled it while my hands slid to roll her stockings down her legs. "Elizabeth Darcy." The taste of dormant gardens urged me to loosen the ribbon of her drawers too. "Elizabeth Darcy." I bared her buttocks, as my tongue feasted in the silkiness of her mouth. "Elizabeth Darcy." My teeth lingered on the moans that rose from her throat. "Elizabeth Darcy." I encircled her waist as she abandoned her neck backwards. "Elizabeth Darcy." She grabbed my head imploringly and drove me to her chest.

Once her defenses had melted, I opened the front pins on her gown, one by one. The light from the hearth intruded into our nest, and I could see how the path my touch was drawing was a path of fire. The petals at the summit of her breasts, together with the flames in her pupils, threatened to burn my eyes. Her naked body resembled the depictions of the sunset in the desert — the rebel land that cannot be conquered. I was steadfast in my resolution of claiming my lordship over its vastness. Ambushed into each golden dune of her torso, each secret valley of her arms and each soft curve of her calves, I persisted with insatiable thirst. Her womanly essence was the siren's song that led me to safe harbor. I navigated her flesh until I found the oasis between her thighs. I opened her with both hands and drank from it.

I felt her palpitating for me. *FOR ME!*

I knew I was having all of her; that she was giving herself unreservedly. The promise of her fulfillment slid throughout my digits whilst tasting her sweetness. I was sure she could never look more stunning than now, when I was worshipping her velvety essence. Hence, I claimed my right to tame her gently, until the way she arched her spine and squeezed the robes pulled me to anchor inside her hips. I savored her name with every thrust. "Elizabeth Darcy. Elizabeth Darcy. Elizabeth Darcy..."

Whereas her breathlessness teased my neck, the delirium of her tightness impelled me to sink deeper. Her bare nipples caressed my skin mercilessly. The warmth inside her vessel overpowered me. Our joined moisture launched a new frenzy. I explored her confines, bursting. She fastened me with her legs and, as a sandstorm, infused herself in me. Then, when I believed it impossible for her love to undo me further, she grasped my shoulders roughly and summoned the waves of pleasure that could not be stopped any longer.

I lost my voice and myself in an uncontainable spiral to an endless world.

At some point, from the other side of the abyss, I heard someone say, "That was unbelievable, Fitzwilliam."

Chapter 34

ELIZABETH

The night I found out about my natural father, was when William broke the final wall I had built around myself. He had found me on the terrace, and had kissed me as if this was our wedding night. Fighting the ghosts in my mind with the resolution of vanquishing them forever. Once in our room, he took my clothes off with veneration. He traveled the roads to my soul with a gait that was swift, driving, and determined; hands eager with craving. The small shadow of anxiety that had possessed me before dissolved in the dampness — sweet essence that was the silent witness of his presence inside me.

Oh Lord, thank you! I repeated each time he said my name.

For me, his worry that my insecurities could come to haunt us again, made him more endearing. "Elizabeth Darcy, Elizabeth Darcy, Elizabeth Darcy." The words resounded inside me while we arranged ourselves on the bed, making me aware of his loyalty.

After apologizing for his hurtful words following his uncle's visit, he claimed the only thing he would not stand was if I withdrew from him. The rest we would solve together. As for Wickham being my half-brother, it only strengthened his resolution to cherish me.

I tried to apologize for speaking of annulment, but he would not let me, repeating time after time, "Oh, my love! Please, oh, Lizzy! Never! No! How much I love you!"

With the weight of William's leg bent over my thighs — enveloping me as if to shelter, to keep, to belong — I disclosed what had happened when Wickham's father took off the blindfold and learned my name.

Apparently, they had a heated discussion just before, and he had beaten his son with cruelty. The whole of that day appeared in my dreams while sleeping in the bathtub, prior to being startled by William's presence. I was devilishly angry with my natural father and out of my wits with the knowledge of how he had treated my mother. "You see, my parentage was clear to me the very moment Wickham senior threatened us — the moment that man brought me in front of Mama in Lambton church. My memory blocked this, not wanting to deal with the hurt I thought that *I* had provoked. All these feelings of guilt, of being afraid, had their source in the way she reacted. In the way we ran away from Derbyshire and secrets were kept from me. She must have felt Willoughby's betrayal as a dagger to her gut."

William related his anguish when he imagined, for a couple of minutes, that I was George Wickham's wife.

Oh Dear! How could things be so convoluted? I took in the nightmare my husband experienced before coming to the balcony. "I was asking Jane advice about how to convince you. I did not want you see me scream or curse — not after we had argued. Surely you were going to be incensed. I was preparing to explain that I care not a whit about George Wickham. I only care about us and our family. I was scared you would doubt my ability to be a good example if I was a Wickham and had to help you see I would not be unfit if they truly knew me."

William encouraged me to talk about this, and then, went to my escritoire to compose something in the diary that had remained almost untouched since the encounter with the general. When finished, he handed it to me for my perusal.

"You kept writing all this time?" I was amazed to see the way he described me and how perceptive he was.

"Yes, I wrote during the nights. You could not continue after being injured so badly. Now, I want you to read it and to remember, next time you go through anything like this, there is no 'civil' or 'uncivil' between us; I adore you. I only get more bewitched by that innocent passion of yours. You are my wife. My friend. My partner. You can cry or swear whenever you want. I am not a saint. And I want no saint in my bed."

****

With the balminess of a new understanding still surrounding our bodies, I awoke with the certainty from now on my life was going to be wonderfully different.

His breath was tickling my cheek when a strident, "Mr. Bennet, cannot you stay away from the library for one day?! We are traveling in an hour, for

God's sake!" from my mother, hurrying Papa to prepare for their departure to Hertfordshire, interrupted us.

Opening my eyes at the unwelcome sound, I saw my beloved smile sympathetically. "Shh. Shh. Do not wake. Shut out the outside world, Lizzy. It is just you and me. Nothing else."

"William, it must be quite late if Mama is up. We have little time for the farewells, and we must tell them what we found out before they depart."

"Must we?"

"Yes. She will be shocked at first, but she will become more tranquil when she finds out there is no chance of Willoughby crossing our path ever again."

"Cannot we do that later?"

"No. They are leaving today."

"Agggrrrr," his voice protested while he pulled me atop him. "Well, I will let you wake up if you promise not to leave me for a single minute today."

Why would I deny such a delightful request?

****

The morning began rapidly the instant we heard the rest of the house coming to life, with the rush of the preparation for departure of my parents and the Bingleys. Dismissing my abigail, Fitzwilliam helped me dress, and I helped him, whereas we had time to discuss a strategy for sharing our news.

His plan was simple: to draw a picture of George's father and show it to Mama. It happened to be a good strategy.

"It is he." My mother clutched her heart in shock the moment she saw the portrait. "It is John — my first husband."

"Mrs. Bennet, this is George Wickham's father — John Wickham," Fitzwilliam explained under the attentive ears of both my parents.

She rubbed her temple, unbelieving, and gave the illustration to me as I sat beside her on the couch. "But how? We were married. I knew him. He came to Bakewell often. He wooed me. He... We married in Scotland."

Papa approached us, and was fast to placate what was surely to become a fit of nerves. Calm prevailed in the closed room while she processed the truth. Some scattered voices of my younger sisters, calling for the family, were heard from the gardens a couple of times.

Finally, my father, watching the impact the latest knowledge had on Mama, declared, "Fanny, this is not so terrible. Look at the good side. We did nothing wrong when we wed. You are not a sinner anymore. And that man is dead."

"Yes... But Lizzy is... She is... Oh My! She is *his* sister. That crook's sister! And Willoughby was Wickham. Not Willoughby. He never loved Lizzy or me. He had another family. He left us because we were nothing to him. Nothing since the beginning!"

Papa seemed to absorb these words slowly. He took one of Mama's hands in his and turned to look at me most sternly. He examined me. As a person that reads a book for the first time, he traveled my features. Until, steadily, that somber study became tender. "My child," his first words afterwards. "You are *my* child. I opted to be your father a long time ago. You are not *his* daughter, but mine. I chose you, even if I already had Jane, Mary, Kitty and Lydia. Lizzy, if anyone ever says you are a Wickham, remember you are *my* flesh and blood. Not because of some joke of destiny, like this thing of Willoughby, but because I wished it to be so. I was positive that my home would be blessed with the presence of your caring mother and you. Do not let some silly concepts related to the unfeeling man that fathered you intrude into your happiness. You mean the same as my other four daughters mean to me: Everything." He kissed his companion's cheek tenderly. "And your mother. Well. What can I say? She is the love of my life."

These declarations provoked a cascade of tears from Mama, and even if they were happy tears, it took a while for them to cease. When they did, well, I must say she was up to the challenge. "How do you feel about this? Is this knowledge what had you so distracted since we told you that we saw Willoughby here that day? Did you discern you were Wickham's sister then?"

"No. I had a lot of evidence. I hypothesized about it. Even so, I denied it. I only found out for certain yesterday."

369

Mama was pensive a couple of seconds, sniffing still. Then, she looked in the direction of the portrait of John Wickham that William had drawn and asked him, "Do you have a pencil, Son?"

My husband produced it and she took a book from the shelf nearby, using it as a base. "No, Lizzy, I think he does not resemble himself here. Let us fix this drawing." A determined Mama added a broken tooth to the mouth delineated on the paper. "Better." She cocked her head to invite the rest of us to look at her handiwork.

Papa took the hint directly and filled with a dark shadow a circle around one of John Wickham's eyes, to which William chortled, approaching to improve the representation.

He grabbed the implement enthusiastically and took his time to sketch the silhouette of a horrible mouse eating at one ear. This extracted a contagious laugh from all the family members.

"I think he is not as handsome as you once told me." I stitched a prominent scar on the nose. "Next to this, even a Cyclops is handsome."

"Yes, Lizzy. You inherited your beauty from *me*."

****

This conversation led to the disclosure of Charles and William having found the marriage certificate between a Fanny Gardiner and a John Willoughby the previous day. We speculated about its consequences, but could not come to any conclusive understanding. Thus, the question about being legitimate was resolved to be in some legal limbo, that we sincerely did not care to clarify.

The heartfelt farewells in the main stairs lasted what seemed like a century. However, it was worth it, as I felt myself to be glowing with a new sense of rightness — of acceptance and of optimism.

This day marked a transformation for me, into the lively girl Fitzwilliam had fallen in love while we resided at Netherfield. Solving the puzzle of my relationship with George Wickham (as meeting him so many years after the first fatal encounter was what had triggered my former state of depression) was a great source of relief. Not because of what had transpired — on the contrary, because not knowing was much worse.

****

As the darkness set in that evening, William invited Ana to the balcony to share some of the marvels the firmament had reserved for us.

We were lucky to find a clear sky with Jupiter in the east — in opposition to the Sun. "Look how big and bright it seems. This is a unique occasion. Jupiter has a much wider orbit than others, and is seldom this near to the Earth. Picture the phenomenon of being 'in opposition', equally to the point in which our planet is in the middle between our main star and Jupiter — as if the Earth was trying to make an eclipse on the bigger planet. Of course, the size of the sphere we live in is much smaller, and thus, only makes a diminutive circled shadow; in the rare case in which we found ourselves exactly in line."

Seeing Ana's blank expression and finding his speech was a bit too scientific and confusing, I created a representation to clarify the concept. "Let us suppose that William is the Sun," I put him in the middle between Georgiana and me. "Now you are Jupiter — as you must be larger than the Earth, which I am. The rest of our sisters could be the other planets, but they are not needed for us to understand what 'in opposition to the Sun' means. Then," I paused to indicate how she should move in ample slow circles around William and I orbited closer to, as if I were Earth, "if we keep moving, at some point, your brother will see you behind me. This is the moment when Jupiter is in opposition to the Sun. That is why, these nights, while the sunset happens in the west, we find Jupiter on the opposite side: in the east."

"Lizzy," my sister started to follow my instructions with a dancing step, "compared to yours, the description from my brother looks like boring documents a solicitor would write."

"Georgiana! When did you learn such disrespectful behavior!" William asked, fists on his hips.

"No, my dear," I shook my head, trying to hide the mirth his gaping astonishment provoked. "Do not try teasing your brother, because 'Mr. Darcy is not to be laughed at!' I am perfectly convinced that he has no defect, since he owns that his only fault — pride — where there is a real superiority of mind, will be always under good regulation."

Ana giggled to his face, and William said, "Hmm! I see <u>you</u>, Mrs. Darcy, are the instigator. You will pay dearly for this!" He grabbed me by the waist and pushed me toward the door. "Good night, Georgiana."

Since his playful manner only provoked more silly laughter, he grumbled, "You are not afraid, eh? You seem to have forgotten that you are ticklish, and I can torture you all night long."

Oh, no!

---

*To learn more about what can be found every day in the sky read this page: http://www.skyandtelescope.com/observing/ataglance

EPILOGUE

Pemberley, 10 April 1813

I am starting a new diary today, exactly one year after your proposal in Hunsford. I do it, knowing someday you, Fitzwilliam, will come across it.

No story is written without thinking of the reader. The scenes you wrote only for my eyes were done with the main purpose of making me see myself as you do. The same happens now. I write these words thinking of you: thinking this will be helpful to you when the time is right.

I can only tell my story. We can only write about that what has happened to ourselves. I will never be able to write a tale about conquering the Kilimanjaro or the voyage of a slave to freedom. I can only write how I learned my truth, in the hope that you learn yours. That precious truth that is yours alone.

"What am I to do with the truth?" you could ask. The answer is as personal as each human being.

This is what I did with it:

At the end, it was straightforward to forgive myself. It was natural, yes, because I understood as a child — what does the world consist of, if not of her parents? I loved my mother, and before meeting Papa, I wanted to love — or at least to think well — of my natural father as well. I did it because I needed love as any child. And I needed friends.

My truth told me this was why I agreed to allow George Wickham to blindfold me. Nowadays, my heart says I was right to do that. Since, how could one be wrong when one commits any mistake? How can it be wrong to fall, stand up and learn? How — if this is the way we are expected to go through life?

My truth taught me one lesson can last many years. Thus, after the incidents in Lambton, I learned FEAR. The small Lizzy that still lives in me learned it so well, that fear was what made me reject you in Hunsford. The fear of being loved and being abandoned afterwards (something I knew to hurt too much). Of course, I could not know back then when someone says, "I love you," this person has changed your life forever.

Fear was my reason for running away from home; my reason for cutting my hair short. Fear was even the reason for allowing you to take me away from Cambridge — an instance in which I acted for my own self-preservation.

Fear is an enormous word.

You say fear is one of the reasons why England is at war on the Continent. The government can have some other unknown incentives. But we, the people, are involved in a war far away from our land because we fear Napoleon could gain more strength. We fear this, even when we have no proof of his intention to attack us across the sea.

It is also my guess you were invaded by fear when your father was dying. You lost your mother when just a teen. How could you not fear your father's death when you were my age? I think this fear is what made you get involved with a married woman. You could have been afraid of the challenges before you: raising a small sister and running a vast estate. Furthermore, I am glad you take responsibility for this. However, I wish you took responsibility for your actions alone, and not for everyone else's, as she did not die because of any indiscretion on your part.

Now I know, when it is appropriate, you will read this entry. You will see that fear made me build high walls. Sometimes, they were so very high, I could not see spring blossoming outside. And, no matter that I am grateful for my mistakes, and that life behind those walls might be safer, I am resolute about not living my life guided by fear.

****

"I should draw this ethereal gait of yours someday — your skirt dancing as an extension of the music that subtly dissolves into the air," William told me when I received him on the big staircase, after a long week of work.

My reply should have been, 'A new Mozart concerto Georgiana has being learning during this afternoon is contagious. Sadly, she is already in bed, and you missed it.' As I was finishing the last bits of a special surprise I had prepared, I said instead, "Do you think so? Well, I am not one to contradict you, Mr. Darcy."

"Mr. Darcy?" His brows knitted quizzically.

"Yes. Have you read the new letter from your friend Mr. Sedgwick that arrived yesterday? Are you ready to debate each of his theories, sir? I am eager to express opinions that are not my own, just for the pleasure of the battle."

"Sedgwick's letter? What does it have to do with anything?"

"No? Hmm! Where is it?"

"Somewhere between the piles on my desk."

Pulling at his horsewhip, I guided him toward the study. "Should I use my accomplishments to convince you to peruse it, sir? Should I offer some juicy reward in exchange for this service? I would be happy to perform any task."

"What is to be found in that letter that attracts your interest so?"

"Your friend must have explained the theory about how caves were formed."

"A theory?" My attitude must have lastly reminded him of some irreverent dialogues we had before. "You forget that experimenting is the key to any true understanding. Why study some theory, when there is practice? Why search for the truth in a letter or a book? There is no use for a theory."

Merry at the remembrance of our discussion of this subject, I realized I had created enough expectation. Hence, I sat him down at his desk chair and stood behind him, pushing him to the table (startling him at first, and making him chuckle soon afterwards). "It amuses you to watch how I have to exert my physique, to only transport your weight a minuscule of an inch, eh?"

"Well, you must agree, it is impractical, if you want to make me read anything, to use only brute force. Why do not you come and sit on my lap so that we can do the research together?"

No, no, no. I would not fall into his trap. I was the one in charge of seduction this night. "You forget, Mr. Darcy, there is nothing more useful than a *good* theory." I turned around to present my posterior once again. "For example, you can see Newton was right about force being proportional to mass. I cannot move you because you are too devilishly heavy!"

"You should desist then."

"Certainly not! Hold the flower vase for me, Mr. Darcy." I abandoned the previous post to surround the desk, grabbing it with both hands. "You see? Galileo had another useful theory as well. He said everything is relative. Here. This works the same. Now you are set." The first step in my mission was accomplished.

"What if I refuse to oblige you?"

"In that case, you are resigning the pleasure of observing *me* taking a turn about the room, which is most refreshing, and admire a figure that is to the greatest advantage in walking."

"You are going to meander about the room while I study? This is not to be borne! This is the most unfair exploitation!"

With, "Actually, no. *I* am off. *You* wait for the tray with the dinner I had arranged to be sent to you," a previously written note was pressed into his hand. It said, *"Go to your bedchamber in two hours, Mr. Darcy."*

****

Never had I felt so much expectation as when I prepared this intrigue. After composing uncountable letters, and utilizing the helpful intervention of Mr. Cochran and Mrs. Beth, I had what I needed without William being the wiser. The only things that remained to be accomplished were to be achieved during these two hours.

With Mrs. Reynolds' and Lillian's complicity, following months of careful planning and no less effort from the footmen (in order to move the goods whilst my husband was in the fields) I had managed to prepare an amazing stage in the attic of the Manor. I also had the audacity of asking Georgiana to dine early today, in order to guarantee that William and I would be left alone this evening. Therefore, here I was, writing the next step for my husband to follow after the appointed time.

"Dress." Those were the instructions he would find attached to a parcel lying on his bed.

The package contained a pirate costume, and I could not help the self-conscious giggle at the picture of him discovering an eye patch and a fake hook, together with some peculiar robes.

I prepared another note in my bedchamber. *"I am in the place where you kissed me for the first time."*

My mind sketched what he would do. "The bedroom in London? — No. This cannot be the answer to the puzzle," I said aloud, imitating his masculine voice, and left the note upon the writing table.

Then I wrote another hint on a separate piece of paper, *"The place we slept together first,"* and laid it over the bed.

"Hmm. Is she referring to our wedding night?" he would think.

"Paradise can be hidden below any roof." — The last clue would give him the exact place.

****

Mrs. Reynolds must have instructed all the servants to vanish, because there was not a single soul to be seen or heard as I climbed the stairs to the Pemberley's attic. Once secluded there, with even more anticipation, I bathed in the tub I had installed in this new setting, and worked on my disguise.

When finished, the reflection in the looking glass told me, I had accomplished my daring task superbly. A blue hue covered from my bare feet up my legs, to the waist, resembling a fish tail; a long cashmere veil (the only significant cloth I was wearing), with cyan arabesques covered hair and shoulders, and concealed my bosom without spoiling the disguise.

Would he find all the clues? Would he like this? Would he think I was too wanton?

****

Most likely, I could have stayed a while longer, gaping at my own image, but the darkness and silence in the house indicated I should put the final touches to the scene by pretending an inspection of the skies with the old telescope.

"This is extraordinary!" his silhouette was visible in the door as he entered and closed it, leaving only his voice to be heard. "When did you...? This is why you needed time to keep me busy! So that you could reproduce your room in Cambridge. Look: the steamy bathtub. The huge wardrobe. The gigantic bed. The small escritoire. Even the rocking-chair. How did you accomplish this? Ah. The telescope!" His aura was starting to be distinguishable again while he approached, and I was pleased to see the costume suited him rather well.

"There is the North Star, sir. Do you want to observe it?"

"You remembered I envisioned you as a siren in the cavern!" Bending to touch my knee, he must have discovered it felt smooth and warm. "What did you do to have a fabric that clutches to your body like this?"

"It is paint." I pointed to a set of oil dyes on the floor. "Do you like it?"

"Like it? This is my deepest fantasy come true!" He tapped the colored scales I had drawn on my skin, until he reached the piece of triangular chiffon that covered the most intimate part on the threshold to the hips. "You are naked!"

"Almost." I pulled at the fabric to point out I was not revealing *everything*.

"Really? Do you think you can make a point about being properly clothed, Miss Siren, when I can appreciate your mesmerizing shapes?"

Nodding in response, I felt his other fingers on my neck. Oh, Yes. He liked this seduction!

"You will think differently when I tear it off."

"Are you complaining, Mr. Darcy? I thought you would enjoy having a model of a mermaid. That is why I am here to help you. Nothing else, sir."

"Nothing else? Then, why is *that* here?" He hinted at the bed, while lifting me up.

"I do not know. *You* are the artist."

"I am Pirate Darcy! I have the reputation of terrorizing the Seven Seas. I am no artist, no painter. I am a dreadful and heartless savage. This hammock is the place where I subdue my victims." Grumbling most severely, he laid me upon the mattress.

"Are not you troubled by staining the pristine linens, Mr. Pirate? The tint might spoil them forever. It will not do to…"

"None of your impertinence! This is a rough hammock, Miss!" He seized both my wrists over my head with one hand. "Or I will have to tie you to the main mast."

"Whatever for?"

"To kiss you. All over. As if the world were going to end tomorrow."

****

Feeling that the rivers must have changed their course, the moon had surely shown her other side, and the falling leaves were levitating over the ground during our lovemaking, I started to draw relaxed caresses on Fitzwilliam's chest. "What did you do during these two past hours? Did you stay in the office studying?"

"Only for a while. I could not help being lured to take a bath as well." Mmm. This was why he smelt so nice! "And, I read your new diary while looking for clues in your room."

It appeared to me this happened sooner than expected, but his voice did not betray any anxiety. "And? What do you think?"

He took a strand of hair from my side-whiskers and started to sweep my earlobe absentmindedly. "That you are right. God will put more challenges in our path, but they will not frighten us, as He brought us together."

"Yes. He has been with us all along. He even built a cavern under our feet when we thought the darkest hour had come." The image of that place with the stone draperies resembling St. Mark's Basilica appeared in my mind.

"You found the Cochrans' protection when you ran away. Although, I wonder what would have happened had you not fled from Hertfordshire."

"It would have been most inconvenient. Since, no amount of stubbornness from your part would have prevailed against my wish to hide during every visit."

"Oh, I am sure He would have given me an opportunity. He always has. This is why our mistakes not only make us better; mine also helped you forgive your younger self."

"Your mistakes helped me?"

"In the cave, you saw that, if my dealings with the general led us to almost die, then your naïve childhood behavior was not in fact such a big deal. We all make wrong decisions — it is part of His plan."

I felt elated he saw his mistakes as something Our Father had absolved him for. But, how did they help *me*? My first thoughts about not blaming myself were when he was sleeping in that cavern. When I understood that some faults had unpredictable consequences — like being buried by the general. "Dear Lord, you are correct! I started to see things differently after our conversations there!"

"I am glad to be of service, my lady, even if we have a new problem now."

A new problem? "Which one?"

"We will never be able to play pirates with our progeny."

Those impossible dimples of his attested he was quite happy with this conclusion, and I had to ask, "Why?"

"Because the image of you dressed — or should I say undressed — as a temptress will assault me each time."

"That seems like a huge problem indeed." *You! Cheeky boy!* "It does not matter, though. Love is all children need."

"Right."

William would be there to support me when I made my next misstep. "It takes away any fear. Does it not?"

Apparently his playful woolgathering triggered something else. "Give me a second to put on my breeches."

"Where are you going?" I said, a bit aback, while he fastened the ribbon to hold his undergarment in place.

"Nowhere. I just need to speak to someone."

"Now?"

"Yes. I want to be the first one." He stood up and helped me rise as well. "It is time to show our daughter how much we wish her to be part of our life."

I pulled at the counterpane and enveloped myself with it. "Our daughter?" Of whom was he speaking?

He set one knee on the floor and spoke the next words to my belly. "Little one, I do not know if you are there already. You even might be beginning to exist this very moment. I hope that you are, but if you are not, it does not signify. I vow to repeat the same every month until you can hear me: Welcome to Pemberley!"

_____**The End**_____

THINKING ABOUT MY WORLD
Appendix by Ph.D. María de Lourdes Ballinas

Since human beings appeared on Earth, there is a continuous interest in explaining how things happen, why the Sun shines, why the matter exists, why there are so many differences among people and in nature. In the late 1800s, science was growing in its interpretation about all the chemical and physical phenomena. These questions were strictly asked by men; there were only few bright women involved. Antoine Lavoisier, known as chemistry's father (1743-1794), demonstrated there is some special composition in organic matter (with his wife's help). His work was, at first, only divulged by hand scripts, which were sent to other specialists.

For a woman, it was almost forbidden to question about science, even more to have some written information! It was necessary to send letters of request, inquiring about some news on the scientific research. This was a very slow process!

Science evolves at the same time in many human minds. Let me put this in our context:

One of the biggest events in chemistry was the statement of The Principle of Conservation of Mass, which was known to be outlined by Lavoisier. Mikhail Lomonosov (1711-1765) had expressed very similar ideas before, in 1748, but he wrote them in Russian. Even our Elizabeth cannot understand the complexity of this language! And there is evidence that Joseph Black (1728-1799) and Henry Cavendish (1731-1810) had anticipated this law as well. As a matter of fact, this idea likely came as an inspiration for many scientists at the same time.

Why is this law so important? Maybe it sounds like a heavy science lecture, but it is not. Have you ever thought why, when you burn a piece of paper, it disappears? Have you ever noticed that, it is not the same to have water or to have oil, in contact with soil? What happens? Why the different compounds and matter behave so differently? So many times our deafening world cannot let us think about simple things with so great power! In the 19th century, there were no noisy distractions which perturbed our mind, and our imagination.

The law of conservation of mass explains how matter does not disappear. It always remains constant (the same as our most beautiful memories). This simple principle was not obvious during those days. And, it is such an important event that Chemistry could never change into modern Chemistry without it. Alchemy transforms into this Science in a great extent, thanks to this discovery and thanks to the work done for its verification.

In the moment that chemists were able to measure substances and realized they never disappeared, they began to understand how the transformation of substances occurs. These are known as chemical process, just like the ones happening in our body when we eat, or in the photosynthesis which, at the end, allows us to breath. Chemistry can explain how the simplest reaction can change the whole structure of the initial matter into a completely different compound, such as the dream of the princess, where we can transform a frog into a charming prince. This is Chemistry.

ACKNOWLEDGMENTS

I was born in Cuba. Yes, that little island that gets into trouble so easily. I suppose you have heard as many unpleasant things about my beloved motherland as I about capitalism. For example, when I was about 8 years old, the Soviet propaganda was focused on saying that a Nuclear War was imminent. So, I grew up thinking that USA, UK, Canada, Argentina, Colombia, Australia, etc. were places where many evil people lived. Please, take into account I was only 8 years old.

And, what does it has to do with this novel?

The thing is that I was taught to not trust, to not believe, to be suspicious of any person from a capitalist country. I was taught that if someone from those countries befriended me, it was because they had some obscure interest. I hope you are laughing at this notion, because I find it absurd nowadays.

And why it is so ABSURD?

Because both sides in the Cold War were wrong. Because the team that supported me while writing this story: ***Beth, Debra Anne, Lynne, Mariana, Romina, Luly, Erika, Linda, Anaelu, Grace and Barbara***, dedicated to this job uncountable hours for free. Sometimes for a person they haven't even met. And they are from all over the world.

This is one way I have to say "thank you" to them. To say THANK YOU for the support and also, for changing irrevocably the way I see human kind.

The other important lesson I have learned so far is the product of belonging to an amazing family and to my Mr. Darcy. They taught me to love.

Finally, I must confess my undying gratitude to Miss Jane Austen.

17649266R00225

Made in the USA
Lexington, KY
20 September 2012